THE HIGHGATE DEAD

Gordon Ian Barrick

Published by Gortfordshire Books
Copyright Gordon Ian Barrick 2013

ISBN: 978-0-9926490-5-0

THE HIGHGATE DEAD

CONTENTS

Prologue: Hampstead Heath 1997

A distant flare of pursuing headlights illuminated the road ahead as Tom ran on, his shadow springing suddenly into life and elongating in the pale glow now before him. To either side the bordering tree lines bloomed into a muted grey: twisted branches and boles framed, like Tom, against the further darkness. Plucked from the obscurity of the night, Tom felt his fear rise again – knotting his stomach and gripping his tired body like some tangible presence. They had found him.

Beneath Tom his shadow strengthened as the car drew nearer: distorted, stretching and contracting rapidly in a grotesque mirror of his movements. Exhausted and shambling he ran on, desperately trying to out pace the onset of the lights.

Through ragged breaths, a strangled cry rose up from Tom's aching lungs as the headlight-lit road grew ever brighter. It was a pathetic sound, barely louder than his gasps yet the noise spurred him on – made him clutch the book he carried even tighter and harden what little was left of his resolve. He had to go on! With a stumbled turn, Tom aimed himself at the southern tree line and ran headlong into the bushes bordering the roadside.

The noise of the pursuing car became lost amongst the crash and crack of ferns as Tom flailed his way deeper into the undergrowth. Heedless of the sounds, he was only aware of the manic beating of his heart and the safety the darkness offered: an immediate release from the glare of the lights. Brambles ripped his face and tore at his hands as he ploughed obliviously onwards, but with every stride the brush became thicker and more resistant to his movements. Tom's panic rose again; and the realisation that the car must now be close added ferocity to his flight. Running for his life, Tom fought on deeper into the darkness.

He did not get far before the tangled, black expanse of a thorn bush denied him further progress: its thick, spiny sprawl yielding little to his efforts of breaching its heart. They must be close now, Tom thought: running for him, reaching for him. His body shivered with the perceived threat of his pursuers drawing near and so, ignoring the savage rips to his flesh, Tom flailed desperately into the bush.

He gained a step, pushed out against the surrounding branches to gain another before his leading foot felt the ground give way beneath it. Unbalanced, Tom toppled forwards into the heart of the thorn bush and continued to fall, crashing painfully to the bottom of an unseen incline with the twisted remnants of the thorn bush still gripped in both hands.

Tom lay where he had fallen, his chest heaving in spasms – arms and face bloody and burning like his lungs. Slowly, with stunned senses refocusing on his danger, he crawled from beneath the broken bush and searched for the book which he had lost in the fall. Tom became aware of a numbness in his right leg as he groped blindly in the darkness and the soft rustle of his hands against the undergrowth contrasted sharply with the strained wheeze which emanated from his mouth. Tom attempted to kerb the wretched sound and in doing so realised he could no longer hear the car – realised how noisy his progress into the wood must have been. He could not hear them but he knew they would be coming: following the path he had gouged through the undergrowth. And when they caught him, he thought as he frantically felt the ground; they would do to him what they had done to the others. He had to keep moving, get away – but he had to find the book first – the proof that would make people believe.

As if responding to his silent pleas, his hand felt something solid and angular beneath it. Tom clutched at the book and, with a sigh, drew it close to his chest. In the same movement he forced his body to rise, to move and send him onwards and, despite a sudden sharp pain in his leg that made him wince and stagger, he stayed upright: refusing to give in to the sensation. Hugging the book even tighter, Tom stumbled on into the safety of the night.

A short rise brought him to the top of a knoll level with the surrounding tree line and Tom paused to evaluate the silence, desperate to rest a few seconds and consider his next direction. He placed the book gently on the ground and bent double, his lungs clanging hollowly as he massaged his injured leg. Whatever the fall had done it hurt like hell but, though it felt wet, Tom could not be sure if it was blood or merely the sweat which slicked his palms. He retrieved the book then straightened up and groaned as the pain in his arms, hands and face began to join with that of his leg. Tom knew his body could not take much more punishment yet he knew he had no option but to keep on moving.

Barely discernible from the feeble glow of a cloud swept half-moon, Tom could see that beyond the knoll stretched Hampstead Heath, a black and grey patchwork of tree lines and grassy spaces. Dark and silent, it seemed accentuated by the sight which lay beyond as London, bright and dazzling from a million lights, sprawled brilliantly past the southern edge of the park. It was a world away for Tom, the night seeming bleaker and more isolating for the contrast, yet he had no choice but to head for the distant brightness and pray it held his salvation.

With no clear path to follow, Tom determined to head directly south into the deep wood which lay beneath the rise. He forced his body into motion once more and quickly found that, on the far side of the knoll, the ground dropped away again. It seemed a gentle slope but, with Tom's leg flaring with pain, the obstacle proved too much. Within moments, Tom had lost his footing and tumbled down the hill. Too weak to halt his motion, Tom continued to roll down the incline, his spinning senses vaguely aware of the rustle of leaves and snap of twigs which marked his passage. With a painful thump, his descent ended abruptly against the bole of a tree and he sprawled stupidly at its base, winded and too exhausted to stand.

A breeze picked up, briefly cooling the bloody burning of his face and hands and Tom blinked up at the stars through the gently moving branches above. All around, the creak and rustle of the wood soothed his nerves while he fought for breath and, in the back of his mind, another reassuring thought came to the fore. There were no sounds of pursuit.

Tom lay for a while beneath the tree until at last he was able to catch his breath. The smell of earth was strong in his nostrils, the sounds of nature tranquil, but Tom fought the compelling void of tiredness which threatened to overwhelm him. Gripping an arm around the trunk of the tree he slowly inched himself upright, then tested his injured leg while he scanned the darkness in a vain attempt to get his bearings. The yellow glow of street lights could just be made out through the foliage and, though he still had some distance to go to reach them, Tom considered what to do once he exited the park. He knew he was a long way from being safe but, with no sound of his pursuers, a vague sensation of hope began to ease his fears.

Tom had originally intended finding a Police station but, being a stranger to North London, he was unsure where the nearest one was. But would they believe him, he wondered? Even with the book would they believe the whole story? Perhaps it would be wiser to try and contact his sister first. Tom had no money on him but that was the least of his concerns. If he could make it beyond the heath and to the lights then he would find a phone box and reverse the charges. Or break into a house if he had to, and make the call from there. Claire would not believe him either of course, but she would come. She always did. Then he would phone the Police and give himself up – commit himself to their safekeeping. What would happen after that he could not guess: but he knew one thing. He would be safe.

While considering these actions Tom limped slowly down the slope. Clutching out at every branch and bole he could find he was able to stay upright and relieve the pressure on his leg but then a sound from the darkness froze Tom to the spot. Barely audible, yet totally out of place with the murmurs of the forest, it was an unnatural noise: and it seemed to have come from the top of the rise.

Tom's panic flared back into life; stronger than ever because he recognised the sound and what it signified. It meant he was going to die. Here in the darkness, alone and helpless amongst the trees.

Ignoring the pain, Tom launched himself into motion and, with gravity aiding his last reserves of energy, was just able to keep upright as he fled down the slope. He was screaming now, from both pain and fear but, though the sound cut through the night, it was muffled by the trees.

He reached level ground and stumbled on, clearing the wood to find an expanse of long grass before him. Agony and exhaustion cried out for him to stop but fear propelled his body woodenly onwards. Survival was now Tom's only consideration.

The figure was before him suddenly. Rising up from the night to block his path. Tom registered the movement too late to turn but knew he stood no chance. No one ever did. The first slashing blow struck before Tom could fill his lungs to raise a final scream. The second before he could catch his last breath.

Beyond the darkness and the tree lines, London – for all its appearance of life – slept on. For most of its inhabitants Tuesday was a good five hours away.

Chapter One

Mikey walked the path until he neared his favourite spot on Parliament Hill. He was early. He stopped for a moment to check his watch and for the third time in as many minutes pulled a lock of red hair away from his eye line. Delving deep into a pocket of his military jump suit, Mikey fished out an elastic band. With deft, well practised movements, he strangled the offending hair into a ponytail.

Military Mikey. It was a nick-name he had incurred from friends for his peculiar dress sense, or Captain Camera from Fleet Street editors with tricky photo assignments. Mikey's ability to get the perfect picture was as predictable to those editors as what he would be wearing when he delivered it: the same grubby, army surplus fatigues he always wore.

It was a simple enough affectation – to Mikey at least – with a practical application for a particular line of photography which had taken him around the world's trouble spots in just a few short years. It was also born of the same hero worship that captivated most children's hearts. Only with Mikey the hero worship had been a little different.

Mikey's idol had been neither a singer nor a film star, though the latter description could be applied in one sense. For a photographer's son who seemed to have silver iodine running through his veins, there was only one man who captivated young Michael Dayville's imagination: filling his mind with adrenalin-charged images of humanity. A man who captured the savage reality and horror of warfare like no other. Tim Page: war photographer. What the young Mikey had seen in his father's books had made up his mind there and then. To follow Tim Page's example and, if he was lucky, experience something close to the dreams which those pictures filled his head with so often as a child.

Now, with the Middle East, South America, China and the Balkans under his belt, at the age of twenty seven Mikey had gone a long way to fulfilling those dreams. But at a price. The pictures he had idolised in his youth had never shown the life behind the camera; never communicated the sacrifices and strength needed to capture such moments. Mikey found with experience what a dangerous existence Tim Page had lived – a separate world where war was the backdrop of your career and life always bordered upon the brink of destruction. All to get the perfect shot and show the world humanity's dark underside.

Such risks had not abated his enthusiasm at first, the rewards having – to his mind – more than compensated for the dangers. Mikey's sorties to China and South America had earned him respect and recognition in almost every quarter – the pictures syndicated world-wide. His skills had also made him financially secure: swelling his bank account and allowing him to buy a house in Hampstead. But with time the constant immersion in horror tainted such gains and repeated exposure to the suffering of the world began to make Mikey question his actions, his involvement. Life itself became a little less worthwhile.

Such thoughts were already running through his mind when he had accompanied the award-winning journalist, Geoff Freeman, on a clandestine investigation into the continuing plight of the Kurdish tribes in Northern Iraq. It had seemed a simple enough brief: cross the mountain border from Southern Turkey, meet their guides and then travel on to the hillside villages around Ruwandiz. But such a trip, however well organised and planned beforehand, was always going to be a risky venture at best. It was Geoff and Mikey's bad luck that their investigation had swiftly degenerated into a fight for survival.

Their guides, positive they could take the pair to their destination unhindered and happy with the money they were given, robbed and deserted their charges thirty miles past the Iraqi border. Geoff suffered a broken ankle in the assault and, unable to walk, was carried by Mikey as they crept their way around Iraqi border patrols. They returned to Turkey with nothing to show for their troubles but their lives.

The trip, though a disaster, had still given Geoff material for a well received magazine piece and their experiences formed a firm friendship between the journalist and the photographer. Searching for an opportunity to work together again, the pair had teamed up a year later to join the perpetual media throng in the Balkans. A week into their assignment, outside their small hotel in the troubled Macedonian town of Kumanovo, Mikey and Geoff were on hand when a local man was hit by sniper fire whilst crossing the street. Stunned, Mikey's instincts had brought his camera into action to capture the aftermath of the event and it was through his viewfinder that Mikey then saw Geoff suddenly enter the frame. Frozen with fear, Mikey could do nothing but keep clicking as his friend ran to aid the fallen man. Mikey had yet to develop the role of film which catalogued Geoff's subsequent death at the hands of the same sniper.

Cutting across the bleaching grass, Mikey headed toward his usual spot in the shade of an oak tree: one of a row which dotted the brow of the hill. He slumped down, deposited his rucksack and camera bag beside him and let out a sigh. The grass was longer and lusher around the oak's base and Mikey ran his pale hands through it: felt the tingle of the greenery as it passed his outstretched fingers. He wanted to put Geoff from his mind for a while, forget about the pain he felt and the funeral he had attended only two days before. His only desire now was to block out the sorrow in the sunshine of the day. That, and spend some time with Jane.

Before him the hill dipped down from the line of oaks, steeply at first, then a gentle curve which petered away as it approached the tarmac path, the swimming pool and the running track at the bottom of the heath. Beyond that lay London, beautifully framed by the southern tree line, its towers and spires basking in the warm June sunshine.

Mikey leaned back on his arms to take it all in. The city was a patchwork of hazy browns and greys – the darker greens of nature peaking out here and there. Then there was the lighter, faded green of the heath beneath him; well worn by a thousand pairs of wandering feet and edged by the oaks which shimmered in the silent breeze. Above it all was a blue and brilliant sky, empty apart from a noonday sun. Thank God I'm home again, thought Mikey.

Beneath him, where the grass flattened out, the park was beginning to fill with the first influx of lunching workers – fanning out as they passed the tennis courts and the pavilion in search of their own little piece of nature. The chance to while away a lazy hour with a pre-packed sandwich and a can of warm coke. They dotted the hillside, singly or in groups, but few ventured up as far as Mikey. It was too hot for the effort – took up time better spent enjoying the sunshine.

Mikey had always loved his particular spot for that very reason. It never got crowded and from the shade of the oak he could see absolutely everything that went on below. The interplay, the quirks, the individuals, he could see it all. And, with a telescopic lens, he rarely failed to capture it all. But then, Michael Dayville – photographic wunderkind – rarely failed to capture something good anywhere. It was why the press could never get enough of him.

With the heat beginning to penetrate the cover of the leaves,

Mikey rolled up the sleeves of his olive drab jump suit then debated whether or not to unzip the suit halfway. He was beginning to relax, but not that much, so instead he decided to have one of the beers in his rucksack. In the process Mikey unpacked the blanket and the food he had brought in Hampstead a short while before.

He spread the blanket and tossed the food unceremoniously before him, regarding the assortment with a disbelieving stare. The cheese, French stick, nachos, dip, apples, beers and packet of cigarettes were unsurprising in themselves, but what left Mikey speechless was the cost. He had stared open mouthed, dumbly counting out the money, when the woman at the till had asked for twenty five pounds. Twenty five quid! They must have seen him coming, he thought, shaking his head. Hampstead prices, even after more than a year of familiarity, still made Mikey cringe. He could afford it – that could not be denied – but that was not the point. Being someone who had grown up in the working class world of Kilburn, just a stone's throw away, he knew that he could get the same things down the road for less than half the price. Ahh well, thought Mikey. As my father's so found of telling me: that's the price you pay for decadence.

He took a beer bottle from the jumble and, placing its neck against the oak tree, banged it sharply with the palm of his hand to remove the cap: impaling it into the bark in the process. He took a swig and regarded the other bottle caps stuck in the same spot: every one a memento of his previous visits. He counted them and found that there were seventeen in all. Perhaps I should cut down, Mikey pondered, examining the scars, I might be harming the tree.

Mikey looked up into the depths of the leaves and lay back – the beer bottle perched on his chest. He watched the swaying branches wink shafts of sunlight on and off then groped for his cigarettes: not wanting to shift his gaze. His hand clutched randomly at the blanket, the packet illusive, and was finally forced to sit up. He ran the cool bottle across his brow as he located the Gauloises and stretched to take them, rummaging through a deep pocket as he did so for his lighter. He took another swig of beer and then lit up, drawing the heavy pungent smoke deep into his lungs as he tossed away the cellophane and silver paper. Mikey drew his legs up, clutched them with his arms, and gazed back down at the ever-crowding heath.

It was busier now, the steady flow of lunchers now a torrent. The grass and base of the slope were littered with prostrate bodies: the air alive with the murmur of voices. Pseudo-seaside, thought Mikey, like some land-locked beach. Pigeons for gulls and a distant ocean of brickwork.

Shifting his gaze Mikey noticed that a party of children had come out to the pool. They broke their ordered formation quickly and leapt carelessly into the water. How they must be envied, Mikey thought, by the sweltering 'suits'. Without thinking, he reached into his camera bag, removed a Nikon camera with a zoom lens and turned it towards the pool to get a closer look. The children were young, no more than six or seven and, judging by the water-wings most were wearing, not yet used to the water. They splashed and screamed silently as he looked on: little explosions of foam surrounding each body. On the pool side, 'Miss' was trying to dodge the liquid eruptions whilst attempting to instil some form of order to the chaos. Unsuccessfully it seemed: the children too enamoured with the novelty of the pool to even notice her waving arms. Beside the teacher huddled a towel-wrapped girl, regarding the water with nervous eyes. There's always one, thought Mikey, and reeled off some rapid shots, catching the moment.

Despite himself, Mikey was beginning to enjoy the day.

14

Doing what he liked more than anything in the world and capturing only happiness. Here was life at its unconcerned best. No pain, no hardship. No bloodied faces pleading for comfort. Just unrestrained joy. He panned across the pool, snapping the frantic action as he went, then pulled out, dragging the focus away to jump more randomly around the grass. Flicking here and there he joined the little sun-baked groups of workers, capturing the gesticulations and expressions. Lost amongst the throng.

Jane found him in the same position half an hour later, still clicking and zooming, his bottle of beer unfinished. She tapped him gently with the toe of her shoe to get his attention, then crouched down to kiss him.

'You're late,' he said smiling, disengaging momentarily.

'Some of us have to work,' she replied, instantly regretting the remark. Unfazed, Mikey held the smile.

Thankful she had not upset him, Jane gave him a final short peck before regarding the beer.

'Now that's just what I need,' she said, grabbing a bottle.

Jane stepped over Mikey to repeat his procedure with the cap on the tree and took a welcome swig. The beer was warm from the heat and gassy, making her burp involuntarily. She patted her chest and looked accusingly at the bottle.

Mikey laughed and shook his head. 'You've got the manners of a docker.'

'Yes,' agreed Jane with a sly smile. 'But not the body.'

Mikey had to agree. Jane had the type of slender build only fasting could attain, but a metabolism which allowed her to eat almost anything without affecting it. Her short cropped, auburn hair framed a delicate face and tiny crease lines around the mouth and eyes revealed a countenance almost always on the verge of a smile.

Jane gave Mikey her best smouldering look and sat down

beside him, her free arm resting on his lap. She took another swig of beer, Mikey joining her.

'So what was more important than the picnic?' Mikey asked.

Before replying, Jane picked up the French stick, broke off an end and moved the piece to her mouth before realising she was not hungry. She looked at Mikey, wondering for a moment how he would take the news.

'There's been a murder,' she said quietly.

Mikey's fragile peace of mind was shattered.

'Shit,' he said softly, almost to himself. 'Where?'

Jane pointed to the ground, hesitated. 'Here...The heath,' she said. She dropped the bread back onto the blanket.

Mikey's mouth compressed to a thin line. He looked around, scanning the slope beneath as if expecting the murder site to be within view. He nodded. 'When?' he asked with a sigh.

Jane understood Mikey's feelings completely, and when she replied her tone bordered on the apologetic. 'Last night, apparently,' she said. 'Up by the east vale.' She pointed a thumb behind her. 'The Police have it completely cordoned off and, so far, no journalists can get in. I managed to speak to one of the constables standing guard. He said I didn't want to.'

Mikey looked towards the tree line behind them. 'God,' he whispered. 'Poor bastard.' He turned back. 'Any idea who it was?'

Jane shook her head. 'None. The constable said a statement would be issued to the press as soon as they've done their stuff up there. But I wouldn't imagine they'll release any name for a couple of days at least.'

They were silent for a moment, staring into space. Jane easily guessing the thoughts racing through her boyfriend's mind.

'Too bloody close to home,' said Mikey, breaking the silence but addressing no-one in particular. Jane nodded but said nothing. 'It happens,' Mikey continued with a shrug. 'I know it happens… Jesus, I've made a fucking career out of documenting it. But… I expect to find it there,' he pointed his beer bottle towards the London skyline. 'Or abroad. But not here.' He gestured around him.

Jane gave a sardonic smile. 'I know,' she said. "England's green and pleasant".

Mikey mumbled an 'Mm' through his beer bottle.

'I've been feeling crap since I heard about it this morning,' continued Jane. 'For the same reasons. Even worse when I spoke to that policeman. It sounded nasty.' She took a sip of beer. 'I just pray it wasn't one of those ritual killings.'

'Oh god!' said Mikey, shaking his head. 'That's the last bloody thing we need.' Though he had been abroad when they had happened, Mikey had read all about the murders which had taken place in London over the last three weeks: six so far. The media had talked of little else. Even Jane, though she worked for a local paper, had covered the third murder for the Hampstead Chronicle

'I'm going to need some pictures…' Jane said sheepishly after a pause. '… For my piece.'

Mikey's jaw dropped.

'I don't mean that,' she continued hurriedly, realising her words had been ill chosen. 'I mean I need to borrow a camera. Our photographer is off sick again.'

Mikey was silent for a moment. 'I'll do it,' he said, not really sure why the words had come out.

Jane pulled herself close and put her arm around his waist. 'You need a break,' she said, kissing him gently on the cheek. 'Some time to rest.'

'I know,' said Mikey with a nod. 'I don't know why I volunteered.' He let out a sigh. 'I think it's just that, well… I don't know. Doing it might help to exorcise some ghosts. Does that make any sense?'

Jane nodded. 'Perfect sense. But only if you're sure.'

'Yeah,' Mikey replied with a shrug. 'I wasn't up to much this week anyway, and you can't take a photograph to save your life.'

Jane laughed and hugged him even tighter, happy that Mikey's spirits had improved since the funeral.

The picnic lay discarded before them, their appetites failing to return. Instead they kept the same close embrace, opened some more beers and sat watching the hillside scene: Mikey pointing out people he had spotted earlier to Jane.

'Now there's something you don't see every day,' Mikey said, pointing down into the crowd. Jane followed the line of his finger.

'What?' she replied, seeing dozens of people in the indicated direction.

'The priest,' said Mikey, still pointing. 'See him? All in black with the hat on. He must be boiling in that outfit.'

Beneath them, wending his way circuitously through the crowd Mikey watched as the black-clad clergyman trudged on, his face down turned, shadowed by the wide brim of his black hat. Hampered by the prostrate bodies, he made slow progress in his attempt to climb the hill.

'Where?' Jane asked, still unable to spot the figure.

'Directly beneath us – see? Just passing the old couple with the bright blanket.'

Jane continued to scan the hillside and found the couple that Mikey was pointing at. 'I can see them. But I can't see a vicar.'

Mikey frowned, giving his girlfriend a sideways glance. 'You're joking, right?'

Jane shook her head, laughing, and reclined on the grass. 'No!' she protested. 'Honestly, I can't see him.' She pulled gently at Mikey's shoulder in an attempt to make him join her.

Mikey resisted the move and looked down at his girlfriend, then back down at the priest. He laughed and picked up his camera. 'Okay, have it your own way. But a tenner says he's down there. Wanna bet?'

Jane shrugged, smiled up at Mikey as he toyed with the camera. 'Sure. It's your money,' she said.

'Right. You're on.'

Mikey swung the camera to his eye, practised hands already adjusting the focus to bring the dark figure into large and sharp relief. The clergyman had stopped about a hundred yards below and the hat brim rose slowly to expose a pale, thin face. Eyes gazing directly at Mikey.

'Smile!' exclaimed Mikey, fingering the shutter release.

Down the slope, the priest smiled.

The auto-wind whirred twice then stopped. Mikey lowered the camera from his face.

'Forget the tenner,' said Jane, still grinning. 'Why not just buy me dinner?'

Mikey did not reply and continued to stare down the hillside.

'Hey, copper-top,' said Jane, tugging at his sleeve.

'Uh? What?' Mikey seemed lost in thought.

'Buy me dinner,' repeated Jane.

'Yeah. Dinner… Right…'

Mikey gazed into the crowd still milling and roasting beneath them, searching intently for the priest. He had a clear view of the entire area – from the tennis courts in the east to the tree line and houses way over to the west. But no matter where he looked, the priest was nowhere to be seen.

Inspector Fletcher patted his pockets and pulled a face.

'Bugger,' he mumbled to himself, removing the unlit cigarette from his mouth and turning to his sergeant. 'Got a light, Pete?' he asked. 'I've left mine in the car.'

Sergeant Peter Rose drew his narrow shoulders into a brief shrug.

'Given up guv',' he said. 'A week tomorrow.' Sergeant Rose did not bother to hide his pride.

'Great,' replied Fletcher with a sneer.

Turning slowly on his heel, the Inspector scanned the assembled uniformed and forensic officers for active smokers.

'I'll tell you what, Pete,' he said over his shoulder as he advanced on a constable who proffered his cigarette stub. 'I bet you a fiver you'll be back on the weed before this case is out.' He took the burning cigarette and lit his own, a cloud of smoke rising as he puffed the tobacco into life.

The sergeant shook his head. 'I might start using more patches, but not fags. Sharon'd kill me.'

'Well, we wouldn't want that,' said Fletcher, walking back. 'One murder is enough.'

A few yards behind them, where foot high grass met the enclosing tree line of the hollow, two medics were struggling to place a misshapen corpse into a body bag. Their white overalls, gloved hands and boots were smeared red with blood and both scowled and cursed as they attempted to manoeuvre the slick and deformed figure. A police photographer stood to their right and, keeping his distance from the pervading odour, took final shots of the blood soaked grass. Beside him, another pair dress in white, paper overalls stood debating and making notes about the patch. At length the shorter of the two men broke away from the discussion and, with a brief frown aimed at the men with the body bag, strode towards the inspector. Drawing near he drew a clear plastic bag from his pocket.

'I think you'll want this, inspector,' said the Forensic Pathologist, handing the item to Fletcher.

The inspector looked blankly at the blood soaked brown

wallet inside the bag and passed it to his sergeant. He looked at the pathologist and nodded towards the matted grass.

'Any thoughts, doc?'

The pathologist turned to see the body finally disappear into the bag. He bit his lip and placed the pencil he held to his mouth, chewing it for a few seconds in absent-minded contemplation.

'Too early to say, really,' he said, finally removing the sodden pencil end.

Fletcher raised his eyebrows at his sergeant, who mimicked the gesture. Same old line, the inspector thought. Never ask forensics to give you a snap decision. They'll always want to test everything three times and call you back in a fortnight. Meanwhile Fletcher and those like him were supposed to fend off the inevitable media feeding frenzy with the well worn and rarely satisfactory 'continuing enquiries' routine.

The pathologist caught the silent exchange between the officers and knew instantly what it meant. The old story, he thought. The boys in blue were always too hasty and his long association with the Metropolitan Police had shown it to be their unwavering way. Get it cleared up quickly – get on to the next case. No time to wait. Though he was sure they understood that accurate, conclusive medical evidence took time to collate, it never stopped them from demanding it instantly. But it was an unfortunate fact that they sometimes got it. How many times had he seen cases thrown out of court due to police impatience for a conviction? How many rushed and pressured guesses? Far too many for his peace of mind. Well this one, he knew, was going to have to be different. It was going to take time – and lots of it. He could see no other way. And, on the initial evidence, he doubted that the police would be happy with the results. Doubted they would manage a conviction. The doctor let out a resigned sigh.

'I can give you some preliminary results in a couple of days,' he said. 'Detailed stuff will take longer.'

'Uhuh,' replied Fletcher flatly.

The intonation was not lost on the doctor and as he moved to follow the departing stretcher, he stopped and wagged his pencil at the two policemen.

'I can tell you though, that you would be well advised to contact London Zoo,' he said with a grim half-smile. 'They may be able to help you.' With that oblique parting shot, the pathologist continued on his way. Fletcher and Rose exchanged bemused frowns before strolling after him.

'What the bloody hell is that supposed to mean?' called Fletcher.

The doctor halted and gazed silently at the inspector for a moment. Though he had never met Fletcher before, he knew him. There were hundreds just like him in the Metropolitan Police. Carbon copy detectives with the same dour attitude and expression, the same dress sense and the same hunched posture. Premature grey hair from the stress and the look of a fifty year old when they had not yet touched forty. Here was a prime example of the journeyman copper and the pathologist did not need a sixth sense to see that this one was worried. Hampstead and Highgate were, considering their proximity to London, a bit of a backwater as far as killings of any type were concerned – let alone something this grim. It was more indecent exposure and burglary around these parts. And now, thought the doctor, he's got a nasty murder on his hands and everybody's attention.

The pathologist sucked his teeth and attempted a more conciliatory tone. 'My initial examination of the deceased leads me to believe that the assailant – or assailants – either inflicted the many parallel wounds we found with some unusual multi-blade instrument or...' The doctor paused and

22

bit his lip. '…Or the numerous lacerations were inflicted by a large, clawed animal. Possibly a cat. Unfortunately – unless the attackers wanted souvenirs – the absence of the major internal organs seems to point to that fact that the cat was hungry.' The doctor looked briefly round the glade while Fletcher and Rose stood dumbly digesting the doctor's conjecture. 'Almost perfect habitat for a large feline, I suppose,' he mused, lost in his own thoughts. He shrugged and patted the silent inspector on the arm. 'But, as I'm sure you understand, I wouldn't like to swear to that without running some tests to confirm my hypothesis. I'll be in touch.'

With a casual wave of his hand the doctor walked off into the trees to catch up with the stretcher.

They watched his portly frame disappear into the greenery before Fletcher turned to his Sergeant, a tinge of exasperation in his voice.

'Right… Pete,' he said with a sigh. 'Before we spread the men out further, comb the wood again. See if you can find any evidence of paw prints – missing organs – that sort of thing. I'll go back to the car and put out an alert for the public to be on the lookout for the fucking Wolf man.' Sergeant Rose gave a wry grin in response and tramped off to collect officers for another search.

Bob Fletcher began following the course of the doctor into the trees, heading back up the hill to find his car. He stuffed his hands into the pockets of his coat in search of his cigarettes before remembering he did not possess the means to light them. He grimaced and put his head down, watching his feet as they swished through the grass: thinking hard. He did not care for the doctor's escaped tiger scenario, or for the doctor come to think of it. Daft old twat, thought Fletcher. How does a large, savage animal escape from anywhere without the alarm being instantly raised? And how would it get from

London Zoo to Hampstead Heath – on the bus? The Inspector smiled to himself. He would get some constable to check the relevant establishments just to make sure, but he knew that, whoever the murderer was, they were more dangerous than any wild animal.

Even in the shade Fletcher found it was hot: the midday sun fiercely beating through the trees. The heat wafted the sickening odour from the murder site up the hill and the Inspector grimaced at the sickly smell. He walked on in search of fresher air and removed his coat to sling it over one shoulder. This is not turning into a good day, Fletcher thought and wondered what they would say back at the station.

Chapter Two

Mikey ran on, out of control: his breath coming in large, ragged gasps. He felt no pain from the exertion but could hear all too well the laboured pants and manic thumps as his heart beat time almost perfectly with his rapid footfall. All he could feel was the fear – colouring every sense he possessed – tainting, twisting and distorting them until he became unable to bear the escalating panic nor digest the vague jumble of images which flew before his eyes. He felt like an unwilling passenger of himself, powerless to stop or rationalise his situation before his body and senses sped onwards.

He was running. But where? Why? It was too dark to see. Night-time? Something told Mikey it was night. Shapes flashed past but they were indistinct and Mikey felt a brief dizziness as his dark world seemed to tumble. If only he could stop for a moment! His fear told him that would not be wise. Whatever happened he should not stop running.

A ticking began, soft yet insistent, gradually rising above the clamour of his heart and lungs. A clock? It's coming from behind me – counting down. The ticking is something to do with the fear but I mustn't turn around. Still running. Got to keep moving. Must outrun the fear.

More grey shapes loomed large before him, blurring quickly to the sides of his vision before he could bring them into focus. His sight wandered vaguely. Moonlight. Trees? Someone's behind me! Stumbling forwards, can't stop. Feel dizzy. The ticking is louder, closer. I'm down. Oh God! My heart, please stop.

'Over here.'

Fuck, someone is there! Move! Run! Escape the ticking. Get up! Christ! Please get up! Why won't my body move?! Move! Fucking move!? At last!! Got to keep going.

'Here. Over here.'

I don't want to stop, but I must think! I'm sure I know the voice! Where is it? Can't see in the darkness. I think something is in the trees. Can't contain the panic. My heart is racing like the clock. Too fast – can't control it!

'Michael.'

It's to my left but my eyes won't obey. Please, please look to the left? There! There!

Oh my god it's him.

Mikey sat bolt upright in the darkness of his bedroom and pushed aside the sweat soaked sheets with a single frantic movement. The images in his head were vague but the emotion was strong and his heart still laboured from the fear. He swung his legs round and stood up from the bed, making another swift motion to switch on the bedside lamp. The room filled with its feeble glow, making the night seem stronger, the bordering shadows of the room more encroaching. Naked, he strode across the littered floor to reach the main light switch and flooded the bedroom with a brightness that removed all traces of the dark. Hands to his face, Mikey massaged away the sleep and felt the clamminess of his sweating cheeks as he wiped his face. He took a deep breath to calm himself and by degrees felt his heart beat slow to normal.

Another fucking nightmare, thought Mikey with a sigh. He glanced around the room to reassure himself with its familiarity and noticed for the first time that Jane was not in bed. In the same instant he heard rapid motion on the stairs and within seconds Jane was in the room: jumping when she encountered an ashen faced Mikey standing naked by the door.

'What's up?! I heard a noise,' she said, looking anxiously at the nervous, blinking figure.

Mikey said nothing. He stepped forward and wrapped his arms around her, feeling her warmth soak through her dressing gown. Breathing her scent. He let out a shallow sigh.

Jane held him tight, pressed his head against her neck and spoke softly. 'It's okay,' she said. 'Everything's okay now.'

Mikey began to cry.

Mikey sat curled in the corner of his sofa in the living room and listened to Jane pottering about in the kitchen. The noise stopped. Jane's head appeared around the doorframe and she waved the uneaten French stick at him.

'Sure you're not hungry?' she asked with a frown.

Mikey waved back with his cigarette.

'They're very nutritious,' he mumbled and put the cigarette back between his lips.

Jane opened her mouth to comment, reconsidered, then disappeared back into the kitchen.

Unfocused, Mikey stared across the living room, his mind trying to clarify images which less than ten minutes ago were vivid enough to scare him awake. Phantom like, they eluded his attempts – slipping from focus to hang tantalizingly close to recollection. The harder he tried to form the images the more insubstantial and vague the memories became. All he was left with was a bleak and uneasy feeling, made worse by the knowledge that it had not been the usual nightmare: the recurrent scenario his mind had tormented him with since Kumanovo. That was firmly etched into his consciousness, and always followed the same harrowing line.

He would stand beneath the weathered colonnade outside their hotel, watching the bright lines which illuminated the street before them. Geoff would smile and step down onto the broken tarmac, then waving, walk towards the man lying in the midst of the beams. The light would play around the pair for a moment and puzzled, Geoff would turn to look back toward his friend. That was when Mikey raised his camera to his eye to catch the moment the lights began destroying the reporter.

A small flash on the side of Geoff's head – the shutter closing. A ripple of concussion sweeping across his face – the features distorting. The black of the shutter. Violent movement from an exploding swell of flesh, Geoff's eyes shocked and wide, head jerking sideways. Black shutter. A portrait of blood and pain: a streamer of red radiating from a dark blast hole in Geoff's cranium. A scream. Piercing and shrill – emanating from the slack mouth of the dead man as the impact threw him out of the frame. It was always then that Mikey awoke, realising the sound had come not from Geoff's dead lips, but his own.

This dream, however, had been different. Mikey had neither screamed himself awake nor woken to feel the pain of those awful memories: his usual guilt or bitter remorse. This time it had been an unsettling sensation of terror.

Mikey shook his head. It was gone, he could not recapture this new nightmare and was not really sure if he wanted to. He would wait until morning before (if at all) he tried again and Mickey felt certain that – in the bright light of day – the whole event would seem much less unnerving. Then again, why not put it down to stress as Jane already had and forget all about it. It's about time my unconscious had some time off anyway, Mikey thought, drawing on his cigarette.

He snuggled up into the folds of his dressing gown and, with daybreak only a few hours away, thought about taking an early walk on Hampstead Heath. Mikey yawned. Perhaps I can convince Jane to take a dawn stroll, he thought, it's an age since we last did that. He stubbed his cigarette out in the ashtray before him and yawned again. That's what we'll do, he thought, go out as the sun rises. He closed his eyes, picturing the glint of dew on the grass and the fresh smell of the woodland. Jane returned from the kitchen a minute later to find that her boyfriend was fast asleep.

Pete Singleton resigned himself to the fact that Miss Henshaw would be putting him in detention again. It was her standard punishment for a pupil who was late for school more than once in a week and, as Pete had arrived late on Wednesday and Thursday for the last three weeks, tonight would be the evening he would have to stay behind. Too bad, he thought, I'll have to miss rugby practice again. At this rate he would be dropped from the team. Pete's only concern about his repeated detentions was that Mr. Matthews, the P.E. teacher, would catch on to his scam and consult with Miss Henshaw.

Pete meandered along the road that led to South Hampstead Secondary School, checking his pace now and again and taking interest in anything that delayed him in arriving at his destination. He knew it would not do to turn up and find that he had not yet been missed, so he engrossed himself in a banal analysis of everything he passed. There were the trees with pink blossom lining the road: how interesting they were. The cat curled up on a garden wall: fascinating. Pete paused by a queue of old ladies – complete with shopping trolleys – who were waiting for a bus and spent several minutes waiting with them. On and on Pete ambled until the school loomed before him and he began to run out of distractions. He turned into an access road that skirted the woodwork rooms and took the longer, back route to reach his class.

By the mesh fence which bordered one side of the rear playground and close to the hole in the fence which Pete planned to use, the boy found a man in grey overalls standing beside an identically coloured van. I wonder what he's up to? Pete thought, following the same line of inquiry which had slowly brought him up the road. Yet this time he was genuinely interested.

In one hand the man held what Pete could only assume – from this distance at least – to be a miniature television, while in the other what looked like an opened map. Its unfolded vastness prevented the man observing Pete's approach and as he drew nearer he made out a large octagonal shape marked heavily with black ink showing through the paper. Bizarre, thought Pete, moving closer. The man tutted to himself, gazed up at the sky and shook the little box in his hand.

'Whatcha doin' mister?' Pete asked as he sauntered closer, his hands thrust firmly into his trouser pockets.

The man folded up the map and regarded the boy with unconcealed distaste. Pete, oblivious to the hostile stare, craned his neck to see what was on the television but the man was already placing it into a pocket.

'What's that building over there?' demanded the man, ignoring Pete's enquiry.

There was a forcefulness in the tone that stopped the boy in his tracks and Pete swallowed nervously. Suddenly he was aware of the piercing stare and, taken aback by the authority in the voice he dutifully followed the line of the man's arm.

'That's the boiler room? I think,' mumbled Pete, hoping it was a good enough answer. He found, though he had no desire at all to continue, unable to wrest his gaze from that of the man, and something inside him quailed at the prospect of upsetting the stranger. It was not just the voice and eyes that were imposing, but the build of the man and his stern, set features which unnerved Pete more than he thought was possible. As the man continued to regard him unblinkingly, Pete's only desire was to run as fast as he could into class.

The man held Pete immobile for a few more seconds before retrieving the box from his pocket and unfolding the map.

'Aren't you late for something?' he asked, his attention

finally transferring from the boy and back to the device.

Pete was already moving before he managed a mute nod, bolting past the man to skid through the opening in the fence and quickly cross the playground on the other side. He did not care if he got detention for a week, Pete thought as he ran – as long as it meant being inside with people. Even rugby and the security of standing bored on a field amongst twenty seven other boys seemed now to have an appeal. Anything that ensured he did not have to meet that man alone again.

The man watched the boy race across the asphalt before rechecking the co-ordinates of his satellite navigation system. He mouthed the illuminated numbers it showed on its screen then double checked them against his map. Satisfied, he collected a bulky canvas bag from the back of his van and with a grin made his way towards the building Pete had correctly identified as the boiler room.

The phone rang loudly, startling Mikey awake. Morning glowed through the drawn curtains and a bright line of sunshine spilled through a chink onto the living room carpet. He blinked groggily and yawned, taking several seconds to orient himself to his surroundings. It was another few rings before he clambered from the sofa to grab the phone.

'Yep,' he mumbled, rubbing at his eyes with his free hand.

'Oh, you're awake!' said Jane. Her voice echoed slightly and it took Mikey a few seconds to realise that she must using her mobile phone. 'I didn't want to disturb you this morning,' she continued. 'How are you feeling?'

Mikey remembered what he was doing on the sofa. He yawned.

'I feel tired,' he replied. 'What time is it?'

'Half past eleven.'

'Didn't you want me to take those pictures?' Mikey asked.

Jane's voice held concern. 'I thought in light of what happened last night you really needed to take some time off.'

Mikey untangled his dressing gown and slumped back onto the sofa. 'Mm, maybe. But I'd rather be active.' He looked at the filtered daylight on the curtains. 'Anyway, it looks like another lovely day.'

There was silence for a moment, Mikey able to picture Jane biting her lip as she debated his welfare. 'Okay?' she said at last without enthusiasm. 'But I think rest would do you more good.'

'We'll compromise,' Mikey replied, 'I promise to rest tonight. Whaddaya say?'

'I say you're mad.'

'Not yet,' said Mikey, 'but I'm working on it.'

The humour returned to his girlfriend's voice. 'Alright, Mr. Madman, here's the situation. The Police have let down the perimeter tape, so you should be able to get some shots. It's in the East Heath so meet me at the top of Hampstead by Whitestone Pond.'

Mikey grinned, happy to have won Jane over. 'I'll be there in twenty minutes.'

He put the phone down and yawned deeply, stretching his arms and massaging the crick in his neck as he moved to the rear windows and threw back the curtains. The sunshine made him clamp shut his eyes, wincing from the brilliance of the light.

'Ouch!' he yelled, covering his face with his hands.

Regretting his unprepared zeal for the new day, Mikey repeated his actions on the front curtains more cautiously, keeping his eyes tightly shut until he had become accustomed to the light. Outside, the narrow street was bathed in warmth and, with a smile on his face, Mikey hurried upstairs to get changed.

He returned a few minutes later dressed in a clean jumpsuit and walked through to the kitchen to collect the keys to his motorbike. He grabbed an apple from the fridge, his cigarettes, crash helmet and camera bag from the living room then strolled out into the sunshine.

Jane was fiddling idly with her car radio when Mikey found her fifteen minutes later, attempting to pick up newscasts and see how the heath story was developing. He crept up behind the car and tapped lightly on the rear window then ducked down when Jane turned. He reappeared beside the driver door and pulled a face.

'You get more attractive every day,' Jane joked with a smile, winding down the window. Mikey stretched through the opening and kissed her loudly on the cheek.

'You and me both,' he replied with a grin and opened her door.

Jane stepped out of the car and they hugged warmly. Mikey holding her slim frame close as she ran her fingers through his red hair. She smiled and looked deeply into his eyes, her face showing the merest hint of a frown.

'How do you feel?' she asked.

Mikey broke contact and stepped back, flapping his arms up and down and puffing out his cheeks. 'Never better, nurse,' he said, stopping to feel his pulse.

Jane kissed him on the lips and slipped her hand around his waist. 'I'm glad to hear it.'

They left Jane's car and crossed Heath Street to a winding lane which bordered the eastern edge of Hampstead. From here the narrow road snaked and descended between the houses and the wooded border of the East Heath. It was nearing midday and, as the pair strode the narrow pavement which sat beside the Heath, the lane was filled with speeding cars travelling to and from the distant base of the hill. Jane and Mikey veered away from the road a short way down and entered the Heath: following a well worn route through tall grass which brought them eventually to a gravel path. The sun was high and warm and the lush plant life buzzed with insects. Soon both the buildings and traffic were lost to a thick wall of greenery and the sounds of nature.

As they walked, Mikey attempted to humorously recount the events of the previous night before Jane had entered his bedroom. He made light of his sweating, pale body and laughed as he described how he had bolted around the room in his efforts to evade the darkness. He still remembered nothing of the nightmare and the daylight had all but eradicated the unease he had felt at that time. Now he just felt embarrassed by the whole incident.

Jane smiled at his over-embroidered tales but, behind it, Mikey sensed that she was still concerned. He had known her too long and too well to miss the subtle creasing squint around her eyes, and a smile which faded more quickly than usual. Despite her unspoken doubts though, Mikey felt better than he had done in days and the burden of guilt he carried from watching Geoff's untimely demise seemed to have eased a little. Smiling, he held her hand as they walked on.

The ground began to rise as they drew nearer their destination and so too did the number of people. They were mainly locals: joggers, cyclists, walkers with dogs, and all curious to know exactly what had caused the peace of the heath to be shattered. A red and white plastic tape stretched across the brow of the hill to prevent the passers-by becoming any more curious and so the onlookers had to content themselves with the unsatisfying view of a single Policeman standing beside a further brake of trees. Jane spotted an old newspaper colleague moving slowly through the throng, but steered herself and Mikey away from him before they were seen themselves. Mikey, his attention focused like the rest of the crowd on the top of the rise, seemed not to notice the sudden change in direction.

Jane chastised herself almost instantly for the decision – for her weakness in avoiding contact with that period of her life. It was amazing to her that Mikey could brave his fears – as he was attempting to do today – only weeks after a terrible incident, and yet she could not face her past after more than three years. It surprised her that the scars she thought had healed long ago could, with the merest glimpse of someone she had known from that time, suddenly flare again into painful life. Despite her best efforts, Jane found herself recalling her terrifying memories of the London Evening Mail

It had been the London Evening Mail that had facilitated Jane's big leap into first division journalism: a move from a local paper earned through hard work and an instinctive 'nose' for a good story. The editor of the Mail knew talent when he saw it and, like Jane, had every confidence that his newest reporter would quickly blossom into an outstanding journalist. Circumstances however, dictated that the junior member of the news team would meet a different fate.

Life on the London Evening Mail started promisingly enough, with her immediate boss, Colin Ford, ensuring that Jane immediately took on assignments generally handed out to reporters more experienced than her. Sucked into a whirlwind of hard work, tight deadlines and late nights it seemed to Jane that the paper could not groom her quickly enough. Being young, hungry, gifted and ambitious, she readily accepted the challenge. The relentless intensity demanded to achieve such ends shrank Jane's world to include only those members of her paper who kept the same unsocial hours that she did. It meant that rest and recreation was snatched whenever work allowed but Jane, single and more concerned with building a career than a relationship, never noticed any lose. A few chaotic months into her new job however, that outlook changed.

Mikey Dayville had an open brief with the Mail. Having once worked there as a full time photographer, he periodically contributing material to their weekly colour supplement whenever his ever-expanding schedule allowed. After returning from South America with a photo story for the magazine however, he found himself for once at a loose end. Instead of taking the time to relax and enjoy his new Hampstead home Mikey – curious to experience his old job again – and quite attracted to the new junior reporter, accepted an offer from Colin Ford to join Jane on her first murder assignment.

The story itself was nothing extraordinary, but to Mikey and Jane it seemed just the opposite. They talked and joked and laughed endlessly, almost oblivious to the reason that they were together but not wanting their assignment to end. It affected Mikey so much that he found reasons to stay with the paper for the rest of the month, and turned down several assignments that would take him out of the country again. For Jane the extra weeks were not nearly enough and, when Mikey reluctantly had to say farewell to the paper and finalize travel arrangements for a trip to Taiwan, Jane grabbed a few days holiday so that she could be with him before he departed. They spent the following three days in blissful isolation from the outside world and only emerged from Mikey's house for Jane to drive him to Heathrow Airport.

As Mikey kissed Jane goodbye at the boarding gate, he placed in her hand a small gift wrapped box; asking her not to open it until he had gone. She waited tearfully until his plane was a dot against the sky before opening the package and inside found a set of keys. With them she found a note which read: "These are the keys to my house. The keys to my heart you already have."

Six months on, Jane's blossoming relationship with Mikey became complicated when Colin Ford offered her the vacant role of Deputy News Editor. It was a decision which shocked everybody, not least Jane. The move meant a substantial pay-rise and a more than equivalent increase in her responsibilities and work hours but, this time, Jane was not sure she was ready for it. However good she thought she was, Jane knew that there were other, more experienced journalists on the paper to whom the role would be better suited. But when she aired her misgivings to her boss, Colin simply chided Jane for her indecision; commenting that the sooner she stopped measuring her abilities against those of her colleagues the better. Reluctantly, Jane accepted the position.

It was seen as favouritism by some, whilst others maliciously formed the opinion that, with his marriage on the verge of collapse, Colin was thinking with an organ other than his brain. Jane, too busy now to be aware of office gossip, failed to realise that her promotion had engendered quite such an air of resentment within her colleagues. Her only concern was that the extra workload would still leave her some time for Mikey when he returned. Many silently wondered just how long Jane could take the pressure before buckling under the stress.

As summer approached Jane struggled to cope with her position. Finally realising that she was openly resented by her work mates she found her new task a thankless one: isolated and despised as she was by people she had once considered friends.

Only Colin kept his faith in Jane's abilities. Ever attentive and kind, he continued reassuring her that she was doing a fine job but, as summer wore on and the strain of work continued, Jane began to question her own commitment to the task. Even in late June it always seemed to Jane that her working day finished when the sun went down. All that kept her going was a set of keys to a house in Hampstead and the knowledge of who would be there when she opened the door.

Jane could never recall if her wavering interest in her job began to show at that time but it was during the summer that an abrupt change occurred in Colin. His usual, placid manner was replaced by a surly brooding and, with increasing frequency, it flared into violent verbal outbursts. Though Jane was aware, as were many close to the News Editor, that Colin's marriage was continuing to deteriorate, all were at a loss to attribute a definitive cause to such a radical change in temperament. Colin had previously seemed resigned to the fate of his marriage, stoically accepting the fact that he and his wife had drifted apart. Now he seemed consumed by some inner demon and Jane soon found herself the main focus of her superior's vitriolic tirades. Shocked and unnerved by an endless stream of insults and insinuations and isolated by her position, Jane began to consider leaving the paper.

Matters came to a head in late July. Jane, already burdened with her own tasks, suddenly found herself snowed under with Colin's work due to an inexplicable absence. Having never missed a day's work and with no one able to contact him at his home Jane, along with most of the office staff, wondered whether the breakdown that for so long had seemed imminent for the News Editor had finally occurred. The extra responsibilities took Jane even later into the night than usual and, unaided by colleagues, she eventually found herself alone and still busy after the last of the paper's stalwart journalists had left to catch their midnight trains out of London. Tired and stiff as the endless day merged into the next, Jane was more than a little surprised when Colin suddenly entered the news room. Puzzled, yet somewhat relieved that her boss had turned up (however late) to help out, Jane took the opportunity to rest her eyes and grab a coffee. She was hit from behind before she had risen from her chair and when she finally woke it seemed that the world – and Colin – had gone mad.

Jane's head had pounded: a dull throb that flared painfully when she had attempted to open her eyes. Blinking, a little of the fuzziness had left her as she regained consciousness and it was then that she noticed a strong, musty smell in her nostrils. Jane had tried to bring her hand to her temple to feel for a wound but, with pain emanating from both arms, she quickly felt a terrible pressure on first her wrists and then her ankles. Within a second she was wide awake and struggling to stand.

Bound at the wrists and ankles, Jane had writhed on the carpet in Colin Ford's office. Attempting furiously to rise, her efforts only allowed her to glimpse what Colin had done while she had been unconscious. Naked from the waist down, what remained of Jane's blouse was sweat stained, shredded and to her horror she saw smears of blood amongst the material. There was a sore, wet sensation from between her legs and buttocks which told the rest of the story and, as the realisation struck her, Jane had begun to scream.

Appearing from nowhere, Colin had clamped his hand upon Jane's mouth. Though she struggled and bit ferociously, a succession of ringing blows to her head soon left her dazed again. With Jane silenced and prostrate Colin had stood back and leered at his colleague. He too was naked from the waist down and a dark patch of blood covered his groin and flaccid penis. Still stunned, Jane had twisted and writhed in an attempt to break her bonds then snaked herself across the carpet in a vain attempt to escape. Breathing hard, Colin had watched her frantic motion for a moment before picking up a carving knife from his desk and straddling her.

Jane had stopped struggling when the knife bit sharply into her throat and with an expression of triumph, Colin had brought his flushed and sweaty face close to hers. Panting heavily, Colin had forced Jane's legs apart while his free hand attempted to push his limp member back inside her. Frozen with terror, Jane found her eyes locked on Colin's compassionless stare. There had been no familiarity in it – no recognition. It was just the soulless, vacant gaze of a madman and, with the knife digging deeper, Jane found herself begging for her life.

Whether it was her pleas, her tears, or her sheer terror that stayed Colin's hand Jane never knew but, in the midst of her ordeal, Colin suddenly seemed to focus on her for the first time: a glimmer of familiarity returning to his face. He had leapt away from her, dropped the knife as if it had burnt him then, with a scream matching Jane's, began maniacally clawing at his face. It was then that Jane had heard the footsteps and shouts from outside of the office and yelled at the top of her lungs to get their attention. As she resumed her slow flight towards the door, a sudden cool draught from the far end of the room had caused her to turn. Colin, his face cut and bloody, crouched in the open window – his fingertips clinging to the frame – his eyes upon her. For a moment Jane had seen some semblance of normality in Colin's face, and the comprehension of what he had done twisted his expression with pain for a fraction of a second before he pushed himself from the window and disappeared without a sound into the darkness.

They said she had been very lucky when they carried her out on the stretcher a few minutes later and, though she felt so thankful to the Police for saving her life, all that went through her mind at the time, was what a bloody stupid thing it had been to say. It was when she was being put into the ambulance that she overheard the reason for her luck. Colin had beaten his wife to death with a carriage clock less than two hours before, then stabbed and killed both the taxi driver who had driven him to work and the security guard in the ground floor reception.

It took a year of intensive psychotherapy before Jane could fully cope with both the physical and mental scars of her ordeal. A similar period before she could enjoy any sort of intimate relationship with Mikey and a further year before she felt confident enough to apply for another newspaper job. The Hampstead & Highgate Chronicle may not have been in the same league as the London Evening Mail but to Jane it gave her everything she needed now. With her career ambitions gone, the local paper allowed her to write without pressure as well as providing her with time for the man who had been the rock she had clung to throughout her entire rehabilitation. Even more than before, Mikey was the most important thing in Jane's life.

Jane found herself absentmindedly fingering the tiny white scar which still showed on her throat and kept her head down as her ex-colleague from the London Evening Mail passed straight by them. She supposed she might never be ready to endure the stilted pleasantries he was bound to make, or the knowing, sympathetic look that would creep periodically across his face as he did so. For Jane that period of her life was best left in the past and if that meant avoiding vague acquaintances then, she felt, it was a small price to pay for peace of mind. They walked on.

Near the top of the rise Jane and Mikey stopped by the cordon tape, waiting for the constable on duty to amble over. Jane flashed her press card and her smile and recounted the phone conversation she had had earlier that morning with a Sergeant Rose. The officer turned away to mumble briefly into his radio and after a few responsive bursts of replying static allowed them to pass. They stepped over the drooping red and white tape and preceded towards the brow of the hill, the constable obligingly pointing the way.

'Did you see Adam back there?' Jane asked as they walked down the other side of the hill. She wanted to purge the guilt she felt in avoiding him as quickly as possible.

'Mm,' replied Mikey with a nod. 'Though not as quickly as you did.'

Jane gave a rueful smile and shrugged.

'You know how it is,' she said, attempting the statement to convey a lightness she did not quite feel.

'Mm. I know,' replied Mikey with a knowing glance. He put his arm around her waist and kissed her lightly on the cheek as they strode through the grass.

The glade was picturesque, peaceful and bathed in sunshine. On any other day its secluded beauty, flanked as it was on all sides by trees, would have made the ideal retreat for those seeking tranquillity. The presence of two policemen and the roped off patch of bloody grass robbed the area of its usual serenity.

The constables fidgeted as Mikey and Jane approached. Taking turns to frown up at the sky they wiped the sweat from their brows and grimly endured their baking vigil. Jane led the way towards the pair and, with her well honed smile blazing, set about attempting to glean any small piece of information out of them. Both officers were reluctant to divulge anything but, having stood in the same oppressive spot for almost two hours they were bored enough to be more forthcoming than usual. For them, Jane was light relief and they welcomed the distraction as she tried the most oblique questioning approaches she could think of: endeavouring to catch them off-guard.

Mikey sauntered past the group, beginning to unzip his camera bag before he drew level with the murder site. He had seen the rope square as they had broken through the western tree line and though his heart had fluttered slightly at the prospect of what he was about to see he reassured himself with the fact that, from a distance, the scene did not look particularly imposing. Now, with his first clear view of the blood matted vegetation, he was not so sure.

He stopped and crouched down, placing his bag in the long grass and removing a camera. He paused and remained on his haunches, holding the camera with one hand while the other searched his jumpsuit for cigarettes. Shit, he thought as he surveyed the bloodied grass, I shouldn't have come. Mikey lit his cigarette – shook his head as if the action would dislodge the flashing memory of Geoff's fallen, broken body. He sighed, feeling the sadness resurface, the bleakness he had felt before welling up inside him. I really shouldn't have come, he repeated to himself. I thought I was ready, but I'm not. Not yet. He looked down at his camera, glanced over to where Jane still chatted with the policemen, catching the odd word from their conversation. He knew she would understand. If he put away his camera and did not take the pictures, Mikey knew Jane would understand completely. But would he? Hadn't he insisted on getting back into the swing of things? What did you really expect, he thought, chastising himself: did you really think it was going to be so painless? That you could loose a close friend and just forget? Perhaps he had, sighed Mikey, and focused the camera on the blood.

It took about four seconds to get the photos he needed, but Mikey continued to click away, ignoring the matted grass within the rope and shooting randomly at the wooded slope behind the murder scene. He tried to relax his mind, put aside the images of blood by concentrating his attention on some impromptu nature photography. He was also aware that the longer he kept taking pictures, the more time he gave Jane to question the policemen. He returned to his bag, retrieved a second camera and, moving up the wooded slope from the murder site, continued shooting.

It was a relief when Jane ruined one of Mikey's pictures by walking into frame and signalled to him with a discreet thumbs up. Mikey lowered the camera with a smile and strolled down from his position amongst the trees.

'We'd better be off!' Jane said with a grin.

Mikey nodded and returned the camera to his bag then, settling it on his shoulder, led the way towards the eastern tree line.

'So?' Mikey asked when they were out of sight of the policemen. 'What did you get?'

Jane continued to grin and slipped her arm through his. 'More than I expected. Much more.'

'And?'

'Aaand? It would appear that the Met's chief suspect in this case is a wild animal.'

Mikey stopped, taking in the sentence. 'A WILD ANIMAL?!' he exclaimed. Jane's eyes blazed momentarily and she quickly placed a quieting finger upon her boyfriend's lips.

'Shhhshh!' she hissed.

'Sorry,' said Mikey, dropping his voice. He frowned, remembering the stained grass. 'What sort of wild animal?'

Jane walked on a few paces before turning to give another grin. 'I don't know, yet. But you can bet your life it's not a fox.'

She walked on. Mikey hefted his bag on his shoulder and

trotted to catch up.

'So what else did they say?' he asked as he drew level.

Jane shrugged. 'Not a lot. Young man. Very messy attack. They're bored stupid from standing there so long. But I'm pretty sure no-one else knows about the animal yet.'

'So what now? Shouldn't the Police be cordoning off the heath? Warning the public, that sort of thing?'

'Aahh! C'mon Mikey,' said Jane, placing her hand in his. 'You know them better than that. They aren't going to risk looking foolish now are they?'

The pair smiled grimly at the joke. On that first, magical assignment which had paired Mikey with Jane at the London Evening Mail, the two of them had overheard a senior Police officer state to one of his subordinates that the reason they were withholding vital evidence from the public in the murder case was that he personally did not want to look foolish if they got it wrong. Jane had made both the statement and the hidden evidence national news and the ensuing public outcry had instigated a government review of Police-public relations. It seemed the investigation had changed little.

'No, they won't say a thing until they're certain,' continued Jane. 'Alerting the public is my job.'

Mikey nodded and cast his gaze around the bushes and trees surrounded them, wondering just where a wild animal would hide itself. There was certainly the space, but still?

'What's your next move?' He asked.

'Phone London Zoo I suppose,' replied Jane. 'It's the most likely place. If I get no luck there I'll start checking on circuses and fairs. Then I'll get back down to the station and see if I can get a name for the body.' Jane thought a moment then grinned. 'If I get lucky with the phone calls, I may have some interesting questions to ask the Police about their murder suspect.'

'Do you really believe there's a lion or something, roaming

around Hampstead Heath?' Though he had begun to eye the bushes cautiously, Mikey still found the possibility a little far fetched.

'I don't know,' Jane replied, 'but I intend to find out. It is a little hard to believe, and those two Policemen think so too. But at the moment they must have something to lead them to that conclusion. I'll have to see what I can dig up.'

They walked on, gradually making their way back to Hampstead in a wide arc. She had not noticed it, but subconsciously Jane was avoiding the possibility of meeting her old work colleague again.

It was mid-afternoon before Mikey returned home, having left Jane to continue her animal investigations with the promise that he would have the photos developed for her that evening. There was no rush for the pictures, Mikey knew, but after considering his qualms on the heath it seemed best to get them out of the way as soon as possible.

He deposited his camera bag on the sofa and sat for a moment on the padded arm, vacantly watching dust play in the sunshine which streamed through the rear windows. The effect should have been soothing but the first thought which entered Mikey's head was to contact his cleaner – he could not remember the last time she had been round to tidy. Not since the Balkans, Mikey realised and instantly found Geoff Freeman back in his thoughts.

'I've got to try and relax!' Mikey growled, standing and digging his hands into his hair. He slapped his face several times to see if it would help then noticed his answering machine had registered four calls.

Mikey flicked the playback switch and while the tape rewound raided the fridge for a beer. The first two calls were from friends on national newspapers, both asking if Mikey was available later in the week.

'I'm on bloody holiday!' Mikey shouted from the kitchen. He looked around for a bottle opener.

The third message was from his father and Mikey paused in the kitchen doorway to listen. It was obvious from the way the sentence cut in half way and the faltering disjointed speech that his dad still had not got used to answering machines. His father's call finished and the hesitant tone was replaced by the smooth joviality of Cooper, an old acquaintance of Mikey's from his early newspaper days.

'Sooo,' said the voice, tinny yet unmistakable through the minute speaker, 'Captain Camera's back in town! Well, if he can be bothered to look up an old friend when his schedule allows, I've found an amazing new restaurant that you'll just love! The decor's awful, the service is terrible, and the food isn't even worth mentioning. Everybody's going there. Give me a call, Mikey. Hope to see you soon. Bye? Oh, by the way, it's Cooper.'

Mikey smiled. Typical Cooper, he thought. He moved towards the phone and then eyed the sofa where his camera bag still sat.

'Let's get you out of the way first, shall we,' said Mikey. He picked up the bag and headed for his basement.

At the bottom of a narrow set of stairs which ran down from the kitchen, the basement opened out into one large room. The floor was concrete and the blank, plastered walls were all but obscured by a myriad of photographs. The basement was one of the features Mikey had liked about the house when he had bought it, and now it housed his developing equipment. Everything from a state-of-the-art colour processing machine which occupied one corner, to his faithful old black and white rostrum camera which loomed large in another. The centre of the room was taken up with a workbench, on which sat chemical trays and a light box and above that ran a wall to wall clothes line, weighed down with bulldog clips. The whole room was bathed in red light and, although he lived alone, he had installed a warning light which shone above the entrance in the kitchen.

Mikey emptied the films from his cameras then flicked on the radio – humming tunelessly to himself as he placed the film rolls into drums for development. Once done he exited the basement to phone his father.

'I should be so lucky' by Kylie Minogue was playing when Mikey returned to the basement a little later and he leapt at the tuner; muttering curses as he searched for a station which was not playing anything by Stock, Aitken and Waterman. He rubbed his ear, still hot from its confinement on the phone. He had forgotten how much his father could talk. Satisfied the radio was now only going to play rock, Mikey stubbed out his cigarette and went to work on his films.

He had developed four rolls, one hundred and forty four pictures in all and, after releasing them from the drums, he cut the film into strips and began to make contact sheets to decide which shots he would enlarge into prints.

The first film exposed was not one Mikey had taken that day and when he scanned the rows of tiny frames he recognised the crowd scenes he had taken from his picnic spot on Parliament Hill. He smiled. Even at this scale he could tell that the pictures of the children in the swimming pool had come out beautifully, as had the old couple with the beach towel. He put the sheet to one side and began exposing the other three films for Jane.

An hour later Mikey stood in the living room with one hundred and forty four pictures spread before him on the carpet: trying hard to believe his eyes. He had not intended developing them all, just the relevant ones from the murder site for Jane. What he had found on the last three contact sheets however, had first caused him to scrutinise them in curious disbelief, then recheck the frames from Parliament Hill. The curiosity had turned to incredulity when he did so and, unable to accept what he was seeing, Mikey had set about developing them all.

Now they lay before him, a sea of gloss emulsion images, stretching back towards the rear windows. The Parliament Hill photographs were closest to his feet and Mikey scanned them once more, rechecking what he already knew: the omission that was part of the problem. There was the photograph: the couple with the beach towel. Frozen in mid-debate with the man's arm half raised, the woman smiling. That was the shot, Mikey knew it, yet the focus of the photograph was missing. Non-existent. For reasons Mikey could not comprehend, the preacher, the only reason he had taken the picture, was not there. Mikey had scrutinized the contact sheet and then the negatives to double check that this was the shot but, no matter how sure he was, or however many times he stared at the image, the preacher remained noticeable only by his absence. It could have been a fault in the camera, as Mikey had first considered, or a frame lost at the end of the role. Taken in isolation, he would have thought nothing more of the minor discrepancy. Unfortunately the problem of the absent preacher was disturbingly accentuated by the photographs Mikey had taken at the murder site. Of the many photographs he had taken that morning, every one but two contained the preacher: staring directly and intently at the camera in each frame.

Mikey shook his head at the sight and balled his hands into his eyes, rubbing them furiously in an attempt to relieve the strain felt from his continued scrutiny. He reached for his cigarettes and shifted his focus across the room – out of the window to see the warm glow of the summer afternoon. The sight helped to settle him and he walked to the kitchen, trampling over the photographs as he went in an act of contempt for the conundrum they posed.

Mikey opened the back door and stepped out into the sunshine, dusting down a weather beaten wicker chair on his patio to sit and smoke. He recapped the debate he had been having with himself for the last few minutes, abstractly noting in the process that his garden was in danger of disappearing forever beneath weeds unless immediate action was taken. Mikey had neither the time nor the inclination at that moment, his mind fully occupied with the problem of the pictures. He left the plant life to fend for itself and returned indoors, resuming his debate before the photographs. This time he thought aloud, hoping it would make his arguments more substantial.

'Right!' He pointed at one of the frames containing the preacher. 'You, are supposed to be in that picture!' He cast an accusing finger at the black and white photo of the couple with the beach towel. 'But you're not!? And you can't be a double exposure, because it's a separate fucking film!' Mikey took a large swig from the beer he had collected on his way in. Despite his frustration he was also beginning to feel nervous. 'And even if you were a double exposure,' he continued, waving the bottle. 'You aren't in the same pose!' Mikey's voice dropped to a whisper. 'Why aren't you in the same pose?'

He stared at the multiple pictures of the preacher imploringly. 'But you weren't there. You were never there.' The camera never lies Mikey, he thought to himself humourlessly, so where does that leave you?

Dispassionately, the preacher stared back at Mikey from one hundred and ten different angles around the murder scene. He was amongst the trees. On the grass. By the bloodstain. The same intent expression on his face, eyes always looking straight at the camera. At Mikey. And in each picture he was pointing: sometimes to his left or right, sometimes into the trees or straight down at the ground. Mikey shook his head and sipped at his beer. The images made him feel cold, and the more he studied them, the more Mikey realised it was not just the unnatural presence of the preacher which made him feel uneasy. There was something about the trees on the slope, something familiar he had failed to notice while he had been there. A disconcerting sense of recognition. What did it mean? Who was this invisible man?!

Though he had no idea who he was, Mikey had reached the only conclusion he considered plausible as to what he was. And though the realisation distressed him, he felt it the only answer to the problem of how someone – something – could be seen and not photographed and then visa-versa. It was not the first time he had seen something like this, he suddenly recalled, and memories of a long forgotten day flooded back as he sat on the sofa staring sightlessly at the images. Mikey had only known his father to have accidentally photographed a ghost before.

Mikey had been only six at the time, yet the memory of his parents' house in Kilburn, of that day, were still vividly etched into his mind. He recalled the big colour television in the living room and the old wooden-armed sofa on which he would tunnel amongst the cushions. There had been a glass fruit bowl on the coffee table, its bottom permanently filled with foil wrapped toffees, and a large cage in the corner of the room that housed their noisy macaw.

It had happened in the afternoon. Mikey, curled upon the cushions, was watching television when his father, Patrick, had entered the living room with a sly grin on his face: one hand behind his back. Mikey sat up and watched alertly as his dad sat down with his hand still hidden, sensing some form of surprise. He was disappointed when Mr. Dayville, sly grin even broader, held out a large black and white photograph for him to look at.

Patrick Dayville was a professional photographer – weddings and portraits mainly – plus the occasional job from the Kilburn Herald. In his spare time he loved to walk up the long incline from the dusty bustle of Kilburn and wander around the fresher climbs of Hampstead Heath, Highgate; and Highgate Cemetery - always with camera in hand. He would photograph the plant life, the birds or the ornate headstones in the cemetery but his favourite pictures were always of those people who used the heath. It was a passion which in later years he had passed on to his son but, Parliament Hill was, even as an adult, the furthest east Mikey would go. Though so many years had passed, Mikey still never ventured near Highgate Cemetery. The photo his father had showed him that day had subconsciously shied him away.

The young Mikey had looked down at the glossy print in his hand and wondered why his father felt it so important. It showed a group of people standing before a crumbling mock Egyptian facade, part of the open air catacomb of Highgate Cemetery. He had looked up at his father and frowned.

'Tell me what you can see,' prompted Mr. Dayville cryptically.

'Well?' Mikey had begun, studying the photograph more intently.

The picture had been taken at the end of the Egyptian Avenue, the centre piece of Highgate's grand Victorian cemetery. Against a backdrop of weather worn plaster surrounding a rusty vault door, in the middle of the picture stood four people; three adults and a boy of about Mikey's age. A man and a woman stood to the left of the child, the woman holding the boy's hand. The other man, older than the couple, stood directly behind the boy, one hand resting on the child's shoulder. All but the boy were smiling at the camera.

'Well,' began Mikey again. 'The little boy is crying.'

'Yes,' agreed his father. 'What else?'

Mikey frowned in concentration but could find nothing else to comment upon. He shook his head.

'Okay,' Mr. Dayville had said. 'What about the clothes? Notice anything odd?' He indicated with a finger the man on the far left and the man on the right.

Mikey looked. 'That man's got a funny collar,' he observed, pointing to the man on the right.

'Yes, he has, hasn't he,' replied his father. 'Well spotted. And I can't be sure, but I'd say his suit is about a hundred years out of date too.'

Mikey's frown had deepened. 'Why's he wearing a hundred year old suit, dad? Can't he buy a new one?'

Patrick Dayville had laughed. 'No, I don't think he can. You see, when I took this picture the other day, that man wasn't there. It was only the boy and his parents.'

Mikey struggled to comprehend. Failed.

'I think? In fact I'm sure,' said Mikey's father. 'That this man is a ghost.'

Mikey knew vaguely what a ghost was, but the import of what his father was saying only became frighteningly clear as his dad continued. Patrick had been quite exited about his strange discovery and in his enthusiasm to communicate the picture's importance, he failed to realise that he was slowly but surely terrifying his son.

'It's a little bit like if I took your picture now –' explained Mr Dayville '– With you sitting on the sofa. It would just be a picture of you, wouldn't it?'

Mikey nodded.

'But then, what if when I developed it there turned out to be someone you'd never seen before sitting beside you? Wouldn't that be odd?'

The young Mikey felt a coldness spread from the back of his neck all the way to his toes. Tears began to well in his eyes and he looked around the room uncertainly. Was somebody else here? Unseen but watching him? Touching him? His father, leaning back on the sofa and lost in his own thoughts, failed to see how much he was upsetting his son. It was only later, when Mikey sat immobile in the same spot and refused to go upstairs to bed that Patrick Dayville realised the mistake he had made. Mikey vaguely remembered that it had taken a week before he got a good night's sleep but it was years before he had forgotten about the photograph.

The pictures came back into focus as Mikey returned his thoughts to the present, the preacher still staring from almost every photo. The recollection of that other picture seemed somehow to ease the nervousness he had felt and he looked again at the many different shots of the clergyman, trying to fathom what his presence in the pictures could possibly mean. It was possible it was nothing more than coincidence, but then there were over one hundred photos, not just one. Whoever – whatever – this figure was, the evidence seemed to suggest that he was all too aware of Mikey's presence. Mikey thought about Parliament Hill, remembered the look as he had focused on the clergyman – that direct stare back at him across a crowd of many hundreds of people. He could see me then, thought Mikey. And he had smiled at me. It was a chilling thought. A second one followed. The preacher had seemed intent on climbing the hill. Was he, Mikey thought, attempting to reach me?

Mikey grabbed at the photographs and shuffled them into a

pile, obscuring the sight of the clergyman behind the shot of the children playing in the pool. He lit another cigarette and placed the photos amongst the jumble of magazines on his coffee table. That was better. Out of sight, hopefully out of mind. Mikey reached for the phone and attempted to call Jane, desperate for someone to talk to. An engaged tone sounded down the line and he replaced the receiver with a bang. Shit, he thought. He went into the kitchen and attempted to concentrate his mind on domestic banalities, searching the cupboards for food even though he was not hungry. The pictures of the preacher and how they related to him were all he could think of.

Mikey concluded his search by collecting another beer and returned to the sofa. The problem was not going to go away, so he decided to attempt to think it through.

Five minutes and half a beer later, he was massaging his temples in frustration.

'What's the bloody meaning?!' he shouted, exasperated by the thought that he was supposed to be seeing something relevant in the events of the last few days, and getting nowhere past the fact that a ghost appeared to have taken a shine to him.

Somehow there had to be a connection between what he had seen on Parliament Hill and the murder sight photographs. He felt sure of it. But what was the connection? The whole thing made no sense. It took another twenty minutes before he thought he had solved the puzzle.

Mikey had switched on the television to give his brain a rest and watched the late afternoon's children's programmes. After that came the local news and a photograph of Hampstead Heath appeared as the news reader relayed a short item about the murder. Mikey sat bolt upright and stared at the screen, not believing his eyes.

The photo had been taken from the wood above the murder

site and had seemed to have been shot before the Police had lowered the closest perimeter tape. You could see nothing of the glade in which the murder had happened and the entire picture was simply a landscape of trees descending a hill. What hit Mikey was the sudden recollection of his dream from the previous night, in enough detail for him to realise he had seen that wood before from exactly the same angle. Mikey closed his eyes, attempting, as he had tried the night before, to let the images flow.

He had been running through darkness, terrified of something, and had reached the trees. Those trees, he felt positive. Then he had continued on, running yet out of control. There had been a voice! Something, somebody, calling from the woods. It was? It had been familiar, or rather had sounded familiar, and he had caught a glimpse of the caller. He could see him, some vague shape amongst the trees, merging with the darkness. Mikey concentrated, knowing that the images would prove illusive if he tried too hard.

He opened his eyes wide and leapt from the sofa, glaring at the photos on the table beside him. It had been the preacher! He had stood in the trees to the left as Mikey ran past. Beckoning. Calling him by name.

Mikey began to pace frantically up and down the living room, his hand pulling nervously at his chin.

'I don't like this,' he said aloud as he paced. 'I do not like this at all!'

That was the connection. The murder. Whatever it meant, for whatever reason, that had to be the link. He had seen the preacher just as Jane had told him about the murder, and he was there in almost all of the murder site photographs. And now the dream. He had forgotten all about it apart from his fear when he had woken. Now he could recall enough of it to know that it was the preacher again. Reaching out to Mikey, even invading his sleep. But it made no sense! What did he want, this preacher? Was he hostile? Despite everything Mikey felt that this contact was not malicious. Just very, very unnerving.

Another thought struck him, stopped him pacing to stand rigid in the centre of the room – his mouth open wide. When he had run through the woods in his dream, was he retracing the murdered man's path? Was he, could he have been seeing events through his eyes?! That was a terrifying thought.

The sound of the doorbell nearly launched Mikey though the ceiling and he could barely control his racing heart as he answered the door.

'What on earth's the matter?!' asked Jane, staring at the pale face of her boyfriend as the door opened.

'Oh! Thank God!' exclaimed Mikey, clutching at his chest. He let out a huge sigh of relief.

'Are you ill?' Jane asked, stepping through the door, concern evident in her tone. She placed the back of her hand against Mikey's forehead.

'I'm fine, I'm okay,' said Mikey, gripping Jane's hand. He ushered her into the living room and pointed to the pile of photographs. 'Just take a look at those pictures will you,' he said.

Jane still wore a frown. 'Sure,' she replied and sat down, watching Mikey intently as he grabbed the photos from the table and thrust them into her hands. He studied her face as she flicked through the pictures, waiting to see her expression change.

Jane looked up, her brow still furrowed. She cocked her head to one side and stared at Mikey quizzically. 'They're fine,' she said. 'Just what I needed. Did you think they weren't?'

Mikey's face dropped. 'Don't you see him?' he asked.

'Who?' replied Jane, glancing down at the pictures of trees.

Chapter Three

'My husband was in the war, you know,' said Mrs Pleasance, reaching up to tap the man in the grey overalls on the shoulder. The man sighed, dug the spade he was holding into the lawn and resigned himself to another conversation.

'Really,' he replied, not caring if the boredom in his voice was noticed by the old woman.

'Yes,' continued Mrs Pleasance, 'Though, not the big one – that second one – but the other one.'

'The First World War?' replied the man dubiously.

'Not the first!' Mrs Pleasance bristled, 'I may be old, but I'm not that old! No, it was the other one. After the second.' Mrs Pleasance furrowed her brow in concentration. 'Now what was it called..?' she pondered, tapping an index finger on her lips.

'The Korean,' said the man, ignoring the diminutive figure beside him to scan the tiny metal box in his hand.

'Yes, that's right!' agreed Mrs Pleasance, 'The Borean War, that was the one!'

'Korean, you dizzy old tart,' muttered the man under his breath. He gave another sigh and, looking quickly around the garden, smiled pleasantly at the woman and pocketed the box.

'Oh! Stanley did enjoy that!' continued Mrs Pleasance with a shake of her head. 'He was in the artillery, you know.'

'Really,' nodded the man. 'Well I…'

'Nothing better than frightening foreigners, Doris, he used to say to me,' continued Mrs Pleasance enthusiastically. She gave a little laugh. 'Put's the wind up 'em! He always used to say. And Stanley must have been good at it because they gave him a medal.'

The man nodded blankly.

'You're not a foreigner, are you?' asked Mrs Pleasance, suddenly concerned.

'No,' said the man.

'Only you look quite dark.'

'I've just come back from a holiday –' the man pulled a map from his pocket and began to unfold it.

'Ooh,' said Mrs Pleasance with a grimace. 'Was it abroad?' The man nodded. 'We would never go abroad, Stanley didn't like it. He always used to say that the only time he would go abroad was in uniform with a rifle on his shoulder.'

'Senile bitch,' muttered the man from behind his map.

'How long will this thing take?' asked Mrs Pleasance, suddenly changing the subject.

The man lowered the map and indicated the spade. 'As soon as I've dug down far enough, love, I should be able to locate the pipe.' He turned the map and pointed to a large black octagon drawn over it.

Mrs Pleasance nodded. 'You won't damage the lawn though, will you?'

The man shook his head. 'I'll just lift the turf here, and then replace it.' He gave a small chuckle. 'You won't even know I was here.'

'And it's broken, you say?' Mrs Pleasance looked dubiously at the grass.

'That's right,' said the man with a nod. 'But once I've fixed it, it should halve your water bill.'

'And you'll put everything back?' persisted Mrs Pleasance, 'Only Stanley laid this lawn.'

'I can assure you, you have nothing to worry about,' lied the man with his hand on his heart.

Mrs. Pleasance nodded. 'All right, if you're sure.'

The man placed a consoling hand on the old lady's shoulder. 'Trust me,' he said and pulled the spade out from the soil. 'Now I must get on, or my boss'll kill me!'

'All right,' repeated Mrs. Pleasance. 'Would you like some

tea?'

'Lovely,' said the man, beginning to dig. He waited until the old lady had disappeared into the house before checking the contents of his canvas bag. Satisfied, he rechecked his satellite navigation system and continued with his hole.

Late rush-hour traffic clogged the North End Road as Mikey weaved his way towards the North Circular; negotiating stationary cars on a guttural Triumph Bonneville. The sun baked lanes were filled with weary workers, tempers rising with the heat haze as they attempted to escape the city. Envious eyes watched Mikey as he manoeuvred through the static ranks of cars and soon he was picking up speed, heading south towards Richmond. Mikey was over the limit, he knew, but this just would not wait. He had to see his father.

Once through the many jams and congested junctions, Mikey headed for the river; crossing Kew bridge to pass the Botanical Gardens and the Old Deer Park. On any other evening such as this, Mikey would be heading down to the riverside. To sit outside a pub, pint in hand, and watch the sun gently sink as the Thames rose steadily to flood its banks. This evening it was the last thing on his mind.

It took a further ten minutes of short cuts and traffic jams before he was parked on the curb beside his father's house, patting his jacket pocket which held the eerie photos of the preacher. Jane could not see him. Perhaps his father could.

Mikey left the motorbike and strolled up the path; rang the old bell pull and stood waiting for the muffled sound of footsteps in the hallway. He noticed the fir trees standing sentinel beside the door, remembered how short they had seemed the last time he was here. Was it really only six months? He could not recall, so much seemed to have happened since his last visit. Mikey rang the bell a second time, debating whether to tell his father about events in the Balkans. One thing at a time, perhaps, he thought.

The click of the lock broke his line of thought and the door, opening with an almost musical creak, revealed his father: a surprised smile on his face. Mikey grinned back.

'What brings you down here?! Couldn't you wait?!' Patrick Dayville held the door wide and shepherded in his son, hugging Mikey briefly as he stepped into the hallway.

'I know I said next week, dad,' said Mikey, releasing his embrace, 'But I have to talk to you about something.' He walked down the hall.

Patrick closed the door and nodded to his son's receding back.

'Jane not with you?' he asked, instantly trying to ascertain the nature of Mikey's unexpected appearance. His son had disappeared out of sight.

Patrick followed Mikey into the living room to find him slumped in a chair by the front windows. His legs were splayed out before him, eyes heavy lidded and dull.

'You look exhausted,' observed Patrick, walking over to an adjacent seat. Mikey shrugged but remained silent. 'Shall I make some tea?' inquired his father, attempting to coax conversation out of his son.

Mikey shook his head, pulled his cigarettes from a jacket pocket and a large pile of photographs from another. He let out a huge sigh, as if he had been holding his breath since the hallway. Then he spoke, looking at his father as if for the first time.

'I left Jane up at my place...' Mikey said, in answer to his father's earlier inquiry, then added: 'But that's not why I'm here. Jane and I are fine.'

Patrick nodded, pleased that it was not the reason for the visit. He thought of Jane as one of the family.

Mikey let out another, smaller sigh, and lit a cigarette before continuing. 'I need you to have a look at these,' he said, passing the pictures to his father, who caught the intonation in his voice.

Mikey stared across the room. Ignoring Patrick as he flicked through the photographs. Immobile apart from the occasional movement of hand to mouth and an accompanying cloud of smoke.

'Mm,' said Patrick after a time, not really sure what he was supposed to be looking for but conscious of his son's strange mood.

'What can you see?' asked Mikey, finally glancing over.

'Well, it seems to be Parliament Hill and some woodland shots.'

'Can you see a priest?' Mikey asked. He kept his tone light. Not wanting any emotion to show through.

Patrick frowned and returned to the pictures. 'Ah, yes,' he lied, 'Odd chap. Is he a friend of your's?'

Mikey grinned, relief plainly evident on his face. He sat up in his chair.

'No not really,' he said, slowly shaking his head. 'More of a recent acquaintance.'

As Patrick had hoped, Mikey began to recount the events of the last few days.

It was getting darker outside by the time Mikey had finished his story, his father listening intently to every word, never doubting for an instant the integrity of his son's strange tale. It troubled him that he had lied to his son about being able to see the priest, yet he knew from past experience that without coaxing Mikey would probably have kept quiet. There was something vaguely familiar to him about the tale but it was not until the old ghost photo was mentioned that Patrick realised what it was. An episode of their lives, long forgotten, which seemed to be resurfacing. What troubled Patrick was that this time there did not appear to be a ghost.

They took a break. Patrick making some tea, then sat together on the sofa as Mikey aired his views on what he felt the events signified. As he listened, Patrick tried to read between the lines of what his son was saying. In the hope that he would discover the real reason for his son's agitation.

'I'm still sure it connects with this murder... Thank you.' Mikey accepted the cup and saucer his father passed to him.

Patrick perched himself on the arm of the settee and rattled a teaspoon briefly in his cup. He creased his brow. He was not happy with continuing the charade but felt unable now to admit to lying. Instead he tried to steer Mikey's thoughts towards his own. 'You could be right,' he agreed, nodding. 'But perhaps what's more important is to try and fathom the 'how' and 'why'. People don't see this stuff every day,' he added pointedly.

'Jane can't see the figure at all,' Mikey reminded him, unaware of the discomfort his words caused his father.

'Yees...' Patrick squeezed the word through his teeth and quickly took a sip of tea, narrowing his eyes as he stared at the pictures in his son's hand. 'I'll get you that other photo,' he said and left the room.

While his father was upstairs, hunting for the old Highgate picture, a sudden thought occurred to Mikey. He put his cup down and, taking the photographs, began shuffling through the prints until he found the picture of the bloodied ground. Using that as his starting point, Mikey then placed the others around it; putting them in their relative positions so that he began to build a panorama. He had seen David Hockney photos placed in a similar way to achieve a surreal panoramic effect, and although his were not taken to deliberately mimic that, with so many photos taken, Mikey did find a pattern emerging. He swept up the prints and started again, this time omitting those which looked down the slope, working the remaining shots as part of a jigsaw puzzle. He felt a little easier with the images now. Knowing that he was not alone in seeing them.

Using the blood stained grass again as the centre he fanned outwards, overlapping the frames so that they seamlessly joined. He found the preacher pointing right if he appeared in the left hand prints and visa versa. By the time his father came back he had finished, the combined images quite revealing.

'Interesting,' said Patrick. Seeing the large woodland scene over his son's shoulder. 'Does it seem clearer?'

Mikey nodded. All the photos of the preacher, now that they were arranged, pointed from all sides to one photo. In that single frame the preacher this time pointed to his feet. With the surrounding pictures it was easy for Mikey to get a perspective of both the wood and the glade: to see that fifteen feet from the murder sight was something the preacher felt warranted Mikey's attention. The only question on Mikey's mind was what?

'Well, that appears to be the centre of it, dad,' said Mikey, indicating the picture. 'But there can't be anything there that he is pointing to. The Police have combed the entire area.'

'Hhmm,' said Patrick, thinking quickly. 'Well, if he's pointing, it must be for a reason. He must be pointing at something.' In the back of his mind, a half-thought had occurred. If Mikey was to revisit the scene and find nothing there, perhaps it would end his son's present line of reasoning, refocus them on the real causes of his troubles.

Mikey stared at the photos for a moment as his father crouched down beside him. 'Could it be the murder weapon?' mused Mikey quietly.

Patrick frowned and placed a hand gently on his son's

shoulder. 'Possibly,' he said.

To Mikey, one problem still persisted however.

'But how do I, and how does a dead clergyman fit into this?' Mikey could still not fathom why he should be singled out for such a dubious honour.

Mr. Dayville gave a shrug and returned to the sofa. 'Perhaps there is no connection,' he said, then remembered the old black and white photograph in his hand. In light of what his son had said and what had happened when he had seen it before, Patrick was dubious about re-exposing Mikey to it. Yet despite his misgivings Mr. Dayville was willing to take the chance in the hope that the sight would jog Mikey's senses. 'Here's the Highgate picture you wanted,' he said and held his breath as Mikey took the photograph.

Mikey felt a shiver run down his spine as he renewed his acquaintance with the image. It was worse than he had remembered it, somehow more malevolent than those of the preacher. The little boy crying, the parents oblivious to the other man. The apparition smiling as if enjoying his actions. He grimaced and put the photo face down on the carpet.

Patrick waited for a reaction that never came.

'All I can think of,' said Mikey, indicating the pictures of the preacher 'Is that perhaps these things, these spirits, are drawn by death, which is why -' Mikey had reached the conclusion that death was the connecting factor, and was about to mention that Geoff had been on his mind that first time he had seen the preacher. He quickly changed tack. 'It's a local spirit that has found someone aware of it, or possibly the victim of the murder attempting to communicate something important.'

It seemed a bizarre thought to Mikey's father, yet no more bizarre than anything else Mikey had said.

Mikey shrugged. 'Either way. Whatever the reasons behind

it. I don't think I'm going to get a good night's sleep until I've solved, or helped with whatever it is.'

Patrick nodded. 'I think you should visit that spot in the photograph, perhaps what you find there will get you closer to the problem.' He prayed he was right.

They sat in silence, sipping cold tea while Mikey gazed at the multiple figures of the preacher. He wondered whether he would find anything in the wood, and if he did, what the police would say when he took it to a station. Would they believe him or dismiss him as a crank? There had to be something there, though Mikey, some reason for the way the images, like a visual magnet, drew his eye to the central point. It was how Mikey was starting to feel: drawn in. But to what he did not yet know. Tomorrow morning would hopefully shed more light on the problem.

Mikey stayed the night at his father's, phoning Jane to check that she was not angry over his sudden disappearing act. She was more worried than upset, concern easily identifiable in her tone, and Mikey did his best to placate her. He avoided mentioning that his father could see the preacher as well, and said only that they were going to study them for faults. He promised to explain in greater detail what was happening the following day. Mikey knew it would take some explaining, but then he hoped to have some tangible proof by the time they met. He planned to visit the heath the first thing in the morning.

Mikey went to bed late and got a night of untroubled sleep, neither Geoff nor the preacher disturbing his dreams. For his father it was different. Patrick's conscience kept him awake into the early hours, racked by recollections of what he had done to his son all those years ago and chastising himself for not telling Mikey the truth about the photos.

Chapter Four

Though Mikey had gone to bed late, he still found himself awake at six the following morning to see dawn spread slowly across the rooftops of Richmond. Feeling alert and anxious to get to the heath, he grabbed his photos, cigarettes and crash helmet from the front room, left a note for his father in the kitchen promising to update him on developments, then disappeared into the cool of the morning.

It promised to be yet another beautiful day, and the gentle warmth of the rising sun refreshed Mikey even more as he made his way at speed back towards Hampstead. He could not explain why, but this morning he felt on top of the world: calm, alert, totally in control. True, the sun was glinting merrily through the trees as he sped along, and the greenery smelt fresh and strong in the breeze. That had to be a part of it. But at the back of those feelings he felt... Nothing. No guilt, no anxiety. All of the mental baggage which he had brought back from Macedonia seemed to have faded away. Now he could think of Geoff without the associated pain: cherish unburdened the memory of his close friend. And there was something else. Another sensation which tingled through him. Excitement? It surprised him, but Mikey could find no other word to express the feeling. The fear he had experienced in developing the preacher photographs had completely left him, to be replaced by a hopeful anticipation of what he might find. There were still many unanswered questions but he felt good, and he felt confident. He knew he was going to get to the bottom of the mystery.

The heath was practically deserted so early in the morning, enough so that Mikey was able to approach the murder site without encountering any dog-walking early-risers or track suit clad health freaks. He walked down from the north, leaving his motorbike on the pavement by Spaniards Road to follow a winding route around deep scrub and bushes. It was a circuitous path but Mikey felt confident he was heading in the right direction, as if he had travelled the route a thousand times. The thought stopped him in his tracks and he slowly scanned the surrounding plant life. Was this the route he had taken in his dream? If not, why was he so sure of the way? Mikey could certainly not recall ever walking through this part of the heath before. His study of the greenery failed to spark any recollections, and the memories of the nightmare failed to diminish his spirits. Whistling softly, Mikey moved on.

As he passed into the denser shadows of the woods, Mikey considered his actions of the previous evening, his sudden disappearing act from Jane. She had been concerned about his welfare before the preacher episode, now she must think I've gone completely mad, he thought. If it had not been for his father also seeing the preacher in his photographs, Mikey guessed he might be of a mind to agree with that verdict. He hoped she would except his explanation. Or at least just understand it.

The remains of a thorn bush blocked the path he had been following for the last few minutes, forcing Mikey to tramp deep into a brake of waist high nettles which loomed beside the worn mud trail. As he stomped, arms raised, through the weeds, Mikey wondered whether Jane had made any progress in finding out more about the murdered man. Could it have been his preacher? He had been too wrapped up in his own troubles the previous evening to ask. If he found something in the hollow, would that aid the Police in catching the murderer? He felt sure it must, there had to be a connection. But what about the belief that it could be an animal? Mikey still found the possibility a little far fetched. The blood matted grass pointed to violence, that much was obvious. But a wild animal? How did that explain the attentions of his ghostly friend? Too many questions, Mikey thought. Perhaps the officers on duty had been joking with Jane. She had made it plain she was a journalist, so perhaps they had had a little fun sending her off on a wild goose chase.

'Wild lion chase,' Mikey corrected himself aloud with grim humour.

Well, he would soon see, he thought and walked on, brushing greenery from his jump suit.

The terrain became familiar as he cleared a rise in the ground and in an instant he knew for certain he had dreamt of this place. He stopped for a moment, took in the air and the scenery. The procession of oaks which merged into the shadows as the ground dropped away. Yep, thought Mikey, just like the picture on television.

He sauntered down the hill, unfazed by the recollection, and soon stood beside the taped off patch of darkened grass. Mikey looked around the empty glade, getting his bearings; half expecting the preacher to pop up out of nowhere and point the way. He did not appear, and the hollow, save for the swish of Mikey's strides through the grass was still and quiet. Even the birds seemed hushed by the brilliance of the morning.

Mikey walked in the direction the preacher had pointed to, debating briefly whether to consult the photos and make sure he got the right spot. It proved unnecessary. After only a few steps back into the trees Mikey could see the place where the preacher had stood. What puzzled him was how the Police could have overlooked the spot.

On the leaf strewn floor lay a dark brown book, leather bound and clasped with a silver lock. It showed signs of age but seemed well cared for, and from the deep lustre of the binding Mikey could tell it had not been exposed to the elements for long. He crouched down to pick it up, turning it over in his hands to feel its weight and the embossed ridges in the leather. It was old, worn to a blackened shine on its edges, and locked tight. Mikey stood and looked around again. This could not be it, surely. Something so large must have been dropped here since the murder. Mikey could not comprehend how the police could overlook so obvious an item, and yet... He furrowed his brow. It certainly wasn't a murder weapon. Placing the book beside him, Mikey knelt down to examine the ground, brushing away the loose covering of leaves to search for evidence of freshly disturbed earth. There was none.

A few feet away lay a piece of broken branch. Mikey picked it up and used it to scratch at the surface. Perhaps what he was looking for had been long buried. It was slow and laborious work, the soil dry and compact, the stick a cumbersome implement and, after a time, he had to admit defeat. He was not going to uncover any incriminating evidence, just roots. So was the book it? His reason for coming here? He shovelled the dirt back into the shallow hole before stamping the ground flat again and threw the stick into a clump of bracken at the base of a tree. He checked his hands which were now filthy and brushed them on his jump suit in a vain attempt to clean them.

Mikey picked up the book and made his way back up the slope, turning to shake his head ruefully at the spot, irritated that he had found nothing conclusive. Only more questions.

'So what do I do now?' he said quietly to himself as he walked on. 'Go to the Police? Tell them I found a bloody great book that they must have missed?! I don't think so.'

He reached the top of the rise and turned again to view the site one final time. He sighed, perplexed by the turn of events, his good mood diminishing. What do I do now? he thought, and wandered back to find his bike.

The man sat on the window ledge and gazed down into the street. It was a quiet and peaceful scene at most times of the day, but he found nothing quite so relaxing than this time. To watch his hurrying neighbours head for work never failed to provide him with an indescribable sensation of happiness and so he would sit and follow their various courses up and down the pavement secure in the knowledge that he would not, and would never have to, follow in their footsteps. His path led in an entirely different direction. Never to chase the clock, he thought, and laughed quietly to himself.

Occasionally he would shout a jovial 'Good morning!', or simply smile and wave as the 'nine-to-fivers' passed by his short driveway. He did not know whether such behaviour made those he greeted feel good or bad about their coming day, but it gave him the most enormous pleasure. He checked his watch and craned his neck around the window frame to look up the street. Nine o'clock. The morning rush was nearly over. And Garvin was late.

Twenty feet below him, a black and white cat trotted along the wall at the edge of the short front lawn. It froze half way to flick its eyes suspiciously around, suddenly arching its back to let out a guttural growl. The man smiled. Can you sense it? Or can't you? he thought, watching the animal intently. The cat remained immobile, apart from its head which turned to face the house, its gaze slowly climbing to settle finally and unblinkingly on him. He returned the stare, his smile becoming a grin. You don't know what it is, he thought, eying the motionless animal, but you won't dare come any closer, will you? They never did and the man had noted with interest how the wall acted as a mental as well as physical boundary for the local feline population. All the birds in the world would not tempt them to venture onto the grass beyond its boundary.

As the man eyed the cat, his mind was unfocused on the

creature, wandering instead through the house: down the three flights of stairs to the basement. That was where that feeling emanated from, the sensation that the cat was so right to be wary of. He could sense it himself now that he had focused upon it. A low tingling, almost a shiver, far down in the depths of his senses. A tangible thing, radiating out in ever weakening waves from its source. Such power! he thought. Such beauty to be held in something so seemingly fragile. Wonderful!

The chant began. A steady pulse like the beat of a heart, slowly growing in strength and volume. The man could not be sure of its origin for it seemed gradually to rise from nothing on the back of the vibration which pervaded his body. Lilting, it rose through him, gently building until it became all, sweeping the tremor before it, carrying the man up and round, twisting and spinning until he felt it touch his very soul: merge with it. The note changed. A deeper, bass tone crept into the melody and he knew he was now controlling it, orchestrating it. Moulding and shaping the tune into his own song. He carried the theme higher, to a cacophony of overwhelming emotion, felt the very fibre of his body sing with its brilliance. His mind glowed with the power coursing through it. Then he felt it fade. The euphoria diminish and his concentration waver and fail.

Then he was back at the window. Dizzily viewing a day that seemed suddenly dim. Insipid by comparison. He let out a deep sigh and looked down to the wall.

In the flower bed lay the remains of a cat, misshapen and singed down one side. Its eyes appeared to be missing; burnt and hollow sockets gazing vacantly across the grass. The man studied the remains, blinked twice as if unable to believe what he was seeing. He grinned. Garvin will be impressed, he thought, and left the window.

Inspector Fletcher tapped his pen twice on the desk. The second strike clicking the ballpoint into position. He looked up from the untidy jumble of paperwork scattered before him and regarded the young woman who sat opposite. In his best sympathetic tone, he said:

'I'm very sorry, Miss McDonald. I know this is a difficult thing to come to terms with.'

Claire McDonald nodded but continued to stare vacantly at the dark, chipped varnish on the reverse side of the desk. Handkerchief still clutched to her mouth, she vainly attempted to stifle another sob. Fletcher watched her, admiring – despite the understandable show of emotion – her poise and control. He had seen so many distraught people in this situation. Mental, physical wrecks unable come to terms with their grief so soon after identifying a loved one. Some made it past the mortuary door before cracking, some to the slab. A minority, of which Claire was one, got through the entire ordeal without a twitch; the realisation and emotion following after. Yet even then the mental strain showed; a distance of manner, a deadening of tone. Claire McDonald had followed just that pattern when asked to identify the mangled remains of her brother.

The door at the far side of the office creaked open, causing Fletcher to switch his gaze and Claire McDonald to turn; startled at the sudden noise. Sergeant Rose entered the room with a cup-laden tray and placed it gently on the edge of Fletcher's desk. The inspector acknowledged the action with a wink.

'Thanks Pete,' he said, reaching for one of the Styrofoam cups.

'Would you like any sugar Miss?' Sergeant Rose asked, offering a cup to Claire. She shook her head, accepted the tea and sipped at it mechanically.

Fletcher took an exploratory sip from his cup, grimaced as he swallowed and cast an accusing glance at his sergeant. Rose smiled, drank from the third cup and exited with the tray. The inspector put his tea down and looked over at Claire.

'You'll probably feel better if you don't drink the tea,' he quipped.

Claire managed a thin smile but hung onto the cup.

That's a little better, Fletcher thought. He used the opening to press on. 'Just take your time, Miss McDonald. There's no rush, and I know this isn't easy. But when you're ready...' he let the sentence tail off.

Claire dabbed at her eyes with the handkerchief and nodding managed another brief smile. 'I'm okay, thank you,' she said. She clasped one hand firmly in her lap and gazed at the inspector.

'Okay then,' replied Fletcher, smiling back. He picked up his pen and straightened the topmost paper on his desk. 'What can you tell us about your brother's whereabouts over the last week?....'

An hour later Sergeant Rose sat in the chair so recently vacated by Claire McDonald, watching his superior light another cigarette.

'So what's the S.P.?' Rose asked.

Fletcher blew out a cloud of smoke and shrugged, the action ridging the shoulders of his shabby jacket. 'By all accounts Tom McDonald dropped out of university a few months back,' he said, consulting his notes. 'Miss McDonald said she hadn't seen him since five months before that and apart from one telephone call had had no contact from him over the remaining months.' Fletcher made the lines almost lyrical. Conducting and punctuating the sentences with his cigarette.

The sergeant grunted. 'So not much help then.'

Bob Fletcher leaned back in his chair and took another drag on his cigarette. 'Actually, we may have a lead.' He turned his attention from the ceiling to Rose, who made a surprised face. Fletcher continued: 'His sister claims that the reason he left college was to follow some fellow student...a...' he glanced down at his notes, "Peter Bradford", who left the university the term before. Miss McDonald claims that her brother was besotted with him.'

Rose pulled another face. 'Gay?'

Fletcher gave a brief shake of his head. 'Not according to his sister, no. She said it was more like a father figure thing.' It was Fletcher's turn to make a face. 'I quote: "Tom was forever talking about him, trying to behave like him, dress like him". That sort of thing.'

'Obsessive character then, our boy.' Pete Rose crossed his legs and searched his pocket for some nicotine chewing gum. He tried not to keep looking at the cigarette packet on the desk.

'Seemingly,' Fletcher replied. 'Their mother died years ago and Tom didn't get on with his father; big businessman, lives abroad, never sees the kids. Apparently Tom was always looking for a replacement... From a very early age according to his sister. But she said the situation with this Bradford character was a little too weird for her liking. That Tom was a little too involved. She met him once, at..er... "St. Thomas's College, Oxford", and says she did not like what she saw. The inspector scanned his notes with a finger. ' She felt very protective towards her younger brother... Attempted to convince Tom to stay away from him and for a time she says that it had some effect. Blah, blah, blah... Bradford was in the year above Tom and left after finishing his course. Tom had another year to go and so Claire McDonald thought that her brother was rid of him. The next thing she knows he's disappeared from the university... Months later she gets a phone call from him saying he's with Bradford in London and preparing for an expedition.'

'So Bradford lives in London.'

'Possibly, but she didn't know where. The postmark said Westminster.'

'Expedition? What is he then? Some mountaineer, this Peter Bradford?'

Fletcher shook his head and moved back to rest his hands on the desk. 'Nope. Apparently, and here's the interesting part, both McDonald and Bradford studied Egyptology at college.'

Sergeant Rose looked blank. 'How's that relevant to our case?'

Fletcher shrugged the ridges into his shoulders again. 'There could be a connection with another case.' He wagged a finger at his sergeant. 'Ever meet Jack Faber?'

Rose shook his head.

'Went to Hendon with him. Nice enough bloke.' Fletcher twisted round to scan the wall behind his desk; pointed to a graduation photo hanging crookedly above him. 'That's him, next to me. End of the second row.'

Pete Rose squinted at the picture and grinned. 'You've put on weight, boss.'

Fletcher ignored the jibe and straightened the frame.

'Anyway, Faber works down at the Yard and is handling the Sacrificial Murders case, y'know?'

Rose nodded. Like everyone else in the country, he knew about that particular case. The papers and news programmes had talked of little else over the last few weeks.

'I had drink with him about a week back,' continued Fletcher, 'and he told me some stuff that, in light of what Claire McDonald just told me, could – just could mind you – be a connection between the two cases. Have you seen the memos from the Yard about the case. The stuff that hasn't been released to the public yet?'

The sergeant nodded. 'Some axes were stolen from the British Museum, weren't they? As far as I know that's still confidential to eliminate crank callers.'

'Hmm,' said Fletcher. 'Egyptian axes by all accounts, nothing else was touched. And according to Faber the murders have all been carried out with those same axes, and meticulously executed if you'll excuse the pun. Very unusual, Faber says. More so than the press and public know. He's got some bod from the museum on the team but so far hasn't got any real motive apart from a religious angle. The bod thinks the killings have the hallmark of some Egyptian sect, but so far they have no concrete suspects.'

'Has the lab come up with anything concrete on our murder yet?' Rose asked. 'Anything more definite that could connect the cases?'

Fletcher stubbed his cigarette into an overflowing ashtray, lit another, then pulled a manila envelope from the top drawer of his desk. He passed it to his sergeant.

'It came in earlier. Seems our Doctor Shaw has finally made some progress. I've spoken to Faber, who's interested in the case, mainly because of the other detail which points to a similarity.'

'Which is?'

'Well, again this is something Faber hasn't made public yet... And won't be from our case either.' Fletcher paused. 'The major organs were all found to be missing on our boy, right?' Rose nodded grimly. 'Well according to Jack that's been a chief factor in his case too.'

'So Shaw's ruled out his wild animal theory then?' Sergeant Rose flicked through the papers in the envelope.

'Yeah.' Fletcher shook his head in mock disbelief. 'So we can stop interrogating those lions we got from London Zoo now...' The inspector indicated the envelope. 'Shaw reckons death was between two – three o'clock on the Tuesday morning and that some form of unusual clawed implement, or glove was used to carry out the murder -'

'Would that make it sacrificial?' asked Rose.

Fletcher shook his head again. 'Not like Faber's, no. Which is a pity. No evidence of axes being used. That does not mean, however, that there is no connection.'

It seemed to Sergeant Rose that the inspector was a little too concerned about there being a comparison between the cases. Despite such misgivings however, he nodded as Fletcher continued.

'The doc' believes that this glove thing made it look superficially like an animal mauling, but the absence of any bite wounds on the neck apparently rule out that possibility. That and the angles of the initial blows indicate that the attacker was probably taller than McDonald, and the distribution of blood marks show McDonald remained standing for the early part of the assault.'

Rose was silent for a moment. 'What ever happened to plain old stabbings?' he asked, perplexed. 'Why go to the length of making it look like an animal attack?'

'God knows,' replied Fletcher. 'The more I think I know the workings of the criminal mind, the more the sick bastards surprise me. Maybe it was a full moon. Hopefully these curious little details will become more obvious as we get a bit further with this thing.'

Rose jerked a thumb at the lab report. 'Did Shaw find any cotton fibres? Hair?'

'None,' Fletcher replied. 'Which is a sod. So all we have to go on is this Bradford bloke, an approximate height, and the fact that Shaw reckons the murderer was pretty fit. Quite muscular, I think he said. He believes that to pull open a rib cage like that and break it that way would require some considerable strength.'

'Lovely,' Rose grimaced, remembering the body on the heath. 'So if Bradford's a six foot five body builder and owns a wolf man suit he could be our boy.'

'Who knows?' Fletcher leaned back in his chair and stretched. 'But find him.' He yawned. 'See what you can get out of him. In the meantime I'm going to give 'Faber of the Yard' a call and see if we can get him over here.'

Sergeant Rose frowned. The constant reference to Faber was beginning to irritate. 'This could all be coincidence though, couldn't it?' he said. 'The connection with Faber's case?' Rose tried to keep the disdain from his voice.

Fletcher sighed. Rose was still relatively inexperienced, he thought, but he would learn in time. 'Yep,' the inspector replied. 'Every bit of it could be completely coincidental. But at the moment it's all we have to go on. Like old Sherlock says: 'Once you eliminate the impossible, whatever's left, however thingy... Etcetera, etcetera...' Fletcher arched his eyebrows 'Either that or you come up with something on the house to house enquiries.'

Rose nodded. Neither one of them gave much hope to that line of investigation.

The inspector reached to pick up the phone and checked his address book for Jack Faber's number. The meeting was over. Sergeant Rose returned the files to the envelope and left to hunt down Peter Bradford. He had reached the door before Fletcher called him back.

Rose turned to see the inspector muttering something into the phone, his left hand beckoning the Sergeant distractedly as he listened to whoever was at the other end. Rose returned to the desk. Fletcher put his hand over the mouthpiece and said quickly.

'Now we've got an idea of the murder weapon, get the divers to check the ponds again.'

Rose nodded. The inspector's concentration briefly went back to the phone before his hand returned to cover the mouthpiece. He gave the sergeant a quick grin, indicated he should hold on, then rummaged through the clutter of his desk. After a short frantic search and a couple of affirmative grunts into the phone, Fletcher produced a small colour photograph which he passed over to the sergeant.

'Claire McDonald gave me this. Get some posters done,' he said and returned to his call.

Outside in the corridor, Rose took a closer look at the picture. It showed Claire McDonald and her brother posed before what looked like a college entrance, arm in arm and grinning broadly at the camera. He wondered how old the picture was. Not very, judging by Miss McDonald, she looked just the same. Poor bastard, he thought, focusing his attention on Tom. He looked nothing like the bloody, pathetic mess they had found on the heath. Yet despite the devastation wrought upon the body, it was the dull, half-closed stare that had remained the sergeant's most vivid memory. In the picture, Tom McDonald's eyes were bright. Alive. Rose shuddered at the thought of what those eyes had seen before life had faded from them. He put the photograph in the forensic envelope and walked on.

As he made his way towards Highgate station's cramped file room, Rose questioned again the idea that their case was in some way connected with the sacrificial murders. It seemed counter-productive to him to even think such a thing until they had more evidence than the purely circumstantial stuff which Fletcher felt so conclusive. There were more dissimilarities than similarities as far as he could see. And now they had – even if it was tentative – a possible suspect. It irritated Rose in knowing what Fletcher's real motive was. This was a big case, the type that, if successfully investigated, could earn those involved commendations: promotion even. But it was also high profile, the national media and upper echelons of the Met paying close attention to the proceedings. That, the sergeant felt, was the main reason Fletcher was side-stepping the issue. Fear of the limelight. Sergeant Rose's fear was that, by attempting to push the case Faber's way without any real evidence to support it, the attention Fletcher was seeking to avoid would simply focus on him for intentional prevarication. Such a scenario was not going to earn Rose any merit points.

Rose knew the arguments Fletcher thought justified his actions: too many cases, too few men, so he was trying to off-load his work onto somebody with the resources. Yet that lack of manpower was the same in all police divisions, and such motivations were inevitably seen as a poor excuse for bad police work. Rose just hoped they could make some progress before Fletcher accumulated enough circumstantial evidence to make a fool of himself. The sergeant sighed. If he had known that this was how the C.I.D. operated, he would have joined the R.A.F. like his father had wanted.

'What gas leak!?' demanded Bob Holcroft. He squeezed round from behind his cramped counter and, with arms crossed, confronted the workman in the grey overalls.

The man sighed, cast his gaze lazily around the tiny shop then gave a shrug and closed the door behind him.

'I'm not saying you have got a gas leak,' he replied. 'I'm saying you might have a gas leak. That's why I'm here.'

Bob Holcroft frowned and fingered the crystal pendant hanging from his neck. It was already well into the afternoon and so far the only person to venture into his Hampstead 'boutique' was a damn workman!

'I don't have any gas,' he said with finality.

The man in grey lifted his eyes briefly heavenward before fixing the shopkeeper with his stare. He took in the rose tinted glasses, the Hawaiian style T-shirt which strained to cover a portly mid drift and the tortured lycra cycling shorts around his thighs. You're going to be trouble, he thought.

'Do you have a basement?' he asked with a smile.

'I don't see what that has to do with anything,' protested Bob, taking an instant dislike to the man's calm authority. He did not want some workman with an attitude problem disrupting his day. Beside's, he thought, the man, with his tanned skin, blue eyes and square-jawed good looks was far too attractive. After a slow day which had followed all the other slow days of the week, the last thing Bob wanted was some lowly menial standing in his shop who made him feel even more worthless than he already did.

'The pipe runs through your basement,' said the man pointing downwards. 'I have to check that it's okay, otherwise there might be an explosion.'

Bob shook his head. 'Well I was down there earlier, and I didn't smell any gas.'

The man shrugged and held his arms out. 'I'm sorry,' he said, adopting a tone of conciliation. 'But I have to check it. It's my job. I'm sure you're right and there's nothing wrong with your pipes, but I have to make sure. If there's an explosion it could bring your whole shop down. But if you let me check the basement I can be out of your hair in no time. If that's okay?'

Bob, despite the fact that he was in the mood to unleash his frustrations on just about anyone, found himself swayed by the man's plea. He gave a grudging nod.

'Thanks,' said the man with a grin, 'I've just got to get my tools from the van.'

Bob sucked at his lower lip and watched the man exit his shop and cross the road to a grey van. Nice muscle tone, he thought, noting the man's sleek movements: firm lines barely hidden by the overalls. He smiled to himself. His friend Ralph always said that the best ones were the 'bits of rough', but Bob had never mixed in the circles where those types tended to proliferate. Ralph, on the other hand, didn't care where he got his fun from. He could be such a tart sometimes. Here was a bit of rough, though Bob, right on his doorstep: with good looks and a body to match. He withdrew back to his counter as the man closed the van's rear doors and decided to adopt a different tact with him. Perhaps, if he was lucky, today wouldn't be such a loss after all.

The man returned with a heavy looking canvas bag slung over one shoulder and, smiling at the shopkeeper, asked for directions to the basement.

Smiling back, Bob shuffled out from the narrow confines of the counter, beckoned the man to follow and led him through a door at the back of the shop. At the end of a cramped passage, a stairway curved down beneath the floor. Bob flicked at an old brass light switch and led the way to the basement.

'Watch your step,' he said, glancing back.

The workman looked briefly towards the shop door and followed Bob down.

'It's a bit of a mess,' said Bob, swinging an arm to indicate the jumble of boxes and racks of clothes littering the claustrophobic cellar.

The man in grey nodded and pulled a small metal box out from his overall.

'What's that?' asked Bob, pointing at the device.

'Gas detector,' explained the man.

Bob craned his neck to get a better view. He frowned.

'That's a whachamacallit,' he said, trying to remember the name. The man ignored him and, consulting the device, took a few steps towards the wall. 'A satellite thing,' continued Bob, perplexed. 'My friend Ralph has one on his yacht.'

The man, regarding the box in his hand, shrugged and nodded to the shopkeeper. 'That's right,' he replied. 'We use them to detect the pipes.' Bob did not look convinced. The man returned the box to his pocket and removed a wad of paper from another. 'Look,' he said, unfolding a map and turning it so that Bob could see. 'This is the route of the pipe here,' he tapped at a black octagon drawn upon the map. 'It's an old pipe, which is why it's got the leak, and though we know its general location, using the global positioning system we can pin-point it exactly, you see?'

Bob looked at the shape on the map and the eight points circled at each angle. 'And that's my shop, is it?' he asked, pointing to the converging lines where the map showed Hampstead High Street.

'Precisely,' agreed the man. He folded up the map.

'Is it dangerous?' asked Bob.

'Shouldn't be,' replied the workman. 'But if the pipe gives way when I test it, that could be a little tricky.'

Bob nodded. 'Well, I'll leave you to it. Shout out if you need me.' He shuffled as slowly and as close as he could past the workman and creaked his way up the stairs.

The man rechecked the GPS and moved across the floor until the co-ordinates matched those on the map. He pushed a box aside and grimaced when he saw the concrete floor beneath. 'It's got to be in the fucking ground!' he cursed and looked up to the ceiling. A smile slowly spread across his face. 'I am in the ground,' he answered himself with glee.

Above him the thick oak beams which supported the ground floor ran length ways towards the far end of the basement. A single pipe, obviously a later addition, carved its way through them. I bet you're the gas pipe, thought the man with a grin and looked around for something to stand on.

Bob, bored with his empty shop, was fantasising about seeing the man downstairs naked when he heard a faint tapping from beneath his feet. He checked under the counter before realising the origin of the sound and, thankful for a reason to go down, went to check on the workman's progress.

As he reached the first stair, Bob heard the slap of feet on concrete and hurried down into the basement. As the man came into view, Bob saw him returning a metal clothes rail to its place by the wall. Puzzled, the shopkeeper gazed around the basement, wondering for an instant – from the brief look of surprise on the man's face – whether he had stolen anything.

'Everything okay?' asked Bob, injecting some authority into his voice and looking pointedly at the clothes rail.

'Fine,' replied the man. 'All done.' He stooped to pick up his bag and swung it across his shoulder.

Bob regarded the bag. It had been heavy and bulging when the man had walked in: now it appeared to be lighter – less full. Despite the reduction in size, the shopkeeper was curious and spurred by his initial suspicion he asked: 'You don't mind if I check the bag, do you?' Bob crossed his arms and barred the way to the stairs 'I wouldn't want any of my stock to suddenly go missing.'

The man frowned at the implication but unslung his bag and held it out, unzipping it as he did so. Bob peered inside.

'Oh,' said Bob, slightly disappointed that his hypothesis was incorrect. The bag contained only tools. 'So was there a leak?' he asked as the man re-shouldered the bag.

'There was a small crack around one of the joins, but I patched it up. It shouldn't give you any more problems.'

Bob nodded. 'Is it behind there?' he asked, pointing to the

85

clothes rail he had seen the man moving.

'No, up there,' said the workman. He pointed above his head.

Bob looked up and saw the pipe which ran beneath the floor of his shop. Half way along, a small cylindrical object swathed in black tape had been firmly secured to the side of the pipe by three metal bands.

'It's a pressure regulator,' explained the workman, 'It shouldn't give you any problems now.'

Bob frowned, wondering how anybody could be so stupid. 'That's a water pipe,' he said.

The man raised an eyebrow and a smile slowly spread across his face. He looked at the shopkeeper but said nothing.

'That,' said Bob, stabbing a finger in the direction of the pipe, his bad mood returning. 'Is a water pipe!'

'Good,' said the man. His right hand, holding his bag to his shoulder, suddenly released its grip. The shopkeeper had barely enough time to register the bag's descent before the hand had balled to a fist and struck him squarely on the jaw.

Bob stumbled back from the heavy blow, his legs buckling beneath him as he staggered into the stairs. He landed badly and, dazed by the force of the impact, tried to shield his face with his hands as the man advanced and locked his fingers around Bob's windpipe.

'I knew you'd be trouble,' said the man, almost conversationally.

Bob stared, wide-eyed with fear through his fingers as the man fixed him with his gaze. He struggled vainly to breath through the fierce constriction of his throat; to form words that would offer his assailant anything if only he would stop. There was a blurred motion on the edge of the shopkeeper's field of vision and a new sensation suddenly overwhelmed the pain he felt around his windpipe. Bob tried to suck in breath from the shock and instantly attempted to scream. The workman switched his hand from throat to mouth, muffled the fading cry and twisted the knife still deeper between Bob's ribs.

With the scream dead upon his lips, the workman withdrew the knife from Bob's chest and stepped back to watch the body register its final spasms of life. He smiled at the surprise which briefly formed on Bob's face before the muscles slackened, the tiny convulsions of his hands and feet as death spread to the man's furthest extremities.

'Shit.' The workman gazed down with irritation at his overalls, which were, like his right hand, now covered with blood. He kicked the body of the shopkeeper savagely and scanned the clothes rails for something to wear.

Five minutes later, with Bob's corpse hidden beneath a pile of clothes, the workman climbed the stairs in his new attire. He grimaced when he saw his overly-floral reflection in a mirror and then checked to see that no-one was looking into the shop. He opened the door, switched the lock so that the door would shut fast behind him then flicked the OPEN sign which hung on the back of the door to CLOSED.

'Not that anyone's going to notice,' said the man as he exited onto the almost empty street. He checked the road for traffic and crossed to his van.

'The first thing I want to say is that I'm not mad, okay?'

Jane smiled. 'Okay, Mikey. I'll take your word for it.'

The sun streamed brightly through the bay window, illuminating Mikey's back as he stalked to the table to collect his jacket. He had driven straight from the heath to Jane's flat, ringing the bell until, bleary-eyed and yawning, his girlfriend had let him in. Now Jane sat curled in an arm chair by the window, swamped by a striped baggy nightshirt; a pair of dog eared slippers hanging precariously from her feet. Jane checked the clock in the centre of her cluttered mantle-piece. She had been awake for less than ten minutes and Mikey had not stood still for one second.

She watched her boyfriend stomp to the rear of the room, smiled to herself and reached for the coffee she had insisted she have before he explained further. She could tell from his agitated state that he was still full of the same emotional energy as he had been the previous evening. From what little he had said since getting her out of bed and storming around the front room, she knew it was the subject of his ghost which was still consuming him. Yet he seemed a little less fraught than the night before. Less manic. If anything his agitation seemed now to derive not from any major emotional distress, but rather from a sense of extreme excitement. He glowed with it.

Mikey had finished rummaging through his jacket and pulled from an inside pocket the large wad of photos. He turned to face Jane, brandishing them in his right hand.

'Dah, dah, dah, DUM!' Jane exclaimed with a snigger over her coffee mug.

'Oh look, this isn't funny,' pleaded Mikey. He walked towards her and placed both hands upon his hips. 'How would you like to be haunted!?'

'Okay. Sorry.' Jane acted suitably admonished and put down her mug, adding: 'Only trying to make you feel a little less serious.'

Mikey nodded and kissed her gently on the cheek. 'I know. Thank you. But I just need you to understand what I'm going through right now. How weird this is.'

'Alright.' Jane looked up into his eyes, smiled kindly at the earnest face before her. 'I understand...Or rather, I'm sure I will do once you've explained it.'

'Okay.' Mikey, reassured by the warmth in his girlfriend's

voice, turned to sit cross-legged on the floor with his back towards her. Removing the photographs from their envelope he began to place them on the floor. Jane leant over his shoulder to watch the abstract heath scene expand upon the carpet.

In a minute he had arranged the pictures into the same pattern as before at his father's and Jane shifted in her chair to get a better view.

'Right,' she said. 'Now tell me again what I'm supposed to be seeing?'

Mikey craned his neck to look at her. 'Well… It would seem you can't,' he replied with a regretful shrug. 'I don't know why you can't see him. I wish I knew why…' Mikey returned his attention to the pictures and pointed. 'What I can see, and so can my dad thankfully,' he lifted his eyes briefly heavenward. 'Is a figure in every single picture. The same person I saw two days ago on the heath. The preacher.' Mikey paused, knowing how this must sound to someone who could see nothing but woodland. He shifted his position to give Jane an unrestricted view and leaned his chin upon the arm of the chair, motioning her to look. Jane nodded and studied the photographs quietly for a moment. Mikey watched her intently; saw the beginnings of a frown.

'What's he doing in the pictures, this... this man?' she asked. 'Just standing there?'

Mikey shook his head and stood up, stepping over the pictures to stand in the centre of the room.

'He's doing this.' Mikey imitated the various pointing gestures of the preacher. 'And in that centre frame,' he indicated the central photo with the toe of his shoe, 'He's doing this –' Mikey pointed to the floor.

'Hmm,' responded Jane with a bigger frown. She studied the photos again. 'And your dad can see him as well?' Despite her best intentions, Jane could not help sounding dubious.

'Yep.' Mikey could hear the doubt, but persevered. She had to believe him.

'Now take a look at this photo.' Mikey went back to his jacket, returning with the old black and white picture his father had taken. He handed it to Jane, and mimicked the words his father had spoken to him all those years before. 'Tell me what you can see.'

Jane looked at the picture, then at Mikey. 'Is the preacher in this too?' she asked.

'No,' Mikey slapped his forehead; grinned. 'Don't worry,' he said, 'I'm not trying to catch you out. Just tell me who you can see in the picture.'

Jane looked closely at the photograph. 'All right, what can I see?... A couple... An old man. And a child. Yes?'

Mikey let out a sigh. 'Congratulations,' he said. 'You've just seen your first ghost.'

'Hurrah!' said Jane playfully, 'Do I win a prize?' She fixed Mikey with a sudden, smouldering gaze and arched an eyebrow: its intention not lost on her boyfriend.

'Yeah,' said Mikey, laughing. 'You win the grand prize,' he returned the look. 'Come into the bedroom and I'll let you unwrap it.'

With a broad smile, Mikey took Jane's hand and, giggling, led her through to the rear of the flat. In the front room the phone began to ring. They ignored it, their attention elsewhere and after three rings Jane's answer phone cut in.

'Oh!' exclaimed Jane from the bedroom, her voice drowning out the message. 'I thought my prize would be bigger!'

Later, glowing and happy, they sat in bed as Mikey explained about the photo his father had taken. The conversation turned to the subject of the preacher, and Mikey spoke about the conclusion he had reached about its appearance in the murder site pictures.

'So you think it could be a murder weapon buried there then?' Jane asked.

'Nope,' Mikey shook his head and made a dramatic pause. 'No murder weapon there at all.'

'You've gone back and checked?!' Jane's eyes grew wide.

Mikey grinned and nodded. 'First thing this morning.'

Naked, he leapt out of bed and disappeared in the direction of the living room, his voice drifting back from down the passageway. 'I just couldn't wait!'

Jane draped herself across the warm depression he had left and shouted. 'So what did you find? Anything?'

Mikey stuck his head around the doorframe and winked. 'I found... this!' he said, gleefully dancing the book before him.

Jane sat up as Mikey clambered onto the bed, depositing the book in her lap. She turned it over in her hands, cautiously. Like Mikey before her she felt confused by its presence.

'Where did you find this?' she asked.

Mikey lit a cigarette. 'Exactly where the preacher was pointing to. And not buried either, it was just sitting there.'

Jane put a hand to her head and absentmindedly pushed at her fringe. It instantly fell back. She held the hair up with her hand and studied the binding closely; examined the clasp. 'If the Police didn't find it,' she said, 'then it must have been dropped after the murder.' Jane continued to scrutinise the ornately embossed leather, wet her finger and began to rub at a raised oval on the cover.

Mikey had been pondering the same problem as he had driven to Jane's. 'I don't think it was dropped by anyone after the murder,' he replied, 'I think it more than possible it was dropped by the victim himself.' It was the only conclusion that made any sort of sense to him.

'So why didn't the Police find it? And why didn't it show up in your photos?' Jane stopped rubbing at the leather and looked at her work. Mikey puffed thoughtfully on his cigarette.

'I don't know,' he said. 'Perhaps for the same reason you can't see the preacher.' He shrugged. 'I don't pretend to understand what's going on, I'm simply struggling to find some rational explanation for it. And the only conclusion I've reached is that I was led to find the book and that somehow it connects with the murder.'

Jane reached out and clasped Mikey's hand. She wasn't convinced that this was anything more than a coincidence, and in light of what Mikey had been through recently was not sure that such an intense preoccupation with 'mystic' events was going to help him. Yet, Mikey seemed positive that he was onto something, and that feeling had been compounded by his finding the book. No matter what, she thought, he's going to follow this thing through to the bitter end. And, like it or not, I'll do my best to help him. Jane only prayed that the end would not be too bitter.

'I do know one thing,' she said, holding up the book and twisting it in the light. 'If the murdered man was carrying this book, it didn't belong to him.'

Mikey looked quizzical. Stubbed out his cigarette. 'How do you know?'

'I managed to get his name out of the Police yesterday evening: 'Tom McDonald'. This book appears to belong to someone with the initials "M.T.W."

'Let me see.'

Jane passed the book back to Mikey and pointed out the fine scripted letters, all but worn away in the centre of the oval.

'Hhmm.' Mikey stared silently at the initials for a moment; Jane reached for her dressing gown and climbed out of bed.

'If it does have something to do with the murder,' she said

from the foot of the bed, 'you really should hand it into the Police.' Mikey ignored her. 'You know that don't you?'

Mikey nodded, lost in thought.

'It could be the clue that leads them to the killer.'

Mikey nodded again. 'But why wait for me to pick it up? If it was visible to them why not let the Police find it?' He glared at the dull brown leather, willing it to start explaining itself.

Jane stood in the doorway, adjusted the sash around her waist and looked at her boyfriend. She could see the frustration written broadly across his brow. 'I'll make some coffee,' she said and left him alone.

Mikey ran a finger around the silver clasp and bit his lip. He had been putting it off, not wanting the situation to get any stranger, yet he had to do it. Even if he did pass the book on to the Police, said he had found it on the heath, he had to know what was inside.

Mikey glanced around for Jane's nail file, clambering over the duvet to take a closer look at the fragrant rubbish tip which covered her dressing table. The sound of a cup smashing to the floor distracted him from his search, and hopping into his jump-suit he made his way back into the living room.

Jane was crouched and picking up broken china by the table as Mikey entered. 'Are you okay?' he asked. Jane nodded and indicated the answer phone. She looked pale.

Mikey checked the box beside the phone and, seeing the flashing red 'message waiting' light, looked questioningly at his girlfriend before pressing rewind. Jane stood up and grasped his hand tightly.

The tiny speaker on top of the answer phone burst into crackling life, heavy static almost drowning out the thin voice which spoke just three words. It was a strange, chilling sound; something indefinably odd about the whispering pitch, the strained enunciation. The hair on the back of Mikey's neck stood up at the sound and he felt Jane's grip grow even tighter. The message ended, the speaker falling silent. Mikey pulled Jane close and hugged her; she looked up, still pale.

'I don't know who that was,' she said, an air of nervousness in her voice. 'But I think I'm starting to believe you.'

Mikey nodded silently and looked back at the answer phone. How could she not? Something inside both of them knew the call to be more than coincidence. Just three little words were all that had been spoken, but they could not have come from a random call, a wrong number, or arrived so opportunely. Three little words: 'Marcus Tenneshaw Wright.'

Chapter Five

Paula Frost shouldered open the front door and with relief dropped the shopping bags onto the hallway floor. She kicked the door closed with a well aimed heel and turned to switch off the alarm beeping insistently on the wall.

'What a day!' she said, picking up the shopping to trudge through to the kitchen at the end of the hall. She put the bags down for the final time and began to empty their contents onto the breakfast table.

It had been one of those days that never seemed to end or improve. From waking and arguing with Sam; so much so that he refused to give her a lift to work and had made her late, to being unfairly criticised by her boss for not getting the audits completed on time. What a cheek! To cap it all the supermarket was so busy Paula had queued for what seemed like hours to get out and then had to walk home because Sam was too busy working to give her a lift. What a bastard! Paula removed a string bag of oranges from the pile of miscellaneous shopping she had been building and took them over to the wooden block containing the kitchen knives. She selected a small blade, held the bag aloft and with vigour plunged the knife into it.

'That's for you, Mr. Know-nothing Peterson! You fat pig! Shove the audits up your arse!'

The knife sank deep into an orange; squirted juice all over Paula's hand. She pulled it out and stabbed again, relishing the feeling as the skin yielded to her thrust and the liquid gushed past the blade.

'And that's for you, Sam! You dickless twat! How dare you question my fucking commitment to this relationship!'

Paula continued to stab at the fruit. Punctuating each lunge with a curse, each curse with a smile, until the floor was wet with juice and the bag finally gave out under the frenzied onslaught. With mangled shreds of peel at her feet Paula let out a deep satisfied sigh, and regarded the tattered dripping remains in her hand. Paula grinned. Who needs psychotherapy? She thought, and dropped the bag into the bin.

Feeling much better, Paula rinsed her hands and, taking a towel, threw it onto the sodden jumble on the floor. With a single swipe, she deposited the mess, towel included, into the bin. Paula sighed again, happy that the anger, the pent up frustration of the day was out of her system and returned to empty the shopping bags.

There was a scratching sound from the kitchen door. Paula looked up from the fridge and walked to let in the cat.

'Alright. Alright! Coming…' She twisted the key and opened the door just enough to let George through.

The cat sped through the gap like a rocket, skidding wildly on the lino as its paws sought for purchase. It gained a grip and accelerated into the hallway, its galloping footfall diminishing as it hurtled up the stairs.

'Had a bad day too, have you?' Paula asked as George disappeared. She shook her head, opening the door wider to let in some air. Mad cat, she thought, probably been annoying next door's dog again.

Paula stepped out into the garden and took a deep breath of the gentle scent from the lavender bush beside the door. Bees were busily flitting around it and she watched with interest as they went about their duty.

'Doing some late shopping too?' she asked, and went back inside to continue filling the fridge.

It was a little later when the door bell rang and Paula reluctantly dragged herself from the sofa to answer it. It couldn't be Sam, she knew, because his door key was with his car keys. Perhaps it was Mrs. Oscar. God! thought Paula as she walked to the door, I hope not. I don't need anymore recipes or Tupperware.

The patterned glass in the door obscured her view of whoever was standing in her porch, but Paula could see enough detail and colour to surmise it was thankfully not Mrs. Oscar. She opened the door.

Two grey suited men stood in the porch and gazed impassively at Paula as she peered cautiously around the frame. They had short hair, bad suits, but above all the demeanour of people of authority. When the taller man spoke, it confirmed Paula's suspicion that they were policemen.

'Good evening madam,' he said sombrely. 'Sorry to trouble you at this hour. But I'm afraid we have bad news.'

'Oh, Christ,' whispered Paula. 'Sam?'

Both officers nodded solemnly.

'If we could come in for a moment?...' The taller officer gestured towards the hallway.

'Yes...Yes,' muttered Paula. Distracted by a thousand vague and unpleasant images, she led the policemen into the living room.

Paula sat on the edge of the sofa, cupped her face in her hands and waited nervously as the officers occupied the two arm chairs by the front window. The tall one spoke again.

'This is not an easy thing, I know, Miss. But I regret to inform you that your husband died earlier this evening.'

Frozen, the statement thudded into Paula's mind, each word a door to plans and dreams now slamming shut for ever. Locking her into a world of darkness. Her mind swam, her mouth moving numbly.

'He... He was my boyfriend,' she muttered, unsure why. 'He wasn't my husband. We...' Paula's voice became swept away as the emotion swelled and overwhelmed her. She hid her face in her hands and let the tears flow, her body shaking as the loud sobs spilled out.

The two men sat quietly, not wishing to disturb her, letting the emotion take its course. After several minutes the tall officer moved to the sofa and offered Paula a handkerchief.

She accepted it dumbly and wiped her eyes, bit her lip to stop her jaw quivering.

'If it's any consolation,' said the officer beside her, 'he would have felt nothing.'

It was no consolation at all! Paula collapsed back into the sofa and shook her head frantically. As if the denial of what she was hearing would make it untrue. The policeman touched her lightly on the knee.

'Is there anybody we can phone? Any relatives or friends nearby who can come over?' The tone was calm, tinged with the right degree of concern.

Paula shook her head, fought away the tears and mopped her streaming eyes.

'What happened?' she managed to whisper.

'It was a car accident. He was taken to the hospital, but...'

Paula nodded woodenly and rapidly blinked her eyes. Her senses were scrambled, her thoughts like lead. She struggled to take the information in. Poor Sam, she thought. Why?! Why!?...Why today?! I never told you I loved you today.

The ringing phone acted like an alarm call: Paula instinctively standing and walking to the hall before being conscious she had done so. She was in no fit state to talk to anybody, yet anything was better than trying to deal with her feelings and her subconscious leapt at the chance of distraction. Anything to muffle her thoughts for a few seconds. She picked up the phone, heard her voice speak shakily somewhere in the distance.

'Hello?'

'What's the matter with you?' said the caller. 'Did somebody die or something?'

Deep within Paula's mind a door unlocked.

'SAM??!!' she cried. Her legs felt very weak.

'Of course it's me! What the hell's the matter?!'

Paula could hardly get the words out. So many emotions were fighting to express themselves. 'But! You were –' Paula remembered the policemen, turned to point in the direction of the living room as if to explain visually the situation to Sam down the phone. Her voice died away.

Standing in the hallway was the smaller officer. His tanned face was tilted to one side, an amused look on it as he advanced towards her.

'I realise this must come as a shock,' he said, smiling.

There was a flash of movement from his right arm and Paula barely registered the action before the axe struck her on the temple. A thought, unbidden and seemingly out of place, entered her head as she realised the arcing blade would connect. She thought of oranges.

It was approaching eleven in the morning by the time Mikey reached central London and the steady growl of traffic quietened to a murmur as he parked his motorbike in a cul-de-sac near Russell Street. Unstrapping the book from the rear of the seat, he walked quickly out into the noise and sunshine and, checking his watch for a second time, hurried round to the entrance of the British Museum. He was late.

Both he and Jane had spent the previous day studying the pages of the unlocked leather bound book, in the hopeful belief it would bring them closer to whatever it was the preacher was attempting to communicate. If the answer was contained within the pages however, it had defied their attempts to deduce it.

The book was full of hieroglyphics, page after page of

lovingly rendered pictograms and pictures with hieroglyphic notes written into the margins. To Mikey and Jane, though they recognised it as probably Egyptian, it was as far as they could get with deciphering the book's content. The numerous illustrations which ran throughout the text were only marginally more accessible. Beautifully drawn, meticulously detailed plates appeared to show the interior of a temple, or more likely a tomb. There were side views of corridors covered in friezes, details of columns rich with colour and dozens of plan views of rooms and chambers. All were accompanied with cramped hand written notes, but as they too were in the same incomprehensible language as the rest of the text, whatever information they conveyed was as far beyond Jane and Mikey's linguistic grasp as the rest of the book. After studying the pages all morning they had to grudgingly admit defeat. The pair had spent the afternoon wracking their brains to find an alternative course of action.

After much cajoling, Mikey agreed to Jane's suggestion that he should contact the British Museum in central London. After all, Jane argued, with such an extensive collection of Egyptian antiquities, if anybody could decipher the book's secrets, surely it would be them. Mikey was uncomfortable with the idea, partly because he felt such a major institution would not be interested, but mainly because he did not want to field any persistent enquiries about the book's origin. Jane suggested another course of action, but as that involved taking the book to the police, Mikey felt the former plan held more merit.

It surprised Mikey to find the British Museum's number in the phonebook, and though it was late, after a few innocuous questions it surprised him even more to get an appointment for the next day. When he left Jane's flat the following morning, it was with the promise that she would endeavour to track down the name of Marcus Tenneshaw Wright.

As he turned the corner into Russell Street, Mikey paused to take in the massive Greco-roman structure which loomed beyond the perimeter railings. The museum was an impressive sight, built at a time when British imperial wealth had known little limitation, and the British imperial mind had seen no just reason why the ancient wealth of other nations should not be theirs. The Victorians, Mikey supposed, had felt akin to those great civilisations whose relics they coveted. Saw some parallel between their society's achievements and those that had gone before. It was ironic, thought Mikey, that the building itself was now a part of the same history.

Tourists milled around the forecourt as Mikey walked on towards the entrance gate, students and holidaymakers trooping in and out of the main door, or standing for pictures upon the steps before the colonnade. Mikey turned at the outer gateway to join the throng and stopped just inside the railings: overcome by the strangest of sensations.

He felt as though he should remember something, or was it a sensation of deja-vu? The fleeting impression was vague. Mikey closed his eyes for a moment and, attempting to concentrate his thoughts, stepped back onto the pavement. He felt drawn somehow, compelled into the actions he was undertaking as if wading in water and attempting to walk with the flow. He twisted on his heels and opened his eyes, found himself staring in the direction he had come from.

Some part of him was disappointed not to see the preacher standing before him, nothing in view except tourists and a phone box. Shrugging, Mikey turned once again and took a step towards the gateway. The sensation came again. This time hitting him like a bullet. His head span wildly, suddenly, causing him to stagger, his equilibrium catherine-wheeled off balance by some unknown force. Mikey crashed into the railings by the phone box, one hand shooting out to grab at the bars while the other attempted unsuccessfully to keep him upright. His legs collapsed from beneath him as his shoulder struck metal and he fell onto all fours; breathing hard more from shock than exertion. Mikey took several deep breaths and closed his eyes, the feeling of disorientation dissipating with every racing beat of his heart. What the fuck was that?! he thought as he gripped at the railing he had missed the first time and pulled himself upright.

'You alright, son?' said a deep, gentle voice behind him.

Mikey looked round and nodded weakly at the concerned tourist standing over him, accepted the steadying hand offered and lent back against the railings.

'Best take it easy in this humidity,' said the plaid dressed man, 'It'll get ya every time.'

Mikey nodded and gulped a few more deep breaths, waving as the man took a final look in his direction before disappearing through the gateway of the museum. Mikey shook his head slowly and collected his wits. Whatever it was seemed to have disappeared as quickly as it had come, leaving only a wary apprehension in Mikey about what would happen when he passed the same spot again. Mikey sighed, just what I need, he thought, another mystery. He took a deep breath and ran towards the museum.

Mikey reached the entrance without further incident and after briefly explaining who it was he had come to see, an usher escorted him along the main corridor towards the west wing. Past the exhibits and the ever meandering tourists, the usher kept a brisk pace, pausing only to hold doors open as Mikey repeatedly trotted to keep up.

For Mikey the museum and its contents were a step back into his own past, rekindling long forgotten memories of trips he had made here in his youth. He found himself distracted as he marched behind the usher; continually slowing his pace to take in the impressive sights he strolled by. The usher, perhaps used to such distractions in others, waited patiently at the next door until Mikey drew level.

The corridor ended at a wide stone stairway and curled its way down around a totem pole before passing into the lower level of the museum. They walked on until, by a wall lined with glass cases, the attendant indicated Mikey should wait. The usher slipped behind a rope barrier and disappeared through a white-washed door. Mikey passed the time by glancing at a cabinet full of flint arrowheads until the usher returned and led them on through the door and down a spiral staircase. The journey ended in a cramped passageway lined with cupboards.

'Mr. Trent is through the second door on the right,' said the usher with the flicker of a smile. He turned and ascended the stairway.

Mikey strolled along the passage and considered again what he would say if asked how the book came to be in his possession. The truth, he felt, would only complicate matters, so an old book shop was the current favourite. Mikey's worst fear, and one that had persistently nagged him since entering the museum, was that the book might have been stolen from the room he was about to enter. He stopped at the door and put the notion out of his head. Things were peculiar enough without those sort of thoughts. He knocked and, before waiting for a reply, stepped inside.

The room was gloomy, the walls cupboard-lined like the corridor, and lit by a single desk lamp upon a wide table in the centre of the room. The surface of the table was crowded with drawers removed from the walls, white cloth spilling everywhere. It looked to Mikey as if the place had been ransacked and, here and there amongst the jumble, he caught the dull glint of metal. Beyond the light came the sound of a chair scraping against the flagstone floor and a dingy figure beckoned Mikey forward.

'C'mon over, take a seat,' said Mr. Trent, reseating himself. He moved the object he held towards the lamp and resumed his study.

Mikey sat, glancing around as he waited and got a better impression of the jewellery strewn across the table. Each drawer was packed with tightly wrapped bundles, the opened bundles strewn across the table revealing intricately crafted jewels and precious metals. Mr. Trent turned the piece in his hand slowly and, popping a watch-maker's eyeglass from his eye, placed it reverently back into its wrapping. He turned and gave Mikey a grin.

'Snap!' he said, pointing at Mikey's jumpsuit.

Mikey, now that his eyes were growing accustomed to the feeble lighting could see that the Egyptologist was wearing the same dark military fatigues as he was.

'We must have the same tailor,' Mikey replied, returning the smile.

'Must have.' Trent held out his hand. 'Pleased to meet you. I'm Danny Trent.'

'Michael Dayville,' Mikey replied, shaking the man's hand. 'Mikey to most people.'

Danny nodded. 'Well, welcome to the warehouse.' He spread his arms wide. 'A veritable Aladdin's cave of knick-knacks and bric-a-brac.' He picked up the item he had been examining and looked at Mikey questioningly. 'I don't suppose you know anything about Tuthmosis the third, do you?' he asked.

Mikey shook his head.

'No,' said Danny, putting the piece down again. 'That makes two of us.'

The comment, and the general demeanour of the man, surprised Mikey. He had expected to encounter somebody as stuffy as the atmosphere in the room, as ancient as the exhibits stored within it, and not the genial figure who now sat before him. This man was young, barely older than Mikey himself. Danny Trent turned and clasped his hands in his lap, continuing:

'Not really my specific area of expertise, this stuff, but unfortunately the man who should be doing it is, shall we say, on another case.' He paused, sighing quietly. 'Anyway, that's enough of my troubles, what can I do for you?'

Mikey drew the old leather book from his bag and placed it on the table. 'I was wondering if you could tell me a little about this?'

Danny nodded sagely and, picking up the book, ran a hand briefly over the embossed surface before opening it. He flicked through several pages then stopped and put the book down. Mikey, looking on curiously, noticed the quick sideways glance in his direction as Trent pulled the lamp closer. He began to go through the book again, slowly this time, minutely studying the text. A broad smile spread across his face.

'This is very good,' he said, looking up from his examination to give Mikey a wink.

'What's very good?' Mikey asked.

'This,' said Danny. He sat back in his chair and pointed to the text. 'Somebody has a very good imagination.'

Mikey shuffled his chair closer, intrigued. 'I'm sorry,' he said, shaking his head. 'I don't understand.'

Danny picked the book up and indicated a line of pictograms. 'I don't know where you got this from, but somebody went to an awful lot of trouble to make this read like it was some form of pre-hieroglyphics. It really is very, very good.' Danny held up a finger. 'Almost convincing.'

'You mean it's a fake?' Mikey stared at the opened page.

'A good one. But yes, a fake none the less.'

Mikey shook his head. 'How, I mean, what makes you think

it's not authentic?' Mikey could not believe the book was not genuine.

'Okay.' Danny put the book back on the table. 'What someone seems to have done is produce, for want of a better word, a 'teaser'. It used to happen occasionally. They've invented a none existent subject, i.e. this temple here,' he pointed to one of the illustrations. 'And put it across as an authentic undiscovered site. With me so far?'

Mikey nodded.

'But what these notes appear to say, and what the hieroglyphic style points to, is that this temple predates all other Egyptian sites of a similar type. Which is impossible.'

'Why impossible?' Mikey asked.

'Imagine you found a book which described in great detail how jet planes where developed for the first world war. This is a little like that. A site with an architectural sophistication of this nature is at odds with the pictogram style depicted on the walls. Conclusion: an amazing find to turn early Egyptian history on its head. Unfortunately, the supposition is impossible.'

Mikey frowned. 'Why, if it would be spotted so easily would someone go to such lengths to record it in a book? Why bother?'

Danny shrugged. 'Well I really couldn't say for sure.' He scratched at his chin thoughtfully for a moment. 'The book itself is old, say, I don't know, turn of the century. Maybe older. Taken at face value back then it might have passed examination with flying colours. Convinced people it was the record of a unique find.' Danny nodded to himself, warming to his hypothesis. 'But whatever the reason, the author of this masterpiece knew his stuff and he's been clever with his approach.'

'In what way?' Mikey asked.

Danny picked up a pencil and taped the book. 'Because the premise of this information is so preposterous he's attempted to sweeten the pill, draw us into the charade by taking basic Egyptian hieroglyphics and pissing around with it.'

Mikey furrowed his brow. 'I don't follow,' he said.

'Right, well take a look at this line here.' Danny pointed to some glyphs. 'It looks to the untrained eye like hieroglyphics, but it isn't. The characters are slightly wrong.' Danny could see Mikey's blank look and attempted to explain. '...It's a bit like writing a capital 'A' but without the central stroke. Do you follow?'

Mikey nodded.

'Right. Well what we're supposed to deduce from this text is that it is an early hieroglyphic form, taken from a site which contains other examples of the same language.' Danny patted the book with admiration. 'They've even gone to the trouble of writing notes in the margins which look like attempts at translation.'

Mikey still found it difficult to believe the book was just a worthless fake. 'Is there no way it could be genuine?' he asked.

Danny gave Mikey a grin. 'Believe me, when I first flicked through this book I thought, for a few moments at least that it could be authentic. Like I say this piece of work is almost perfect. The illustrations are intriguing to say the least, and the text is mesmerising. I can only understand a small proportion of the glyphs, which of course is the whole idea of them; to grab your attention. And if that was it I would be willing to spend more time considering that this site could exist.'

'So why don't you?'

Danny raised a finger dramatically and placed it with a flourish onto the book. 'Because of that!' he said theatrically.

Mikey leaned over to get a better look. Above Danny's finger he could see a group of five pictograms surrounded by a squashed black oval. It meant nothing to him. 'What is it?' he asked.

'Too clever by half,' Danny replied and removed his finger. 'It's the one thing that completely ruins the authenticity of the work. I can only assume that the person or persons behind it got a bit too cock-sure of themselves. It may have fooled somebody back in Victorian times, but nowadays we know a little more.'

'So what is it?'

'It's a cartouche. A device that contains, in this case, a divine name. The name of a god. And it's mixed up with all the other gods, from Isis to Osiris.' Danny pointed to other black ovals on the page. 'But this particular god: 'Hathnos', is where the whole thing starts to fall apart. He never existed.' Danny closed the book and swivelled on his chair. 'As I said, too clever by half.' It seemed to Mikey that the case for the prosecution was rested.

'So, okay,' said Mikey, attempting to get a picture of the book's origin and purpose, 'What you're saying is that somebody, probably in the nineteenth century, compiled this book about a temple that didn't exist with a language that never existed in order to pass it off as a genuine site. Yes?'

Danny nodded. 'That's about it.'

'I still can't see why. Why go to so much trouble?'

Danny considered the question. 'Do you know anything about Tutankhamen? About Carter's excavations during the nineteen-twenties?' he asked.

Mikey nodded. 'A little.'

'Well, Carter had a sponsor; Lord Carnarvon, who put up the money for the original expeditions. A lot of money. It's a very expensive business, archaeology but, if you're looking for international prestige, worth the investment. Egypt has always been a good crowd puller, right back to Napoleon's time. So, say you're an unscrupulous opportunist, who sees a way of making easy money by hoodwinking some glory seeking old aristocrat. This book's contents could well be the bait to hook him. But not any old bait, oh no,' Danny shook his head. 'This is the one that points to something no-one else has ever found.'

'So it makes it that much more seductive, right?'

Danny nodded. 'Exactly.'

Mikey sat for a moment considering the implications of Danny Trent's scenario. How did a book about a fake Egyptian temple link to a dead preacher and a murder victim? If there was some connection it was doing its best to elude him. He remembered the faint initials on the cover of the book. The strange phone call.

'Have you ever heard of anyone called Marcus Tenneshaw Wright?' Mikey asked.

Danny leaned back in his stool, a puzzled expression flitting briefly across his face. 'Sure,' he said. 'What do you want to know about him?'

A low, mechanical murmur greeted Jane when she arrived at the offices of the Hampstead & Highgate Chronicle: the relentless, slow turn of fans flicking across the paper littered surfaces. It was the same scenario – so she had been told – every summer. The fans would be brought out of storage, dusted down and started, and then, as one, the journalists would begin raiding the deepest recesses of their drawers in search of paper weights for their overburdened desks.

The offices were virtually empty, the humidity oppressive enough to send most of her colleagues in search of fresher air. Jane greeted the few brave, sweating co-workers who had decided to endure the tropical climate and sat down to finish her murder story.

Jane enjoyed working for the Chronicle. It's lethargic pace, so different to that of the London Evening Mail, suiting her present needs more than she would ever have admitted to her colleagues. In the few months that she had worked on the local paper, Jane had come to feel more at home with the environment and the people than she had ever done at the Mail. Here, she sensed no vindictive envy of her skills, quite the opposite in fact: there was an open admiration for her abilities. It was a small but important boost to her confidence as she took her first steps back into what she saw as the 'proper' working world. Above all, working for the Chronicle made Jane feel safe.

Sometimes, she could read the curiosity in the faces of her co-workers: the unasked question of why, if she was as good as she seemed, was she there? Not once had anybody broached the subject, and Jane was thankful that politeness, so far, had left the question unspoken. Her editor knew, but that was as far as the information had gone. It seemed that if there was a story there, her colleagues felt it was her business and left it at that. It was another of the reasons Jane enjoyed life at the Chronicle and, ironically, why none of her fellow reporters would ever make the big time.

Jane finished her piece and sat back, catching a faint breeze from the fan as it rotated to face her. The minute drop in temperature served only to exacerbate the intolerable heat in the office so Jane grabbed for the bottle of cold water she had bought; now warming steadily beside her computer. She punched at her keyboard to download the story to her editor's machine, then ran the bottle across her brow before taking a sip. Jane closed her eyes as the fan swept back and, considering what excuse she could use to get out into the open, she remembered Mikey and the promise she had made to him that morning.

The thought brought her mind back to the murder. Not the one, it seemed, which she had just written about using the facts at her disposal, but the stranger scenario Mikey appeared so anxious to pursue: which she herself was now getting dragged into. She sighed. She had said that she would help but now, with a new day and the comforting familiarity of her surroundings, it all seemed a little far fetched. Silly even. She thought back to the phone call. Jane could not deny the fact that it had been odd, or that it had shaken her up at the time. But really! A ghost?! There had to be a more logical explanation. At the back of Jane's mind was the nagging suspicion that someone, somewhere, was playing a cruel and very joyless joke on Mikey.

'Hi, Jane,' said a voice. 'How ya doin'?'

Jane straightened in her seat and looked up to see the sweaty, dishevelled figure of the paper's junior reporter, John Parker, standing beside her.

'Better than you by the look of things, John,' she said, grinning. 'You look like you've just taken a shower.'

John nodded and pulled his tie even further away from his collar. 'If this heat gets any worse I'm going to shrink,' he said, puffing his cheeks and blowing. The effect momentarily ruffled his wispy fringe.

'Mm,' said Jane, still lost in her own thoughts. She switched off her computer, which she now realised was blowing hot air at her and moved to stand beside the fan. 'Has Doug been in at all today?' she asked, giving a brief glance towards her editor's empty desk. She turned back and grimaced as John attempted to un-stick his shirt from his stomach.

The reporter gave up his efforts and shook his head. 'He phoned earlier and left a message for you.' John walked the few paces back to his desk and, lifting paperweights, began sifting through the clutter on its surface. 'Doug said,' explained John as he searched, 'that if you finish the murder piece, you could have a treat.'

'Sounds ominous,' Jane said, side-stepping to follow the fan.

'Ah! Here it is!' John retrieved a yellow post-it note from underneath his phone and held it up triumphantly.

'So, what is it? A fortnight in Acapulco?'

John shook his head. 'Your next assignment, 007,' he said with a smile and handed Jane the note.

Jane turned the paper the right way round, read the hurried scrawl and grinned broadly. 'Excellent!' she said. 'How long has it been in town?'

John shrugged. 'Since last night, I think.'

'Brilliant!' Jane replied. 'I'll get right on it.' The subject seemed a little lightweight for Jane's attention but she was not about to question Doug's decision. Visiting a Fun Fair down on Hampstead Heath was the perfect way to spend the afternoon.

'Doug said there was some problem with the fair's legality,' said John, pointing at the note. Jane looked quizzical. 'The council have no record of them applying for permission,' he continued. 'Doug thinks they might be trying to cash in on the murder.'

Knowing the morbid curiosity of the British public, thought Jane, it seemed a logical enough conclusion, and as such something a little more demanding of her talents. She moved to collect her things then, remembering Mikey, followed John as he returned to his desk. 'What are you working on at the moment?' she asked warmly, attempting to decipher the information from the jumble spread before him.

John pulled a face. 'Council notices!' he said with unmasked distaste.

Jane tutted. 'Oh, that's a shame,' she said, inflecting just the right degree of disappointment.

John swivelled in his chair: his interest peaked. 'Why?' he asked.

'Oh. nothing really,' Jane said, starting to move away. 'It's just that I need some research done on my murder story.'

John leapt at the opportunity. 'I'll do it!' he said, and as Jane turned smiling he swept a hand dismissively across his desk. 'This is nearly finished anyway!'

Jane pretended to ponder the offer. 'Are you sure?' she said.

'No problem at all,' replied John, smiling hopefully. 'What do you need to know?'

Though John Parker was young, of all her colleagues at the Chronicle, Jane considered him to have the potential to go further. He was not a great reporter yet, but as a researcher he was already one of the best she had ever met. Though not reflected in either his dress or his desk, John possessed a meticulous mind which, once directed in a particular area, never failed to discover details and connections other journalists would simply have overlooked. If anybody could find information on Marcus Tenneshaw Wright, it was John.

'I need you to trace this man,' said Jane, scribbling the name onto a note pad. She handed it to John, adding: 'It's for some background on the heath story. Possibly nothing, but find out all you can.'

John nodded and mouthed the name on the pad. 'Consider it done,' he said and picked up the phone.

Well, thought Jane as she collected her things, that's that. There's nothing more I can do. She remembered the photos Mikey had given her for the story, pulled them out of her bag and, flicking through them, shook her head. Nothing but greenery and a blood stain. She selected one and took it over to her editor's desk, left a note on his computer about the story and waved her goodbyes. As she exited, she wondered how Mikey had fared at the British Museum.

Chapter Six

'Nice house,' said Constable Wright from the back seat of the Police car, craning his neck to view the four story town house they had just stopped outside.

Sergeant Rose nodded and pulled on the hand brake. 'Mm,' he mumbled. 'And I bet our Mr Bradford worked his arse off to get it.'

'Now, now, sergeant,' said Fletcher, wagging a finger from beside him. 'Let's not go colouring our judgment. Innocent until proven guilty. We're not to throw the book at him until after we've spoken to him.' The inspector winked at Rose and opened his door. 'C'mon,' he said. 'Let's see if he's in.'

Sergeant Rose wondered at the sudden change of heart of his immediate superior. Was it that Fletcher's old college friend Faber thought as Rose did? That there was no evidence to support the idea of similarities between their respective cases. Or was it to do with the place of residence of Mark Bradford: less than a mile from the scene of the crime? Rose imagined it was probably a little of both, but whatever the reason, Fletcher had got the scent of blood in his nostrils and was determined to interview the suspect personally.

The trio climbed slowly from the car, Constable Wright putting his helmet on as he walked round the bonnet behind Fletcher. The inspector stopped on the pavement and turned to regard the immense Constable who, helmeted, now stood 6'8". Fletcher indicated the car.

'Grab one of those posters and do a house-to-house, see if anyone saw McDonald recently.' A tiny smile played on Bob Fletcher's lips as he indicated Mark Bradford's house. 'If we need some back up, I'll bring you in to frighten the life out of him later.'

Constable Wright nodded, took the keys from Rose and

squeezed himself back into the car.

Fletcher pointed to the front door. 'C'mon, sergeant,' he said, and strode briskly up the short driveway.

Rose rang the doorbell, the pair turning to take in the small garden and the street as they waited for sounds of movement inside.

'I don't know what he does to criminals, Pete,' said Fletcher as they waited. 'But he scares the shit out of me.'

'Who? Wright?' asked Sergeant Rose, watching the towering constable wander away from the car.

'Yes,' replied the inspector. He grinned. 'He gives the term "Long arm of the law" a whole new meaning.'

Fletcher rang the bell again: measured footfalls coming from beyond the door as the single chime faded. Rose took a step back and brought out his identity card as the lock clicked. Fletcher kept his hands in his pockets to let his sergeant do the introductions.

The door opened, revealing a cramped stairway leading up to the next floor and a pale figure wincing and blinking at the sunlight. The man, slender and tall appeared more like a victim than a perpetrator: one hand using the door for support while the other touched at a large white bandage smothering his forehead.

'Mr. Peter Bradford?' Rose asked. The man nodded, still clutching at his head. 'I'm Detective Sergeant Rose of the Metropolitan C.I.D. and this is Detective Inspector Fletcher.'

Bradford eyed the pair, grimaced and nodded slowly.

'We're conducting an investigation into the murder of Tom McDonald,' continued the sergeant, ignoring Bradford's obvious discomfort. 'I believe you were acquainted with the gentleman?'

Bradford nodded again and pushed the door wide. 'Please,' he said weakly and motioned the officers to enter, turning as they did to walk slowly up the stairs.

Rose and Fletcher followed until they reached a small landing and watched as Bradford, not looking back, disappeared through the first of several doors which led off from the landing. The inspector paused on the final stair and quickly took in his surroundings.

The landing appeared to be the heart of the house, three doors and two more stairways leading off of it. One flight twisted up onto another story while the second curved precariously down behind the first towards the back of the house. Old, thought Fletcher, noting that despite the pristine paint work and the plush white carpets there was a decrepit air about the place: the musty signature of a house over one hundred and fifty years old. Fletcher ended his brief appraisal and, leading the way, followed Bradford into the room. The sight beyond the door momentarily baffled him.

It was a small and narrow room, gloomy from the drawn curtains at the front and cluttered with an odd mixture of furniture, potted palms and ornaments. A slit of light from between the curtains provided what little illumination there was, but it was what the sunlight fell upon that both Fletcher and now Rose found so intriguing. Clocks; dozens and dozens of them, covered the far wall from one end of the room to the other. They varied in size from antique pocket watches to what looked like official station timepieces, yet all shared the same peculiarity. Each second hand, each minute hand, was set to twelve o'clock. And not a single one was ticking.

Refusing to get side-tracked, Fletcher shrugged off his curiosity, returned his thoughts to more immediate concerns and sat on a leather sofa behind the door: Rose following suit a moment later. Bradford returned to what appeared to be a makeshift bed in the window seat beneath the curtains and looked as crumpled and pale as the sheet which half covered him. He sat patiently in the half light waiting for the officers to settle themselves, one hand still repeatedly touching at his forehead.

Fletcher crossed his legs and sucked at his teeth.

'So, Mr. Bradford,' he said gazing levelly at the drawn figure opposite. 'What appears to be the problem with your head?'

Peter dropped his chin, avoiding the inspector's piercing stare. 'Car...Car crash,' he stuttered. Fletcher nodded.

'Uhuh. Drink driving, was it?' asked Fletcher. Slowly Bradford shook his head.

'Uhuh,' said the inspector. 'No one else hurt though, I hope.' Again Bradford shook his head.

Fletcher nodded to himself and, finding his attention returning to the wall, said: 'Your clocks' appear to be broken, Mr. Bradford.'

'Perhaps he can't afford to have them repaired,' sneered Rose.

Peter Bradford ignored the remark and attempted to turn his head in the direction of the wall, saying weakly: 'I've always liked to collect timepieces, but that many make too much noise. That's why I keep them unwound.'

His curiosity satisfied, Fletcher searched his pockets for his cigarettes. 'Do you mind if I smoke?' he asked, waving the packet at Peter.

Bradford coughed: an involuntary reaction which creased his face with pain, compressed his lips to a thin line. 'I'd rather you didn't, please,' he managed to say.

'Uhuh,' said Fletcher and lit up.

'Now...' said the inspector, after a lengthy and pointed examination of the glowing end of his cigarette. 'Where were we?' He raised his brow in mock confusion then, looking around for somewhere to deposit the ash, found what appeared to be a likely receptacle on the small table beside him. 'Oh yes!' he said, and flicked his cigarette. 'Your late friend, Mr. McDonald,' Fletcher pointed the cigarette at Bradford. 'You didn't appear too surprised when we mentioned his death –'

'– Or too bothered,' added Sergeant Rose. He got up to examine more closely the contents of a cabinet at the rear of the room.

'Yes,' agreed the inspector, nodding curtly at his sergeant's back. 'When exactly did you hear about his demise?'

Peter Bradford looked blankly at the policeman and let one arm drop towards the floor, his hand pointing as he did so to a folded newspaper almost lost in shadow at his bedside. Fletcher, though his eyes had become adjusted to the half-light in the tiny room, shifted forward in his seat and strained to make out the topmost headline. It read: 'Sacrificial Murder: Fifth victim is claimed.'

Inspector Fletcher sat back and sneered with distaste at the article. It was the same one he had reluctantly read that morning and did indeed mention Tom McDonald by name; but where they had got ideas about a link with the sacrificial case God only knew. Bloody press! thought Fletcher. He wanted there to be a connection with Faber's case as much as anybody, but couldn't they at least wait until he had some more proof?! Perhaps, he thought, looking across the room, that might not be far away.

'Where were you on the evening of Monday the fourteenth?' asked Fletcher, almost conversationally.

Bradford coughed and wiped his eyes. 'I was, er... At a dinner. In –' He winced and clutched at his head; bit his lip against the pain. Rose, turning from his investigation of the cabinet looked on impassively. Inspector Fletcher puffed on his cigarette and waited.

'– At a dinner in Chelsea,' Bradford finished. Regaining his composure he let out a sigh. 'You must please excuse me, officers,' he said, fumbling a bottle of tablets out from amongst the bedclothes, 'The last few days have been very difficult. I have a gash on my forehead... An apparent fractured skull... My physician advised me to rest and now this, this awful thing happens to Tom.' Bradford shook out a pill and reached for a glass which sat beside the paper.

'Where in Chelsea was this dinner?' asked Fletcher.

Peter returned the glass to the floor and wiped at his mouth with the back of his hand. 'Jennifer Pearson's.' His voice sounded tired, almost emotionless as he recited the address. 'Lanford Road – Fifteen Lanford Road. I was there all night.'

Sergeant Rose pulled out his notebook and, returning to the sofa, jotted down the details.

'What time did you leave?' the inspector asked.

'In the morning. As I said I was there all night.'

'Uhuh,' said Fletcher. 'And when was the last time you saw Tom McDonald.'

Bradford turned his eyes to the floor, seemed to gaze sadly at the tabloid headline. 'Not for a while...' There was a wistful tone in his voice before it tailed off and for a few moments he held the same static pose. 'Things had been difficult with Tom for quite a while,' he said at last.

'Difficult?' queried Fletcher. Bradford caught the intimation and looked up as the inspector continued. 'Why don't you tell us all about it?'

Peter Bradford pulled a flattened pillow out from behind him, replaced it, and attempted to sit more upright. 'I don't know how much you know about my relationship with Tom, Inspector,' he said, 'But it had stretched to breaking point long before I left college.'

'That's not what we have been led to understand, Mr. Bradford,' replied Fletcher. He tutted and shook his head. 'By all accounts you and Mr. McDonald were very close. Do you deny that?'

'No.' Bradford nodded gently, a slight smile flickering briefly on his face. 'Tom and I were close once, but his behaviour towards me became too much in the end, and I was forced, sadly I may add, to shun him.'

'What behaviour would that be?' asked the inspector.

'Obsessive behaviour,' said Bradford, a tinge of regret evident in his tone. 'Very obsessive.'

'Uhuh,' Fletcher replied. 'And how exactly did this, "Obsessive behaviour" manifest itself?'

'It's a long story, inspector.'

Fletcher stubbed out his cigarette, checked his watch and glanced at Rose beside him. 'We're not in a rush, are we?' he asked. Rose shook his head. 'Well then...' Fletcher grinned a friendless smile at Bradford and spoke through clenched teeth. 'Get on with it, please… Sir.'

Bradford sighed and smoothed some creases from his bed sheet. 'I first met Tom when I was at Oxford, studying archaeology. He was a year below me but, like myself and several others, had a particular passion for Egyptology. That, more than anything, drew us together and we became firm friends. In the time that followed however – as I got to know him, and his situation, a lot better – it became apparent that he, for some reason to do with his mother I think, began to focus his affections, for want of a better word, upon me.'

'In what way?'

'Well, for a while we were inseparable: shared rooms together. It was good fun for a time, but that's where I really began to find out about him and also where the problems began.' Bradford took a deep breath. 'To begin with he would always be wherever I went, just turn up out of the blue when I was with other friends, or girlfriends – which was okay – we were good friends too, so I didn't originally find it an intrusion.

I can't say my friends were as accommodating though, they thought him a little odd. Then he began borrowing my clothes, saying that he preferred my wardrobe to his–'

'– And you didn't like that?' queried Fletcher as he lit another cigarette.

'To be honest, at the time I was flattered,' Bradford shrugged. 'Nobody had ever complimented me on my dress-sense before, let alone want to wear my things, so I took it as a compliment. But then the fun seemed to slowly drain from the relationship. On evenings when neither of us were going out and we'd maybe had a drink or two, he would always turn the conversation to the subject of me, then himself, before launching into furious tirades against his family. His mother who he despised for leaving him, his father whom he despised even more for not caring, and his sister who he envied for coming through the same situation unscathed. It became increasingly apparent to me after several such conversations that he seemed to be placing me on a pedestal, raising me up as some form of emotional saviour for him… It was shortly after this I began to notice the mannerisms, or rather it was pointed out to me –'

'– What mannerisms, Mr. Bradford,' interrupted the Inspector.

'Mine, inspector. My mannerisms,' Bradford cocked his head to one side. 'My girlfriend noticed it first I seem to remember, and once spotted it was terribly difficult to ignore. I think he felt that if he had the same friends, the same clothes, all he needed was to act like me and he could be me; somehow escape from himself and his troubles.' Bradford paused and raised a tentative hand to his head before continuing. 'I tried speaking to him about it, but he refused to listen, got quite angry about the whole thing. Perhaps he really couldn't see it then, I don't know. It was only when his sister came up to visit that he seemed to see some sense.'

'I thought you said he didn't like his sister?' Fletcher asked.

'No, I said he envied her, Inspector. There was definitely some bond there. Though she certainly didn't care much for me. I got the impression that she saw my closeness to Tom as interference. Meddling. But I think it helped knock me from my pedestal in Tom's eyes, gave him a shot of much needed reality for a time. Unfortunately once she had gone he slipped back into the same pattern. I moved rooms shortly afterwards in the vain hope things would improve, but instead the situation became worse.'

'In what way, Mr. Bradford?' asked the inspector.

'He became really obsessive – dangerous to know – and I tried to keep a distance from him for both our sakes. My exams were close so I busied myself with them and stayed away from him. So Tom began, what I can only describe as a 'hate campaign' against me: slipping nasty notes under my door when I was out, following me to classes that he shouldn't have attended. He also ruined an archaeological dig near the college which I had organised for my exams. Finally my girlfriend, who roomed in the block near me, was attacked one evening on her way home. I mean really badly assaulted. We called in the police but it had been dark and she couldn't identify her attacker, so it went no further. But both she and I were suspicious of who it could have been. Anyway, a few days later Tom slipped another note under my door which seemed to hint that he knew something about the incident. It was stupid of me not to have called the police then and there, but I was so furious I went immediately round to our old rooms with every intention of beating the hell out of him.'

Inspector Fletcher tutted. 'I take it you saw better sense.'

'I banged on the door like a maniac when I got there and got no response,' continued Bradford, 'I knew he was there because I could see light from under the door but he didn't answer. It was when I stopped pounding the woodwork that I heard Tom's voice faintly through the door. It didn't sound right. I broke the door down to find him collapsed on the floor with his wrists slashed.' Bradford blanched at the recollection. 'There was blood everywhere, inspector. Tom was covered in it and in a bad state but the mad bastard had taken the trouble to decorate the floor with dozens of scrawled symbols, written in blood, before becoming too weak.'

The inspector arched an eyebrow. 'What kind of symbols?'

'Power symbols,' explained Bradford. 'It's a kind of old Egyptian magic, protection from evil, strength from the Gods, that sort of thing. I think Tom was at the stage where he would try anything.'

'So what did you do?' asked Fletcher. 'When you saw Mr. McDonald lying there?'

'I panicked. Tried to think straight, and eventually bandaged his wrists before bolting off to get help.'

'You called an ambulance?'

'Yes. I had to call from another floor because Tom's phone had been disconnected, but they were fairly prompt and took him away within the hour, thank heaven.'

'Which hospital?' Rose asked, his pen poised above his pad.

'The Royal. I think, though it was a while back and not something I've been keen to dwell on since.'

'Understandable, I suppose,' said the inspector. 'And was that the last time you saw Tom?'

'No, I still had my exams to finish so I saw him around when he came out of hospital, but we kept our distance. I think he was ashamed about what had happened and I just wanted to forget all about it. Tom had begun to hang around with some creep from his year named Stephen Knight, possibly the only boy in college odder than Tom. So neither myself or any of my friends were troubled anymore with his attentions.'

'And was that the last you saw of him?' queried Fletcher.

'Yes, to my knowledge.'

'So you wouldn't know what he was doing in London? In Hampstead? Or how he happened to meet his end less than a mile from your house?!'

Bradford shook his head. 'I wish I knew inspector, but I never gave Tom my London address.'

'And you never spoke to him, on the phone perhaps? Or communicated with him in any way?'

'No, inspector,' replied Bradford. 'As I say, he did not know I lived here.'

Fletcher sucked at his bottom lip. 'You mentioned a...' he glanced over at the sergeant's note pad. '... Stephen Knight. Who you describe as odd. What was so odd about him?'

Bradford shrugged, winced and sat silently holding his head for a few seconds. 'Excuse me,' he said, removing his hand. 'Er, yes, Steven Knight. Well, he was one of those types I think you find at most colleges.' Fletcher and Rose looked blank. 'An occultist,' continued Bradford, 'At least I think you'd call him that. You know, black magic, secret societies. If I remember correctly he had some pathetic sect called 'The White Knights', or something, who were into the cosmic powers of the ancient Egyptians. We used to joke about what they did during their meetings,' Bradford smiled to himself. 'Wrapping each other up in bandages if I remember rightly...' The two policemen sat stony-faced. Bradford quickly straightened his and said hurriedly, 'Anyway, I think that's where Tom learnt the symbols he scrawled on the floor that night.'

'Uhuh,' said Fletcher. 'And what happened to Stephen Knight?'

'I've no idea. I never spoke to the man. Not really my type.'

They sat in silence for a time, Fletcher drumming his fingers on the arm of the sofa and staring at Bradford who blinked continually and held his head. Rose studied the clocks.

Fletcher's fingers reached the end of their quiet tattoo and he stood, adjusting his overcoat as Rose put away his notebook.

'Thank you for your co-operation, Mr. Bradford,' said Fletcher with a pained smile.

'Not at all, anything to help.'

'We may need to ask you some more questions, so –'

'– Don't leave town?'

'Something like that,' said Fletcher. 'We'll see ourselves out.'

Following his sergeant, the inspector reached the landing before returning to the room. 'Just one other thing,' he said from the doorway.

Bradford looked quizzical. 'Yes?'

'Your accident. When was that exactly?'

Bradford gave a small smile. 'On the way back from Chelsea, Tuesday morning.'

Fletcher nodded, looked around the room one final time and then left Bradford to his gloom.

The cramped bulk of Constable Wright greeted the pair when they returned to the car. 'Any luck, sir?' he asked as Rose and Fletcher sat down.

Rose looked at the inspector, who shrugged. 'God knows,' said Fletcher. 'How about you?'

Wright shook his head. 'Not a thing, no-one remembers ever seeing Tom McDonald around here, and they say Bradford's a nice, friendly chap.'

'Hhhmm,' said Fletcher looking back towards the house.

'He's certainly not a body builder,' said Rose, recalling their earlier hypothesis about the heath murderer.

'No,' replied Fletcher with more than a touch of chagrin. 'I noticed.'

'So what now?' Rose asked. 'Do you think he's involved?'

'Do you?' asked the inspector, irritated. He drummed his hands upon the dashboard for a while, mulling over the conversation with Bradford. 'Before we can get anywhere with that one I want his alibi checked, otherwise he could be out of the picture. At the same time I want Stephen Knight found, Claire McDonald requestioned and Tom's autopsy report re-examined,' Fletcher raised his eyes heavenward. 'And that's just for starters.' The inspector pulled a pained face. 'Why can't anything be easy?' he said and twisted in his seat to face Wright. 'Constable,' said Fletcher with a grin. 'Pop in there and beat a confession out of him, will you? I can't be bothered with all the paperwork.'

Wright grinned nervously at the suggestion. Rose raised his eyebrows in alarm and started the car. Fletcher, smiling, turned and wound down the window. 'Okay,' he said, 'let's do it the slow way and go back to the station.' Fletcher glanced at his watch. 'What time is it?' he asked, looking across at Rose.

Rose checked his watch, as did Wright.

'Quarter to one,' said the constable from the back seat.

Fletcher nodded but continued to look at his sergeant.

'Bloody odd,' muttered Rose, holding his watch up to his ear. His watch, like Fletcher's, read twelve o'clock.

Mikey sat on a bench outside the British museum staring sightlessly at the patch of blue sky above the buildings before him. Beside him, two German students, backpacks at their feet, consulted a map and discussed in accented English which sight to visit next. Mikey was oblivious to the conversation, indeed to their presence, so occupied were his thoughts with the conversation he had just had with Danny Trent.

He stubbed out his cigarette and sighed, the same question

coming back again and again to nag him. What now? True, he had moved a step further by visiting the museum but, he thought, where the hell was it leading him?

Danny had told Mikey the little that he knew about the late Marcus Tenneshaw Wright: wealthy landowner, Victorian entrepreneur and explorer. He had made a fortune in the shipping and spice trades, (supplementing his considerable inherited wealth), and while in the Middle East had become obsessed with collecting Sumerian and Egyptian artefacts, an occupation which made him one of the pioneer amateur archaeologists of the nineteenth century. After his death in 1849 the collection he had amassed over his short lifetime was donated to the British museum by trustees of Tenneshaw Wright's estate. Given his concern about the possible origin of the book, Mikey had nearly panicked when told all Tenneshaw Wright's archaeological possessions had been passed on to the museum. The situation was made worse by Danny's aside about a recent theft in the Egyptian rooms and Mikey had fallen quiet while the archeologist talked on, debating in his head whether to come clean and explain where the book had been found. Danny abruptly gave him a reprieve, the potential association of Tenneshaw Wright with the book redirecting his curiosity.

'If this is connected with Tenneshaw Wright, we may be able to verify it by comparison with material in our possession,' Danny had said, unconscious of the fact that he was rubbing his hands. 'Though the public rarely gets to see it,' he continued, 'we have an extensive collection of books and papers down here in the vaults,' he tapped the leather binding. 'We don't however have very many fakes of this calibre, and if it does turn out Tenneshaw Wright was somehow involved with this it would be a fascinating addition to our library.' Danny had paused and placed his hands possessively upon the book. 'Would it be possible, at all, to hang on to this for a while?' he asked, quickly adding: 'If we can verify its origins it would be just marvellous!'

Mikey considered the proposal for roughly a second before agreeing. What was he going to do with it? It was gibberish to him. If Danny Trent could confirm its origin and a connection with Tenneshaw Wright it would not exactly be what Mikey had been hoping for but, then again, Mikey was not at all sure what he had been hoping for.

'The address of a preacher, maybe,' said Mikey quietly to himself as he gazed up at the sky. The German students stopped their conversation to give him a sideways look.

'Excuse me?' said the one holding the map

Mikey broke from his reverie and noticed the Germans for the first time. He blinked and looked quizzically at the pair. 'What?' he said, slightly irritated.

The students, more satisfied with his glassy stare than his outburst, returned to their map.

Mikey stood up and looked around, still not quite focused on his surroundings. What do I do now? he pondered as he strolled towards the gate. He knew he should phone Jane to check on her progress, his father to keep him updated, but he didn't feel the immediate necessity. He had done more than enough for the moment as far as he was concerned and the search was at a halt until Danny Trent came back with some results. What else could he do? He was no detective. I need a break, he thought, something to get me out of this weird situation for a while.

'I'M ON HOLIDAY!!' he shouted as he approached the main gate, the sudden eruption of sound startling him to a halt. Shocked by the ferocity of the unexpected outburst, Mikey placed a hand to his heart, felt its beat thumping wildly within. He ran nervous fingers through his red locks and looked around, at once realising that he had silenced and focused the entire forecourt of the museum on himself. He put his head down and exited hastily.

Mikey walked back to his motorbike, attempting to figure out his mood as he strode through the dusty streets. Gone was the euphoric rush he had experienced the previous morning when he had left his father's: the inner calm he had felt after finding the book. Now there was a sense of gloom, of despondency which the photographer felt unable to shake. There was no question in his mind that it was connected with the lose of his friend, and the more he thought about it the more he realised just how much he had been avoiding the grief he felt over Geoff's death. He had willingly pursued the distraction caused by the preacher as a means of blocking the pain which had accompanied him back from Kumanovo. Now the distraction had reached an end, and his subconscious, overriding his desire to lock it away, had returned the melancholy he had pushed to one side.

And there was something else. The unaccountable and growing sense of agitation, as manifest in his angry outburst a few minutes before What was the cause of that? Somewhere deep inside Mikey, a tiny rage seemed to be flickering. He could not account for it, yet he could feel it: like some minute, buzzing itch getting ready to flare into violent life. It isn't right, Mikey thought. He knew he was going through a bad time, but never before had he experienced such pent up ferocity: it was not in his nature. That line of thought led him to another nagging question. The reason for the strange dizzy spell he had experienced outside the museum. Was it stress? Whatever it was, Mikey hoped it was an isolated incident.

As he debated, Mikey passed a phone, and stopped in his tracks a few feet beyond the glass panelled box. On impulse he decided to call Cooper. If anyone could divert his attention for a few hours, Mikey knew Cooper was the man, and he had been meaning to return his call for days. He back-tracked to the box and, checking his pocket for change, pulled open the door and reached for the phone. It began to ring.

'Hello?' said Mikey, automatically lifting the receiver.

There was a whistling on the phone line, more akin to the wind than some mechanical phenomenon and Mikey felt his spine tingle with apprehension at the sound. He recalled Jane's answer phone message and cursed himself for touching the phone, an inner voice urging him to quickly replace the handset. The sounds, however, seemed to coalesce before he could move, and blended to form a voice, though barely discernible, sighing amongst the breeze.

'Time... Michael... Not much time,' hissed the voice.

Mikey froze, his muscles stiffening as he recognised the speaker: not wanting to hear, repelled by its presence. He dropped the phone as if burnt by its contact and shot backwards out of the booth: the call disconnecting before the flex had pulled taut. Mikey failed to hear it, the tiny rage inside him erupting to the surface.

'LEAVE ME ALONE!!' he screamed, an avalanche of noise and emotion escaping him as he faced the telephone box.

The savage sound seemed to reverberate within the tiny space, visibly shaking the structure as if some beast of air and vapour where trapped within; the ringing in Mikey's ears a physical force as one by one the glass panes of the phone booth cracked and shattered. Mikey watched, stunned in disbelief as the small windows – fracturing in unison – blossomed in every direction before falling. A silent, glittering cascade hit the pavement, its noise lost amongst a greater tumult.

Mikey stood by the curb, shocked and confused as he took in the devastation he appeared to have caused, saw the handset rocking gently on its cord behind the ragged panes. He managed to take a breath and immediately felt the anger lessen, the rage diminish against this thing, this preacher who haunted him. His body was shivering uncontrollably now, yet he felt some semblance of clarity return. What did it want from him!? What more could he do?

'Oy! Mate!'

The voice came from directly behind him and Mikey turned to see a black cab parked beside the curb, its driver leaning out of his window and pointing accusingly at the damaged booth.

'Was that you?!' he asked, contempt in his voice.

'Fuck off,' replied Mikey bluntly. He re-entered the broken phone box to call Cooper.

Le Mars, a recently opened restaurant on the back streets of Green Park, was fast becoming the place to be seen by discerning London socialites. The proud proprietors matching an expensive menu with an inventive interior that by their own happy admission had cost the best part of a quarter of a million pounds. The decor, if it could be termed as such with its cracked plaster walls, exposed support girders and smashed tiling, had been described by the interior designer as a destructive art house mix of fifties beat bar and seventies kitsch. It reminded Mikey of a Balkan war zone.

Still shaken after his destruction of the phone box, Mikey had felt it wiser to leave his motorbike where it was and so, after a brief and reassuringly jovial conversation with Cooper, had caught a cab over to the restaurant where his friend would be lunching. Now, an hour, a meal and several drinks later, Mikey had brought Cooper up to date on the strange events of the last few days.

'An unusual tale,' said Cooper after Mikey drew his monologue to a close. 'And one all the stranger because the

131

very same thing happened to me only last week.' Cooper winked and cracked a broad, infectious smile which Mikey could not help but mirror.

'But do you believe it?' asked Mikey. Even he found it far-fetched.

'Knowing you as long as I have, I see no reason to disbelieve,' Cooper replied, "More things in heaven and earth" and all that. In fact I have an uncle who used to tell the most hair-raising stories about a woman who haunted his manor house in Berkshire. So you're not alone.' Cooper frowned and patted his jacket, removed an address book and leafed through it. 'Aha!' he said after skimming through the pages.

'Aha, what?' asked Mikey through his wine glass.

'Do not despair, Captain,' said Cooper, patting Mikey gently on the hand and grinning. 'I think I have the very person to cure your particular ailment. I'll give them a call.'

Intrigued, Mikey watched as his friend – mobile phone in hand – delicately negotiating his considerable bulk from his chair then waddled to the back of the restaurant in search of privacy to make his phone call.

Colin Hooper, affectionately known as Cooper to close associates due to his barrel-like frame and love of real ale, was one of the capital's leading, not to mention feared, restaurant critics. In his early thirties, the thinning hair, stout build and florid complexion had the effect of – to the casual observer at least – placing him in late middle age. It was only after closer inspection that the assumption was generally revised, usually after exposure to his eyes which sparkled and blazed with a youth and ferocity unmatched by his countenance.

The former attributes were ones which Cooper never tired of exacerbating during his work, whilst beneath the genial demeanour and playful irreverence of his 'bumbling old fool' act, hid a savage wit which many an unfriendly and unsuspecting restaurateur had had the misfortune to fall foul of.

Mikey saw his friend disappear behind a jagged, badly constructed wine rack and returned to studying the assorted half-eaten dishes spread upon the messy tablecloth. I'll say one thing for Cooper, Mikey thought, examining the various blotches and sauce stains on the white linen, he may have impeccable gastronomic taste but it's countered by his table manners.

As he waited for Cooper to return, Mikey picked at his own untouched plate. He still had no appetite, but after an hour in Cooper's cheerful company he felt the gloom that had weighed so heavily upon him lessen.

He had first met Cooper at a party thrown in the offices of the national paper they were both working for at the time. Having just flown back from an assignment in Israel, Mikey had travelled straight to the office to deliver his photos only to find himself adrift in dusty combat clothing amidst a sea of suits engaged in an office function. Uncomfortable, and unable to find the editor who had commissioned him, Mikey attempted to remain inconspicuous by skulking around the buffet table in the vain hope the man would turn up. It was here he had noticed a large, cherubic looking man with ruddy cheeks poking dubiously at a vol-au-vent.

'If you're one of the caterers that would explain the food,' Cooper had said, dropping the pastry back onto the plate and looking suspiciously at Mikey. 'Fundamentalist reactionaries never make the best cooks.'

Before Mikey could explain, Colin Hooper had thrust out his hand and grinning said: 'You're the man with the golden lens, Michael Dayville, aren't you? I'm Colin Hooper – food terrorist – pleased to meet you.'

Mikey had been taken aback by the recognition, even more by the appellation and stood dumbly as Cooper vigorously attempted to dislocate his shoulder. Mikey's incredulity reached its peak when, after letting go of his hand, Cooper pointed to his olive drab jump suit and said: 'You look like Tim Page. I'm a big fan of his Vietnam work.'

The friendship had blossomed there and then, the pair talking and joking non-stop well into the early hours of the following morning. Mikey remembered little more of that evening. His most vivid and indelible recollections were that of waking up opposite Colin on his kitchen floor some time the next day and the hang-over which kept him tea-total for a month.

'Right,' said Cooper, returning to his seat and flipping his mobile phone shut. 'Your troubles are over!'

Mikey straightened in his chair, lit a cigarette and raised a dubious brow at his friend's beaming countenance. 'Who have you phoned, Coop',' he asked with a smile. 'The exorcist?'

Cooper shook his head and laughed. 'He was engaged I'm afraid, so I've got you the next best thing.'

Mikey nodded. 'Who?' he asked. Cooper caught the seriousness in the tone.

'A medium. A friend,' he said, then added, 'well... A friend of a friend. Or should I say friend of an acquaintance? Anyway,' he continued with a theatrical flourish, 'she's very good and wants to see you now.'

Mikey tapped thoughtfully on his cigarette and stared at the overflowing ashtray. 'What did you tell her?'

'Nothing. Not-a-thing. She didn't want to know any details other than your name.' Cooper placed a reassuring hand on Mikey's and looked him in the eyes. 'I really think she can help, Mikey.'

Mikey shrugged. 'If she can tell me who the hell this preacher is, I'd be very grateful.'

Cooper threw his hands into the air. 'WHO WILL RID ME OF THIS MEDDLESOME PRIEST!?' he bellowed with a grin, and went of to pay the bill.

Chapter Seven

The colourful sprawl of fairground stalls and rides sat incongruously upon the almost level field at the top of Hampstead Heath. Bright paint work blazed in the afternoon sun and the cheery lilt of a dozen fairground organs drifted across the expanse of grass. Closer still and the music tempered with the noise of milling spectators and the laboured murmur of diesel generators.

There was something wrong with the fair. Jane knew it was unscheduled and likely to be closed down at any moment but, as she wandered slowly amongst the rides, trucks and caravans she could not help but feel that there was something amiss, some fundamental flaw with it all which, though she sensed it, she was at a loss to explain. There was the usual collection of stalls: the coconut shy, the hoopla, and perennial rides such as the waltzer and merry-go-round, yet despite such repetitive familiarity Jane found that the whole thing, somehow, did not seem right. It irked her journalistic sensibilities that her intuition could be no more specific.

Get a grip! she chided herself, stopping to take a sip from her warm bottle of water. You're letting Mikey's behaviour get to you. She had found her thoughts straying repeatedly to Mikey since leaving her office earlier, and now, as she glugged down a mouthful of water, she wondered for the umpteenth time how her boyfriend had got on at the museum. She hoped (or was it prayed?) that he had found some logical explanation for the book, or at least something to ease his agitation. More than anything, Jane wanted him back to normal.

'Perhaps that's it,' she said softly to herself as she recapped the bottle and returned it to her bag. There's really nothing wrong with the fair, she thought, it was just her perception of it. It was her that was wrong. Her, and Mikey.

Jane wandered past the straggled perimeter of stalls and against the light influx of newcomers made her way towards the line of oaks which all but bisected the field. She sat in the shade, weary from the heat and, as the shadows cooled her, watched the fairground scene. Before her, a queue had begun to form alongside an ice cream van: sweltering children impatiently waiting their turn as the vendor passed down melting handfuls of '99's'. Jane resisted her initial temptation to join the queue as the vendor, his apron grey and grime stained, the van battered and rusty, made Jane wonder what sort of germs where being bred and passed on. It was such a contrast, she thought, to the pristine paint work of the rest of the fair, almost clinical in its cleanliness. Jane shrugged, and turning her back on the scene, continued her debate.

What would Doctor Frencham make of Mikey's troubles? she wondered, considering his behaviour over the past few days. The question surprised her and Jane realised it was the first time in over a year she had thought at all about the psychiatrist. Such a kind man, such a kind and helpful man, she thought, recalling the long and stressful sessions after her rape, the slow but steady progress she had made in that stuffy third floor room. Both he, and Mikey, had brought her back from her breakdown. Bit by bit restoring her confidence and faith in a life shattered by her experiences at the London Evening Mail. It was a testament to Doctor Frencham's abilities, as well as Mikey's love and understanding that she was now a journalist again: happy again. But what about Mikey?

Was it possible, Jane wondered, that Mikey's loss of his friend in such terrible circumstances could be akin to the events that had affected her? She tried to review the information logically, to remember what she had read in the books on Freud, on Jung, which Doctor Frencham had given her. Something about archetypes? Dream analysis? It had been a long time ago. Mikey had spoken of recurrent nightmares since returning from the Balkans, the same scenes repeated every time. That was easy enough to explain, Jane thought, such experiences would doubtless be hard to forget. Yet, after seeing the preacher, Mikey had had a totally different nightmare. What did that signify? Jane tried to recollect what she had read, feeling sure she was on the right track. She lay back on the grass, closed her eyes and began reviewing events from the afternoon on Parliament Hill.

Mikey was sure he had seen a ghost that afternoon, thought Jane, yet she hadn't. Didn't Jung also write about seeing ghosts? That they were manifestations of repressed subconscious desire or something? Jane could not quite remember the details. Next, Mikey had had the terrible dream, a nightmare which he later believed to be about the heath murder: also involving the preacher. So the man in black again. After that, and Jane cursed herself for allowing it, she had made the mistake of letting Mikey take the photos at the same site, and again he had seen the preacher, this time only on the photographs.

Jane sat up, surprised by the brightness of the day around her. That was it! she thought, why hadn't she seen the connection sooner? It had been there all the time, but she, like Mikey, had been distracted by the symptom, not the cause. The heath murder was the catalyst, the heart of Mikey's problem: an all too present reminder of his loss in Kumanovo. What was it he had said that afternoon? Something about the murder being too close to home? How right he was! If only she had realised – if Mikey had realised– what his statement had really meant. His experiences in the Balkans had affected him far more deeply than either one of them had suspected, and they (Jane felt herself far more guilty) had compounded the problem by getting more involved with a similar event. Yet Mikey's subconscious had known the danger, and brought out the preacher: appearing more and more often as he pursued his misguided quest. There was no ghost: it was simply the embodiment of an encroaching psychosis – a cry for help from Mikey's subconscious – manifesting itself in ways that seemed real to him. Mikey was haunting himself.

Jane rummaged through her bag, searching its depths for her mobile phone and her address book. Another thought had struck her, a problem which, if it were true, could undo her hypothesis. She was sure that her theory was correct, yet there was one person who had supported Mikey's claim of seeing the preacher in the photographs. His father. If she could eliminate that problem then everything made logical sense, and the book and that odd phone call could be discounted as mere, what was the word? Synchronicity. Jane knew that Mikey would not have lied about what his father had seen, but had his father lied? It was a long-shot perhaps, but more productive, she felt, than chasing ghosts.

Jane fished out the small leather filofax, her equally minute phone and, after placing them beside her on the grass, took another swig from the tepid water in her bottle. She began to leaf through her list of addresses, humming contentedly to herself as she flicked the pages; happy now that things were making sense. Though she wished she had spotted Mikey's symptoms earlier – and she of all people should have – she knew now. And that meant that Mikey would soon know, and he would start getting back to normal. Jane found the page, and with a smile phoned Patrick Dayville.

Twelve year old Ralph Chivers – "Spiv" to his friends – felt the same unaccountable strangeness with the fair that Jane had. However the tawny-haired, moon faced youth found a more expressive way to encapsulate his feelings towards it.

'What a load o' fuckin' shit!' he said, waving the stick he had found in the grass in the general direction of the ghost train.

John and his younger brother Dave, reclined on the grass before him, followed Ralph's gaze and nodded.

'Yeah,' said John, squinting against the sunlight to look at Ralph crouching a few feet away. 'I get more shit up when old 'Bloodshot' chases us.'

Ralph laughed and banged his stick repeatedly against the ground until its tip snapped off.

'Who's 'Bloodshot'?' asked Dave, flicking his glance between the older pair. Ralph ignored the question, John scanned the milling crowd. 'Who's 'Bloodshot'!?' he repeated, tapping his brother's leg with a foot to gain his attention.

'Eh?!' said John, suddenly turning.

'Who the bloody hell is 'Bloodshot'?!'

'Council bloke. Ya know. One at the church, down the 'ill.' John jerked a thumb in the general direction of Belsize Park.

Dave opened his mouth wide. 'Oh, 'im,' he said, satisfied.

'Yeah,' said Ralph with a broad smirk. 'Looks like e's face is gonna explode when he gets goin'.' Ralph began pumping his arms as if running on the spot and puffed out his cheeks. 'Come back 'ere ya little bastards!' he panted. 'I'm gonna bleed on yer!'

John and Dave exploded with laughter at the impression. Ralph kept up the impetus and pounced on Dave, pinning his arms behind his head.

'An when he gets yer,' said Ralph, bringing his face close to Dave's who struggled, laughing, against his grip. 'He says: "Got ya boy! Now me cheeks are gonna go BOOM!" Ralph mimed his face exploding with both hands before rubbing them into the younger boy's face.

Dave spluttered beneath the grubby palms and with his arms now free, rolled sideways into his brother. Ralph slumped, giggling, onto the grass beside him.

'Eeergghh!' exclaimed Dave, spitting and wiping at his face. He pushed himself to a sitting position and grinned at his laughing companions. 'Eeerrghh,' he repeated, ''e don't really do that, does 'e?'

'Aaaaww, yeah! Dimwit! Corse 'e does!' chastised his brother, pulling a face and slapping Dave playfully round the back of his head. 'All the bloody time!' John tutted loudly towards Ralph who echoed the sound.

'Well I dunno, do I?!' Dave retorted, his pitch rising. 'I've never seen the bloke.'

'Only 'cos you bottled it last time we all went down there,' said Ralph. He clasped his hands before him and screwed up his face. "I'm not goin' in there," he said in a high, whiny voice. "I've gotta go 'ome for me tea!"

'I never said that!' protested Dave as the older two collapsed into hysterics again. 'I fuckin' never said that! You lyin' bastard, Spiv!' In exasperation he kicked out at Ralph, who lazily rolled away to avoid the blow.

"Boohoohoo!" continued Ralph as he moved clear, his voice choked with laughter. "Boohoo!" He wiped away imaginary tears from his eyes and quivered his bottom lip.

Dave's lips compressed to a thin line, frustrated in his inability to think of a suitable riposte. He hated it when he was picked on. He was always being picked on. He couldn't help being younger and smaller.

John delivered the coup de grace.

'When 'e got 'ome,' said John, his face red and his sides aching. 'Mum had to put 'im in the bath, because –' He couldn't quite finish the sentence and spluttered. Ralph, catching the humour in his friend's voice began to giggle anyway. 'Because... Because –' repeated John, desperate to finish the sentence. 'Because 'e'd shit 'imself!'

Howls of laughter escaped the two boys as they gripped their sides and rocked upon the grass. Dave, indignant, crimson faced and furious jumped to his feet and contemptuously surveyed his companions.

'I fuckin' did not you liar!' he spat, staring down at his brother curled helplessly at his feet. 'Just wait 'till I tell mum!'

The statement only made John and Ralph laugh more ferociously, and in frustration Dave aimed a size three Reebok at his brother's exposed groin.

'Ooow!' cried John, curling up even tighter as Dave's blow struck home: the dull pain mixing with his laughter. 'Aahahaoow!'

Dave sprinted off into the crowd.

'Ahee...ahee!' sniggered Ralph, attempting to catch his breath. He pointed to where John had been kicked. 'John, ahee!... Mind yer bollock's don't explode!'

Dave heard the renewed eruption of mirth as he fled the scene, weaving through the growing crowd to get as far away from the taunts as possible.

He stopped running only when he had cleared the far side of the fairground and come to a sturdy fence which barred his progress. On the other side a gravel track ran parallel to the fence before veering right behind a brake of trees. It snaked on up to Kenwood, the old manor house which housed the concerts every summer. Dave followed its line downhill, tapping the wooden planks every few feet with a broken branch he had picked up. It would be time for the concerts soon, he thought, gazing into the woodland beyond, another golden opportunity for the other boys to take the piss out of him again. Just like last year.

The classical concerts were held at dusk during the summer

141

in the field below Kenwood House, the orchestra playing to a large crowd from a small bowl set on the far side of an ornamental lake. On those still, warm evenings the sound of the music travelled far, past the confines of Kenwood and the heath to reach the houses beyond. It had been John's idea to trace the sound, eventually bringing the six of them to a thicket which bordered the lake. From here, lying hidden amongst the greenery they had seen the orchestra; strains of Beethoven drifting across the water to the assembled mass on the far bank.

'Fuck me,' said Steve Jenkins, crawling through the undergrowth to get a better view. Like all the others he had never really heard classical music before and seeing it performed left him a little awe-struck.

'This is the one from that car advert,' said Ralph nudging Dave beside him. He seemed unfazed by the grandeur of the scene. 'Y'know,' he continued, 'the one for Ford's?' Dave tittered nervously and looked back into the trees.

John was watching the people on the other bank, in particular a group of well dressed men who appeared to be drinking from bottles of champagne.

'Poncy fuckers,' he said to himself, sneering at the audience. He twisted his neck to find Dexter Harris, crouched with Pete Singleton in the bushes behind him. 'Oy, Dex!' he hissed. 'Did you bring your air gun?'

'Oh, don't!' pleaded Dave with a whisper. John ignored the outburst.

Beside him, Ralph moved his mouth to Dave's ear and whispered: 'Poof.'

Dexter spat and shook his head. 'Nah mate,' he said. 'Left it at 'ome.' John nodded and returned his attention to the crowd. 'C'mon,' continued Dexter, tapping John's leg. 'This is fuckin' boring.'

John nodded, moved back into the bushes and began to thread his way through the trees towards the orchestra.

'Where ya goin'?' asked Ralph, as his friend crept off into the half light.

John stopped and looked back. 'I've got a brilliant idea!' he said and grinned. Ralph giggled and beckoned on the others.

'Whatcha gonna do?' asked Steve when the other four caught up.

John grinned even wider and picked up a stick. 'Join the orchestra!' he said and resumed his course through the trees.

All but Dave laughed and followed, picking up their own projectiles as they walked on. Dave hung back.

'Don't!' he pleaded as the last figure began to fade amongst the deepening shadows.

Pete Singleton turned and regarded the younger boy. 'Shut the fuck up, ya little queer,' he said, then disappeared into the gloom.

Dave stood, uncomfortably wrestling with his conscience, before edging back the way they had come. He didn't want to leave his brother, or the others, but he just could not bring himself to go with them. He got another few steps before the music stopped abruptly and whoops and wild crashes sounded in the forest behind him. He ran for his life: not stopping until he had cleared the heath and reached the bottom of his road.

He couldn't help having a conscience, Dave thought as he walked on, or help being frightened. He threw the stick over the fence and dug his hands deep into his pockets. Like that bloody church. Now that was frightening. He cared deeply that they berated him for not going in there: that they labelled him a coward. It was so unfair! Dave knew the others were almost as scared as he was about the place. It having taken the combined bravado of four of them – John, Spiv, Steve and Dex egging one another on – to get inside its crumbling facade.

Dex had later confided to Dave that they had run back out only five minutes later, so why did he keep getting all the flack!? He had had to endure his brother's taunts when he had returned home, and though he didn't let it show, had listened with envy when John described the creepy thrill of the church's interior. Dave so much wanted to be able to say that he had seen it with his own eyes, be able to taunt someone else for not doing what he had done. John had confidently said that the next time they went in they would climb the old clock tower, but their encounter with the council man, 'Bloodshot', had ended that excursion. Ralph still talked of going back to write his name in the tower, but no-one so far had taken him up on the offer. For all his boasts and jibes he too felt uneasy about re-entering the church a third time.

Dave walked on, unable to prevent his mind from running through his back catalogues of 'failures' as he went, but always his thoughts returned to the old church. That was his most unforgiven crime in the eyes of his friends, who could see the recollection upset him and maliciously exploited it. It was his bane and had been ever since he had made his feeble excuse and walked away. Only five minutes inside and he could have been accepted, gone up in the estimation of the others. Dave supposed that was why the taunts hurt more, why he had replayed the scene over and over in his head since that time, changing each recollection until it was only him that had gone inside, racing to the top of the bell tower to write his name and come back down a hero. That would be all it would take, he thought, five minutes inside and he could be the one to boast.

Dave's journey had now taken him well towards the middle of the heath. Just a short walk away, at the bottom of the hill, lay Hampstead Green. Around the corner from that, past the hospital and by the main road, was the root of his troubles – St. Anne's. Dave's feet seemed inexorably drawn towards the

144

church, his mind contemplating the impossible: for him to venture inside. Not just to look around and bolt out, that would gain him nothing, but to climb the tower and write his name. That would be impressive. A real feat. Of course his brother would never believe him, nor would Spiv, Dex, Steve - any of the others. But that seemed to be the greatest thing about the scheme slowly shaping in his mind. To prove him a liar, and they would believe nothing else, they would have to go and look for themselves – do what they had not so far plucked up the courage to do. It seemed to Dave the most wonderful of scenarios and, as he approached Hampstead Green, his spirits were high. Redemption was at hand.

He would go with them when they went to check his tale, he thought, tag along and then refuse to go in. Dave smiled to himself. That would really convince them he was lying, make them all the more eager to prove him wrong. Then Dave would stand outside and wait, wait for the doubters to come back outside and apologise. Brilliant! There was only one small flaw in the immaculate plan, and as Dave passed the small green and turned the corner, he found it waiting for him at the top of the road.

Derelict, St. Anne's loomed large before him, its square redbrick bell tower soaring past the trees which nestled in its shadow. Dave slowed his pace, his neck slowly craning back to take in the tiny blank windows, the grey slits of the belfry and the rusted iron clock faces which forever read twelve o'clock. His legs felt like lead, his heart quickening as Dave realised the true scale of his task. He could not go inside before, and not now. The weather beaten facade contained too many nameless terrors for his will to overcome. His brother and everyone else was right: he was a coward.

Dave walked slowly along the pavement beside the church, past the tiny side door behind the tree which he knew would get him inside. He followed the low boundary wall until he came to the dilapidated metal gates which stood at the junction and lent against them. A rusty cry issued from long disused hinges as Dave leaned back before the heavy padlock which secured the gates stopped their backward swing. Dave watched the traffic: cars slowing and accelerating at the lights beside him and tried to rekindle his courage.

Five minutes! Five fuckin' minutes! he thought. That was all it took! Dave stamped his foot involuntarily and caused a man in a stationary van to look him up and down. Dave was oblivious to the attention, his inner rage in full flight. What was going to happen in five minutes?! he thought. Think of the faces of the others! What they'll think! He so much wanted to do it, to be the hero, to be brave. If only for five minutes. That was all it would take. Not for them, for John and the others. If they were here he would have an excuse to back out – they expected it from him. No, not for them, for him. Prove it to yourself, Dave, he thought, take just five little minutes and change your life. He pushed himself away from the gates and looked around. It was a nice day, a lovely day. Lots of people about, busy, and he would only be a few feet away from them. What could possibly happen? It was a bloody church after all!

Dave returned to the road beside St. Anne's and, checking to see he was not noticed, vaulted the crumbling brick wall. He dashed behind a tree which stood in the small grass border beside the church and crouched nervously at its base, feeling his pulse quicken, the adrenalin start to surge. Before him, from the age weary walls, a dozen sandstone gargoyles gazed down: their features washed and whittled by centuries of rain. Dave did his best to ignore their grotesque leers and kept low as he made his way to the old wooden door at the base of the bell tower. A tiny voice inside him prayed it would be locked.

Five minutes. Five minutes. Over and over in his head Dave chanted the same refrain as his hand reached out to grasp the verdigris covered door handle. Trembling, he gripped and twisted, his heart pounding as the lock clicked and the door eased back. Fuck! Fuck! Fuck! Fuck! Five minutes! Five minutes! He slipped inside before anyone spotted him and silently closed the door.

A short flight of dusty steps led up to a second door. Partially ajar, Dave could see a sliver of warm light beyond. He crept closer, holding his breath until his face was level with the opening and got his first view of the interior of St. Anne's.

Dereliction had taken its toll on the church: litter, leaves and grime obscuring the lustre of what once had been a glorious marble floor. Pews lay scattered around the nave, dashed upon the columns of the aisles as if some storm had raged ferociously through the broken stained glass windows. God had long since forgotten this place yet, for all its dilapidation, Dave found the scene enchanting. He pulled back the door, took a few hesitant steps inside and stood spellbound amongst the coloured shafts of light streaming through the windows.

Beautiful. It was the only word Dave could find, yet he knew it did not adequately describe the grandeur of the sight before him. Sunlight, blazing from countless leaded windows, illuminated the bright biblical scenes; culminating in a dazzling circular display at the far end of the church. Dave shook his head. How could anybody be afraid of this? He took a few more steps to reach the centre of the floor and held out his hand to catch a beam. Yellow and orange light played across his palm and he smiled. How stupid he had been. How lucky to have finally ventured in. John had mentioned nothing of this when he had returned that first time; only the mess and the mouldy smell. This wasn't frightening, Dave thought, it was bloody beautiful!

He turned to see the chancel, through the high arch at the opposite end of the nave, and was again greeted by the same rich sunshine. He walked towards it, passing as he did the ornate pulpit, its wood dark and battered, dusty from the years of neglect. He drew level with the arch and, as he climbed the low white steps towards the alter, he realised he no longer felt afraid. Dave stopped and held out his hand again, saw it steady before him. He placed it to his heart and felt the slow beat. A broad grin spread across his face and, as he gazed up happily into the light, he began twisting slowly on the spot. A pirouette of joy and triumph.

As he span, in the corner of his eye Dave spotted a patch of darkness against the wall. He stopped his rotation and turned to his right to see another open doorway. It was dark beyond, but Dave was sure he could make out the shape of stairs climbing up into the gloom.

He walked over to the entrance and confirmed his observation, a set of worn stone steps spiralling upwards before him. The tower! he thought. This must be it! Being careful not to make too much noise, Dave gripped the iron hand rail and began to ascend.

The staircase was steep and cramped, its only light source narrow Gothic windows which lit the way intermittently. Winding tightly as it climbed, the staircase afforded Dave little warning of what might lay beyond the next turn. He watched his feet to avoid lumps of plaster which had fallen from the walls and, as he rose, Dave felt a little of his fear return.

There was no beauty here, only half-light and neglect and Dave breathed a quiet sigh of relief when he reached the entrance to a hallway which led off at a right angle to the steps. It was just as dishevelled as the spiral staircase, and the pale planks of the floor looked less than safe yet, at its far end, daylight shone welcomely through a large, broken window pane. Dave looked above to the shadowed curve of stairs and estimated that he still had quite a way to climb. He decided to calm his nerves and take in the view.

Dave crept along the corridor towards the daylight. He was conscious that the old boards beneath his feet would be prone to squeaking so he watched his step until he reached the broken pane. Dave felt a warm breeze touch his face but, before looking down at the world outside, he checked the door which stood opposite the window. There was a splintered hole where once a lock had been and Dave hooked his finger into the space to open it. The door swung back with a muted creak and revealed a second, straighter stairway, again leading up. Dave listened for any tell-tale sounds beyond but all was quiet. He left the door ajar and returned to the window, satisfied that he was totally alone. Just wait 'till I tell 'em! he thought to himself, leaning his elbows on the rotting window frame and gazing out. Below him a high angular roof jutted down from the body of the church, cracked red tiles obscuring the small and overgrown graveyard below. Dave shaded his eyes and peered down at the traffic still crawling by: the grey van parked on the road beside the church. A thought suddenly clouded his happiness. What was he going to write his name with?! He stepped back from the window and slapped his forehead. Bollocks! he thought. Now what do I do?

As if in answer to his heartfelt plea his gaze fell upon the remains of the lock, lying broken on the bottom stair beyond the doorway, and in particular the heavy screws which had previously held it in place. Brilliant! Dave thought, grinning at his own ingenuity. He could scratch his name. He crouched down to pick up one of the screws and as he did so the plank beneath his feet groaned ominously. The noise startled him, its sound rumbling through the stillness, echoing loudly in the confines of the spiral staircase. Quickly, Dave hopped off the plank to stand in the doorway opposite the broken window. He let out a long sigh but felt his pulse racing again, his adrenalin surge into overdrive when a second sound came from above. OHMYGOD!! he thought, his eyes suddenly growing wide, MUSTBETHATBLOKE! MUSTBEHIM! OHSHIT! OHSHIT! BLOODSHOT MUST BE HERE!

He flicked his eyes around frantically, panic overwhelming his senses as the sound was repeated. Dave's head felt light, his legs just the opposite, and he stared through the broken window, desperately trying to think. What if it wasn't Bloodshot?! What if it was some old tramp? Jesus! Or a druggie?! What then? Maybe he could call for help. Or jump? Maybe he could slide down the roof?! He heard what sounded like footsteps on stone and realised with terror that whoever had made the noise was now coming down the spiral stairway.

Dave felt his heart clatter in his chest at the sound. OHNO! OHNO! PLEASE NO! DON'T LET HIM FIND ME! His fear rose when he realised the open door beside him would give him away and spurred on by that horrific thought he bit his bottom lip and reached to close it behind him.

It seemed to take forever, the pounding of blood in his ears almost covering the slow but steadily approaching footsteps. Dave ignored the taste of blood in his mouth as he inched the door towards him.

He found himself in gloom as it he finally closed the door. Just a sliver of light from the broken lock to illuminate the stair he stood on. Dave held his breath and attempted to stay upright, his legs drained of all energy. His mouth was numb, and blood welled from his lip to trickle down his T-shirt. Dave wanted to cry, but something deep inside told him to hang on; to cling to whatever reserves he still had left and stay silent. He heard the footsteps stop.

Dave bit his lip again, the pain seeming to hold his

rampaging fear in check just enough for him to stay alert. His eyes stung, and he strained his ears against the silence, positive that whoever was there was now level with the passageway. He tensed himself against the anticipated creak of floorboards and tried to hold his breath for as long as he could. Dave let it go when the footsteps resumed and faded away down the staircase.

He tried to quietly catch his breath, wiped his tear-filled eyes and held his hand against his labouring heart. The danger seemed to be over for the time being, but how was he going to get out?! He couldn't stay here: old Bloodshot was sure to find him eventually. But how was he to get down from the tower? Dave looked up the stairs behind him, saw a little light filtering down. Perhaps that led to another way out, he thought and, sucking the blood from his lip, began to climb.

The stairs led to the belfry, hugging the wall as they skirted the filthy assortment of bells and ropes. The soft coo and flutter of pigeons greeted Dave as he crept cautiously up the steps which wound around the central framework of the clock tower and he stopped to peer nervously into the darkness ahead. He felt trapped. Not wanting to continue, he moved reluctantly upwards to get as far away from the spiral staircase as possible.

The light grew brighter again and Dave found himself stepping up into a wide sunlit walkway, the outer wall of which was lined with narrow stained glass windows. He appeared to be in the middle of a passage which ran right around the top of the tower and, looking left, he saw the windows and walkway disappear around the central wall. Before him, blue sky peeped through a single broken window and Dave noted the coloured glass on the floor as he turned to look to his right. At the far end of the walkway, an opening with an iron handrail marked the top of the spiral staircase.

151

Dave froze at the sight, then at the sound of footsteps. He was coming back up! He struggled to think clearly against the returning panic, to stop himself from running frantically down the walkway in the opposite direction. He had to get out! He had to get away! Dave felt the tears beginning to well again before a glimmer of hope held them back.

If he doubled back, down past the bells to the door, he could get around him. YES! That was it! Bolt down the corridor and the stairs and he would be free! If he timed it right, Bloodshot would never catch him. He had to be sure he timed it right though, there was no margin for error. But how long could he stay here to make sure the footsteps had passed the other passageway? Dave bit at his lip again and winced, his eyes looking down as he put a hand to his mouth to check the flow of blood. His attention was seized by a face amongst the broken glass, a little face with a halo that seemed to gaze serenely back at him. Before he had time to think, Dave found his hand had shot out and retrieved the fragment. He held it up and saw how it matched the top of the hole in the window, a severed head marking its absence. He put it in his pocket and slipped back down towards the belfry as the footsteps grew louder.

Dave could not believe his luck. He was positive he never wanted to return to St. Anne's but, by some miracle, he now had definite proof that he had been there. And what was more, he thought, a bit of evidence which could only have come from one place: the top of the bell tower! The knowledge soothed his ragged nerves as he cautiously descended to the door by the open window.

He stopped in the beam of light from the broken lock, held his breath and listened. Nothing but the faint coo from a pigeon greeted his ears and so, chewing on his lip again, he gently pushed open the door.

Beyond was nothing more frightening than sunlight and the distant murmur of traffic on the street outside. Dave breathed a sigh of relief. He knew for sure that Bloodshot was far above him, so he was almost home and dry. All he had to do was descend the spiral stairs and then bolt across to the exit: easy. He stepped off of the stair and trod upon the same creaky floorboard as before.

This time, the ensuing groan was not answered by the same measured tread, but a rapid pounding, echoing from above. Something possessed of a greater urgency, Dave realised with horror, seemed to be descending. And if he did not move – right now – he would find out what it was.

Dave, his legs filled with an energy that only terror could provide, sprinted down the passage and hit the stairway flying: not caring for the noise he made or the small frightened whimpers escaping him as he fled. His only thought was of escape as he span round and round the stairway. His feet were a blur, barely connecting with the stones beneath and he prayed he would reach the bottom before whatever was behind him caught up. Though he tried desperately not to dwell on it, his mind conjured up all manner of horrors as he sped on, for – in the confines of the staircase – it did not sound like a man descending the steps. But whatever it was, it was coming down fast.

Dave reached the final curve and saw the small door closed beneath him. Without a second thought he launched himself from the steps towards it and recoiled loudly from the woodwork. The door remained shut. He scrambled off of the floor and attacked the small knob with both hands, sobbing frantically as he twisted it to and fro. With dread Dave realised the door was locked.

'Oh fuck!' he gasped, slumping to a heap against it: a sharp pain flaring in his shoulder. The pain was instantly forgotten when a noise sounded from the stairs.

It was a kind of snort. A sudden, short expulsion of air which made Dave's skin tingle with fear, his blood run cold as he looked back towards the curve of the stairs. He was terrified, yet some little part of his mind seemed curious to know how a horse had got into the church.

The thing which stepped slowly around the bend did not in any way resemble a horse, nor anything else Dave had ever seen. In the half-light, as the creature descended the few remaining steps and he tried to catch his breath to scream, Dave got an impression of flaking grey skin, sinuous limbs which despite their pallor seemed to bulge with strength as they reached out towards him. But it was the face which held his terrified attention. A single eye, burning with a hellish inner light, set above a sneering hole of shark-like teeth. The image stayed with Dave for the rest of his life – scant seconds as the monster bore down on him.

Chapter Eight

'So how do you know Catherine Robson, Coop'?' Mikey asked as the taxi pulled into a Kensington back street.

Cooper returned his gaze from the window and looked blank, momentarily at a loss to remember. He nodded his head in silent computation for a few seconds before the recollection struck.

'Do you remember Peter Thomas?' he asked. Mikey shook his head. 'Oh, well, never mind,' continued Cooper. 'Catherine Robson is his younger sister.'

'Oh, right,' replied Mikey, none the wiser.

'Or was she his wife?' Cooper scratched at his thinning hair. 'Anyway, the main thing is that she can help. She's a medium. No...' Cooper shook his head vigorously. 'Not a medium. A psychic, that was it. I always kept her number because Julia – remember Julia?'

Mikey nodded. How could he forget Julia?! The buxom temp whom Cooper had chased so passionately, won so happily, then lost so suddenly. Mikey had spent many long nights with his friend consoling him. He was surprised that Cooper mentioned her so lightly.

'Well, Julia always planned to hold a séance,' Cooper continued, seemingly unaffected by the recollection. 'She was into that sort of stuff: and I thought Peter's sister –'

'– Or wife,' corrected Mikey.

'Yep, or wife, whatever... Well I thought she would be ideal for that type of thing so I hung on to the number. Anyway, when Julia buggered of with that estate agent – God what a bitch!' spat Cooper suddenly. He noted the surprise on Mikey's face and managed a rueful grin. 'Sorry,' he shrugged and continued as if nothing had happened. 'Anyway, she buggered off and so I thought: won't be needing that now. But you know what I always say,' he wagged a knowing finger at Mikey.

'Bitch?' responded Mikey with a shrug.

'No!' Cooper laughed. 'The other thing I always say; "Always keep a phone number –"

"– because you never know where your next meal might be coming from." finished Mikey. He patted Cooper on his bulging stomach and smiled. 'You must walk around with the telephone directory.'

'Yes,' said Cooper looking down. 'Such a pity I don't keep it under there.'

They laughed as the taxi pulled up.

'Is this it?' asked Mikey, looking around.

The taxi driver twisted in his seat. 'Elm Road,' he said and waved a hand at the houses.

They stepped out, Cooper paying the cabby while Mikey faltered at the gate of a large redbrick house. He was beginning to have second thoughts about seeing a psychic.

'I feel like I'm visiting the dentist,' he said quietly to himself, picking at some flaking paint work on the gate. He watched as the taxi pulled away. 'Here?' Mikey queried, jerking a thumb at the house.

Cooper checked his pockets, pulled out a crumpled scrap of paper and checked the number on the gate. 'Yep,' he said, taking Mikey's arm. 'Come on, she'll be expecting us.'

As they started down the flower lined garden path, Mikey spotted a small face at the bay window of the living room. He moved his hand to wave but the child disappeared into the darkness beyond the glass.

'Has Catherine got children?' he asked as they reached the front door.

Cooper shrugged. 'I've no idea, I've never met her,' he said. 'But if she was married to Pete Thomas, probably not.' He arched his eyebrows cryptically and rang the doorbell. Mikey was about to pursue the matter when the lock turned.

The door was opened by a short woman with neatly cut blonde hair framing an elfin face with bright, piercing blue eyes. She smiled, a warm yet disconcerting gesture, Mikey thought: conveying as it seemed, something more than just friendliness. That aside, the overall impression was one of almost mischievous happiness and the pair could not help but return the smile as she ushered them inside.

'You must excuse me,' Catherine said, waving a trowel, 'I just have to re-pot a pelargonium.' Still smiling at the blank stares, she retrieved a walking stick from beside the door and leaning heavily on it, led her visitors through to the rear of the house.

Past the kitchen was a large glass conservatory filled with a riotous assortment of plants. There was a garden beyond but, so prolific was the plant life within the confines of the glass, details were difficult to pick out. Catherine pointed Mikey and Cooper towards a large wicker sofa amongst the spilling foliage.

'Help yourselves to lemonade,' she said, indicating a glass jug on the low table before the sofa. 'I won't keep you a moment.' Humming quietly to herself Catherine continued with her repotting.

Mikey sat stiffly while Cooper poured out some lemonade, unable to relax despite the pleasant surroundings and the gentle scent of flowers. He felt a terrible sense of foreboding, a nagging uneasiness which had grown steadily since entering the house. Something felt very wrong and the pleasing normality of the conservatory, of the house and Catherine herself merely acted to exacerbate Mikey's state of mind.

Cooper became aware of Mikey's stiff posture as he sat back and, handing him a glass whispered: 'Relax, she won't bite.'

Mikey managed to curl the corners of his mouth and gulped

down the lemonade.

The job finished to her satisfaction, Catherine returned to her guests and seated herself in a high backed chair opposite the sofa.

'Would you like some more lemonade?' she asked, pointing to the jug.

Cooper held out his glass. Mikey, about to follow suit, felt his head spin violently: the same disorientation he had felt before making him gasp at the severity of the sensation. His grip on the tumbler slackened as dizziness and a wave of nausea overwhelmed him and he dropped it to the floor. As the glass smashed against the flagstones, Mikey clutched at the arm of the sofa for support and tightly shut his eyes.

'Are you alright?!' Cooper grasped Mikey's arm, frowned with concern as his friend toppled forward.

'Quickly!' said Catherine, rising suddenly from her chair, her tone urgent. 'Help him inside.'

The emotion in her voice drew Cooper's attention briefly away from his prostrate friend and he turned to see Catherine's face creased as if sharing Mikey's pain. She made rapid motions towards the kitchen door. 'Quickly! Quickly!' she yelled. 'Take him into the living room!'

Cooper shifted his weight and lifted Mikey to his feet. He was still conscious but his head slumped limply, his shoes dragging against the floor as Cooper manhandled him inside.

'Lie him there,' said Catherine, pointing to a large padded settee in the living room. 'I'll close the dining room doors.' She hobbled to the rear of the room and pulled at the sliding wooden doors as Cooper gently lowered Mikey onto the settee.

'What's wrong with him?' Cooper asked, puffing hard with the exertion. He made a mental note to join a gym and gazed down at his friend. Mikey now appeared to be unconscious.

'I don't know for sure,' replied Catherine as she returned.

'But I felt something.' She looked down at Mikey and checked his pulse: found it racing.

'Felt what?' asked Cooper, wiping his brow.

Catherine ignored the question and got Cooper to draw the velvet front curtains while she rummaged through an old oak cabinet on the far side of the room. She returned clutching a box of thin candles and an incense burner. 'There's a small circular table against the wall in the dining room,' she said pointing to the closed doors. 'Bring that and two chairs in please.'

Cooper, muttering under his breath about the exercise, found the collapsible table and set it up as directed before the sofa. Retrieving the chairs a few moments later, the pair sat down.

Catherine emptied the candles onto the table and placed the incense burner at its centre. From a pocket she took out a box of matches and lit the burner. Cooper wrinkled his nose as a strong, pungent aroma rose from it.

'This should bring him round,' said Catherine. Cooper nodded and tried to hold his breath as Catherine picked up the candles and handed him three. She gave him the box of matches. 'Stick the candles on those circles there,' she said and pointed to the table top.

Looking down, Cooper could see a fine inlaid pattern on the table's surface, thin white swirls radiating out from the centre Amongst the pattern was a circle of smaller circles – six in all – and putting out a hand to touch them Cooper felt the bumpy residue of candle wax. He lit a match and let the candle drip before securing it in place. Catherine lit her candles from his and covered the three circles on her side of the table.

As the last candle was secured in place, Mikey gave a groan and sat bolt upright. He clutched at his forehead and looked blankly around for a few seconds before his eyes focused on the pair beside him.

'What happened?' he asked, squinting warily at the circle of candles.

'I think you just experienced some form of psychic 'episode',' explained Catherine, 'Very unusual. I felt something myself.'

Her tone was matter-of-fact, and reassured, Mikey managed a weak smile. He swung his legs under the table, resting his elbows on its surface as he massaged his temples.

'Attention seeker,' said Cooper. His tone was light, yet Mikey could hear the concern in his voice.

Mikey nodded and addressed Catherine. 'I hope I didn't upset your daughter,' he said, dropping his hands to the table. Catherine looked puzzled. 'The little blonde haired girl I saw in your window earlier,' explained Mikey. He pointed towards the curtains.

'Aah,' said Catherine. 'You mean Penny. No you didn't upset Penny, she's quite used to that sort of thing.'

It was Cooper's turn to look puzzled. 'What little girl?' he asked.

Catherine ignored his question and fixed Mikey with an appreciative stare. 'You were right to bring your friend here, Mr. Hooper,' she said, studying Mikey's face. 'He possesses a rare and unusual gift.'

'I do?' said Mikey.

'Indeed,' continued Catherine. 'Natural psychic abilities are a very rare commodity.'

'Psychic?!' Mikey couldn't keep the humour from his voice, it vanished when he saw the serious look on Catherine's face. 'I'm not psychic. Am I?'

'Perhaps you'd better tell me why you needed to see me,' said Catherine. She leaned forward and rested both hands on her stick, her eyes seeming to blaze as she gazed intently across the table.

Mikey took the cue. 'Well...' he began with a resigned shrug. 'It started up on Parliament Hill...'

'...So I left the phone box and went to see Cooper, that's when he decided to call you.' Mikey finished and looked at the thin candles, now burnt down to stumps. 'Do you mind if I smoke?' he asked, suddenly feeling the urge.

'Not at all,' replied Catherine. She rose from her chair, massaged her leg before limping to fetch Mikey an ashtray.

Cooper, having heard the tale before had disappeared to retrieve the lemonade from the conservatory. He returned to the table with three glasses and passed one over to Mikey.

'Thanks,' Mikey said, for both the ashtray and the lemonade. He pulled a crumpled packet of cigarettes from his pocket and lit one from a candle. 'So what do you think?' he asked as Catherine resumed her seat.

'Interesting,' she said, looking thoughtful. Catherine watched the smoke from the tobacco swirl and rise around the candle flames for a few moments. 'In all my years of paranormal investigation,' she said, breaking the silence, 'I can't think of another case quite like it.'

'Paranormal investigation?' said Cooper and Mikey in unison.

'Mm,' said Catherine. She swung her gaze between the pair. 'You knew that's what I did, didn't you?'

Cooper shrugged. 'Well, not as such...'

'Not that it makes any difference,' added Mikey quickly, 'It's just I'm not really sure what it means.'

Catherine grinned. 'You wouldn't be the first.' Her voice assumed an almost confidential air. 'I have certain psychic abilities which lend themselves to helping in cases such as yours. But I do not read palms. And I do not tell fortunes.' She banged her stick against the floor to emphasise the points. 'I'm

161

not that theatrical. I have affiliations with the British Paranormal Institute and it's usually on their request that I carry out investigations. Everything from hoaxes to hauntings. Occasionally I involve myself with cases that take my interest, but you must understand that my approach – despite my psychic talents – is to deal with each case in a rational, scientific way and not to try and sensationalise it.'

'You mean you try to find logical reasons?' queried Mikey. He felt the last thing that could be applied to his experiences was the term 'scientific'.

Catherine waved a hand. 'Not in the way you mean, no. I mean that with every case I encounter I always assume an objective attitude, to try and separate the emotions from the experience.' She shook her head. 'You would be amazed at the number of times 'things that go bump in the night' are nothing more than creaking joists.'

'So what about me?' asked Mikey. 'What about my priest that goes bump in the night?'

Catherine smiled and was about to reply when Cooper pointed to the candles. 'If you take a rational, and not theatrical approach,' he said. 'What were the candles for?' There was a mildly scathing tone in his voice but Catherine's smile did not waver.

'The rational approach as far as paranormal investigation goes may not seem immediately apparent to an unfamiliar onlooker. In this instance, the candles were there to aid me in a little experiment. I was about to attempt to discover the reason for Mikey's loss of consciousness.' Cooper mouthed an apologetic 'O' as Catherine continued. 'My usual course is to interview the subject, but until Mikey woke up I had intended to conduct a kind of makeshift séance.'

'So you believe my story then?' asked Mikey.

Catherine nodded. 'I can't give you a reason for it as yet, but

I felt a little of what you experienced. Enough to convince me something preternatural was affecting you.' She paused and Mikey caught a strange look in her eye. 'You've also seen Penny,' she added.

Cooper raised his eyebrows. Mikey felt the hairs on the back of his neck rise.

'Penny's a…?' began Mikey, making vague gestures with his hands.

'A spirit, yes,' Catherine replied. 'She lived in this house right up until she was killed during the blitz, poor thing, and returned – or rather made her presence felt – when I first moved in. She's a very sweet child and a great help to me.'

Cooper voiced something Mikey had not really considered.

'Why is Mikey suddenly being affected by this? Why now?' he asked.

Catherine shrugged. 'I don't know. In some people psychic ability is always present, in others not at all. Others, as it would appear in Mikey's case, develop the ability later on in life.'

'But there seems to be some specific purpose to this preacher's appearances,' responded Cooper. 'They don't seem to be chance sightings. How do you explain that?'

'As I said,' Catherine replied, 'if all that Mikey has experienced is true, then this is a most unusual case. The photographs, the dreams, the phone calls. And the phone box. It's quite beyond the usual case study.'

'I am not a case study,' Mikey replied: an unintended forcefulness in his voice.

Catherine held up her hands apologetically. 'Sorry,' she said. 'I didn't mean to sound quite so clinical.'

Mikey nodded, the error already forgiven. 'What can I do?' he asked.

Catherine drummed her fingers on the table for a second. 'I think you are already doing the right thing,' she replied, looking up from her hands to meet his eyes. 'Attempting to find out about the book is a good avenue to follow, I'd probably have done the same thing in your situation.'

Mikey sensed a hesitation. 'But...?' he asked.

Catherine shifted in her seat. 'There is a quicker, more direct route to the heart of this problem.'

Again the hesitancy, this time Cooper prompted. 'Which is...?'

'Talk to the preacher.'

'Talk to him?' Mikey saw Catherine's eyes move pointedly towards the table.

'Aah.' said Cooper, realising the intention. He shifted his chair back slightly.

'Is there any risk?' asked Mikey. He was not sure he felt comfortable with the idea of a séance, but neither did he relish the prospect of blacking out again.

'I've yet to encounter any in all my time investigating such phenomena. It can be a little unnerving, but what you must always bear in mind is that we have total control.'

Mikey shot a sideways glance at Cooper. He did not look convinced. Mikey sighed. Get it over with, he thought. 'Okay, what should I do?'

Catherine searched out another box of candles from the cupboard and stood them in the warm wax of the previous six. Cooper and Mikey sat tensely watching as the last one was lit.

'Just place your finger tips on the edge of the table,' she said, her voice conveying a calm neither man could share.

Mikey took a deep breath to settle his nerves. Cooper found that splaying his hands before him reduced their shaking.

'Good,' said Catherine in the same warm tone. 'Now simply relax, close your eyes if you want to, and leave the rest to me.'

Mikey shut his eyes. Saw the warm glow of the candlelight through closed lids. What the hell am I doing?! he thought. I don't want to be here. I want to be out in the sunlight. With Jane. Not here. He heard Catherine begin to speak and tried to concentrate on the words.

'Penny?....Penny?'

The voice still held the same calm assurance. That at least was some comfort, Mikey thought as Catherine repeated the call. He could hear his heart beating calmly now. A slow and steady pulse which seemed to keep time with the psychic's speech. The effect relaxed him even more. 'Penny?....Penny?' Mikey felt warm, comfortable with the soft, repeated words all tension slipping away. Gentle, soft sound. Like some far eastern mantra, over and over, over and over; carrying him along with its soothing melody.

There came a faint lilting laugh. Pleasant. Child like. Happy. It curled between the words as if floating on a wind from far away; drifting lazily on a serene breeze. Mixing with the steady beat, it grew louder, more persistent. Separating from the chant to become a voice. Oh shit! thought Mikey, realising the source of the sound. He opened his eyes.

A little girl in a beige dress ran through the closed wooden doors. She stopped as if surprised by the trio at the table and her gaze fell on Mikey.

'Hello,' she said.

Mikey could see Catherine and Cooper framing the girl on either side. Cooper had his eyes tightly shut and Catherine's mouth appeared to move silently. The psychic's eyes were open and she was staring straight towards him, but the gaze appeared glassy and unfocused. Neither seemed aware of the girl's presence.

'Are you in trouble?' asked Penny. She moved her attention to the carpet and twisted slowly round on the spot as if following the pattern. She looked towards the doors and laughed. It sounded nervous.

165

Mikey's eyes widened at the question but he felt too shocked to reply, his mind still attempting to accept what his eyes told him was there. He held out a hand and waved it before Catherine's face. The psychic, oblivious to the action continued to mouth silent words. Why wasn't Catherine seeing this?! Mikey thought.

Penny took a step closer to the table. 'He says you've got to go home.' She looked back towards the doors and nodded. 'He can't reach you here,' she said. 'And you have to get back before it starts.'

'Before what starts?' asked Mikey, finally finding his voice. 'I don't understand.'

Penny ignored Mikey's question and began backing away from the table, her eyes firmly fixed on something the photographer could not see. He heard the sound of steady, approaching steps and recoiled in horror as Geoff Freeman sauntered through the doors.

'Hello, captain,' said Geoff conversationally as he walked towards the table. Penny kept her distance.

Mikey shook his head in disbelief: his mind numb at the sudden appearance of his dead colleague. 'I don't...?' was all he managed to say as he took in the bearded figure before him, saw the livid wounds which still riddled his head and body.

'You look like you've seen a ghost,' said Geoff with a slight smile, the action lop-sided due to a gaping hole in his right cheek. He twisted on the spot and held out his arms, regarding them. 'I'd forgotten,' he continued, holding his hands before his face. 'It seems so strange.'

'What, what's going on?' Mikey stuttered, uncomfortable with the sight of his shattered friend and unable to keep the nervousness from his voice.

Penny moved a step closer to the table. 'Get him to go back,' she said, addressing Geoff. The journalist nodded.

'Something's going to happen, Mikey,' he said. 'Something bad. We can all feel it.'

'Geoff!' pleaded Mikey, 'I don't understand! What's going to happen?'

Mikey switched his attention to Penny as the little girl began to blur, her body writhing as its shape bent and deformed: black swirls overlaying the beige of her dress. She seemed to expand, her height growing until it matched Geoff's, her features reforming until her face was that of the preacher. The mouth moved, and again Mikey heard the vague whistling he had heard before.

'Hurry,' whispered the preacher, his body instantly dissolving back into the little girl.

Penny screamed, her arms rising quickly to her face as her cry reverberated around the room. Mikey looked on, panic stricken as Geoff grabbed the child into his arms and started running towards the velvet curtains. Mikey extricated himself from the table in a second and moved to pursue them.

'Geoff!' he shouted, 'Wait!'

Geoff turned, Penny now clinging to his neck, and stared at Mikey. There was terror in his eyes. Mikey, confused by his expression, moved a step towards him.

'LOOK OUT!!' Geoff shouted and tried to shield the child.

Mikey turned to see the sliding doors explode as a wall of flame, hurtling like an express train, raced across the room towards them. He barely had time to register the shock before a feeling of intense heat overwhelmed his senses, and a crushing impact threw him from his feet. He span through the air, his vision skewing wildly from the jolt, as the screams of Geoff and Penny filled his ears. He hit the floor by the sofa and, winded and dazed, watched in helpless terror as the wall of fire consumed his friend. Their cries became lost in the roar of the flames.

Chapter Nine

'I'm so glad you've come,' said Patrick Dayville as he ushered Jane into the living room. 'This thing has been gnawing at my conscience since Michael came to see me.'

Jane gently squeezed the old man's hand and kissed him affectionately on the cheek. The worry was plain in Patrick's voice, and his posture – head bowed, shoulders hunched – made him seem in some way penitent.

'Everything will be fine,' said Jane in an attempt to reassure him and, leading him by the hand, they sat side by side on the sofa.

'How is Mikey?' Patrick asked, his eyes slowly rising from the carpet to meet Jane's gaze. 'Is he okay?'

Jane knew her smile was forced but tried to convey some measure of comfort with it. She squeezed Mr. Dayville's hand again and gave an involuntary shrug. 'He's alright, I think. But I need you to help me help him. Before it gets any worse.'

Patrick nodded and looked sad. 'I know I shouldn't have said what I said to him about those pictures –'

'– The pictures of the preacher?' Jane interrupted.

'Yes,' sighed Patrick. 'Those pictures. I was wrong to encourage him when I knew there was nothing there, but... He was agitated, and I wanted him to talk to me. I wanted to be supportive. Then, when he mentioned my old photograph, well, I felt I was doing the right thing. Helping him.'

'Mikey told me about the fright it gave him when he was a child, but I'm not sure I understand its significance. Why would his mention of it convince you to lie to him?'

Patrick gave a deeper sigh, hunching his shoulders even more. 'It wasn't just that old photograph. It was his insistence on having seen the preacher again.' Jane's eyes widened. 'I don't know how much Mikey told you – how much he remembers,' continued Patrick. 'But... Well, it was an episode of his life I hoped was long forgotten.'

Jane shook her head slowly. 'Mikey didn't tell me anything about that,' she said. 'But if I'm to understand what he's going through I think you ought to.'

Patrick Dayville's fingers drummed briefly on his knees as if an inner debate was rapidly progressing. He nodded to himself and rose to his feet.

'I'll explain as best I can,' he said. 'But I need to find something as well... C'mon, it won't take a moment.' Patrick held out a hand and led Jane back to the hallway.

'The child psychiatrist believed it to be delayed shock brought about by my wife's death,' said Mr. Dayville over his shoulder. He stopped in the hallway, opened the cupboard door which sat beneath the stairs and reached into the dark recess. 'Could you point this at that pile there?' He asked, handing Jane a torch and indicating a pile of boxes stacked in the darkness.

Jane nodded and shone the torch onto the boxes while Mikey's father crouched down and rummaged through the stack.

'You took him to a psychiatrist?' Queried Jane as Mr Dayville shuffled the boxes around in the cramped space.

Patrick removed a large tin container from the pile and backed out of the cupboard, pushing the disturbed boxes back into the space with his foot. He brushed dust from the box and nodded.

'I was advised to by our doctor,' he replied with a frown. 'For what little good it did.' Mr. Dayville seemed distant for a moment then took the torch from Jane and placed it back in the cupboard before closing the door. He noted the concern written on Jane's face and managed a rueful smile. 'Come back in here,' he said. taking her hand. 'I'll try to explain what happened.'

169

They returned to the sofa in the living room and Jane felt a nervous curiosity as Mikey's father placed the tin box on the coffee table and sat back down beside her. Patrick ran his hands through his grey hair, lent back and gazed at the ceiling for a moment: collecting his thoughts.

'Mikey would have been about six, I suppose,' he began, fixing Jane with sad eyes. 'And it started on the night I showed him that damn photograph.' Patrick shook his head. 'He had been scared – I could see that – after I'd shown him the photograph and so I read him a story when he went to bed.' Mr. Dayville smiled to himself. 'Thomas the Tank Engine, probably,' he said. 'Mikey always liked those stories… Anyway, Mikey drifted off, I left him fast asleep and – at about midnight – I was off to bed myself and thought I'd check on him as I passed his door.' Patrick paused, his brow furrowing as the memories came flooding back. 'I could hear – something – even before I pushed the door open and when I turned on the light I found Mikey sitting in the middle of the floor surrounded by his toys.'

'He couldn't sleep?'

Patrick shook his head. 'He was staring at me the moment I pushed the door open but, to this day, I still swear he was fast asleep.' Mr. Dayville waggled his fingers. 'He wasn't playing with his toys – he was dismantling them – and though he stared at me when I asked him what he was doing he gave no reply, just looked at me blankly and continued to pull his toys to pieces.' Patrick sighed. 'So I asked him again what he was doing, then told him to get back into bed. He didn't move so I picked him up and put him into bed myself. Mikey didn't make a sound, didn't resist and I sat on the edge of his bed and watched him as he lay there, staring at the ceiling.' Mr Dayville shook his head. 'I must have sat there for god knows how long, talking to Mikey and trying to get him to respond, but he never said a word to me – he just lay and stared at the ceiling until finally he closed his eyes. I left him to go to bed myself but I hadn't even reached my bedroom door before I heard him again.'

'He'd got up again?' asked Jane.

Patrick nodded and snapped his fingers. 'Instantly,' he replied. 'So I went back and threw the door open this time, expecting Mikey to dart back into his bed, but there he was again; in the middle of his broken toys and staring at me vacantly. And that's when it struck me that he'd been taking his toys apart in complete darkness.'

Jane frowned. 'So what did you do?' she asked.

Patrick shrugged. 'There were times as a child when Mikey could be mischievous but I sensed that this was different – unusual. Like I say, though his eyes were open, he didn't seem to notice me at all: even when I threw the door open. It was like he was sleepwalking.' Mr Dayville scratched his head. 'So, realising something was wrong, and remembering that old wives tale about not waking sleepwalkers, I put the light on again and watched him from the doorway while he continued to pull his toys apart. I couldn't for the life of me begin to fathom what on earth the problem was but, I must admit, I did find his behaviour a little unnerving'

'Why?'

'Because he was looking at me the whole time, not at what he was doing, but was still able to deftly dismantle the things around him,' replied Mr Dayville. 'And six year old boys shouldn't know a thing about electronics.'

'Electronics?' echoed Jane.

Patrick nodded. 'The toys he took apart were all his electronic games: a Speak and Spell if I remember rightly. battleships – y'know the sort of things kids like. Anyway, the more I watched the more I noticed that Mikey's glance would

171

occasionally move away from me to another part of his bedroom, then he'd pause, nod, return to staring at me and continue dismantling.'

'Did you not think to intervene again?' Jane asked, not sure that she would have allowed such a situation to continue unchecked.

'I was torn between just picking him up again,' continued Mr Dayville, 'and letting the thing – whatever it was – run its course. I suppose in the back of my mind was the thought that Mikey would soon tire of his destruction and simply fall asleep again so, though it was certainly disconcerting, I simply looked on.' Patrick reached forward, opened the tin box and pulled out a small object made of metal and wires. 'And, as I watched, Mikey built this,' he said and passed the object to Jane.

Jane turned the thing over in her hands and frowned at Mikey's father: Patrick nodding at the unasked question.

'Yes,' he said. 'I know it seems strange but Mikey built that right in front of me.' Patrick took the object back from Jane and pointed to a liquid crystal display strip and a small speaker which made up part of the device. 'This is the Speak and Spell thing here,' he said, 'and when Mikey had put all this together he sat it on the floor and turned it on. It said "All right" or "All clear" – something like that – and Mikey left it where it lay and went straight back to bed. By the time I'd crossed the room he was fast asleep.'

Jane shook her head and took the device back. She looked at the blank LCD display and noted that there was a second, LED display, sitting above it and a pair of orange, Ever Ready HP7 batteries almost fused into the base. 'It's certainly amazing,' she said, turning the object over in her hands again.

Mr Dayville sighed. 'And that was the start of it. The next morning Mikey came down to breakfast in tears and told me that "The Preacher" had come into his room in the night and broken all his toys. When I asked him to describe the man he did indeed describe a clergyman – dog collar and all. He remembered doing none of the damage himself but insisted that this preacher had done it.' Patrick shifted in his seat and put the device back in its box. 'Mikey was agitated all day so I kept him home from school and that night I had him sleep with me in my bed…'

'And?…' Jane sensed by Patrick's tone that there was more.

'And the same thing happened that night. I woke up to find Mikey gone and searched the house to find him in my darkroom dismantling my cameras.' Patrick tapped his chest indignantly while Jane hide a smile behind her hand. A child breaking his own toys was one thing, she thought, but breaking the toys of a grown-up was an altogether different matter.

'Because of the chemicals in there,' Mr Dayville continued, not noticing Jane's smirk. 'I'd always kept the darkroom locked, but somehow he managed to get in. I found him on the floor again but this time surrounded by my photographic equipment.'

'Did you wait to see what he'd build?' asked Jane with a straight face even though she already knew the answer.

'Nooo,' Patrick replied with a shake of his head. 'I had him off the floor and out of that room so fast that I was locking the door shut before I even realised I'd done it.'

'So Mikey had found your key then?' said Jane, her journalistic instinct briefly getting the better of her politeness.

'No, it was still on it's hook above the door where it always was – out of Mikey's reach,' answered Patrick. 'But the lock was damaged because, when I put Mikey down, he made straight for the darkroom door and pushed it open again.'

Jane shook her head in wonder. 'And he still seemed to be sleepwalking?'

'Yep, the whole time,' said Patrick. 'He struggled a little

173

when I held him but that soon stopped and he drifted off to sleep in my arms. The following morning I took him to the doctor who recommended the child psychologist.'

'Who said it was caused by the loss of Mikey's mother?'

'Pretty much, yes. He said the preacher was most likely caused by the minister at my wife's funeral and that Mikey – being so young – perhaps saw that figure as responsible for the loss of his mother.'

'What about the toys?' asked Jane.

Patrick shrugged. 'Guilt? Subconscious emotions? It was something like that.'

'And did the psychiatrist help at all?' Jane inquired.

'Nope,' replied Patrick dismissively. 'I spent the next three nights stopping Mikey from sleepwalking down the street and by this time the poor boy was so overwrought during the days that I had to plead with the doctor to give him sedatives. I couldn't leave him alone for a minute because he was so frightened.' Patrick sighed. 'He'd just sit in the corner of the living room in his pyjamas, crying and begging me not to leave him alone with the preacher.'

'I'm surprised you encouraged him this time,' said Jane.

Mr Dayville nodded. 'On reflection I'd say you were right but...' Patrick frowned, searching for the words. 'Mikey seemed so positive this time,' he continued, looking earnestly at Jane. 'A week after the original events Mikey was as right as rain – and seemed not to remember a thing about it. When he mentioned the photograph and the preacher to me a few days ago – like I say – he seemed positive, resolute. I thought that letting him follow his theory might help him get over the death of his friend.'

Jane nodded. It was obvious that Mikey's father genuinely felt he had been doing the right thing: perhaps a natural response considering this new information. And it reinforced

Jane's own theory about Mikey haunting himself. The preacher was a deep rooted symbol of Mikey's remorse, resurfacing when his emotions tried to cope with death. Unfortunately it had been compounded by his discovery of the book but perhaps, thought Jane, she could help. Maybe, like Mikey constructing the – whatever it was – out of his toys, his pursuit for information was his attempt to reach some kind of psychological resolution. Jane picked the thing that Mikey had made out of its box.

'You say that when Mikey had finished this he went straight back to bed?' Jane asked. Patrick nodded. Jane turned the object over in her hands, thinking. 'Can I borrow it?' she said after a few moments.

'Well, yes… I suppose so,' Mr Dayville replied. 'Do you think it might help?'

'I'm not sure,' replied Jane distantly then smiled reassuringly at Mikey's father. 'It might,' she said brightly and stood up, placing the object in her handbag. 'Well, I'd better get back.'

Patrick stood up and walked her to the front door. 'He's a lucky man, my son,' he said, pecking Jane on her cheek.

Jane smiled back and returned the kiss. 'Don't worry,' she said. 'Mikey's going to be just fine.'

Jane smiled and waved her way down the front path then returned to her car; her mind occupied by the plan of action forming in her mind. The toy she had taken was a last resort: a possible shock tactic if all else failed. But, until then, she was going indulge Mikey like his father had done all those years ago. The quicker Mikey's line of enquiry reached resolution, Jane thought, the quicker he would get over the death of Geoff.

Jeremy Thacker sighed. Why did people do it? He wondered,

gazing at the fun fair sprawled across the field before him. There were official sites for this sort of thing: procedures and channels available for any registered show of this type. It wasn't a difficult process. Yet here was a group who could not be bothered with anything so inconvenient as a license and had just turned up and set up. An unregistered, unauthorised event on a part of the heath which never had – and was never supposed to have – any such activity taking place. Did they really think, Jeremy wondered, that no one from the council would notice?

The council official unfolded his arms and picked up the briefcase at his feet which contained the eviction notice. Let's hope they can be civil about this, he thought as he strode across the grass. He had the sneaking suspicion however, that this was not going to be an easy eviction.

'Oh well,' he sighed. He would just have to come back with the police and do it the hard way.

Jeremy made a beeline for the nearest stall and noted absently that, even at this time of the afternoon, the fair was attracting a crowd. There was the usual raucous noise of a dozen different sound systems, mixed with the clunk and whirl of the various – garishly painted – rides. Beneath it the cries of the stall holders were all but drowned out.

'Excuse me,' said Jeremy, putting down his briefcase and addressing the man in the Hoopla stall.

'Yes,' replied the man. 'Three rings a pound... mate.' He waved the yellow plastic rings in his right hand by way of explanation.

Jeremy twitched a humourless smile in response. 'I'm looking for the owner,' he said.

'Oh, yes,' replied the man blankly.

'Yes,' repeated Jeremy with several nods. 'I'm from the council.'

Unimpressed, the man shrugged and lent across the counter. 'Do you see that Winnebago back there?' he said, pointing past the rides to where the trucks and caravans were parked.

'You mean the big camper van?' Jeremy asked. He was not really sure what a 'Winnebago' was but instantly spotted the huge American camper van parked right at the back of the fair.

'Yees,' drawled the man. 'That's the one. Well, you go there, knock on the door, and ask for a Mr Garvin.'

'He's the owner, is he?' asked Jeremy.

'Don't ask me, mate,' replied the man with a smile. 'I only work here.'

Jeremy picked up his briefcase and sauntered between the rides and stalls, loosening his tie as the humidity of the day began to make him feel uncomfortable. He had half a mind to stop and buy a cold drink before delivering the eviction notice but felt, on reflection, that such an action would be hypocritical. The fun fair was illegal and he was here to close it, not use it.

As he wove between the crowd and the rides towards the caravans and lorries beyond the fair, Jeremy wondered which of the various excuses this "Mr Garvin" would use to attempt delaying eviction. Although it was not the mainstay of Jeremy's job, his particular talent for confronting such individuals personally had amassed him a rare mental catalogue of excuses and lies. There were even some wits in his particular department who claimed that, in a former life, Jeremy had been a Traffic Warden.

Jeremy ran briefly through the list as he skirted a half-empty waltzer at the very rear of the fair. 'I can't do anything until I've spoken to the owner,' was a popular choice he thought, as was searching for the paperwork which Jeremy knew they did not possess. Occasionally – as with the previous year's rash of hot dog vendors – they would even pretend that they

177

could not speak English. Of all the excuses Jeremy had heard though, his favourite was still from the man who had broken into an empty shop to begin trading illegally and, when Jeremy had confronted him, had stated quite calmly that a Mr Jeremy Thacker from the council was the person to contact to sort the problem out. It was a slim hope, but Jeremy hoped Mr Garvin would use that same excuse again: it had made him laugh out loud the last time.

Beyond the fair the grass was covered by cables which snaked away towards chugging diesel generators. There was a greyhound cocking its leg over the wheel of a lorry but, apart from that, Jeremy encountered no one until he reached the door of the Winnebago.

He was about to knock when a thought struck him and he walked to the front of the enormous camper van to check the registration number. As he had suspected the vehicle appeared to be brand new. Jeremy walked back towards the door and cast his gaze back at the fair. He had not realised it before but everything seemed new. Every single ride and booth was gleaming with pristine paint work. He shook his head in wonder: he had no idea the fun fair business could be so profitable. Well, he thought to himself, they'll get no more money from this site. With a growing sense of indignation, Jeremy rapped firmly on the door.

Almost instantly the door was opened and Jeremy stepped back as a tanned man in a grey boiler suit swung the door outwards.

'Yes?' said the man.

'Mr Garvin?' asked Jeremy.

The man smiled. 'That's right,' he said.

'I'm from the council, Mr Garvin,' Jeremy continued. 'I'm here to serve a notice of eviction for this –'

'– Just one moment,' interrupted Mr Garvin with a raised

hand. Before Jeremy could continue he had disappeared from the doorway.

Jeremy sighed, pulled the eviction papers from his briefcase and stepped up into the interior of the Winnebago. 'I wouldn't bother looking for your permit, Mr Garvin,' he said wearily. 'We both know you haven't got one.'

The fairground owner was standing by an open cupboard a little further down the spacious interior, his arms obscured by the cupboard door. He nodded in response to Jeremy's statement, closed the cupboard door then blew a large hole in the council official's chest with the silenced .45 Colt he was now holding.

'I wasn't looking for my permit,' said Garvin as he strolled up through the drifting smoke to crouch beside Jeremy Thacker's splayed corpse. He waved the bulky Colt pistol before the dead man's face. 'I was looking for my silencer.' Garvin indicated the large cylinder attached to the square barrel.

He stood up, closed the door and briefly checked through a window that nobody had heard the muffled shot. As he had suspected, the sound had been completely obscured by the greater noise from the fair. He tapped the gun barrel on his chin for a moment as he debated what to do with the corpse then placed the pistol on a chair and grabbed a cloth to remove the spatters of blood which had hit the window. After cleaning the glass to his satisfaction, Garvin regarded the remaining blood specks which had fanned out over the interior of the camper van. He shrugged, threw the cloth down beside the gun and went to get a towel.

With a little effort Garvin placed the large, dark blue towel under the dead man's midriff to soak up the worst of the blood still pooling around him then crouched beside the body to admire his handiwork. The Colt .45 had always been a personal favourite of Garvin's but he made a mental note to try out his new .44 Magnum Desert Eagle as soon as possible. It was a slightly smaller calibre but, apparently, it made an even bigger hole. He wondered idly how long it would take before the dead man would be missed – how soon it would be before the local authorities sent somebody else. Not soon enough, Garvin thought. The fun would already have started by then.

His attention returned to the livid entry wound and the slack expression on Jeremy Thacker's face. Garvin's own countenance was suddenly split by a broad grin and he chuckled down at the corpse.

'What a perfect idea!' he said to himself.

Still grinning, Garvin exited the Winnebago to tell the ghost train workers about the latest addition to their ride.

Jane reached Mikey's house in the early evening. Seeing that his motorbike was not parked nearby she was surprised to find that anybody was home. That surprise passed quickly through shock to reach anger as soon as Cooper had explained to her what had happened to Mikey during her absence.

'It's my fault, Jane! All my fault! Blame me, not Mikey!'

Cooper, flushed and anxious was standing in the middle of the living room; his usual ebullient demeanour replaced by one of abject apology. His hands hovered near his mouth as he saw Jane's frown crease her expression even further.

'I DO BLAME YOU!!' she barked. 'What the hell did you think you were doing, Coop'!? And what the hell is the medium doing here!?' Jane's finger stabbed in the direction of Catherine Robson who had so far remained merely an observer to the conversation.

'Believe it or not Miss –?' began Catherine.

'– Marshell,' added Cooper.

'Miss Marshell,' Catherine continued. 'I'm trying to help.'

'Help?!' echoed Jane incredulously. 'My boyfriend is lying upstairs – unconscious,' she ticked the words swiftly off on her fingers, 'and you say you're trying to help?!'

'Your boyfriend was the victim of an extreme psychic encounter, Miss Marshell –'

'– The only thing Mikey has been the victim of is you two!' countered Jane angrily. 'Thank God one of you had the good sense to call a doctor.'

'We had no idea anything like this was going to happen, Jane,' explained Cooper. He shook his head vigorously.

'Well that still doesn't excuse –' Jane began before the sound of somebody descending the stairs diverted her attention.

A short man wearing a misshapen tweed jacket, black trousers and brown brogues reached the bottom of the stairs and entered the living room to stand beside Jane. He placed a bulky leather bag on the floor by his feet and flicked his gaze quickly between the other people in the room.

'How is he, doctor?' asked Jane as the man's gaze fell on her.

'Well, he'll be better if you can keep the yelling down a little bit,' the doctor replied. 'But for the moment I've given him a sedative and he should sleep right through 'till morning.'

Jane nodded.

'Mr Hooper told me about your friend's activities today,' the doctor continued. 'And, considering Mr Dayville's recent experiences in the Balkans, I'd say it was fairly obvious that he's suffering from a severe case of stress and nervous exhaustion.'

'How does stress explain him shattering every window in a phone box?' asked Catherine.

Jane, though she had not been told that piece of information, scowled at the psychic. The doctor managed a humourless

181

smile.

'I have neither the experience nor the interest in such matters,' replied the doctor. 'And couldn't really comment on such an act of vandalism... But,' he continued, 'in my professional opinion I'd say that such an act was a clear indication of Mr Dayville's mental instability.'

'What can I do to help, doctor?' Jane asked.

'I've left a bottle of pills by his bedside,' replied the doctor. 'He's to take one twice a day. Apart from that he needs several days rest and no excitement.' With that the doctor picked up his bag and, with a curt nod to Catherine and Cooper, turned to leave.

Jane followed and at the front door the doctor paused.

'It may be a wise decision to convince Mr Dayville to see a psychiatrist,' the doctor said quietly. 'In a situation like this bed rest and sedatives can only do so much.'

Jane nodded, thanked the doctor as she closed the door behind him then returned to the living room.

'I'm sure Mikey'll be fine, Jane,' said Cooper as she came back in.

Jane ignored him, gave a huge sigh and slumped down in a chair by the front windows. She massaged her temples for a moment and then fixed her attention on Catherine.

'I'd like you to leave,' said Jane wearily then switched her gaze to Cooper. 'Both of you.'

Cooper, mumbling apologies made straight for the front door. Catherine followed but stopped as she drew level with Jane.

'I think there is more to Mikey's condition than simple stress,' she said.

Jane regarded her in silence for a moment. 'I don't care,' she replied with a fractional shake of her head. 'Now would you please leave.'

'Of course,' the psychic said with a nod.

Jane let out another sigh as she heard the front door shut behind the pair and stared blankly for a while across the room. Rousing herself from her torpor she left her chair and climbed the stairs to check on Mikey. She knew that there was little she could do to help – especially while he was sleeping – but her concerns for his welfare overrode any practical considerations. She would just watch him sleep for a while.

Jane pushed the bedroom door open and then stepped back with shock – one hand to her mouth as she took in the scene. Naked and sitting cross-legged on the floor, Mikey stared back blankly at his girlfriend. Spread before him were several of his cameras and, though he did not shift his gaze from hers for a second, Mikey's hands continued to deftly dismantle the objects.

'Oh, Mikey...' whispered Jane. She felt tears well up in her eyes as she looked down at her boyfriend and the realisation struck her of how helpless Patrick must have felt all those years ago when he had witnessed the same scene. She took a step closer and was about to crouch down before him when she remembered the object she had brought back with her from Mikey's father. Jane turned on her heel, bolted down the stairs and within a minute was back with the device the young Mikey had made in her hands.

Mikey's vacant gaze was still set on her when she returned and, holding the device before her, Jane moved closer. Suddenly, Mikey's gaze focused on the object. He grinned and snatched it from Jane's hand before she could stop him. Slightly shocked by Mikey's sudden lunge, Jane looked on as Mikey turned the device over in his hands. He studied it for less than a second, ripped the corroded batteries from their housing then pulled the rear cover from a flash gun which was lying by his knee. He pulled the Duracell batteries from where they sat in the flash gun, clicked them rapidly into place on the device then sat back with the object on the floor before him.

The whole process had taken less than five seconds and Jane was dumbstruck by the speed at which Mikey's hands had moved. Now, like Mikey, Jane's attention was focused on the device which bleeped before a tinny, emotionless voice sounded from the speaker.

'SEVEN... TEEN... HOURS... AND... TWENTY... THREE... MINUTES... AND... COUNTING...'

Jane looked up to see Mikey's attention was now back on her.

'Oh shit, Jane,' he said quietly and slumped backwards, unconscious before his head hit the floor.

Chapter Ten

Detective Sergeant Rose kicked the filling cabinet and swore loudly at the ceiling. Before anyone in the cluttered file room could enquire what the problem was the policeman had stomped off into the relative seclusion of Inspector Fletcher's office. Pete Rose slammed the door behind him, threw himself into the inspector's vacant chair and dismissively cast the papers he was carrying onto the desk.

'Balls,' he muttered, his head in his hands. 'Balls, balls, bollocks, fuck.'

He gave a deep sigh, gazed at the ceiling in silent prayer for divine intervention then span the chair round so that it faced the wall.

'You were right, weren't you? You old bastard,' he said, staring at the graduation photo which showed Fletcher. 'All that hard work and I end up proving you right.'

The sergeant shook his head and twisted round to re-examine the evidence he had painstakingly collected. He hoped he might have overlooked something which would change the unwanted outcome.

Sergeant Rose had spent the last few days diligently investigating and verifying the details which Peter Bradford had given about Tom McDonald. As their only vague lead in the Hampstead Heath murder, Rose had been certain he would find something to connect Bradford to McDonald's death but, the more he delved, the more it had seemed likely that his particular lines of enquiry would do nothing except confirm Bradford's innocence.

St. Thomas's College in Oxford – where both Tom and Peter had studied – had been extremely reticent in divulging any information over the phone and it quickly became evident to the sergeant that they simply did not want to divulge any information at all. Rose had found himself being passed from one disinterested party to the next until finally the secretary to the Deputy Vice-Chancellor agreed to take his call.

After explaining who he was and the reason for his enquiry, Rose was informed that any such information – even if it existed – might prove detrimental to the reputation of the college. "Hallowed halls" and all that,' the secretary had told him. It had taken a lot of patient persuasion, an explanation of the criminal consequences of hampering official Police enquiries and finally the threat of St Thomas's "hallowed halls" being swarmed by policemen with warrants before Rose could even get confirmation of the attendance of McDonald and Bradford at the university. However subsequent questions about the attack on Peter Bradford's girlfriend and Tom McDonald's attempted suicide were met with disbelief, denials and ultimately derision.

'I suppose we will just have to endure your 'swarm', sergeant,' the secretary had said and promptly put the phone down.

Fuming, Rose had considered making the two hour drive to St. Thomas's that instant to confront the secretary in person but, several minutes internal debate and a cup of coffee later, the sergeant found himself pursuing more productive lines of enquiry.

First, Rose had contacted the Oxford Royal Hospital who had managed – after some nagging – to unearth the gruesome admission details of a T. McDonald. Next he had got in touch with a Sergeant Banham from the Oxford branch of the Thames Valley Police and, after searching their files, Banham had provided Rose, via fax, with the case notes from Jennifer Pearson's assault. Sergeant Rose had scrutinised both documents thoroughly but found nothing in them that conflicted with the story Peter Bradford had already given.

The assault against Miss Pearson was still unsolved and Tom McDonald had indeed been admitted to the hospital with severe lacerations on both wrists. There was a dated note attached to his admission stating that he had later been interviewed by the Police over the incident and Rose made another call to Sergeant Banham to see if there was any record of the interview.

'You should really try contacting St. Thomas's if you want more information,' Sergeant Banham had said after agreeing to send over anything he could find. In response Rose explained about his single lack of progress with that particular line of enquiry.

Banham had laughed. 'You learn to handle the colleges with kid gloves after a while,' he said, 'and I wouldn't be at all surprised if they send some snotty message to your chief complaining about "Police brutality" or something. But, if you really need to know anything about these Bradford and McDonald characters, I might be able to find you the name of someone in the college that could help.'

Rose had waited while Banham searched: listening to the muted noises of the Oxford station down the line. The solid click of plastic on Formica signified the return of the sergeant.

'... It's one of the first things you learn down here,' announced Banham as he picked up the phone. 'Never speak to the dons or deans about college matters. Always go to the people in the front line, so to speak.'

'So, who's your contact?' asked Rose, intrigued.

'The Head Porter at St. Thomas's,' Banham replied. 'A... Mr Childs apparently.'

'You don't know him personally then?' enquired Rose.

'Noo,' said Banham, 'ya never know 'em all – we have a fair few universities down here in case you didn't know. But pretty much every one of them has a porter who knows what's what and is always willing to tell all. They're the chief source of gossip for the whole town.'

Thanking the sergeant for his time Rose took down the Head Porter's number then gathered up the faxed statement Banham had sent relating to Tom McDonald's suicide attempt. He studied the first page absently as he returned his desk to make the call then something in the text caught his attention. He read through the statement carefully then re-read the notes he had made during the interview with Peter Bradford.

In his statement at the hospital, Tom McDonald had cited depression as his reason for attempting to take his own life and thanked the quick actions of Peter Bradford and Stephen Knight for saving it. Yet Peter Bradford's statement made no mention of anyone but himself helping McDonald, and his references to Stephen Knight had branded him as an odd, pathetic creep who was into the occult and who he would have nothing to do with. So what, Rose had wondered, was someone Bradford claimed to despise doing there that night? And why had Knight's presence completely slipped Bradford's mind? It wasn't much to go on, but it gave Rose an excuse to drag Bradford in for questioning.

Sergeant Rose had waited until the following morning to call the Head Porter of St. Thomas's College and, though he expected very little from the call he soon found himself making reams of notes as Mr Childs told all about the time Bradford and McDonald had spent at the college.

'They were an odd group, I recall,' Childs had said. 'But always polite – especially Mr Bradford. What did they call themselves…?'

'Who?' asked Rose.

'Mr Knight's gro – that was it!' Sergeant Rose had heard the faint snap of fingers down the line. 'The White Knights – that was it. Funny things kids do, eh?'

'Mm,' said Rose. 'And do you remember who was in this group?'

'Well,' replied the head porter, 'like you've already said: Mr Bradford, Mr McDonald and Mr Knight amongst others.'

'Are you saying Peter Bradford was in this group – this White Knights thing?' Rose asked.

'Well,' Childs replied. 'I couldn't swear to it, but they were always together. There were about five, six of 'em in all I seem to remember – girls as well.'

'Jennifer Pearson wouldn't have been one of the girls, would she?' Rose asked.

The porter had laughed. 'Seems you know as much as me, sergeant. Yes, Miss Pearson, Miss Jackson and er... Mr Harrison if I remember rightly –'

'– First name?' interrupted the sergeant as he scribbled notes.

'Er, Kev – no, Colin Harrison I believe and Celia Jackson. Though we usually don't refer to our ladies and gentlemen by their first names of course.'

'Of course,' mumbled Rose.

'Yes,' continued the Head Porter, 'it seems like an age ago now but you still hear them mentioned occasionally.'

'Why's that?'

'Well, apart from the incident with poor Mr McDonald which, from what I hear, is rapidly attaining the status of a ghost story, they all used to dress the same way, were always together and, apart from Mr Knight, they all left at the same time.'

'What's so unusual about that?' asked Rose.

'Well most of them had yet to finish their degree courses, you see,' the porter replied. 'Most still had a year to go until their final exams.'

'So they all just dropped their degrees and left?'

'Yep, just like that.' The sergeant heard another click of fingers. 'And nobody's heard a thing about them since. And, though Mr Knight stayed on, even he left before his finals. And now we have some very nasty rumours flying round the college about him.

'What rumours would they be?' Rose had asked.

'Well, it really is only gossip,' replied Childs, 'but the rumour is he was one of those 'sacrificial' murder victims down in London.'

Rose had frowned. 'I think you'll find that really is only gossip,' he said. 'Nobody called Knight has been listed.'

'Oh, no,' replied the porter. 'You're quite right. But apparently Mr Knight changed his name to Croft straight after leaving St. Thomas's – but I'm sure you're right, sergeant. It's the college you see,' he explained. 'The truth has no chance against rumours like that.'

Sergeant Rose had put down the phone and sat staring at his notes, not liking the suspicions which were creeping into his mind and their obvious connotations. A man named Roger Croft had been the third victim of the Sacrificial Murders and, if that turned out to be someone originally named Stephen Knight, then Sergeant Pete Rose had just stepped closer to solving the case. Only it was the wrong case, and that meant Inspector Fletcher would be able to do what he had been set on doing all along – dump their investigation into his friend Faber's lap.

Rose had slapped his pockets for his nicotine chewing gum then, finding none, grabbed at a packet of cigarettes discarded on the table opposite. The packet was empty.

Cursing, Rose had slumped back down in his chair and stabbed at his computer keyboard: logging on to the Metropolitan Police Network. Constable Pearce, sitting in the far corner of the room with WPC Linden, asked if the Sergeant was alright but Rose ignored the enquiry while he quickly accessed the Public Records Office database. It took seconds to get into the Deed Poll section which dealt with name changes and, with his Police clearance, Rose was soon running a search for the name 'Stephen Knight'. It came up within moments: Stephen Knight, AKA Roger Croft. Appended to the file was a death certificate less than a month old.

Rose grabbed his paperwork from the table, kicked the filing cabinet behind him then swore at the ceiling before stomping off to Inspector Fletcher's office. Fletcher found him still there half an hour later.

'You alright, Pete?' Fletcher asked when he saw his sergeant sitting sullenly behind his desk. The Inspector closed the door behind him and threw his coat onto a hook on the wall. 'Wassup? Ya havin' trouble with this Heath thing?'

Rose, his face crumpled and leaning on his fist, gave a slight shake of his head as Fletcher planted himself in the chair opposite. The sergeant gave a sigh, lent back and pointed to the papers spread before him. 'No,' he replied. 'I think I've solved it.'

Fletcher looked confused for a second then grinned at his sergeant. 'But that's good, isn't it?… Isn't it?' He repeated when Rose shook his head again. 'Ah, c'mon, Pete,' said the inspector. 'Tell your Uncle Fletcher all about it.'

The inspector listened patiently while Rose outlined his enquiries and the connection he had found between the McDonald murder and the sacrificial case.

'… And,' concluded Sergeant Rose after several minutes, 'when you add to that the fact that your mate Faber reckons it's some cock-eyed, religious sect doing these murders with Egyptian axes… Well, it's pretty bloody obvious – isn't it? What I don't understand is why 'Faber of the Yard' hasn't

191

already arrested Bradford.'

Fletcher shrugged and pulled his cigarettes from his pocket, gave a smile when Rose took one. 'Well,' he said, 'I think I can tell you one of the reasons why.' The inspector crossed his legs and drew on his cigarette, snorting the smoke out through his nostrils. 'Our friend Faber has an accurate photo-fit of the man they're looking for – and I've already told Faber that his suspect looks nothing like Bradford. This bloke's swarthy – either Arabic or with a sun tan – and dresses up like a fuckin' copper to do the murders.'

'You're joking?!'

Fletcher shook his head. 'Nope. I've just been to see him this morning, to tell him more about our own murder. Faber says they now have several eye witnesses who have confirmed the description but of course it's difficult for them to make it public.'

Rose nodded. 'You can't tell the public to beware of Policemen.'

'Exactly.' Fletcher paused. 'Faber was saying there was another Sacrificial Murder a couple of nights ago – nasty apparently.' The Inspector grimaced. 'Same M.O. as the rest – y'know – organs missing, stuff like that, but this time the sick fuckers decided to gouge out the poor girl's eye as well.'

'Lovely,' replied Rose with distaste. 'But that doesn't mean Bradford's not connected,' he added. 'There are too many coincidences.'

Fletcher nodded. 'I agree, Pete. I think you've done a sterling job. And if you'll give me my chair back, I'm gonna tell Jack Faber just that.'

Sergeant Rose sighed and pushed himself out of the chair, passing the Inspector as he walked towards the door.

Fletcher put a hand on the sergeant's shoulder, halting him. 'I'm sorry, Pete,' he said earnestly. 'I know you didn't want this outcome but, if it's any consolation, I'll be singing your praises to Faber.' Rose managed a pained smile and nodded as Fletcher slipped behind his desk. 'Oh,' the inspector added, looking up. 'Get Bradford in for questioning will you?'

Rose brightened. 'Can I arrest him?'

Fletcher grinned back and nodded. 'And, if Faber doesn't want to do the interview, you can – you certainly deserve it.'

Sergeant Rose returned the smile and left to get Constable Wright and a squad car. It wasn't the same as being the head of the investigation, but being the arresting officer of someone Rose was certain was involved in the Sacrificial Murder case would be a major feather in his cap. Perhaps he'd even get a commendation. Sergeant Rose rubbed his hands together and went looking for DC Wright. This was not going to be such a bad day after all, he thought.

Mikey woke up to find the concerned face of Jane staring down at him. He frowned and rubbed a hand across his face.

'What time is it?' he asked drowsily.

Jane gave him a half-smile and glanced at the clock on the table beside the bed. 'Nearly ten in the morning,' she replied. 'How do you feel?'

Mikey pushed himself up into a sitting position and gave the question serious consideration. 'Tired?' he volunteered, not quite sure if that was the right answer.

Jane's smile softened and she placed her hand on his. 'And what do you remember about yesterday?' She asked.

Again Mikey concentrated on the question, trying to remember what on earth had happened to him. He vaguely remembered going into London and at some stage had met up with Cooper… Then?… Had he got drunk? Mikey felt a little drained but there seemed to be no trace of a hangover so –

'– I give up,' he said, reading the patient expectation on his girlfriend's face. 'What did I do?'

Jane shook her head. 'It doesn't really matter,' she said and squeezed his hand. 'But I think you were more affected by Geoff's death than you realised. The Doctor –'

'– Doctor?!'

Jane nodded to the bottle of pills beside the clock by way of explanation. 'The Doctor says you're probably suffering from nervous exhaustion, and you need a few days rest.'

Mikey tried to recall what on earth had happened the day before. He dimly remembered being with Cooper and was suddenly struck by a fleeting image of himself standing by a broken phone box: a cabbie shouting at him. Oh God! Thought Mikey.

'I didn't get into a fight, did I?' he asked sheepishly.

Jane laughed. 'No,' she said. 'You just went out with Cooper and… Well, you collapsed. Cooper brought you back here and called a Doctor.'

Mikey nodded slowly, his face a frown. 'And what are these?' He asked, picking up the bottle of pills.

'Sedatives. You're to take two a day.'

'Two!? I'll be walking around like a fucking zombie!'

Jane pursed her lips and took hold of Mikey's hands. 'You're not supposed to be walking around, Mikey,' she said, gazing earnestly into his eyes. 'That's the point. You need bed rest – no excitement – Doctor's orders.' She held his gaze until Mikey's frown became a resigned smile.

'Alright, Nurse,' he said. 'If I promise not to leave the house, am I at least allowed out of bed?'

'Only to lie on the sofa,' Jane replied, her tone serious. 'I mean it, Mikey. You need rest.' She sighed, patted his hand and stood up. 'I'm going to collect some stuff from my flat and then I'll be back to keep an eye on you.' She wagged a finger at him. 'I'm going to make sure you stay in bed.'

Mikey shrugged. 'I don't feel ill,' he said glumly.

'And I don't want you collapsing again,' Jane replied. 'So stay in bed, you'll have less distance to fall if it happens again.'

Mikey smiled. 'Did I really collapse?'

Jane nodded, walked to the door and checked her watch. 'I'll be gone about half an hour,' she said. 'And when I get back I expect to find you right where I left you.'

Mikey grinned. 'Are you going home to collect a nurse's outfit?' he asked.

Jane gave him her best smouldering look. 'Only if you promise to stay in bed.'

Mikey leant back on his pillow and rested his hands behind his head. 'Consider it done,' he said.

Jane closed the bedroom door and trotted down the stairs. Knowing Mikey, he would get up as soon as he heard the door close, so she made sure there was nothing lying around that might spark off any bad memories. She collected all the photos he had taken on Hampstead Heath and stuffed them – along with the old black and white photo his father had taken – into a carrier bag. Into another she placed the dismantled cameras and talking clock then, satisfied that the house was now free of anything hazardous to Mikey's mental health, Jane took the bags out to her car and headed for home. Hearing the door click shut, Mikey counted to one hundred then went downstairs to phone Cooper.

It was only a ten minute journey back to Jane's Highgate flat but the Spaniards Road – which crossed the top of Hampstead Heath – was congested with late morning traffic. Stationary, Jane drummed her fingers on the steering wheel and guessed that the hold up was the usual problem: the single lane bottle-neck beside The Spaniards Inn – the centuries old pub which

195

sat at the end of the road.

In fits and starts the traffic crawled forwards every couple of minutes before stopping again: each move met by a few cars travelling in the opposite direction. Jane – like most people who used the road regularly – wondered if the bottle neck problem would ever be resolved. It was a simple problem, with an equally simple solution. All that had to be done was to move the ancient toll booth – which sat opposite the Spaniards Inn – back a few metres. But, though the squat, unassuming building seemed little more than an inconvenient oddity to most people who manoeuvred their cars around it, it's historical connection with the notorious Highwayman, Dick Turpin meant that it was a listed building: protected from anything so problematic as traffic congestion. Jane sniggered and shook her head. Only the English, she thought, would preserve the place where Dick Turpin had occasionally stabled his horse so that he could continue to hold up traffic centuries after his death.

Another few metres of space opened up before Jane's car and the smile died on her face as she moved forwards and spotted the Police sign positioned beside the road. MURDER was written in large luminous letters across its top and it gave brief details of Tom McDonald's 'vicious' demise on the heath. It offered a reward of ten thousand pounds for anyone helping the Police gain a conviction and called for any eye witnesses to use the telephone number at the bottom of the sign. On any other day the sign would have prompted Jane to investigate how the Police were progressing with their investigation but instead it reminded her that she would have to think of a good excuse when she told her paper she would not be in for a few days.

It took another fifteen minutes before she finally squeezed past Black Bess's old stable to find the opposite side of the road still jammed with traffic. She pulled over as a Police car, it's siren wailing, flashed along the wrong side of the road then found almost no traffic as she made her way home. It was ironic, she thought, that the cars attempting to drive the Spaniards Road were forced to move slower than the horses they had superseded. Somewhere, on heaven's great highway, Dick Turpin was probably laughing.

Deciding that honesty was the best policy, Jane's first action when she finally reached her flat was to contact Doug – her editor – and explain her reasons for staying out of the office for the next few days. She set up her lap top next to her phone, plugged it into the socket on the wall and accessed her work email system. She noted that there was an email for her from John Parker but typed off a quick, explanatory note to Doug before she opened it.

Jane had completely forgotten that she had asked the Chronicle's junior reporter to investigate Marcus Tenneshaw Wright's background. She had, Jane vaguely recalled, mentioned that it was to do with her heath murder story but the first line of John's email jokingly explained that her instincts, for once, had let her down. Marcus Tenneshaw Wright had been dead for over a century.

Jane skimmed quickly through the information John had managed to find out about the Victorian shipping magnate and read of the man's achievements and his fascination with Egyptology. He had made a fortune running vessels to and from every corner of the empire and had used his vast naval network to transport ancient artefacts back to London. Wright had been one of the founding patrons of the British Museum – where most of his collection was still kept – and had also been the chief architect of Highgate cemetery. Jane had smiled at the last few lines of John's note.

'… Wright died right after Highgate Cemetery was

completed and, like the pharaohs who he so admired, was laid to rest within his own personal tomb in Highgate Cemetery's Egyptian Avenue. As in life, Wright's fascination with the pharaohs continues after death.'

At the very bottom of the email was an attached file labelled: 'Britain's Most Wanted!' Jane double clicked the document and watched as an old, black and white photograph drew itself line by line down the screen. It showed a man leaning against an ancient Egyptian sarcophagus on what appeared to be a dockside. Beside the dock the black expanse of a ship's hull stretched up and out of the picture and a thick mooring rope curved through the top right of the frame. The man was dressed in white with a high, collarless shirt fixed with a black tie and held a pith helmet in his right hand. Jane had seen such photographs before – old, faded images of Empire – but there was something peculiar about the scene which took Jane a few moments to realise. Of all the pictures she could ever remember seeing from the Victorian era, Jane had never seen one where the subject smiled at the camera before. They were always austere, stiff-backed and formal and always seemed to have their hats glued to their heads. This man was smiling, relaxed and for a moment Jane wondered whether the picture was from a later period. John had scrawled 'Marcus Tenneshaw Wright – Britain's Most Wanted!' across the bottom of the image so Jane had to assume that this was the man in question. Yet something still bothered her and she frowned at the frozen, smiling face for a few seconds more.

Jane leant back, shrugged and switched her lap top off. She had more pressing things to worry about than a long dead entrepreneur. She left the computer on the table and went into the bedroom to collect some clothes, raided the bathroom then returned to the living room carrying a large black nylon holdall. Jane scanned the room briefly for her lap top case but, not finding it, she simply stuffed the lap top into the holdall and returned to her car.

Half way down the road, Jane suddenly slammed on the brakes.

'Shit!' she exclaimed.

Wide-eyed she pulled on the car's hand brake then twisted round to reach the carrier bag full of the photographs she had taken from Mikey's house. Jane frowned into her rear view mirror momentarily – realising she had stopped abruptly in the road – but the street behind her was empty of traffic. She rifled quickly through the photographs in the bag and was soon staring at the old black and white picture which Patrick Dayville had taken of the family in Highgate Cemetery. The one that had terrified Mikey as a child.

'Oh, fuck,' Jane mouthed. There, his hand resting lightly on the shoulder of the crying boy was the grinning ghost of Marcus Tenneshaw Wright.

If it were at all possible, Sergeant Pete Rose would literally have walked on air. Peter Bradford was in his custody and was also – so he claimed – ready to confess to the Sacrificial Murders. Rose could not believe his good fortune and, as he all but skipped down the corridor to Inspector Fletcher's office he felt his cheek muscles ache from the grin he had worn since arresting Bradford on his doorstep almost twenty minutes earlier. Somewhere, the sergeant knew, somebody high up in the force would notice his actions.

Rose tapped lightly on the inspector's door then, not waiting for a response, pushed it open and beamed in the direction of Fletcher's desk.

'Got the bugger, boss –' the sergeant began then stopped as the blank faces of three men turned to regard him.

One, Rose knew, was the fabled 'Faber of the Yard' but the

other two men did not look like Policemen at all. One appeared to be dressed as an archetypal teacher – complete with brown corduroy jacket, grey beard and bifocals – while the other, dressed in green combat fatigues looked more like the student type. Faced with this unexpected audience Rose's smile faltered. Looking sheepishly at the floor he coughed and tapped on the door again.

From behind his desk, Fletcher gave his sergeant a thumbs up while he nodded to the phone clasped in his other hand.

'Yep... Yep,' nodded the inspector. 'That's fine, doc... Yep... Whenever, yep... Whatever – okay...' Fletcher put the phone down and shook his head. 'I don't know how good your forensic boys are, Jack,' he said. 'But our's are shite.'

Inspector Jack Faber smiled at his old friend. 'Problems?' he asked.

Fletcher shrugged and held up his hands. 'I've no idea. Apparently our forensic team were doing a DNA – something or other – on the wounds of our heath victim. Now they say they've got to completely restart the process and check their entire lab because the results have been contaminated.'

'That is shite,' agreed Faber.

'Yeah, well... Never mind.' Fletcher grinned at his sergeant still standing by the door. 'Perhaps we won't need any of it, eh Pete?'

Rose nodded. 'Bradford's in Interview Room One and ready to talk.'

Inspector Faber turned on his chair and frowned at Rose. 'Are you telling me this Bradford character is going to confess?'

Rose nodded again. 'So he says. Bradford says he wants his lawyer present but, apart from that, he says he'll tell you everything you want to know about the Sacrificial Murders.'

'Sacrificial Murders, Pete?' observed Fletcher. 'Or the Heath murder?'

Sergeant Rose grinned. 'Sacrificial. But I'm betting it's a dead cert he was involved with the heath murder too: he must have been. Then, on our way back in the squad car, Bradford says: "Don't you want the axes, Sergeant?"' Rose mimicked Bradford's well spoken voice and frowned while the two inspectors exchanged a glance. 'If it wasn't for that bandage wrapped around his head,' the sergeant continued, 'I would have smacked 'im one.'

Fletcher gave a half-hearted smile. 'Maybe later, eh Pete,' he said then raised his brows at Faber. 'Axes, Jack. That sounds like your boy.'

Faber shrugged. 'One of them, maybe… We'll see.' The inspector stood up and walked to the door, turned and indicated the other two men in the room. 'In the meantime, could you…?' he said to Fletcher.

'Yep,' replied Fletcher. 'No problem.'

Faber gave a curt nod. 'Where's this Interview Room, sergeant?' he asked Rose.

'Just down the hall, sir,' said Rose, pointing. 'You can't miss it – there's two PC's standing guard outside.' Faber nodded silently and strode off as the sergeant shut the door.

Fletcher waved Rose into the vacant chair. 'Good work, Pete. C'mon in, take a seat.' The inspector lit a cigarette and waved it at the strangers. 'These men are from the British Museum. They've been helping Jack with the Sacrificial Murders case.' Fletcher pointed first to the man in corduroy and then to the one in fatigues. 'This is Professor Taylor and this is Danny Trent.'

The three exchanged silent nods while Pete Rose inwardly congratulated himself on correctly identifying the pair as master and student.

'Now,' continued Fletcher. 'Yesterday, some bloke named –

' the inspector pointed to Danny Trent.

'Michael Dayville,' Danny responded.

'Yep, Michael Dayville,' Fletcher replied, 'walks into the British Museum with a book.' Professor Taylor held up a large, leather bound tome. 'That book,' continued the inspector. 'Now, we don't know where this Michael Dayville got it from, but we want to find out.'

'Why,' asked Rose.

Professor Taylor opened the book and held it up for the sergeant to see. Rose looked blankly at an old illustration of several slender axes surrounded by hieroglyphs. 'I'll try not to bore you with the details, sergeant,' the professor said. 'But these are illustrations of the axes which were stolen from the British Museum and used in the Sacrificial Murders.'

Rose nodded. 'So you think this Dayville character could be involved?'

The professor shrugged and closed the book. 'I really couldn't say. Personally I find it strange that someone would knowingly bring this book to us but it is vitally important that we find out how he got it. You see, this is one of several missing volumes of work from one of the founding fathers of the British Museum – a great man named M.T. Wright. The axes that were stolen were also part of Wright's collection, so you see –'

'– There's a connection.' said Rose.

'He's also local,' added Fletcher. 'Which is another connection.'

The sergeant shrugged. 'So… Do you want me to bring him in?'

'If you feel it's necessary, yeah. But for the moment I want you to take these gentlemen over to see him and have a word with him yourself – see what he says. It may be nothing but I think there are too many coincidences for us to ignore.'

Rose nodded and stood up, opening the door for the two men who trooped out into the corridor. 'Are you going to help Faber interview Bradford?' The sergeant asked Fletcher as the room cleared.

Fletcher shook his head. 'First I've got to get a search team over to Bradford's house, then,' he replied with a grimace, 'organise a party to search Hampstead Heath again. Some little kid's gone missing.'

Rose frowned. 'Jesus, what's going on 'round here?'

'God knows,' replied the inspector. 'Never rains but it pours, eh?'

Jack Faber was not a happy man. He had spent the last few months attempting to track down the Sacrificial Murderer using every resource available to the Metropolitan Police. He had used forensics experts, criminal psychologists, Egyptologists, cultists, occultists and a team of thirty officers working around the clock to crack the case. So far, all he had to show for his efforts was an extremely nasty collection of incident photographs and one photo-fit. Now some local Detective Sergeant – who wasn't even working on the case – claimed that the person now sitting across the table from him was their man. The inspector was loathed to admit that he might be proved correct but what was most irksome was the fact that this was the first suspect he had interviewed – and he looked nothing like Faber's photo-fit.

Across the table, Peter Bradford sat calmly. Though a lumpy bandage still circled his temple, the previous pallor of his complexion had gone and he seemed alert. Dressed casually in a white shirt with cream trousers his relaxed demeanour was in stark contrast to the brooding presence of the inspector opposite.

Faber stared at his one and only suspect in silence for several

203

minutes, hoping that the air of tension generated would make Bradford uncomfortable. The inspector knew the man had agreed to co-operate and tell all but, if life in the force had taught him anything, it was to beware of criminals bearing gifts. With the magnitude of the offences Bradford claimed to have been involved in, his entire manner made Faber instantly suspicious. He looked too comfortable – too confident and, despite the inspector's best efforts, remained that way. Perhaps, Faber mused as he watched Bradford check his watch for the third time, that very confidence might be made to work against him. With that in mind the inspector reached into his jacket pocket.

'D'you know your lawyer's number?' Faber asked lightly. He slide his mobile phone across the table.

Bradford took the phone and gave the inspector a slight smile. 'Of course,' he replied, quickly punched in a number then held the phone to his ear. 'Hello?' Bradford said, adjusting his posture so that he faced the corner of the room. 'This is Peter Bradford. I'd like to speak to my lawyer please... That's right... No, I'm at the Highgate Police Station. Can you – that's fine.' Bradford flicked his left arm up and glanced at his wristwatch. 'I know,' he said with a smile. 'No, I'm fine... Okay.' Bradford took the phone away from his ear, switched it off then passed it back to the inspector. 'Thank you,' he said. 'My Lawyer will be here in about ten minutes.'

Faber raised a brow. 'Local, is he?'

Bradford nodded.

'Right, well,' began Faber, noting his suspect still appeared completely at ease. 'Obviously you should be interviewed with your lawyer present but, while we're waiting, perhaps you could save me some time by repeating what you've already told Sergeant Rose about the murder weapon?' The inspector indicated the bulky dual taping device which occupied the far side of the table and hovered a finger above the record button

Bradford checked his wristwatch again then leaned forwards. 'Certainly,' he nodded. 'It will pass the time. What would you like to know?' He asked conversationally. 'How I got the axes out of the British Museum or why I used them?'

Bradford's frankness momentarily silenced the inspector. Was a confession really going to be this easy? His surprise turned to an amused sneer – this really was his man!

Faber held off from pressing record on the tape machine for a moment longer, narrowed his gaze and drawled. 'I don't know who the fuck you think you are, Bradford. But, for what you've done, you're gonna be passing the fuckin' time staring through iron bars.'

Bradford smiled.

Mikey's fragile peace of mind had been shattered by his phone call to Cooper and the unnerving events of the last few days were once again dominating his thoughts. At Mikey's frank insistence, Cooper had cautiously recounted what had happened the previous afternoon and, though Mikey still only had vague memories of all his activities, several disturbing recollections had resurfaced. There was the phone call outside the British Museum, the little girl who should not have been there and finally a wall of fire which had knocked him off of his feet. If that was not bad enough, Cooper was now saying that Catherine Robson was desperate to talk to him.

'Why, Coop'?' Mikey had asked numbly.

'She says she can't get in touch with the – er – other side,' Cooper replied. 'I can't say I really understood the problem but, well… It seems her spirit guide has disappeared.'

Mikey laughed humourlessly. 'Disappeared? Isn't that what they're supposed to do?'

'I suppose,' Cooper responded. 'Look, I'm really sorry,

Mikey. I didn't – well, you know…'

Mikey sighed and lent back on the sofa – rubbing a hand across his eyes. He felt drained. 'I know, Coop'. I know you didn't mean any of this to happen. It's not your fault.'

There was a tangible hesitation from the other end of the line. 'What should I say to Catherine?' Cooper finally asked.

Mikey frowned. 'I don't know, Coop'! Tell her to get her fucking line checked or something! But tell her to stay away from me. I don't need this shit right now.'

There was another pause. 'Y'know,' Cooper began, attempting to sound light-hearted. 'Someday we're going to look back at this and laugh.'

Despite himself, Mikey guffawed at the thought. 'Hey, listen!' he replied tersely. 'I'm laughing right now!'

It was Cooper's turn to sigh. 'Sorry, that probably wasn't the right thing to say.'

'It doesn't matter, Coop',' replied Mikey, his anger fading completely. 'I'm just… I'm just tired.'

'Then perhaps,' Cooper volunteered, 'I should stop annoying you and let you get back to bed.'

Mikey agreed, said his goodbyes and put the phone down. He flopped back into the sofa: arms limp, legs stretched out on the carpet before him and sighed loudly at the ceiling. Was this just stress? He wondered, or was he really suffering some form of breakdown? He stared sightlessly at the ceiling rose for some time; his thoughts meandering without real direction as he attempted to block out his memories of the last few days. It did not help. The harder he tried to ignore the strange pattern of events, the more Mikey found himself focusing on them.

It also bothered him that there were things he could not remember. Mikey trusted Cooper implicitly to tell him the whole truth but still he knew that there were gaps in his recollection: dark clouds across his mind where the landscape beyond could merely be glimpsed at. It left Mikey feeling uncomfortable – he felt he should remember – and that was coupled with a sensation of restlessness: a nagging suspicion that he was supposed to be doing something specific rather than staring blankly at his ceiling.

That thought tugged Mikey from his malaise. What he should be doing was resting, rather than groping – however unwillingly – through his memories. But how was he to rest if it meant his mind simply started sifting through his thoughts again?

Mikey frowned. 'So,' he said, addressing the ceiling rose. 'I am going mad.'

He shook his head. He had to do something – anything – to keep his mind occupied so he stood up and began to pace the room, humming tunelessly to himself as he strode back and forth. Mikey stopped, glanced around for his camera bag, then went back upstairs to search for his cigarettes.

Dressed, and now puzzled by something completely new, Mikey came back downstairs a minute later with his empty camera bag. He frowned at the living room. Where the hell were his cameras? With the curtains drawn at both ends, the room was dingy so Mikey walked to the rear windows to let the daylight in. On his way to repeat the process at the front of the house he looked again to see if his cameras were in view and suddenly realised that the pile of photos were also missing. He shook his head. Was this Jane's idea of ensuring he take things easy? Still puzzled, Mikey threw back the front curtains then screamed at the sight of the preacher standing right outside the window.

'JESUS!' cried Mikey, throwing himself backwards as the gaunt figure vanished as quickly as it had appeared. He hit the floor and scuttled across the carpet, his heart pounding as he stared wide-eyed at the space where the preacher had been.

'What the –? What the fuck?!' Mikey gasped as he backed into the sofa, then his heart leapt again as the phone rang beside him.

Mikey snatched at the handset. 'Get away from me! Leave me alone!' he spat.

'Mi – but,' was all Catherine Robson managed to say before Mikey had slammed the phone down.

The second Mikey replaced the receiver, the phone rang again. He backed away from it onto the sofa, willing it to stop as he drew his legs up and hugged them tightly. After six rings his answer phone cut in and Mikey stuck his fingers in his ears, screwing up his face as his message played. It didn't help – Mikey could still hear – so he leapt forwards before his message ended and, with a violent tug, ripped the phone from its socket.

Now back on the floor, Mikey heard a click from behind him and a low hum quickly replaced by the sound of static. He rolled over, the disconnected phone still grasped in his hands and gazed open-mouthed as he saw that his television had switched itself on.

'Help me Michael. In the name of God, help me…!' wailed a plaintive voice from the speaker as white static filled the television screen.

Mikey stood up and screamed in reply, his body rigid with anger, ferocity welling like a volcano inside him. He clamped his eyes shut as he bellowed at the television and for a second it seemed to him as if the whole room shook from his rage.

The noise from the television stopped and, as he became aware of the silence, Mikey's anger subsided. He opened his eyes, saw the television screen cracked and sparking and then realised with a sinking heart that all the windows in the room were now shattered. On the verge of tears, he hung his head and slowly sank down onto the floor – wanting it to all go away.

'Hoy! You!'

Mikey shook his head fractionally in disbelief – the memory of an irate cabbie suddenly returning to him. Not you again, he thought. With a shuddering sigh Mikey opened his eyes, faced the front windows and saw, framed in a broken pane, a figure he did not recognise.

'D.S. Rose,' said the man, staring back at Mikey with unconcealed animosity. 'Metropolitan C.I.D.'

Rose had held up an identity card which he now withdrew and he regarded the broken windows for a moment before fixing his gaze back on the crouching figure of Mikey.

'What the fuck do think you're doing?' he demanded.

Mikey's eyes were wet with tears and he shook his head. 'I don't know,' he whispered.

With arms crossed, Inspector Faber listened with increasing anger as Peter Bradford gleefully recounted his murder spree onto tape. There was now no shadow of a doubt in Faber's mind that the man was guilty, but his unrepentant zeal for detailing his actions left the Inspector not only disgusted but also convinced that Bradford was insane. Who else but a madman would happily confess to such bloody, senseless crimes?

As the sickening catalogue of horrors went on, Faber found himself giving serious consideration to picking up his chair and striking Bradford with it. He knew he could not cover his actions by switching the time indexed tape machine off and then back on again after he had hit Bradford, but his growing rage was such that he was beginning not to care.

If he was to do it, Faber wondered just how long he would get to repay the pain and suffering Bradford had caused before his lawyer turned up. He would get around the problem of the tape machine by saying it had been knocked onto the floor when Bradford had suddenly turned violent. Though his suspect would be bruised and battered, there was already enough evidence on the tape to prove that Faber had not beaten a confession from the man. The inspector was reaching to turn the tape deck off when a strange thump sounded from somewhere outside the interview room. Bradford instantly fell silent and Faber's attention fell on the door as a second thump sounded. Bradford began to laugh.

'Ooh dear, inspector!' said Bradford, his face a mask of unconcealed joy. 'I do believe my lawyer's here!'

Holding his sides, Peter threw his head back and guffawed at the ceiling while Faber switched off the tape machine, threw his chair back and raised a fist to strike the man. But his attention was taken as several more thumps sounded from outside – this time accompanied by the noise of screaming metal. A chill ran down Faber's spine as he suddenly realised what the thumps signified. Somebody was firing a silenced gun inside the station!

Without a word, the inspector backed away from the grinning Bradford towards the door. He could hear shouts from outside as he reached for the handle and he opened it to find several confused policemen standing frozen in the corridor.

'What the fuck's going on?!' Faber barked at the closest officer.

The constable turned to see the inspector then flinched as a louder thump sounded at the far end of the hallway. He turned his attention back towards the sound then hurried to the inspector's side.

'I dunno, sir,' he said. 'I think it's gunfire.'

Dumbstruck, both men stood immobile as a man in a blue, pinstriped suit came round the far corner of the corridor. In one hand he carried a long barrelled automatic pistol which he instantly raised at an officer who was rapidly backing away along the wall. The silenced shot blew the policeman off of his feet and, just before Faber let the constable inside the interview room and slammed the door, he saw the man discard the bulky pistol to pull a large, silver weapon from his waist band. Something else struck Faber as he ducked back inside the interview room: the man's tanned face closely matched the Sacrificial Murderer's photo-fit.

With the door now closed, the inspector reflexively reached to lock it then cursed when he remembered that all such rooms only locked from the outside. He turned to the constable, snapped his fingers and indicated the overturned chair on the floor. Quickly the pair jammed the chair as best they could against the door before discarding it in favour of the interview table. There was an horrendously loud shot from somewhere in the corridor and both men ducked, wedging themselves against the outer table legs.

Throughout all of this frantic activity, Peter Bradford sat calmly on his chair. With his legs crossed and hands resting in his lap he looked a picture of serenity as the shots and screams continued through the Police Station.

Seeing the man's total indifference, Faber spat: 'That's him, isn't it!? Your fuckin' partner! You really think you can get away with this?!'

Bradford seemed to be inspecting the shine on his shoes but looked up to face the inspector. 'Partner?' he replied in an amused tone. 'Please, inspector, don't insult me. Garvin's a trusted employee.' Bradford glanced at his watch and grinned. 'As for "getting away with it",' he continued. 'You have no idea… But,' Bradford said, reaching a hand up to his bandage, 'perhaps I'll give you a taste of what's to come.'

There were several more shots from outside, interspersed with the muffled sound of what Faber could only imagine were doors being kicked open. Wherever this 'Garvin' character had come from, he seemed to have had some form of military training. He was methodically working his way along the corridor: eliminating every single person he encountered. It was only a question of time before he reached their room.

Trapped, fearful and with his thoughts reeling, the inspector finally remembered his mobile phone. He pulled it from his pocket and quickly punched in the number which would connect him to an Armed Response Unit. He doubted they would arrive in time but it was all he could think to do. He had his finger on the call button when a gasp from the constable made him look up and he froze, open-mouthed when he saw what Peter Bradford had kept concealed beneath his bandages.

At first it was difficult to make out quite what the injury was, but the bloody, badly stitched wound in the middle of Bradford's forehead was an appalling sight. Then the lump in the centre of the injury twitched and a blue, bloodshot eye opened and stared back at them.

'What the fuck?!' whispered the constable.

'Jeesus...' mouthed Faber. 'Oh God...' The horror of the sight was compounded by the instant recollection of the final Sacrificial Murder. The killer had deviated from his usual routine and it had baffled the investigating team as to why Paula Frost's right eye had been gouged out. Now he knew and, impossibly, that missing eye was now blinking back at him from Bradford's forehead.

Bradford chuckled but his voice sounded strained. 'Peek-a-boo, inspector...' he said through gritted teeth. 'I...see...you.'

All other considerations forgotten, Faber reacted. He threw his phone as hard as he could towards Bradford then leapt sideways, grabbed the discarded chair by its leg and swung it with all his strength at Peter's head. Caught off guard by the sudden attack, Bradford managed to raise an arm as the chair struck but the blow still knocked him from his chair. He cried out in pain, sprawled onto the floor, then covered his head as best he could as Faber pressed home his assault.

The inspector managed three more savage blows with the chair before the room resounded to several deafening blasts. With his ears ringing, Faber turned to see wisps of smoke around the shattered door lock and blood pouring freely from a gapping wound in the constable's head. Then the door was thrown back with a mighty shove which toppled the dead policeman to one side and skidded the table away. Faber barely had time to register the suited figure of Garvin in the doorway before the latter raised the bulky Magnum Desert Eagle and fired it at almost point blank range.

The impact bounced the inspector off of the far wall, the hole in his back leaving a bloody imprint as he fell sideways – eyes vacant – and hit the floor. Garvin smiled, put the barrel of the gun to his mouth and blew.

'It's the cavalry, sir,' he said with a smile. 'You can get up now.'

Garvin's smile faltered. His employer, Peter Bradford, did not move.

Chapter Eleven

Dressed in regulation blue overalls, Constables Marsh, Foster and Barnes stepped out of the back of the police van parked outside Peter Bradford's house. With empty plastic evidence bags clutched under their arms they gazed up at the narrow, three storey house until the towering figure of Constable Wright appeared from the front of the van.

'Got the key, Tiny?' Marsh asked Wright.

Wright grinned and held up the two foot long ram he was carrying. 'Shall we go?' he replied and led the trio up the short path to Bradford's front door.

A single, firm whack with the battering ram broke the Yale lock and one by one the policemen trooped up the stairs to the central landing of the house. Constable Wright had been given a rough layout of the place by Inspector Fletcher and now he directed the others to search.

'Marsh,' he said, pointing to the rear stairway which descended towards the back of the house. 'You search down there. Foster as well. Barnsie, you can search this landing while I do upstairs.'

Each man nodded and went in their assigned directions but a call from Constable Barnes brought them all back to the central landing.

''ere, boys!' exclaimed Barnes. 'Come'n 'ave a look at this!'

Barnes was standing on the threshold of the narrow front room where Fletcher and Rose had previously interviewed Bradford. He pointed, grinning, to the countless clocks hanging on the far wall.

'What the fuck is all that about?! Eh?' he said with a shake of his head.

'Fletcher mentioned them,' Wright observed.

Foster checked his watch. 'Are they all fast?' he asked,

214

noting that they all read twelve o'clock.

Wright shook his head and cupped a hand to his ear. 'Listen,' he said. 'Can you hear ticking?'

The others all mouthed silent 'O's while Foster frowned and put his watch to his ear.

'Oh balls,' he said. 'My damn watch's stopped.'

Matching his frown, the others all checked their wrist watches. All now read twelve o'clock.

'That is so fuckin' freaky!' exclaimed Barnes. The others murmured agreement.

'Yeah, well,' began Wright, as perplexed as the rest. 'Whatever the time is, we've got a job to do, so let's not piss about – okay?'

'Maybe it's magnets,' volunteered Marsh.

'Magnets?' frowned Foster.

'What the fuck've magnets gotta do with it?' asked Barnes.

Marsh shrugged. 'I dunno. It's the first thing that came to mind.'

Barnes shook his head. 'Fuckin' magnets!' he sniggered. 'I ask ya…'

'Alright,' said Wright firmly. 'Who cares? It can be solar fuckin' flares for all I care. Whatever the time is we don't have much of it, so let's get searching.'

Constable Wright turned and began to climb the stairway to the next floor. The others dispersed and Wright heard Foster as he and Marsh proceeded down the rear stairway.

'I think it's about ten to twelve anyway…'

Shaking his head and muttering curses to himself, Wright ascended the narrow stairway which curved around the rear wall to reach the upper floor of the townhouse. At the top he found a short landing from which two bedrooms, a bathroom and a study led off of as well as another short flight of stairs to his far left which ended in a closed doorway. The bedrooms, study and bathroom doors were all half ajar and from the front of the house sunshine spilled onto the white walls of the hall. Unable to contain his curiosity, Wright ignored the open rooms and headed straight for the closed door which he guessed led up to the attic.

He climbed the five steps which rose to the door, rattled the handle to find it locked then shrugged and nudged the ram he was still carrying against the flimsy lock. There was a sharp crack of wood – the door instantly giving way – and Wright pushed it back to peer up into the half-light beyond. An old, brass light switch was fitted on the wall beside the doorway which Wright flicked at automatically. He was half way up the stairs when all hell broke seemed to break loose.

First, there came the startling sound of countless bells chiming in unison below him – instantly followed by an enormous explosion from outside which shook the house. Instinctively, Constable Wright gripped the wooden hand rail as the building shuddered and froze as the torrent of noise rumbled through the air over the continuing chimes. In seconds the thunderous wave diminished and Wright – all thoughts of exploration gone – turned on his heels.

He was passing back through the attic door when a cry from Barnes sounded below. Wright ran to the top of the curving stairway, intent on aiding his colleague, then stopped dead in his tracks. The constable regarded the upper landing; a deep frown etched into his brow as he noticed that the previously sunlit walls were now coloured a fierce orange.

Through the half opened bedroom door, Wright caught a glimpse of the view outside and he walked numbly into the room to stare out at the Hampstead skyline. The entire horizon was ablaze.

There was the sound of rapid footsteps on the stairs and Wright had to wrench his eyes away from the numbing sight outside as Barnes clattered his way into the room.

'The fuckin' clocks wen' off, Tiny!' he cried, shaking his head frantically. 'All of 'em! Every fuckin' one!' Constable Barnes' nervous energy had left him panting and he took a huge breath to calm himself before the fiery panorama outside the house began to register. 'What the –' he gasped, then fell silent to join Wright at the window.

What had been bright sunshine was now a flickering, orange glow – fuelled by a high wall of flame which stretched off into the distance in both directions. As both officers looked on open-mouthed they could see dark columns of smoke rising above the outlines of buildings in the distance. The faint sound of a multitude of alarms carried through the air towards them.

'A–atom bomb?' stuttered Barnes, blinking rapidly.

Wright shook his head fractionally, still unable to accept the sight. 'Don't know, don't know,' he mumbled.

There was another rapid footfall on the stairs but it was almost impossible for either officer to pull their attention away from the catastrophe outside.

'We should…' Wright managed faintly. '… Y'know. Get back to the station.' He glanced back to address the new arrivals. 'Don't you thin–!' he began.

There was a strange note in Wright's curtailed sentence which, despite the unbelievable view, instantly grabbed Barnes's attention. It sounded like panic. He flicked his gaze towards his colleague in time to see Wright's head smash backwards through the window then leapt away in terror when he saw the monstrosity which had just rushed across the room.

It was as tall as Wright, but its unearthly appearance was like nothing Barnes had ever seen before. A whole catalogue of animals flashed through his mind as he back-stepped rapidly away from it. Wolf? Horse? Dog? Crocodile? There seemed to be echoes of all those animals and more within the beast, but the sum of its parts was something altogether more horrific.

The creature's skin was an ashen grey, yet this pallid, deathly complexion belied its strength and speed. Above its muscular body, a single eye of almost luminous red sat atop an elongated head all but split in two by a gapping mouth lined with razor-like teeth. Apart from the arms – which ended in knife-like hands – there was one further point which Barnes noted in the frantic second it took him to reverse into the cabinet beside the brass-framed bed. The entire front of the monster was covered in blood – and only some of it was Wright's.

As Barnes saw his friend torn apart in a flurry of vicious, slashing blows he ran for his life: hurling himself across the bed in a desperate attempt to reach the door. There was a deafening roar from the monster and, as the policeman threw every nerve and muscle into propelling himself forwards, his flight was suddenly stopped dead. Barnes felt an unbearable pressure around his temple as the creature's hand clamped onto his head and, though he struggled for his life, he was instantly wrenched around to face the monster. Terrified but still thrashing, Barnes felt his feet leave the ground to find his face mere inches from that of the creature.

There was a loud snort from the bloody countenance as the monster appeared to sniff him and Barnes smelt a putrid stench fill his nostrils. The policeman flailed his arms and legs to strike the creature repeatedly but still the unbearable grip held him firm. Then that terrible mouth seemed to form a sneer and, for the briefest second, Barnes felt himself being swung – pendulum like – towards the ceiling.

As Barnes's feet arced upwards the creature twisted its arm to send the policeman the other way and instantly Barnes' neck was broken. Without a second thought it tossed the dead body into a corner of the bedroom then turned to view for itself the burning skyline. It was hard to be certain, but the monster's mouth seemed to form some semblance of a smile.

At the stroke of midday the peace of London was shattered as rumour broke out in the city that some unbelievable disaster had befallen the residents of Highgate and Hampstead. Though initial details were scant, within minutes the word had spread throughout the city and a rising panic soon brought the capital to a standstill. Worried workers and residents alike rushed to their nearest televisions while those with a more elevated vantage point crowded the windows to scan the northern horizon. Though it was not difficult to locate the cause of the disturbance it was (for those dumbfounded onlookers) almost impossible to rationalise what on earth they were seeing. Terrorist attacks, gas explosions and nuclear detonations were all put forward to explain the disaster but no single theory appeared to fully explain why a massive, shimmering wall of fire was now towering into the sky around what had only minutes before been the leafy climbs around Hampstead and Highgate.

If the distant view of the fire wall was disconcerting, it was nothing compared to the mayhem and trauma caused at ground zero. At exactly twelve o'clock the fire walls had erupted: cutting a deadly swathe through houses, fields, roads and railways alike and cutting off anyone unlucky enough to be in the general vicinity of the heath. Through the back streets of Highgate, through Hampstead and Belsize Park the line flashed in an instant, carving a blazing path as it encircled the heath and leaving nothing but death and destruction in its wake. It seared through buildings like butter; fusing brickwork into glass in a shocked heartbeat and incinerating everything which lay close to its line. Across roads, railways, fields and woodland the same pattern was repeated: one instant the scene was normal, the next an explosion of heat had cut the scene in half. Cars were colliding and smashing to a halt as the roads before them turned into fire. Shoppers were diving for cover under sudden avalanches of masonry and gas mains were spontaneously erupting everywhere. Hell, it appeared, had settled on North London.

The same catastrophe had stopped Sergeant Rose in his tracks. One moment he was staring through the broken window at a crouching, tearful Michael Dayville, the next he was rocked on his heels by a thunderous roar from a nearby street. Now, like Mikey, he was crouched on the floor and, as the explosions subsided into an ominous rumble, he looked up to see that the blue sky was now a glowing orange.

'Jeeeesus…' he muttered, then noticed that Michael Dayville was now standing by his open front door.

'Get inside!' barked Mikey. He waved frantically at the sergeant, then did the same to the two Egyptologists who were spread-eagled on the short path before his house.

'What…?' began Rose. He climbed slowly to his feet but his eyes were still fixed on the sky.

'I don't know,' replied Mikey, guessing the policeman's unfinished question. 'But I think you'll be safer inside.'

With wary glances upwards, both Danny Trent and Professor Taylor instantly took Mikey up on his offer. Sergeant Rose however, stayed put. As if in a daydream he shook his head at Mikey's suggestion and frowned as a light rain of ash began to fall. His eyes grew wide.

'Get inside!' he snapped, seemingly oblivious to Mikey's earlier suggestion. Before Mikey could respond, Rose had darted towards his car.

Shocked locals were beginning to open their front doors and wander onto the street, craning their necks up at the sky and exchanging questioning, worried glances. Seeing this, and noting the continual fall of ash, Rose hollered out an order advising everybody to remain indoors by their televisions and radios.

'NOW!!!' thundered the sergeant as the residents hesitated.

Shaking his head at their reticence – but unable to do much else – Rose jumped inside his car and called the station. He received nothing on the radio but static. Rose tried different frequencies only to find the same white noise then threw the handset down in frustration and got out of the car.

Mikey was still at his door and the sergeant made straight for him.

'I need to use your phone,' he said briskly.

Mikey nodded absently and stepped back to allow the policeman through. He intended to follow Rose into the living room but paused and stared (as he had been for the last few minutes) at the glow above the rooftops. He could not quite put his finger on it but, apart from the fact that the heavens were ablaze, Mikey felt sure that there was something else not quite right with the sky.

Sergeant Rose tapped Mikey on the shoulder and held the disconnected phone up before his face.

'Is this supposed to be some sort o'fuckin' joke?!' he demanded.

The forceful question seemed to return Mikey from his reverie. He blinked, took the phone from the sergeant without a word and then reconnected it back into the wall. Rose snatched the phone from Mikey, picked up the receiver then slammed it down again in frustration. He swept his gaze around the room.

'Does anyone have a mobile phone?' he asked, trying to keep the worry from his voice. 'The phone isn't working.'

Both Danny and the Professor had been standing dumbly in

221

the centre of the room, both men's attention fixed on the grey fall of ash outside. Now Danny Trent patted his pockets and pulled out a slim, grey phone. He passed it to the sergeant.

'Just press that red button at the top to switch it on,' he said. 'Punch in the number – then press green to call.'

Rose followed the instructions and sounded a huge sigh of relief even though the LCD display informed him that there was no signal.

'Problem?' Danny asked, hearing him sigh.

Rose shrugged. 'There's no signal but your phone's working,' he answered cryptically. Danny looked blank. 'Batteries…' added the sergeant. He jabbed the phone at the ceiling. 'If that explosion had been nuclear the batteries would have had their …' he waved his hand as he searched for the word.

'Polarity?' volunteered Professor Taylor.

'That was it,' agreed Rose. 'Their polarity would have been reversed and your phone wouldn't've worked. So… I don't think it was nuclear.' The two men from the British Museum grew wide-eyed at the thought. 'I thought the ash might have been fallout,' continued the sergeant. He let out another sigh. 'But, I think it might just be ash.'

'Do you have any idea what it could have been?' asked Professor Taylor.

Rose shook his head. 'Not yet. I've not been able to get in touch with the station, but I'm going to take a look around and see what's going on. Maybe you could –' The sergeant was about to advise the pair to switch on the television while he was gone but now he stared in disbelief as he saw smoke wisping from the cracked screen.

'Hey!' Rose shouted angrily. He turned to see that Mikey was peering out of the front windows, his head cocked at an angle as he scanned the sky. 'Dayville!' snapped the policeman.

'Mm?' answered Mikey distantly.

'I think he might be in shock, sergeant,' advised Danny.

'Mr Dayville,' said Rose, softening his tone. 'Are you alright?'

When Mikey turned there was a confused expression on his face. He pointed out of the window. 'There are people in the sky,' he said.

The others were silent for a moment before Sergeant Rose moved forward and took Mikey gently by the elbows. 'Why don't you sit down for a bit?' he suggested, guiding Mikey to the sofa. 'Just rest for a minute, eh?'

Mikey did as instructed and sat. He stared blankly ahead, blinking occasionally but remained silent. Rose put his hands on his hips and regarded the others.

'I'm going to take a look outside,' he said. 'If you two can wait here until I get back and look after...' He nodded in the direction of Mikey. '... I'd appreciate it. If I get detained I'll have somebody from the station come and pick you up but in the meantime it's probably best if you both wait here.' Both Taylor and Trent nodded.

With a sideways glance at Mikey, the sergeant left the house and returned outside. On the pavement he paused for a moment and listened to the clamour of distant alarm bells, then turned in the direction he knew led to the bottom of Hampstead High Street.

Though the sky still retained its peculiar luminosity, the closer Rose got to the main road the more choked the air became. At first the sergeant thought it was smoke fading the high street to a pale grey but, though there was a distinct acrid tang in the air, Rose quickly realised that the thickening fog was formed by fine ash. The reason for it became obvious as he reached the junction.

The entire high street was covered in a thick layer of dust and detritus, the shop fronts across the road nothing more than cracked silhouettes with wall mounted alarm units winking red periodically. There were figures running, shouting, screaming amongst the rubble which filled the street and rounded grey lumps scattered up and down the road marked the positions of abandoned cars. An inner voice told the Policeman that he should be doing his duty to help the stricken, the injured, the terrified: yet the sight which he now glimpsed across the road took his full attention. Ignoring the devastation for the time being, he crossed the street to investigate.

A short, paved walkway cut through the northern side of Hampstead High Street to connect to Heath Street, but it too was now cut by a glowing orange wall which sprang from the ground to rise through, then above the surrounding buildings. Superficially the wall resembled flame but, despite its radiance and shifting patterns, it neither gave off any heat nor appeared to be spreading its destruction. It simply sat there.

Rose followed the line of the wall, attempting to fathom the cause of so peculiar a phenomenon. On the flanking sides it had melted the brickwork into wax-like rivulets while the same fused line ran across the paving stones before him. The sergeant wondered just what sort of temperature was required to turn brick into glass and why that same heat was no longer present.

The remains of a large tree – now scorched black and smouldering – sat to the left of the walkway and beneath it Rose spotting a twisted branch jutting from amongst the rubble. The policeman picked it up and prodded the fire wall with it.

Though the barrier gave off no heat, its effect on the branch was dramatic. There was no resistance to his thrust but the wood instantly burst into flame. Startled, the sergeant pulled it back to find the tip of the branch had been completely consumed. With a frown, Rose hurled the remainder of the branch at the wall and watched as its shape flared white for an instant before evaporating. He was about to search for something else to test the fire wall with when a deep rumble from the building behind the tree announced its collapse. Rose hurried back into the high street as the wall crumbled down into the walkway.

Having escaped the falling masonry, the sergeant turned to see rubble and dust fill the space behind him. He squinted through the spreading cloud and could just make out bright flares of white where bouncing bricks were striking the fire wall. Rose grimaced at the strange sight, shook his head and turned away. He had to get back to the station.

A little further down the devastated street was the Hampstead Police Station. The sergeant made straight for it and saw with some relief that there was a flurry of activity outside as uniformed constables gave what aid they could to the injured. The scene in front of the shattered station resembled a war zone and Rose counted dozens of grimy, bloodstained residents sitting on the pavement. Many were tearful, some were screaming, but most just sat there shivering – their eyes wide with shock.

Rose approached the nearest constable and flashed his ID card. 'Where are the fire engines? The ambulances?' he asked

The dishevelled constable, his head crudely bandaged with a white shirt sleeve gazed dumbly at the sergeant for a moment. 'We don't know, sir,' he replied finally. 'We can't raise anyone and…' He pointed down the cloudy road towards Belsize Park. '…That fire's everywhere – the whole area's been hit.'

'Did you see it?' Rose asked. 'Any idea what happened?'

The policeman shook his head. 'I was in the station when it happened – but no one seems to know what the hell's going on.'

Rose nodded. 'Is there anyone in charge in the station?' he asked.

The constable gave a glance towards the station entrance. 'I don't know where our chief is, but somebody should be in there – the place is packed with wounded.'

The sergeant skirted around the injured on the pavement and stopped for a moment beside the station entrance as two shirt-sleeved policemen came out carrying a makeshift stretcher. He watched them trot of into the thinning dust clouds then turned expectantly as the noise of a car engine sounded from up the hill.

Through the chaos of Hampstead High Street a grey van wove its way carefully through the rubble and abandoned cars. Rose squinted through the windscreen as the van drew nearer and was shocked to see that the driver appeared to be wearing some form of bright yellow hazard suit. He moved closer as the van stopped before the Police Station and his fears were confirmed when the side door of the van drew back to reveal two more people dressed in the same, billowing suits.

'Who's in charge here?' said one of the figures, his voice slightly muffled by the enclosing plastic helmet.

The many people gathered on the pavement had all fallen silent as the van drew up and now a middle-aged policeman stepped towards the roadside.

'Who are you?' he demanded.

'Hazard Bureau,' came the terse response. 'Have these people had their tablets?'

The policeman turned to regard the injured for a second. 'What tablets?' he asked, confusion plain on his face.

The man in the suit seemed to heave a sigh while his partner pulled out a box filled to the brim with hundreds of small white tablets. 'Anti-radiation tablets,' explained the first man. 'Have they been given them yet?'

At the first sound of the word 'radiation' a collective gasp went up from the crowd. Someone muttered: 'I knew it! I fuckin' knew it!' While others simply hung their heads. The middle-aged policemen, his features flitting between concern and disbelief, finally said:

'What do you mean, radiation?! You mean that's −' He pointed beyond the van to where the sky was beginning to clear to a bright orange.

The man in the suit nodded. 'That's right,' he said patiently. 'It's radioactive. And we're here to hand out anti-radiation tablets before your exposure goes too far.'

'If that's atomic,' announced Rose; pointing to the sky as he walked closer to the van. 'Why has the electricity not been affected? I thought −'

'− Did I say it was atomic?' interrupted in the man in the suit. 'Did I say it was nuclear? No. I just said it was radioactive. Or did you think I was wearing this suit for fancy dress?'

Rose frowned at the sarcasm. As a policeman the only people who ever derided him were usually wearing handcuffs soon afterwards. Instinctively, he thrust a hand in his pocket, pulled out his ID and held it before the man's face.

'My name is Detective Sergeant Rose,' said Rose. 'I'd like to see some identification.'

The man's shoulders hunched visibly at the demand while the second figure in the van turned away. When he turned back it was to press a sub-machine gun against the sergeant's head.

'There's my ID, Sergeant,' sneered the first man. 'And it says that, under Emergency Law, I am to carry out my duties without let or hindrance.' The man crossed his arms. 'Now,' he continued, 'do you want to fuck around playing 'Bobby-on-the-beat' or do you want me to save these people's lives?'

Rose, shocked by the sudden turn of events cast a glance at the startled face of the policeman beside him. He sighed, lowered his ID card and stepped back.

'Thank you,' responded the man with a curt nod. 'Now, if you would be so kind as to take this box of tablets, we can get on and help other people.' He prodded the box with his foot.

Reluctantly, and with the gun following his every move, Rose leant forward and picked up the box. He passed it instantly to the middle-aged policeman beside him.

'Make sure everybody gets one – but one only,' advised the man in the suit. 'You'll have to make them go round.'

Unnerved, but still not convinced, Rose asked: 'So what has happened? Are we at war?'

The man in the suit gave a humourless smile. 'I'm not at liberty to divulge that information, sergeant. But let's just say that we are experiencing an extreme case of friendly fire.'

With that the man pulled the side door shut and the van began to drive slowly away. Rose let out a huge sigh and shook his head as the vehicle departed.

'Should I hand these out, d'you think?' the middle-aged policeman asked.

Rose cast a glance at the curious sky and then at the worried faces watching him. He was out of his depth in this situation and he knew it. Who was he to question those that were trying to help? Just because he'd never heard of the Hazard Bureau didn't mean they weren't genuine. And if they were – as he was beginning to suspect – part of the Ministry Of Defence, then it was no wonder they behaved as they did. As a policeman he himself knew enough about emergency contingency laws to know that normal rules did not apply. The people in the van were most probably military, and charged with performing a specific task in this bizarre situation: and that meant that he was probably lucky to still have his head in one piece. Rose gave another sigh, reached his hand into the box and took out some pills. He popped one into his mouth instantly and nodded to his companion.

'You'd better hand them out,' he said then turned away as the crowd impatiently waited to be given a tablet.

Rose walked back towards Mikey's house and his car. He felt adrift; powerless. He needed to drive back to his own station, check in with Fletcher and see if there was something he could do. And then he needed to contact his wife: let her know that he was okay. Or would that be a lie? Were the men in suits right about the radiation? If so, had he been over-exposed already? He hoped the pill – whatever it was – would help, but still he found it hard to believe that what he had seen was the result of something radioactive. What had the man said? Friendly fire? What was that supposed to mean? Were the Americans dropping bombs on London? It made no sense.

Rose paused and looked up at the sky which was still tinged with the same orange glow. It made no sense, yet it was definitely there and logically, he reasoned, there would have to be some form of plausible explanation. But what that explanation could possibly be was far beyond Rose's comprehension.

The sergeant grimaced and leant against the low brick wall he had been walking besides: a sudden wave of nausea washing over him. He swallowed hard, feeling bile rise and fought the extreme sensation of sickness. Rose took a deep breath, the urge to vomit now subsiding, and set himself back on his path. If that had been the start of what he feared it was, then he may not have much time. Rose quickened his pace, hoping he could reach his wife before the radiation killed him.

Chapter Twelve

It was instinctive curiosity which took Jane down to Highgate Cemetery, that and the fact that she was less than five minutes away from it by car. But Jane had been so stunned by the picture of Marcus Tenneshaw Wright's ghost that she was half way down the tree enclosed hill which ran beside the cemetery before she became consciously aware of what she was doing.

Jane stopped her car on the quiet lane outside Highgate Cemetery and looked around. To her left the larger, later and less picturesque side of the cemetery sprawled while, to Jane's right, the original part sat behind its redbrick and sandstone facade.

With her hands still on the wheel, Jane gazed absently through the railings at the overgrown cemetery beyond. She remembered taking the tour many years before; wandering (with her guide) along the twisting pathways which climbed the cemetery hill and marvelling at the dereliction which had turned the place of rest into an ivy-gripped forest curiously dotted with lichen covered headstones. She also remembered the ramshackle sight of the Egyptian Avenue - the centrepiece of the cemetery – and how its cracked plaster columns and weathered walls seemed a pale imitation of pharaonic glory. Now, Jane knew the reason for the imitation and that thought brought her back to the question which had nagged her since she had stopped the car. What exactly was she doing here?

Jane picked up the photograph which she had placed on the passenger seat and looked once again at the intriguing scene of family and ghost. There was – she had to admit – no real doubt in her mind that what she was looking at was a genuine image because she could not believe for one moment that Mikey's father would have faked such a thing. It also seemed to explain why, when all the adults in the photograph were smiling, the little boy (the one whose shoulder the equally beaming Tenneshaw Wright had a hand upon) was crying. Wasn't there something about small children being more aware of spirits? Jane mused but, despite her total conviction, her rational mind still held a nagging doubt. That, Jane realised, was why she was here. To ask if anyone else had ever witnessed the ghost of Tenneshaw Wright.

Jane scanned the space beyond the railings once again and spotted two figures walking towards the small chapel which sat to the left of the main cemetery gates. Jane instantly opened her door but then paused to check the clock on the dashboard. It was five to twelve. She had been gone several hours; was she leaving Mikey alone for too long? This was important, she thought and, grabbing the old photograph, she hurried across the road. From the back seat of Jane's car – slightly muffled by the carrier bag and the cameras piled on top of it – a tinny voice chimed out from the strange gadget Mikey had built as a child.

'FIVE…MINUTES…DANGER…FIVE…MINUTES… DANGER…'

Jane was already on the other side of the road.

'Excuse me!?' she exclaimed as the overalled pair behind the gates disappeared into the chapel. Jane gripped the wrought iron gates with a hand and smiled as the two figures reappeared.

Both were young – early twenties Jane guessed – and both were dressed in the same grey overalls. The man was taller, with mousy brown hair tied back in a straggled pony tail and a round face which sported slab-like side burns. The woman was pretty, elfin faced and slim and, though the overalls were drab and unflattering, the effect contrasted enormously with the immaculate five point bob which her hair had been cut into. It fleetingly crossed Jane's mind how someone working in what essentially was now a wood, could manage to keep their hair that pristine. The thought was instantly forgotten as the dark-haired girl spoke.

'We're not open today.' she said flatly.

Jane smiled and nodded. 'That's okay,' she replied. 'I didn't want to take the tour – I just wanted to ask you a few questions…'

The pair exchanged quizzical glances. 'Oh,' responded the man. 'What about?'

'Well,' began Jane. 'I'm not sure how long you've worked here, but have either of you heard of a man named Marcus Tenneshaw Wright?'

The blank expressions on the pair became instantly more animated and again they exchanged a brief glance. The dark-haired woman shook her head.

'Should we have?' she said.

Jane could see they appeared to know nothing but persevered. 'Well, you may not know of the man,' she said. 'But do you know anything about his ghost?'

'His…ghost?' echoed the woman.

Jane held up a hand. 'I know it sounds odd but…' The realisation suddenly struck Jane that she must sound like some mad crank. She blushed and, now suddenly desperate to prove that she was not, she held up an apologetic hand and said: 'One second, I can explain.' With that she dashed back to her car.

Jane quickly opened the boot of her car, pulled her laptop from the top of her holdall and switched it on as she walked back to the cemetery gates: quickly accessing the email photograph which John had sent her. She was relieved to see that the pair had not moved.

'Right,' said Jane with a smile as she turned the screen to face the pair. 'This man here was a Victorian businessman and Egyptologist named Marcus Tenneshaw Wright –'

'– "Britain's most wanted"?' read the man with a frown and with that the dark-haired girl shook her head and walked away into the chapel.

'Oh, yes,' muttered Jane. 'Sorry. Ignore that. That was just one of my colleagues –' Jane grimaced, having completely forgotten the words John had scrawled across the bottom of the picture and realised that, instead of helping her story, the picture had now convinced the girl that Jane was indeed mad. 'I am sorry,' she repeated. 'Just bear with me.' She smiled as winningly as she knew how and was pleased to note that the man, at least, was not frowning at her in some condescending fashion.

'This man,' she continued, 'built Highgate Cemetery and, soon after it was built, was buried up in the Egyptian Avenue…' Jane paused, watching the man's face for any flickering signs of impending ridicule. She smiled with relief when all he did was nod blankly and went on. 'But this picture –' Jane pulled Patrick Dayville's photograph out from where she was holding it underneath the laptop and placed it beside the computer screen. '– This picture was taken about twenty years ago… Notice anyone familiar in the photo?' asked Jane.

The man's gaze met Jane's and held it for a second but Jane had difficulty in reading whether his expression conveyed indifference, understanding or plain incomprehension. Before she had time to dwell on the subject however, her attention was taken by the return of the woman. If the beautifully cut hair had seemed odd, it was nothing compared to the black, angular pistol which she now carried in her hand. Jane looked on dumbly as the woman pointed the gun squarely at her head and, with the smallest of smiles said:

'Shall we continue this inside?'

Jane, her mind numbed by the shock of seeing the dark and deadly gun barrel level with her eyes, felt frozen to the spot.

233

She wanted to blurt out that there had been some terrible mistake, and that whatever it was they were doing their secret was perfectly safe with her. She wanted to run but her muscles seemed locked and all her attention was focused on the black circle of darkness at the end of the gun which could – in a split second – end her life. It slowly dawned on Jane that an entire lifetime of familiarisation with the handgun as a movie accessory did not prepare you for the chilling reality of having the real thing pointed at your head. As the man with the sideburns began unlocking the thick chain which secured the cemetery gates, Jane was sure of only one thing: she was not about to make any sudden moves.

One second Jane was staring nervously at the wrong end of a Walther P99, the next her subconscious sense of self preservation had thrown her unceremoniously to the floor. The air was full of bellowing sound which seemed to signify that the world had exploded.

As she sprawled on the tarmac in front of the gates – blindly discarding the laptop and photograph – Jane had just enough time to deduce that it was indeed the world and not her head that had exploded before the survival instinct she had not known she possessed had her back on her feet and running as fast as she could away from the cemetery. She did not care how, she did not care why, she just thanked her lucky stars that she was free.

With all the pace her panic allowed, Jane sped away from the cemetery gates and up the wood-lined hill of Swain's Lane. She was not aware of pursuit or gun shots and only vaguely did she register the orange tint in the sky above or the violent thrashing of the trees around her. The air was full of the deafening sound of devastation but Jane's mind was occupied with one thought only: survival.

She kept on running, the shady incline now tinged the colour

234

of sunset, then quickened her pace even more when she saw that a car had stopped a little further up the hill. Jane was already pleading for help before she reached the bonnet of the stationary Jaguar and her garbled cries continued as she raced around to the driver's window and pounded frantically upon the glass.

'Help me! Help me!' Jane screamed, attempting desperately to open the car door. 'There are people at the cemetery!'

Jane stopped and wrung her hands, attempting to control herself as the driver's window whirred downwards.

'Can I help you, Miss?' asked the driver calmly.

Jane tried to stem her tears but her sobbing refused to be curtailed. She stamped her foot in frustration and gesticulated wildly down the hill. 'There are –! There's –!' she managed but her articulation had deserted her. She shook her head. 'Please let me in!' she begged.

The driver nodded, then turned his head towards his passenger. Jane had not even registered that there was somebody else inside the car but now a bruised and battered face leant over to regard her. Then the livid wound in his forehead split to reveal an eye and Jane felt herself falling.

Garvin leaned out of the window and regarded the slumped form of Jane. 'Is she dead?' he asked.

'No. She fainted,' Peter replied with a sneer. 'But she'll be dead soon enough.'

'Sounds like she was down at the cemetery,' observed Garvin. 'Do you think she knows something?'

Bradford gave a pained smile. 'Who's she going to tell?'

Garvin returned the smile then grinned up at the orange sky. 'God moves in a mysterious way, Mr Bradford.'

'Mm,' replied Peter, seemingly uninterested. 'And all to order.' He held a hand up to his bruised face, grimaced and pointed down the road. 'I need some pain killers,' he said, 'so let's get on with it.'

Garvin nodded, started the engine and drove on down the hill leaving Jane prostrate in the middle of the road. As they cleared the trees and approached the cemetery Garvin got his first clear look at the fire barrier he had painstakingly positioned and smiled to himself. The fun was just starting.

Professor Taylor and Danny Trent sat perched on the edge of the coffee table which sat in front of the sofa: watching Mikey intently for the merest sign that he was coming out of his stupor. However, in the brief time the pair had been attempting to coax their patient into conversation, the most they had got from Mikey was a vacant nod.

'What's good for shock?' asked the professor.

Danny looked blank for a moment. 'Tea?' he suggested.

Taylor shrugged and peered once again at the discoloured sky. 'I suppose we should try to find out what's going on out there,' he mused. The statement seemed more of an afterthought than a genuine show of concern.

Danny followed the professor's line of sight then glanced around the living room. 'Do you want me to look for a radio?' he asked. 'There must be one somewhere.'

'Mm,' replied Taylor distantly. He reached into his briefcase and pulled out the leather bound book which Mikey had left with Danny at the British Museum. 'I'm going to try asking him about this again, I think.'

'Do you think there's any point – I mean – in his state?' Danny hitched a thumb at the impassive Mikey.

The professor shrugged. 'If it's shock, he's bound to snap out of it sooner or later and, with whatever it is that's going on outside, I'd rather not stay around here for too long…' The professor sighed, tapped the book and looked earnestly at his understudy. 'I just have to get an answer, Danny.'

Danny nodded, stood up and went in search of a radio. He had known the professor since he had first joined the British Museum's research staff but, in all that time, he had never seen the Head of the Egyptology Department become quite so animated about a subject before.

With Professor Taylor advising the Police on the Sacrificial Murder case it had been left up to his junior researcher to cover for him at the museum and, because of that, it had been Danny – not Taylor – whom Mikey had encountered on his visit. So it was not until the professor had returned to check on Danny's progress that the truth behind the book had come out.

Taylor, an archeologist with over forty years experience had, like Danny before him, flicked half-heartedly through the leather bound tome: initially satisfied that Danny's hypothesis had been the correct one – the book was a fake. But then his cursory gaze had happened to fall upon one particular illustration.

The effect on Taylor had been uncharacteristic. The veteran professor, so stoic, rational and matter-of-fact about the most exquisite and rare of artefacts, had one moment been briskly skimming pages, while the next he seemed suddenly frozen. After the same immobile state had continued long enough for Danny to firstly wonder if his mentor was suffering some form of heart attack and then enquire if he was alright, the professor had looked up, mouthed the words: 'Oh my god!' then rushed off to his office with Danny in close tow.

Puzzled, Danny had seated himself in the worn leather chair before the professor's cluttered desk and watched in bemusement as Taylor attacked his book-stuffed shelves. Muttering: 'No… No…No…' He proceeded to flail through his extensive private library until, with a triumphant 'YES!' He grabbed a thin volume from the shelf and threw himself into the high-backed chair behind his desk.

'Oh. My. God, Danny,' beamed the professor, seeming to notice his junior for the first time. He slapped the book Danny had given him with a loud whack then shook his head, chuckling at some unspoken joke.

'Have you found something?' Danny enquired. He pointed at the book.

Taylor returned a playful look, held up a silencing hand then opened the book he had taken from the shelf. He leafed through it quickly, found the page he was looking for and hunched over to study it intently: his head shaking rhythmically as he did so. He looked up suddenly.

'Ever hear of the El-Quirassi dig?' Taylor asked, the same joyous expression on his face. Danny shook his head and the Professor's smile grew even wider. 'Why should you?' he chuckled. 'And why should anyone remember it?'

With one hand the professor span the book he had been studying and thrust it across the table for Danny to look at. While he did so, Taylor returned to ransacking his shelves.

Keeping one wary eye on the professor's abnormal, dervish-like behaviour, Danny checked the cover of the slim volume before returning to the article which had so absorbed the professor. The book was an obscure compendium compiled for the British Museum and had been printed in 1963. The article in question was entitled 'The El-Quirassi Octagon' and reported the accidental discovery of an ancient site buried in the desert several miles outside Memphis in Lower Egypt. Danny was just perusing a murky photograph which showed two archaeologists standing by a deep trench when the professor flew back into his chair with two more books grasped in his hands.

'Never throw anything away, Danny!' Taylor said merrily – waving a hand at his shelves. 'You never know when you might need them.' The professor chuckled again, opened one of the books before him and quickly flicked through it.

'Do you think this book might be important then?' Danny asked. 'Even though it's fake?'

'Fake?' echoed Taylor, half to himself. The professor now had all the books open before him and flitted his gaze quickly between them. He gave a deep sigh, rubbed his face with his hands then grinned back at Danny. 'Fake?! I don't think so.' One by one, the professor turned the books before him so that they faced his understudy. Danny, still holding the compendium, looked on.

'Now then.' began Professor Taylor. 'That article you have there concerns the discovery of the El-Quirassi site in 1962. If I remember rightly the locals were digging irrigation trenches and hit a glass channel.'

'Glass?' repeated Danny. He looked once again at the picture from the article. It had not been apparent from the photograph but the caption beneath stated that the central channel of the trench in the picture was indeed made of glass.

The professor was nodding. 'A trench made of fused sand – about two yards wide and several yards under the desert… Now,' continued Taylor, 'the French team that were involved in the dig worked for about two, three years on the site.' The professor held his arms wide. 'They found that the trench was actually a huge channel – miles in circumference – and described a perfect octagon. They also deduced from the depth underground that the glass octagon would have been on the surface no later than 2600 BC – which is around the time of?…' The professor raised a brow at his junior.

'Er,' began Danny. 'The…um, Forth Dynasty.'

Taylor nodded. 'Yes, and around the time of the first step pyramid… So, as you can imagine, the French team were a little perplexed to find an octagon marked in the desert when

239

no other structures of that type existed anywhere else in Egypt – and certainly not at that time. So, once they had found what they considered to be an octagonal boundary they proceeded to dig in the very centre of it: and found nothing.'

Danny frowned. 'So it was just the channel?'

Professor Taylor grinned slyly and shook his head, tapping the central book before him. 'The man in charge of the dig, er...' he craned his neck to read the text before him while Danny leaned forward.

'Jean Mirez?' offered Danny, picking out the name from the French text.

'Yes, that was the man,' agreed the professor. 'Well, Monsieur Mirez, after fruitlessly digging for months, got lucky. Someone from his team literally stumbled over some wood sticking out from the sand close to the right hand side of the boundary and, when they dug down, they found that a massive excavation had taken place.'

Danny's frown deepened. 'What, someone else had already been there?'

Again, Professor Taylor answered Danny's query will a knowing smile. 'Precisely,' he said. 'And from the wood, its closeness to the surface and various bits and pieces they found, Mirez was able to work out the size of the original excavation and a pretty accurate date for when it had been carried out.'

'Which was?'

'Well, the size of the excavation was roughly similar in circumference to that of the great Giza pyramid of Khufu – but octagonal, not square – and the date it had been excavated was, he estimated, somewhere in the first part of the nineteenth century.'

'So some Victorian had been there first?'

'Mm,' replied the professor. 'And all that was left behind were the rotting panels used to shore up the sides of the original dig and a countless number of untouched, ancient grave sites surrounding the excavation.' Taylor leant his elbows on the table, steepled his fingers and rested his chin upon them. 'So, as I'm sure you can understand, Mirez was furious to discover that an earlier archeologist was not only there before him, but had also vandalised the site – completely removing whatever structure had been there.'

'After working on it for two years I think I'd be a bit upset,' agreed Danny.

'Quite,' said Taylor. He could not contain his glee however and grinned broadly. 'Now,' he continued, 'let's move on to this.' The professor pointed to the central book and turned a page. 'These are the completed El-Quirassi field studies of Jean Mirez, and here you can see the plan he made of the entire site.'

Danny looked, noting the vast octagonal boundary, the dotted grave sites and a smaller octagonal outline close to the right border.

'Now look at this.' Professor Taylor turned a page from the book Mikey Dayville had brought in to reveal a plan map identical to the French one. All except for the position of a temple which sat where Mirez had found nothing but a shored up hole. 'Notice any similarity?' asked the smiling professor.

'Are you saying that this book is actually Tenneshaw Wright's site notes?' asked Danny. 'But what about the cartouche? This 'Hathnos' figure that's mentioned?'

The professor held up a hand. 'It's a little too early to say definitively either way but, despite the fact that Hathnos is mentioned here and nowhere else, if you consider the relevant facts, I do find this book compelling.' Taylor picked up the third book he had taken from his shelf and passed it to Danny. 'That is one of Marcus Tenneshaw Wright's field books from his trip to Heliopolis.'

Danny turned the old book over in his hands and found that

the leather bound cover was identical to the one which Mikey had brought in. He flicked through it briefly.

'Now,' continued the professor, 'I'm no hand writing expert but wouldn't you say that the writing style in that book was similar?'

Danny placed the book beside the first one and, examining the annotations contained in Mikey's book, gave a grudging nod. 'Yes, but… Couldn't it still be a fake? I mean it's too unique. Completely out of step with the rest of that period.'

Taylor's grin was even broader. 'The only reason the El-Quirassi site is not up there among the great finds of Egyptology is because Mirez found very little. The glass octagon is unique but, because Mirez could find nothing else apart from an old hole in the ground, the whole site passed into archaeological history as nothing more than a curiosity.' The professor wagged a finger. 'But somebody was there beforehand and took whatever evidence there could have been away. Why couldn't that somebody have been Tenneshaw Wright?' Taylor shrugged, picked up Mikey's book and leant back in his chair, flicking through it with glee.

'But surely we'd know about it,' persisted Danny. 'Tenneshaw Wright would have given whatever he found to the British Museum wouldn't he? He did help to found this place after all.' Danny frowned across the desk but found that the professor appeared to have frozen again.

'Oh, dear,' said Taylor slowly. He had been flicking through Mikey's book with joy but now, as he looked across at Danny, there was nothing but shock on his face. 'You know the sacrificial axes that were stolen were part of the Tenneshaw Wright collection don't you?' he said.

Danny nodded. 'Yes, you've been helping the Police because of it.'

'Well…' The professor, still clutching the book sat up in his chair: he looked uncomfortable. 'We've always known that the axes were sacrificial but they've never been attributed – we've never been able to place them to a site.' Danny gave a half nod while Taylor turned the book around. 'These are the ones, Danny,' he said, pointing to an illustration in Mikey's book of two delicate axes.

The professor had instantly contacted Inspector Faber with the information and both he and Danny were quickly whisked off to aid the police in interviewing Mikey. It had been soon after that the news had come through of a confession for the murders but a dubious Faber had still been keen for the professor's help. Like Sergeant Rose before him, Inspector Faber thought Fletcher was far too keen in off-loading his murder case. Faber had his own leads to follow and did not want to get too side-tracked.

As far as Danny was concerned, their interview with Mikey had one objective: to find a lead for the Sacrificial Murders. He was becoming increasingly aware however, that Professor Taylor's priorities lay elsewhere. The man seemed to have become besotted with the information he had gleaned from the book and now his only concern seemed to be to find out where and how Mikey had obtained it. Although the professor had not voiced any such thoughts, Danny felt sure that Taylor was vainly hoping that Mikey could, somehow, point him in the direction of a missing Egyptian temple.

Standing in Mikey's kitchen, Danny spotted the red light bulb which sat above the basement door. He pushed the door open, stared down the half shadowed steps that descended into the basement then looked for a light switch. Perhaps, he mused as he wandered down to the darkroom, Mikey had hidden a site as big as the Giza pyramids down here.

Danny returned a few moments later clutching the radio he

had found and plugged it into a socket in the kitchen. He sighed. As in the basement, there appeared to be no electricity anywhere in the house and no batteries inside the radio. He cursed silently, turned to go back into the living room, then made straight for the front door at the sound of frantic knocking.

On the doorstep stood a grime-stained, wide-eyed woman with short blonde hair. She carried a walking stick in one hand, a bag in the other and pushed past Danny the second he opened the door.

'Where's Mikey?' she asked brusquely as she passed. She flicked at the dirt on her shoulders and her eyes flitted nervously on the space beyond the door as Danny closed it.

'Are you a friend?' replied Danny but the woman had already turned and stepped into the living room.

'My name is Catherine,' came the reply. 'I'm – Who are you?'

The question was directed at Professor Taylor who rose sheepishly from where he had been sitting beside Mikey. 'I'm s-sorry,' he stuttered. 'My name's Taylor. Er... Mr Dayville is unwell.'

Catherine took one look at Mikey, crouched down beside him, then focused her attention to the book the professor was holding. There was a marked expression of distaste on her face and she stabbed a finger at the professor.

'What the hell is that?!' she demanded.

'This...?' The question clearly made the professor uncomfortable.

'It's a book which Mikey brought to us a few days ago,' explained Danny from the doorway.

'Ah,' replied Catherine. She checked Mikey's pulse, patted his hand and stood up. 'So it's that book.' She regarded Mikey for a moment longer then flicked her gaze between the two men. 'You must be from the British Museum.'

Professor Taylor walked around the coffee table, holding the book before him. 'Do you know anything about how Mr Dayville acquired this book?' he asked hopefully.

Catherine frowned. 'Please,' she said earnestly, 'could you put that down?'

The request was a curious one but Taylor, noting the woman's evident distress, placed the book onto the coffee table. Catherine took a deep breath, grabbed the book with both hands, and limped quickly to the windows at the rear of the room with her arms outstretched. She threw the book unceremoniously onto the floor and walked quickly back to the dumb-struck pair.

'I'm sorry,' she said, shaking her head. 'But something very bad is happening out there...' She indicated the broken front windows then hitched a thumb towards the book at the back of the room. '...And that book is not right,' she added.

The statement was met with blank incomprehension and Catherine sighed. 'I don't expect you to understand,' she continued. 'But all hell has broken loose out there... And I mean that literally, not figuratively.'

'Is it an explosion of some sort?' asked Danny, missing Catherine's point. He patted the radio he was still carrying. 'We heard the bang but it seems to have taken out the mains – I can't get the radio to work.'

Catherine stared at Danny intently for a second. 'The sound you heard...' she said, speaking clearly and slowly. '...Was hell arriving. On earth. Do you understand? Or have you not taken a good look at the sky out there?'

Professor Taylor reached out and patted Catherine reassuringly on the shoulder. 'My dear lady,' he said soothingly. 'Try not to distress yourself.'

'Yes,' agreed Danny, adopting the same sympathetic tone. 'It was unnerving for us all. Mr Dayville even started seeing people in the sky before the shock got too much for him.'

Catherine dropped her head for a moment and when she looked up there appeared to be a calmer air about her. She gave a short sigh. 'Thank you both for your concern,' she said. 'I appreciate it. But, perhaps it might be best if I introduce myself before this conversation goes any further. My name is Catherine Robson. I'm a psychic and a Paranormal Investigator.' She gently removed the professor's consoling hand and moved to stand by the still impassive Mikey. 'Mr Dayville came to see me right after he visited you at the British Museum. He had a problem he wanted me to help him with.' Catherine shook her head slowly before regarding the two archaeologists. 'So Mikey didn't tell you how he found that book,' she said.

'It was one of the reasons we came here today,' replied the professor eagerly. 'Did he tell you?'

Catherine sighed again. 'He did. But, even if I told you, I doubt you'd believe me.'

'It's vitally important I find out how Mr Dayville acquired the book,' insisted the professor. 'It could be the find of the century. Now, I don't care if he stole it –'

'– He didn't steal the book Mr Taylor,' Catherine interrupted with a shake of her head. 'He found it by the murder sight on Hampstead Heath: in the exact place a ghost told him to look for it…' She nodded at the sardonic smiles. 'I know,' she said, 'that sounds quite preposterous, doesn't it? Yet, even so, that's the truth of the matter.' She returned the same smile. 'Just as when Mikey told you there were people in the sky he wasn't joking, and when I say that hell on earth is here I'm not joking either.' Catherine became serious. 'I don't say it's rational. I don't say it's easily explainable, but then the paranormal so rarely is. But, if you can put your conventional logic aside for one moment, you might begin to understand that I am right.

And I pray that you do, because whatever is going on outside is going to get worse before it gets better.'

'Well…' began Danny. 'That's, um…'

'Miss Robson,' said Taylor. 'I'm a professor of archaeology and, in my time, I have studied many of the superstitions of the ancient world. Now you don't seriously expect me to believe that some form of – I don't know (the professor waved his hands) – witchcraft or some such nonsense is responsible for the explosion we heard?'

Catherine shrugged. 'Frankly, professor,' she replied. 'I don't know what caused the explosion. All I know is that there is a barrier of fire surrounding us and that it's full of spiritual energy. How? I don't know. Why? I don't know.' She patted Mikey on the shoulder. 'But I think Mikey does – that's why I came here.'

'And the book, Miss Robson?' The professor sneered. 'Is that full of spiritual energy too?'

'Yes, professor. It is,' Catherine replied with no sign of chagrin. She picked up the bag she had left on the floor and rummaged through it. 'You're perfectly entitled to play with it as much as you want, Professor,' she said, looking up. 'Just don't bring it anywhere near Mikey.'

The two men from the British Museum looked on as Catherine fished out a handful of candles from her bag, a soot stained incense burner and finally what looked like a strange variation on a chess board. Professor Taylor shook his head.

'This is ridiculous,' he muttered. 'I think we should find Sergeant Rose.'

'Didn't he say we should wait here?' replied Danny.

'That sounds like sensible advice,' observed Catherine. 'I really don't think it's safe out there.' To that the professor snorted and walked towards the back of the room. 'Please make sure he doesn't bring that book down here,' insisted

Catherine to Danny.

'Er, sure,' Danny replied slowly. He watched Professor Taylor as he stared from the broken rear widows, then returned his attention to the curious activity of the psychic. 'Can I ask what you're doing?' he said.

Catherine had unfolded the 'chess' board and sat it on the corner of the coffee table. She was in the process of securing candles onto the board and briefly glanced over her shoulder at Danny. 'Wait and see,' she said.

Danny did not have to wait long. As soon as Catherine had secured six candles to the board she lit them and placed the incense burner in their centre. Kneeling by the table, Catherine placed her hands lightly on the edge of the board and closed her eyes. A pungent aroma struck Danny's nostrils then he took a shocked step back as Mikey yelped and jumped up from the sofa.

'WHAT THE FUCK!?' yelled Mikey. The shocked expression he wore turned to a frown as he regarded the others in the room. 'What the hell is going on?!'

Catherine stood up and placed a hand on Mikey's own. 'You had another episode,' she said gently. 'Do you remember what happened?'

Mikey scratched his head, his frown deepening as he looked at the others and took in the broken windows and shattered television. 'Oh, god!' he moaned. 'It was him: that damn preacher again!' Mikey pointed to the front windows. 'And then... Then...' Mikey's voice trailed away as memories flooded back into his mind. He walked quickly to the front windows and peered up at the sky. 'Ooh my god,' he muttered. 'They are there.'

Both Danny and Catherine joined Mikey at the window. 'Can you see them?' Catherine asked.

'Oh yes,' sighed Mikey, downcast as he watched the drifting

248

spirits spiralling in the sky. 'And I don't think we've got much time.'

Jane woke to find herself bound at the wrists and ankles. For a second her addled wits transported her back to her terrifying ordeal at the Chronicle and reflexively she screamed at the top of her voice. The sound echoed around her, shook those old recollections from her head and, as her senses focused on her surroundings, Jane realised she was laying on the cold flagstone floor of a small church.

From outside came the sound of an engine throbbing, the murmur of voices and footsteps on stone. Jane twisted towards the noise until she could see the gothic-arched doorway to the chapel then shuffled herself into a sitting position against the back of a pew. As she did so the doorway opened and the shadow of a man stood framed against a sunset sky.

'So,' said the man, walking forwards. 'You're awake.'

Jane frowned, instantly recognising the man as the one who was driving the Jaguar she had encountered earlier.

'Sorry about the ropes,' said Garvin conversationally. He crouched down in front of Jane and shrugged. 'But we wouldn't want you running away again, now would we?'

Jane took a deep breath and attempted to regain some measure of composure. She guessed that she was inside the small chapel at the entrance to Highgate Cemetery but could make little sense of anything else which was occurring. She voiced the only question which sprang to mind.

'What the hell is going on?'

Garvin smiled in response. 'The end of the world,' he replied 'Or the beginning… It's all a matter of perspective really.'

'The end of the world…' repeated Jane slowly. For a second she thought it was all a sick joke then she remembered the massive explosion which had thrown her to the floor. Jane craned her neck to see an orange tint visible through the narrow chapel windows.

'That's right,' said Garvin, following her gaze. 'Now, to business...' He stood up and walked over to a small wooden table beside the door: returning with Jane's laptop. There was a crack across the bottom corner of the screen from when Jane had dropped it but the computer appeared to be working perfectly. It still displayed the picture of Tenneshaw Wright.

As Garvin settled the machine on the floor in front of her, two more people walked in. The first was the dark-haired girl who had pulled the gun on Jane earlier but it was the second figure which Jane could not wrench her eyes from.

'I can't get in,' announced Bradford despondently. He rubbed at the sides of his temples then focused his attention on the wide-eyed figure of Jane. 'What's she said?' he asked.

Garvin stood and dusted off his hands. 'She's only just come to,' he replied. Bradford nodded. 'Where's Åpep?' asked Garvin.

To this Bradford frowned. 'God knows.' He pointed to the dark haired girl. 'Jennifer sent some people over to collect him but it seems the Police got there first. He's escaped.'

Garvin digested this news. 'He'll make for here, surely?'

'I don't fucking know, Garvin,' spat Peter. He frowned and massaged his forehead again. 'But I shouldn't fucking need him to get in!'

'He's probably feeding, Peter,' observed Jennifer calmly. She placed a gentle hand on Bradford's shoulder. 'We should have guessed he would want to.'

'Yes, well,' muttered Bradford. 'We'll search for him later. He can't have gone far.' Peter gave a deep sigh and refocused his attention on Jane. 'What were you doing with my picture?' he demanded.

Jane, still deeply disturbed by Peter's frightful appearance, looked blank. She shook her head and looked to Garvin for guidance.

In response Garvin fished a hand into his jacket pocket and pulled out the black and white photograph which Mikey's father had taken. He held it in front of Jane and tapped a finger at the small boy.

'That damn picture!' growled Bradford, looking on. 'How did you get it?'

Jane regarded the miserable child in the photograph then turned her attention to the man with the Frankenstein forehead. 'That's you?!' she answered, awe-struck.

'Who did you think it was?!' retorted Bradford. He took a step closer, his body tense. 'I don't have time to fuck around with you! Where did you get it from?!'

'I…' began Jane. She shook her head. 'I don't understand,' she replied – emotion plain in her voice.

Garvin sighed. 'Look, love,' he said, patting Jane's knee. 'Here's how it goes. You tell us everything you know about these pictures and what brought you down here or I'm going to cripple you.' He offered Jane a mirthless smile and removed his hand to pull a large silver pistol from beneath his jacket. He pressed the barrel of the gun against Jane's leg.

'I'm a – a journalist,' stuttered Jane. She found Garvin's matter-of-fact tone chilling and had no doubt his threat was serious.

'And?…' prompted Jennifer.

'My boyfriend found a book on the heath which he thought belonged to a man named Marcus – something – Wright.' Jane nodded her head towards her laptop. 'That man there.'

Jane's statement was met with silence but the information appeared to strike a chord with her interrogators.

'Was it a brown leather book?' asked Bradford.

Jane nodded. 'He said he found it near the murder site on

251

Hampstead Heath but…' Tears were beginning to well in Jane's eyes. 'But you have to understand he's not been well. He brought me that photograph too but he's not been himself.' Jane tried to sniff back her tears. 'He didn't know it was you in the picture; all Mikey was trying to prove was that he'd seen a ghost.' Jane hung her head but suddenly it was wrenched back and the hideous countenance of Peter Bradford was inches from her face.

'Your boyfriend's seen this man!?' Bradford spat, jabbing a finger at Jane's laptop.

'No!' wailed Jane, distraught. 'No! A preacher! The ghost of a preacher!'

Peter released his grip on Jane's hair and stood up. He frowned down at their sobbing captive then waved a hand at Garvin. 'Get back,' he said.

Garvin picked up the laptop and moved away, re-holstering his gun in the process. He stood beside Jennifer and watched as the eye in Peter's forehead fluttered open.

'I want to know where I can find this boyfriend of yours,' Bradford said coldly.

Peter's icy inference was not lost on Jane and, despite her terror and total confusion, she instantly sensed that something was very wrong. With foreboding she locked her gaze on Garvin – expecting to find him taking aim – but instead found him looking on with mild amusement. Jane coughed, her throat suddenly dry then tried to catch her breath to scream when she saw Bradford's vile eye trained upon her.

'Where's your fucking boyfriend?' demanded Bradford.

Jane gagged and toppled over, her bound limbs thrashing as steam began to rise from her body.

Mikey had raced around the house searching for any camera which Jane had not taken with her and piled them, along with his radio and any other piece of electronic equipment he could find in the centre of his living room. He gazed down at his haul, sifted through it and sighed.

'It's not enough,' he said.

'To build these 'things' the preacher told you to?' asked Catherine.

Mikey nodded. 'I need more cameras, more lenses – more everything.'

Catherine, Danny and Professor Taylor were sitting on Mikey's sofa. The professor felt extremely dubious about Mikey's current activity and repeated the same question he had asked only a few minutes before.

'My boy,' he said gently. 'We've all seen that you have obviously been under a lot of strain but… Do you honestly believe that this 'preacher' fellow is telling you to build things in your dreams?'

Mikey was crouched beside his pile of junk. He shrugged and smiled politely at the professor's condescension. 'You're right, professor. I have been under a lot of strain recently. But, whether you believe it or not, that honestly is the truth of the matter. I can't explain it – I certainly don't know what these things are that I've got to build – but, for some reason, they are sitting in my mind.'

Danny inched forwards on the sofa. Unlike the professor's entrenched disbelief towards Mikey's supernatural experiences, his younger colleague found Mikey's frankness compelling. 'Do you have no idea at all what these things are?' he asked.

'It's like…' Mikey stood up, gesticulating with his hands as he paced before his guests. 'It's like travelling a dark road. I know the general direction I'm heading in but, until I get there, I can't be certain of the detail. I know what I need so that I can construct these things but, at the moment I have no idea of their purpose. Does that make any sense?'

Catherine and Danny nodded. Professor Taylor shook his head.

'I really do believe –' the professor began, but his sentence was cut short by the sound of a loud voice from outside.

The four moved to the shattered front windows and watched as a grey van rolled slowly along the ash covered road. On its roof was mounted a small black loudspeaker from which issued a grim announcement.

'Attention. There has been radioactive contamination of this area,' the speaker barked. 'All residents who have not received their anti-radiation tablets should proceed immediately to Parliament Hill... If you do not know the location of Parliament Hill, you are advised to follow this van... Attention. There has been radioactive contamination –'

'So the sergeant was wrong,' said Danny. 'That explosion was atomic.'

Mikey shook his head. 'They're lying. I don't know what those people in the van are playing at, but that orange sky has not been caused by fallout. I don't think there is any radiation.'

'Young man,' chided the professor breathlessly. 'What on earth makes you believe that, in a situation such as this, somebody would bother creating such a hoax? It's not logical!' There was a note of hysteria in his voice. 'It...makes...no... sense!' Taylor continued, slapping his right hand into his left palm to emphasise the words. 'The only nonsense I've heard today has come from you!'

Mikey emitted a short, mirthless laugh, ran a hand through his hair and looked out onto the street. Cautiously, people were beginning to exit their homes and joined the massing throng behind the van. Mikey leant against the window sill and sighed. 'Professor,' he said. 'I've already told you what both Catherine and I can see in the sky and do you know what?'

Mikey craned his neck for a moment and looked up. 'Yep,' he said, 'they're still up there: thousands of phantoms, whizzing around. And do you know what I see when I look at those people following that van? I see the Pied Piper. I don't know what's going on but, if you want to stay alive, I'd suggest you stay here.'

The professor snorted. 'I think you have a very vivid imagination, my boy… And it's probably going to get you into trouble if you don't start listening to reason.' He patted Mikey on the arm. 'Now, if you don't mind, I think I'll go and see what's really going on. Danny?'

Waving his understudy to follow, Professor Taylor turned, left the room and opened the front door. Danny hung back.

'It couldn't hurt to find out what's going on, could it?' Danny said, indecision in his tone.

Mikey's face showed obvious concern. 'I really wouldn't go, Danny,' he said. 'I wish I could explain it better, but –'

'Danny!' snapped the professor from the doorway. 'Come on!'

Without waiting to see if Danny was following, Professor Taylor stomped out of the house and turned right to follow the receding crowd down the street. With a pained expression, Danny dutifully followed. Catherine and Mikey watched disconsolately from the window but, after the pair had walked mere yards along the pavement, they stopped in their tracks beside an ash covered car.

'Oh my God!' exclaimed the professor.

By the time Catherine and Mikey had joined them to find out the cause of the Professor's distress, Danny had opened the door of the car. Sprawled behind the steering wheel was the dead body of Sergeant Rose. He was a pitiful sight: his face a mask of silent pain, his jacket and trousers stained with grime and bloody vomit.

'Oh, god,' muttered Catherine. She put a hand to her mouth and turned away.

'Shit,' mouthed Mikey.

Whatever had killed Rose had been agonising. His body was still contorted with the pain of his death and his still open eyes gazed back vacantly at the group. His mouth was open and bloody and his lips were almost black. Danny shook his head and re-closed the door.

'You see! You see!' Professor Taylor yelled at Mikey. 'We are going to die if we don't get help! Can't you see that now?!'

'Professor I –' Mikey began but Taylor dismissed his placation with a sharp wave of his hand.

'No more!' cried the professor. He turned away. 'Come on Danny, we have to catch that van.'

Once more Danny wavered as his superior marched off. He opened his mouth to speak, shook his head as if in apology and followed the Professor.

'Be careful,' said Mikey.

Though the van had now disappeared, there were still people wandering from their houses at the far end of the street. Catherine and Mikey looked on as Danny and the professor caught up with the stragglers and joined the procession.

'What do you think will happen to them, Mikey?' Catherine asked.

Mikey shook his head a fraction. 'I don't know,' he said with a sigh. 'But, if radiation didn't kill the sergeant, what did?'

'You don't think the professor's right, surely?'

Mikey looked up at the sky. 'No. You and I both know something far stranger than radiation is sitting up there...' Mikey crossed his arms and turned to the psychic. 'I need to get some parts, Catherine.' he said. 'Do you want to come along?'

Catherine frowned. 'For this thing you have to make? Okay,

but where?'

Mikey pointed in the direction of Hampstead High Street. 'There's an electrical shop up there. If we're lucky it will have just what I need but –'

Catherine held up a hand. '– Don't say it,' she replied. 'Let's just hope for luck.'

Mikey nodded and led the way to the high street.

Chapter Thirteen

Fuelled by fear, Professor Taylor raced through the procession so quickly that it was all Danny could do to keep up with him. The professor's nervous energy was such that his obvious panic rippled through the crowd and soon the whole procession began to speed up alongside him. Despite numerous pleas from Danny to slow down, the professor kept up his rapid pace until, after zigzagging their way through several streets, the grey van finally came into sight.

'How... How far do you think Parliament Hill is, Danny?' the professor puffed. His pace had slowed now and his face was a deep crimson. Breathing hard he stopped and dug a hand into his ribs. 'Damn stitch,' he muttered with a pained expression.

Danny, less fatigued by their exertions, looked ahead to where the rapidly advancing crowd were cramming the street behind the van. The previously subdued and ordered procession had become a swift march but their pace was now hampered by the van's slow progress. There were shouts for the van to speed up and, through the rising noise of the crowd, dull clangs could be heard as the more impatient began to strike the van itself in frustration. Some people however, were turning away from the van's congested path and heading down a side street.

'I don't know how far Parliament Hill is for sure,' Danny said in answer to the professor's query. 'But I think it's somewhere on the heath.'

They walked warily towards what was quickly becoming a rabble behind the van and in the process they drew level with the side road. Beyond the short, tree-lined street, park land could be seen.

'I think that may be a short cut, professor,' observed Danny, pointing as more people broke away from the main crowd to follow the same route.

Professor Taylor, still puffing and holding his side, made straight for the side road. 'Not as fit as I used to be,' he said with a grimace. 'Any short cut is welcome.'

The pair turned away from the increasingly agitated mass of people and followed the smaller procession until they reached the heath. From over the rooftops the crowd by the van could still be heard as a steadily rising growl and above this noise the loudspeaker – which had continued to deliver the same message – now suddenly changed its tone.

'PLEASE PROCEED IN AN ORDERLY FASHION… PLEASE!… LOOK, KEEP AWAY FROM THE FUCKING VAN!… I'M WARNING YOU!…'

'Sounds like it's getting ugly back there,' observed Danny.

'I can't say I'm surprised,' replied the professor. He shook his head. 'It's always the common people who are the unsung voices of history, Danny. Remember that, the next time you unearth a royal tomb.'

They were at the base of a steep grass verge which rose up to a straggled line of beach saplings and bushes. There was a dry mud path worn into the verge and, following the other wanderers, Danny and the Professor climbed up onto Hampstead Heath.

Instantly, the ground dropped away again and the lush panorama of the heath was revealed: its tree lines and grasslands rolling in gentle waves towards the distant, half-hidden brickwork of Highgate. It was a beautiful sight, despite the strange, sunset sky and the two men stopped for a moment while Taylor continued to catch his breath. The thin crowd was heading down a long and shallow incline towards a curve of mature beech trees and their massive shapes all but obscured the orange-lit glint of the ponds which lay beyond. Danny's attention however, was focused on the more distant southern horizon.

'Professor,' he mused, 'does this seem right to you?' Danny pointed to the orange glow in the sky which, now that he could see for some distance, seemed to end, curtain-like in a line beyond the heath.

'Don't you start with that nonsense,' warned Professor Taylor. 'Mr Dayville's ravings were quite enough.'

Danny frowned at the sky. He was the first to admit that he knew next to nothing about nuclear explosions but were they really supposed to sit, static on the horizon like that? 'But –' he began before Taylor cut him off.

'– Danny, that's enough!' the professor snapped. 'This situation is bad enough without you starting some – some –' the professor waved his hands in agitation. 'Well, you know what I mean. As soon as we get to Parliament Hill we'll know exactly what's going on so just save your questions 'till then.' Danny gave a grudging nod in response and the pair walked on in silence, following the others as they tramped down towards the ponds.

They passed through a thick tree line to reach the water's edge and saw that some people were crowding around the base of one of the trees before moving on. Still following the others, Danny and the professor walked closer until they saw that a middle-aged man, his clothes ripped and tattered was leant against the base of the tree. Massaging a bloody, bandaged leg, the man was in heated discussion with another party of wanderers and, though they could hear nothing of the conversation, it was obvious from the man's continually shaking head that he seemed to disagree with the crowd. With the path between the trees and the pond less than a few yards wide it was difficult to avoid passing the dishevelled figure but, as they drew nearer, Danny suddenly recognised the man.

'Inspector?!' shouted Danny.

For a moment Inspector Fletcher looked surprised but that was quickly replaced by a rueful smile. With difficulty, he pulled himself up the tree until he was standing. He tested his bandaged leg against the ground then hobbled towards the archaeologists.

'I was making my way over to you,' Fletcher explained. 'Until this bloody leg got the better of me. What are you doing here? Where's Rose?'

'There's been a nuclear explosion, inspector,' replied Professor Taylor. 'We were following these people towards safety.'

'You haven't taken any pills, have you?!' The inspector's tone was urgent.

'No,' Danny replied. 'We understood from the announcements that we'd be given them once we got to Parliament Hill.'

'Announcements?' echoed the inspector. 'Was this from some people in a grey van?' The archaeologists frowned and nodded. 'I'll tell you what I've been telling all these other poor bastards.' The inspector indicated the few people that were still passing by. 'Don't take any tablets from those people, understand? I don't know why, but I think they're handing out poison.'

'Poison? No, no, inspector,' replied the professor. 'They're going to give us anti-radiation tablets.'

'There is no such thing as an 'anti-radiation tablet', professor,' said Fletcher sternly. 'Take my word for it. These grey van bastards are handing out poison tablets – Highgate is littered with their victims.'

'Pied Piper,' muttered Danny to himself. Only minutes ago they had trailed dutifully in the wake of one of these vans.

'But?… Are you sure, inspector?' Professor Taylor's face

261

was contorted with anguish. 'You mean there's no hope?'

'There's hope as long as you don't take the tablets, professor,' Fletcher replied. 'I know enough about poison to know its effects when I see it.' The inspector pointed to his mouth. 'Black lips,' he said, 'you can't mistake it for anything else.'

'Black...' Professor Taylor put a hand to his face. 'Oh my, poor Sergeant Rose...'

'What about Sergeant Rose?' Fletcher asked but Taylor simply shook his head and stared at the ground.

'He went to check Hampstead High Street, inspector.' Danny explained. 'We found him in his car a little later, he...' Danny paused and shook his head. 'His lips were black.' he said with sadness.

Fletcher nodded, his features a pained mask. 'Fuckers!' he spat, his gaze hardening as he looked back across the heath. 'And what about this Dayville character? Did Rose think he was involved?'

It took Danny a second to remember why it was they had gone to visit Mikey. 'The Sacrificial Murders? No, the sergeant didn't seem to think so, but...' Danny hesitated. 'Mikey seems to think he knows what's going on.'

'Does he now,' replied Fletcher.

'He thinks he can see people, inspector,' added the professor with disdain. He pointed to the sky. 'Up there.'

A smile almost broke the inspector's stern expression. 'People, eh?' Fletcher gazed up to regard the orange glow for a moment. 'Yesterday, I would have dismissed that as the ravings of a lunatic but, after what's happened today...' Fletcher shook his head.

'You can't seriously believe that, inspector?!' exclaimed Taylor. 'It makes no sense whatsoever!'

Fletcher winced as he tried to change his stance and hopped

for a moment before Professor Taylor moved in to support him. Spotting a thick branch lying at the base of one of the elms, Danny quickly retrieved it and presented it to the inspector as a makeshift crutch. Fletcher tested his weight against it, thanked Danny and took a few steps.

'Well, c'mon,' Fletcher said moving back the way the archaeologists had come.

'Where are we going, inspector?' Danny asked.

'I want to see this Mr Dayville, and I need to check out the Hampstead Police Station,' the inspector replied. 'If Dayville says he knows something, I want to know it what it is.'

Professor Taylor fell in step beside the limping inspector. 'He's quite mad, inspector.' he said.

Fletcher nodded. 'Do you know what madness is, professor?' he asked rhetorically. 'I'll tell you. Madness is a lone gunmen killing everybody he can find in a police station. Madness is an orange sky, a wall of fire and a street littered with poisoned corpses. This is a day of madness, professor – and perhaps for that you need to find a madman to make sense of it all.'

Professor Taylor sighed. 'He says a ghost is telling him to build things, inspector.'

Fletcher smiled. 'Now I'm really intrigued,' he replied.

Hampstead High Street was familiar to Mikey for all the wrong reasons. It reminded him of a war zone. The dereliction which had shocked Sergeant Rose still remained but now the ash covered cars and the shattered buildings had been joined by the corpses of countless people: each one black lipped and contorted.

'I told the others that hell had arrived on earth,' Catherine said. 'But realising it isn't the same as experiencing it.' She cast a nervous glance at Mikey. 'What could have done this?'

Mikey shook his head and surveyed the High Street. The same pitiful scene stretched in either direction while above the serrated roof line opposite the fire wall continued to burn brightly. There were cracks and groans from the weakened architecture all around them but no sound and no sign of life. The entire road seemed frozen in time.

Mikey finally broke the silence. 'Gas perhaps?' he ventured with a shrug.

Catherine frowned at Mikey's nonchalant attitude. This was a very different individual from the one who had visited her home in search of help. This Michael Dayville seemed unfazed by the situation.

'Doesn't this bother you, Mikey?' she asked.

Mikey nodded, but his mind seemed to be elsewhere. 'C'mon,' he said. 'This way.'

They walked a little further up the hill, passing derelict shop fronts until they reached the small electronics store which Mikey hoped would have the parts he needed. He surveyed the window display through the broken glass with evident satisfaction then stepped through the still open door. Taking a nervous look behind her, Catherine followed him inside.

The interior of the shop was small but its narrow isles were crammed with every sort of electronic device. It was also unlit and covered in dust from the explosion.

'See if you can find some bags,' Mikey said over his shoulder as he advanced towards the small photographic counter.

By the door was a small pile of plastic shopping baskets. Catherine picked one up. 'Will this do?' she asked.

Now behind the counter, Mikey grinned. 'Perfect,' he replied. Before him on the counter top was a bulbous, battery powered lamp. Mikey flicked it on and illuminated the gloom of the shop. He directed Catherine to a second counter beside his and slid the lamp closer. 'See those portable mini disc players in the cabinet?' Catherine moved closer and looked at the display behind the glass. She nodded. 'I want half a dozen of them.' Mikey said.

'Any particular make?' sneered Catherine, still unsettled by Mikey's calmness.

The sarcasm in her voice seemed lost on the photographer. He shook his head. 'As long as they're small it doesn't matter,' he replied.

Leaving the shopping basket on the counter, Catherine instantly found that the glass cabinet was locked. She looked around for something to break the glass with then spotted a set of keys in the open cash till behind her. Catherine pulled them out and, on the third key, managed to open the display cabinet.

Mikey meanwhile had found his display case unlocked and quickly removed every Nikon and Canon SLR he could find. With an expert's eye he checked the lens on each, lined them up on the counter, then removed the only flash grip and telescopic lens he could find in the cabinet. Frowning, he drummed his fingers on the counter and stared down at his haul.

'Problem?' Catherine asked.

Mikey held up the telescopic lens and flash grip. 'I need more of these,' he explained.

Catherine offered Mikey the keys and pointed to the locked white cabinets which sat beneath the displays. 'Try looking in those,' she suggested.

Mikey grinned, took the keys and began testing the locks while Catherine looked on. 'I've got those things you wanted,' she said.

Mikey looked up to regard her for a moment, then closed his eyes. 'Now, I need...' he said slowly, his concentration evident. '… I need blank disks for the mini disc players and as many rechargeable batteries as you can find.'

'Rechargeable? Don't you want normal batteries?'

Mikey stood up and stared blankly across the gloomy interior of the shop. 'No… They have to be rechargeable – empty.' He nodded to himself then smiled reassuringly at Catherine. 'Otherwise they won't store energy.'

Confused but compliant, Catherine searched the shop for rechargeable batteries, returning a few minutes later with bulging basket and a second electric lamp. Mikey was now behind her counter, removing portable CD players from the display and again, Catherine sensed a strangeness in him as he turned towards her.

'We'll need more than that,' he observed bluntly.

Frowning, Catherine dropped her haul into the counter but Mikey instantly threw out all but the AA sized batteries.

'That's all there is,' replied Catherine defensively.

Mikey met her gaze. 'Then we're in trouble,' he said.

Catherine sighed. 'Mikey,' she said, her tone conciliatory. 'If I knew what it was you were making, then –'

'– Catherine,' Mikey cut in. 'My girlfriend is out there somewhere and I need to find her, but I can't do a thing until I've built these contraptions.' He held up the CD player and camera. 'And if I don't have these things built by nightfall, we will be in trouble – Jane will be in trouble. Trust me when I say that our lives depend on finding more batteries.'

'What's going to happen at nightfall?' asked Catherine.

Mikey pointed upwards. 'Can't you feel them? They're getting stronger. And they are getting lower.' He sighed and shook his head. 'I think it has something to do with the deaths but, I'm not sure how or why I – I just need to do this as quickly as I can. Okay?'

Catherine managed a wan smile. 'Sorry, Mikey,' she said. 'I

have been feeling something but, well…' She shrugged. 'You're right. We'll find Jane as soon as we can.'

Mikey nodded and cast his gaze on the shadow hidden rear of the shop. A smile spread across his face. 'Store room!' he exclaimed triumphantly; his left arm an arrow. 'That might have more batteries!'

Catherine followed as Mikey held aloft his lamp and made for the back of the store but he stopped her and pointed to the hi-fi's and video recorders which were racked on shelves beside them.

'Check those things for remote controls,' he said. 'It doesn't matter what they're from, just as long as they've got a remote.'

Puzzled, Catherine began searching the displays while Mikey disappeared into the storeroom. For a moment she looked out at the broken, empty high street; wondering how long it would be before nightfall. She checked her watch. It still read twelve o'clock.

As they walked slowly back across the heath, Inspector Fletcher explained about the bloodbath which had occurred after Taylor, Trent and Sergeant Rose had left the station and how he had gashed his leg jumping head first out of his office window.

'I think the man was pretending to be Bradford's lawyer,' Fletcher explained. 'But, when I poked my head around the door and saw him, it was fairly obvious what his brief was.' Fletcher shook his head and pointed to his bandaged leg. 'It's amazing what you'll do if someone fires a gun at you. I hadn't even considered jumping through the window – the next second I was sprawled on the pavement and clutching my leg.'

'What happened to the gunman?' Danny asked.

Fletcher shook his head. 'I don't know. I crawled away and managed to bandage my leg – passed out – and woke up to

267

find the sky like that.' The inspector pointed upwards. 'That's when I decided to get over here and find Rose.' Fletcher patted his jacket pockets, retrieved a cigarette and lit up. He was glad that neither man had thought to ask why he had not driven over to Mikey's house instead of walking painfully on his injured leg. The inspector did not want to discuss the fear he had felt during the assault, nor his reluctance to re-enter the silent police station afterwards to search for car keys.

They were on the top of the verge which slopped back down to the road when they heard gunfire coming from one of the streets ahead of them. As quickly as he could, Fletcher led the others across the road and under the shade of a large elm.

'That was a machine gun,' said the inspector grimly. He lent against the trunk of the tree, puffed on his cigarette rapidly and massaged his leg.

The clattering noise sounded again, this time accompanied by shouts and running feet. The three men peered around the tree and saw several figures run past the far end of the road.

'Do you think it was the men in the van, professor?' Danny asked. A hawkish look from the inspector prompted an explanation of how Danny and the professor had made their way towards the heath.

Fletcher was thoughtful for a moment as he desperately tried to make some sense of the situation. But more shouts from the end of the street drew everyone's attention. The figures they had seen earlier were now running back.

'I think we'd better find another way round,' suggested Fletcher.

The others immediately agreed and the three of them walked a little further up the hill until another street ran off to their left. Cautiously they checked the road ahead and, seeing no signs of activity, moved as quickly as Fletcher's injured leg would allow them until they reached a junction.

Here the road continued on before them while a side street ran down the hill to their left. At the bottom of the hill a grey van sat abandoned while around it were spread a number of bodies.

'That's the van, inspector,' Professor Taylor explained. 'The crowd were getting ugly when we left.' He nodded to himself. 'Looks like they didn't heed the loudspeaker warnings.'

Leaning on his stick, Inspector Fletcher regarded the scene for a few moments before starting off in the direction of the van.

'Inspector?' said Taylor, realising the policeman's intention. 'Do you think that's wise?'

Fletcher limped on. 'Just doing my job, professor,' he replied without turning. 'And finding out who the fuck I'm up against,' he muttered under his breath.

Six people lay dead on the road around the van: fans of blood staining the tarmac beneath each corpse. Fletcher had seen enough shootings to be relatively unfazed by the sight of the bodies but still he found the nature of the incident unnerving. It was added to the growing list which had marked the inspector's day.

The driver's door was open and Fletcher peered quickly through the window to check that the cabin was empty. Satisfied that the van was deserted, the inspector looked back up the hill to where Danny and the professor had moved a little closer, then climbed inside the cab. There was a flash of yellow from the small glass panel behind the cabin.

'Hey!' yelled a voice from the back of the van.

Fletcher reversed out of the cabin as quickly as he could; winced as his bandaged leg struck the tarmac and grabbed his stick to support himself. The side door of the van was flung aside to reveal a figure dressed in a billowing yellow suit but, before he could raise the machine gun which he carried,

Fletcher had cracked the man squarely on the temple with his makeshift crutch.

The man crumpled, fell awkwardly from the van and sprawled limply upon the road. The hobbling inspector quickly relieved the man of his weapon, adjusted his crutch then stabbed a finger at the unconscious figure.

'Consider yourself nicked!' he spat.

By the time Danny and the professor had reached the van, Fletcher had cuffed the man in the yellow suit and was sitting on him. He winked at the Egyptologists.

'Well done, inspector,' said Taylor, nodding with approval.

Fletcher smiled back then handed Danny the machine gun. 'Could you point that at our suspect while I check for car keys?' he asked.

Tentatively, Danny accepted the weapon and held it nervously while the inspector unzipped the man's suit and checked his pockets. He then moved on to check the van.

'That's odd,' said Professor Taylor. Like Danny he had been looking on during the inspector's examination and now he reached down to remove a strip of cloth which was tied around the young man's neck.

'What is that?' Danny asked as Professor Taylor turned the cloth over in his hands.

'I think it's a protective talisman,' Taylor replied. He looked pointedly at his understudy. 'Do you recognise the hieroglyphic style, Danny?'

Danny shook his head.

'They're the same as the hieroglyphs in Tenneshaw Wright's book,' the professor explained.

The inspector was now in the back of the van but, catching the conversation, he popped his head around the door. 'What have you found, professor?' he asked.

'I'm not sure it's of much help, inspector,' Taylor replied.

He held up the cloth. 'It's an Egyptian talisman of some sort.'

Fletcher nodded, disappeared again then climbed out of the van holding a sports bag. 'Everything's of use, professor,' the inspector said with a smile. He dipped a hand into the bag, pulled out a pistol then showed the open bag to the Egyptologists. It was full of ammunition clips.

'Amazing what the average motorist is carrying these days,' Fletcher quipped.

'Did you find the keys?' Danny asked.

The inspector shook his head. 'No,' he replied.

Balancing himself on his crutch, Fletcher kicked his unconscious captive in the ribs. There was a groan and the man tried to rise.

'Help our guest up please, Mr Trent,' said the inspector.

Wild-eyed, the young man struggled for a moment as Danny and the professor hauled him to his feet. Fletcher jammed his newly acquired pistol into the man's eye.

'See this, sunshine?' he said. 'One wrong move and I'll blow a fuckin' hole in your head, alright?'

The young man glowered back at the inspector defiantly but said nothing. He shifted his focus towards the professor and suddenly found his voice.

'What are you doing with that?!' he asked. There was a nervousness in his tone.

'This?' Professor Taylor held up the talisman: shrugged. 'Why? What's it for?'

The young bit his lip before his mouth compressed to a thin line. He looked suspiciously at his captors and fell silent again.

Fletcher took the cloth from Taylor. 'This is one of Bradford's little games, isn't it?' he said. There was a flash of recognition in his prisoner's eyes but still he remained tight-lipped. Fletcher shoved the man up the hill. 'Get moving,' said the inspector. 'We'll have plenty of time for questions later.'

271

With his arms secured behind his back and his yellow suit splayed around his midriff, Fletcher's captive was urged on through the streets at gunpoint. The glowing sky seemed a deeper shade of orange now and every road they passed through was silent and empty.

It did not take them long to reach their destination but, as the group came in sight of Mikey's house, a figure emerged from his door. Inspector Fletcher took one look at the man and instantly bundled the others behind the cover of a low garden wall.

'Keep his mouth shut!' Fletcher hissed, his tone urgent. He waved his pistol frantically at their captive then cautiously poked his head above the wall.

Still dressed in his suit, Garvin left Mikey's house and walked quickly to the car which he had parked in the middle of the road. Like their captive, Garvin seemed to be sporting a strip of cloth tied around his neck while in his right hand was a large, brown book.

'Isn't that the book you had this morning, professor?' whispered Fletcher.

Taylor looked up for a moment. 'What the hell –!?'

The professor's indignant tone was a little louder than Fletcher found comfortable and both men ducked behind the wall.

'Sorry,' Taylor whispered.

Fletcher snarled in response and stayed low, listening intently for any sound beyond the wall. Danny nudged the inspector and offered him the machine gun.

'This is not a fucking war film, son!' growled Fletcher. He stared daggers at the young archaeologist.

The sound of an engine broke the tension but Inspector Fletcher waited until the noise had died away before standing.

'What the fuck was he doing here?' mused Fletcher.

'Do you know him, inspector?' Danny asked.

Fletcher nodded grimly. 'That's the bastard that attacked the station.' He looked at the professor. 'What did he want with your book?'

Taylor shrugged. 'I've no idea, inspector.'

Moving back onto the pavement, the inspector directed Danny to bring their surly captive, then limped along until he was in front of Mikey's house. He shook his head as he took in the smashed windows and the shattered door.

'Looks like someone's been having fun,' said Fletcher to himself.

Across the street, two figures slowly emerged from behind a wall. Both were carrying shopping baskets.

'Mikey!' called Danny.

Mikey and Catherine crossed the street while Fletcher turned to regard the new arrivals with a frown.

'Mr Dayville, I presume,' he said coolly. Mikey nodded. 'You know that looting is an offence, don't you?' the inspector continued. He pointed at the baskets.

Catherine gave a hollow laugh. 'Do you honestly think that we've just been shopping?!'

'I'm simply observing what I'm seeing, madam,' replied Fletcher. 'Perhaps you could convince me otherwise.'

'Later,' said Mikey brusquely. 'Right now we don't have the time.' He brushed past the inspector and disappeared through his front door with Catherine in close tow.

'I told you, inspector,' said the professor. 'He's quite mad.'

'I think those parts are for the thing he needs to make, inspector,' Danny explained.

'Ah,' replied Fletcher. 'The thing the ghost told him to build.'

The inspector's statement had a strange effect on their captive. Rather than show surprise, Fletcher noted the furtive

273

glance which his prisoner shot in the direction of the house. When he returned his gaze towards the inspector it was to find Fletcher smiling.

'I think we'll humour Mr Dayville, don't you?' Fletcher announced, his eyes still locked on his captive. The man in the yellow suit narrowed his eyes.

'You've got no idea what you're up against.' he replied with a sneer.

Fletcher's smile grew even broader. 'That's why I've got you, chuckles,' he replied and shoved his captive towards the door.

There was no sign of either Mikey or Catherine when Fletcher entered the house. With the aid of Danny, the inspector secured his captive to a radiator pipe near the back of the living room then sent him to find the others. Fletcher moved to sit on the sofa, massaged his leg and checked the makeshift dressing.

'They're in Mikey's darkroom downstairs,' Danny reported a minute later. 'Working by candlelight. Mikey says to keep out until he's finished.'

Fletcher grunted a response and waved a hand at the kitchen. 'Check in there for some bandages – painkillers – that sort of thing, will ya?'

While Danny obliged, Fletcher reclined into the sofa and took a deep breath. Professor Taylor had been staring out of the front windows but now came to join the inspector.

'It's difficult to tell with the sky the way it is,' said Taylor. 'But I think it's getting darker outside.'

Fletcher, who had continued to watch his captive, noticed a distinctly nervous reaction to the professor's words.

'Not afraid of the dark, are ya son?' chided the inspector.

'Not as afraid as you're going to be,' sneered his prisoner in response.

Danny returned with a bottle of pills and a role of bandage. While Fletcher gratefully accepted the painkillers, Danny crouched down to re-bandage the inspector's leg.

'You'd be amazed how many injuries you see on an archaeological dig, inspector,' Danny explained as he set about cleaning Fletcher's wounds.

Fletcher nodded and turned to the professor. 'This book,' he said. 'You thought it might have something to do with the Sacrificial Murders, didn't you?'

Professor Taylor nodded. 'I'm not sure in what way, inspector, but yes. The sacrificial axes used in the murders were illustrated in the book. That's why I got in touch with Inspector Faber.'

'And did our friend, Mr Dayville, manage to explain how he came to be in possession of the book?'

The professor looked uncomfortable. 'He didn't, but that mystic female friend of his did.' Taylor sighed. 'She said he found it on Hampstead Heath by a murder site and that his ghost friend told him it was there.'

'She's a Paranormal Investigator, inspector,' Danny added. 'She said that right after Mikey came to see us he went to see her – I think it was because of this ghost of his.'

Fletcher pulled out a cigarette and lit up. He blew a stream of smoke in the direction of his attentive captive then stared sightlessly at the man for several minutes, mulling over all that Sergeant Rose had told him about Peter Bradford's past. Danny patted the inspector's knee.

'All done,' he said.

Fletcher looked down and lifted his leg. 'Fine job,' he said and stood up, testing his weight on it.

The inspector walked around in a circle, nodded thanks to Danny then went over to his captive. He pulled a chair out from under the dinning table at the rear of the room and sat

275

beside the man in the yellow suit.

'Now,' said Fletcher, flicking ash onto his prisoner. 'How about some introductions? I'm Detective Inspector Fletcher. And you are…?'

The man kept his head down and stared at the carpet. 'Fuck off,' he muttered.

Fletcher nodded, retrieved the pistol from his pocket and savagely clubbed the man on the head several times. With both hands cuffed around the radiator pipe the man was unable either to defend or retaliate. He cried out and a large cut appeared on his temple.

'Is that really necessary, inspector?!' cried Professor Taylor from across the room.

Fletcher returned a humourless smile. 'I'd take him back to the station, professor, only it's full of dead policemen.'

'Well… Even so,' replied Taylor, his voice subsiding to a mutter.

Fletcher grabbed his prisoner's hair and leaned in close. 'Now you listen to me you little fuck and you listen well!' he spat, his face inches from his captive's. 'I've seen an awful lot of good people die today so killing a little shit like you makes no difference to me. As far as I'm concerned, normal rules don't apply. If you don't answer my questions you're wasting my time and if you waste my time I'm gonna fucking well waste you, understand?!'

There was a look of defiance on the man's face. Fletcher removed it with the butt of his gun.

'Alright!' shouted the man after several more blows. His face was now red and blood stained. 'My name's Nigel! Nigel!'

Fletcher sat up and adopted a more conversational tone. 'Nigel!' he replied. 'Now there's a name.' The inspector leaned in again. 'Right. Nigel. Here's how it goes. I'm going to ask you questions: you are going to answer them. If you run out of answers –' Fletcher pressed the pistol against Nigel's head and cocked the hammer. He grinned menacingly. 'Let's get started shall we?... First question: How do you know Peter Bradford?'

Nigel's eyes darted for a moment. He took a deep breath. 'I was at college with him.'

'Ah,' said Fletcher. 'So you were one of the 'White Knights', were you?'

The inspector's knowledge seemed to surprise his prisoner. Nigel's eyes narrowed. Fletcher smiled and waggled the gun as a reminder. Nigel nodded confirmation.

'So,' continued Fletcher. 'Your friend Bradford formed some sort of mystical society at college... What puzzles me is why was it named after Stephen Knight?'

Nigel smiled. Fletcher tightened his grip on the trigger.

'Don't fuck me around, Nige',' he said with earnest.

Nigel's shoulders slumped. 'Stephen had already founded the Knights,' he sighed. 'But when Peter joined it became obvious who the one with the real power was.'

Fletcher frowned. 'Meaning what?' he asked.

'Look outside,' replied Nigel. 'That's Peter's doing.'

The inspector regarded the street for a few seconds: noted that the daylight – strange as it was – was now fading to a deeper red. 'So Bradford's what?' he shrugged, turning back to address his captive. 'Your guru or something?'

Nigel's smile grew broader. 'You have no idea, inspector.'

Fletcher tapped the barrel of his pistol against Nigel's head. 'I don't need ideas, son, I need information – and it sounds like you're running out of answers...'

Nigel swallowed, the inspector's threat clear. 'Peter made a pact with us at college,' he said. 'He promised us that we would be the chosen few...'

'Yes?' encouraged Fletcher.

Nigel paused, blinking as the blood from his temple began to trickle into his eye. 'We all believed him and made a blood pact,' he continued. 'Even Stephen Knight did it. But Stephen got cold feet after we were introduced to Åpep.'

There was a loud guffaw from Professor Taylor.

'Something funny, professor?' asked the inspector.

Professor Taylor moved to stand beside Fletcher. 'Please don't beat the boy for it inspector, but I'm afraid your prisoner is talking nonsense.'

'No I'm not you fucking fossil!' spat Nigel. 'I've seen him with my own eyes! He killed Tom!'

'Inspector,' said Taylor calmly. 'Åpep is an Egyptian legend, a monster from ancient Egyptian mythology who battled against Ra and lost.'

Fletcher nodded, and returned his attention to his captive. 'And you reckon this mythical beast killed Tom McDonald, do you?'

Nigel nodded, his eyes wide and wary of the gun pressed to his head. 'Tom got cold feet right after Stephen had been killed. He took one of Peter's books and ran. I wasn't there, I was part of the fairground group but –'

'– You were part of the what?'

'The fairground group.'

Fletcher frowned. 'Which was what?'

'Peter's rich,' explained Nigel. 'He came up with a plan to get the White Knights and the vans we needed into the area without suspicion. He bought a fun fair. We all travelled to the heath with it a few days ago and worked there until we received the sign.'

'The sign,' echoed the inspector blankly.

'The explosion,' Nigel replied. 'It was set for midday. That was the sign.' There was pride in the young man's voice.

Fletcher was thoughtful for a moment and nodded to himself. 'You were talking about Tom McDonald before you got side tracked,' the inspector said. 'Something about him stealing a book and getting bumped off by some mythical monster, right?'

Nigel nodded and cast a frown up at Professor Taylor who was shaking his head. 'Tom got nervous,' said Nigel. 'He was always a bit highly strung and he'd always liked Stephen. Anyway, after we got Stephen, Tom made off into the night with one of Peter's books.' Nigel shook his head. 'Like I said, I wasn't there, but I know Peter and Garvin went after Tom in the car. They took Åpep with them… Peter didn't like to leave the creature alone.' Nigel sighed. 'From what I later heard, Åpep chased Tom across Hampstead Heath. Peter wouldn't admit it, but we don't think he could stop Åpep from doing it. Peter's got stronger but Åpep still has to be handled carefully.'

Fletcher nodded. 'And what does this mythical 'Åpep' look like?'

'Inspector!' exclaimed Taylor. 'You can't seriously –'

Fletcher waved the protestation away and motioned Nigel to continue.

'He's your worst nightmare, Inspector: big, clawed and very, very nasty,' replied Nigel, his tone earnest.

Professor Taylor gave a sigh while Fletcher cast his mind back to his initial meeting with the Forensic Pathologist on Hampstead Heath. Nigel's description pretty much matched the doctor's original conclusions about the murderer.

'So this Åpep is a kind of wild animal, then?' the inspector mused, remembering the pathologist's joking suggestion that they phone London Zoo.

'Åpep is the gate keeper of the temple,' Nigel replied cryptically.

'What temple?!' exclaimed Professor Taylor. He crouched

down eagerly beside their captive.

'Professor,' said Fletcher testily. 'Do you mind?'

'But you don't understand, inspector!' Taylor cried. He grabbed Nigel's collar. 'You mean the temple Tenneshaw Wright found, don't you?! The one in the book – the one he brought back from Egypt!'

Inspector Fletcher put a hand on the gabbling professor's shoulder and pulled him away from his prisoner. Taylor toppled backwards while the inspector looked to Danny for assistance.

Danny had been perched on the edge of the coffee table watching the discussion but now he came to Fletcher's aid. He led Taylor back to the sofa.

'Come on, professor,' Danny said soothingly. 'We'll have time to talk about that later.'

Professor Taylor shot a murderous glance at the policeman. 'I'll report you for assault, inspector!'

Fletcher nodded but kept his attention on Nigel. 'Tell me about these sacrificial murders in London, Nigel, were they to cover up Stephen's murder?'

'Food,' Nigel replied with a shake of his head. 'Peter couldn't risk Åpep feeding himself so Garvin was sent into London to get it for him. Peter had told Stephen Knight he couldn't leave the group and so Peter saw a chance to kill two birds with one stone. Stephen thought he was smart to change his name but Peter still had enough followers at college to find out about it. We found him easily enough when he moved to London and then he was killed to feed Åpep.' Nigel's entire tone was matter-of-fact. 'The gatekeeper's ancient,' he explained, 'but he needed his strength back to begin powering the temple in readiness for the alignment.'

'And this would be the temple the professor is talking about, yes?'

Nigel nodded and managed a thin smile. 'The Temple of the

Hathnos has sat beneath Highgate Cemetery for over a century – drawing power from the souls of the dead – waiting for the alignment.'

'I see,' said Fletcher. Despite his prisoner's nonchalant attitude towards murder, the inspector had let Nigel continue without much interruption in the hope that this very attitude would reveal enough for the inspector to form a complete picture of events. It seemed to be working but, though Nigel appeared to be talking with complete sincerity, Fletcher was no longer sure he was following the thread.

'And what exactly happens when this alignment occurs?' asked the inspector.

Nigel laughed. His frank admissions appeared to have made him bolder. 'Let me see,' he said. 'You're all going to die and then Marcus and Peter will lead us all to the promised land.'

Professor Taylor gave another loud guffaw but waved away the inspector's questioning look. 'Oh no, inspector!' he said merrily. 'You'll get no help from me!'

'I think Nigel is referring to Marcus Tenneshaw Wright, inspector,' explained Danny. 'He was a renowned Victorian Egyptologist who also built Highgate Cemetery and, it would seem, he was the one who discovered and brought back this Hathnos temple which Nigel's talking about.'

Fletcher frowned. 'You knew there was a temple underneath Highgate Cemetery?' he asked.

Danny shook his head. 'It's news to me, inspector.'

Fletcher sighed and scratched his chin with the barrel of his gun. 'So, Nigel, let me see if I've got this straight. You and your college friends – with the aid of a mythical beast – have been bumping people off to feed said beast so he can get strong enough to power up a temple underneath Highgate Cemetery so a dead Victorian can lead you to paradise. Is that about it?'

'Pretty much.'

Fletcher tried to keep the smile from his face. 'And you and your friends then set off a load of explosives to disrupt the area then went around handing out poison tablets to the locals, right?'

'Yes and no,' Nigel replied. 'The barrier was put in place by Garvin to protect the temple and the cull is necessary to power the temple.'

"Cull"?!' barked Fletcher. 'Is that what you call mass murder?'

'As Peter always says,' Nigel replied with a grin. "Pain is a small price to pay for paradise."

Fletcher clubbed his grinning prisoner with his gun and stood up. 'The only price you fuckers are going to pay is a life sentence!'

Despite his obvious discomfort, Nigel sniggered. 'Why don't you go over to the cemetery and tell Peter that.' He locked his eyes on the inspector. 'Or better still, tell Marcus.'

Fletcher aimed the gun at Nigel's head. 'Why don't I just blow your fucking head off?'

'You do that, Mr policeman,' replied Nigel defiantly. 'And I'll come right back and get you.'

Inspector Fletcher lowered the gun, flicked his gaze to the floor, then stared back at his captive. 'This is for my sergeant,' he said coldly and aimed the gun at Nigel's head.

In the basement, Mikey and Catherine had been busy. Following Mikey's direction, Catherine had laid out the various electronic devices on the wide central workbench while Mikey brought out a battered tool box from the corner of the darkroom and unloaded what remained in their baskets into a pile on the bench. Catherine had placed candles in a row to provide Mikey with as much light as possible and then had stood back as the photographer went into a sudden flurry of activity.

For a moment Mikey had seemed puzzled as he stood beside

the workbench yet in the next instant his hands were flying. A few feet back, Catherine watched over Mikey's shoulder as he deftly disassembled the Mini Disc players one after another before applying the same rapid dexterity to the remote controls, the cameras, flash grips and then the portable CD players. In minutes the various objects were reduced to their component parts.

Intrigued, Catherine was eager to ask if Mikey knew yet what it was he was making, but she held her tongue. Despite Mikey's activity, Catherine sensed a serenity in him – akin yet radically different to his earlier cold mood – which she was loathed to disturb. Curious, she stepped to one side to better see his face and it was only then that she realised Mikey's eyes were shut.

Catherine mouthed a silent 'O' but remained quiet; watching as Mikey now began to remove, reconnect and then reassemble first the circuitry and then the bodies of the devices themselves. From the pile of miscellaneous junk he had placed at the end of the workbench, Mikey now picked out the discarded headphones and combined them deftly with elements he had removed from the remote controls. Next he was tearing off the battery covers for each of the Mini Disc players and quickly fitting the unpowered, rechargeable batteries into the slots.

One by one, Mikey connected the modified headphones to the now complete Mini Disc players, inserted blank discs into each and placed them in a row at the far end of the workbench. His hands had just grabbed out for a CD player and camera when a resounding bang sounded from upstairs.

Mikey blinked, looked curiously at the objects in his hands and frowned.

'What was that?' he asked, turning to Catherine.

Catherine had taken a step towards the stairs but now backed away with surprise as Danny hared down into the darkroom. Professor Taylor was right behind him.

'Inspector Fletcher's killed Nigel!' The professor exclaimed, his face drawn with shock.

'Who the hell is Nigel?!' responded Catherine. She clutched at her racing heart and took a deep breath.

Danny pointed upwards. 'The – the man we caught. The inspector shot 'im dead.'

'Fletcher's a policeman?' said Catherine. Both men nodded.

'I think he's gone to find this bloke who Nigel mentioned,' explained Danny. 'The one who was being questioned at Highgate station.'

Catherine held out a hand. 'Hold on, Danny,' she said. 'Slow down. What man?'

'It isn't safe outside,' said Mikey blankly. He reached for one of the Mini Disc players and offered it to Danny. 'Put this on,' he said and picked up another one. 'When you find Fletcher give him this.'

Danny took the first device but then just stared at Mikey incredulously. 'You want me to wear a walkman?!' he replied.

'The whole world's going mad,' whispered Professor Taylor from the stairs.

'That's enough,' snapped Catherine, catching Taylor's words. She took the second device from a blank-faced Mikey, turned Danny around and steered him gently towards the stairs. 'Let's discuss this upstairs and leave Mikey alone for a moment, alright?'

Both men returned puzzled nods and walked back up to the kitchen. Catherine turned to reassure Mikey that she would only be a few minutes but his eyes were again closed and his hands a blur. Catherine bit her lip and left him alone in the basement.

Despite Professor Taylor's continual interruptions – usually to decry Inspector Fletcher's mental instability – Danny finally explained the chain of events which had led up to Nigel's untimely death.

'From what we can gather from the conversation, this Peter Bradford and his group are over at Highgate Cemetery,' concluded Danny.

'And you think this is where Fletcher's gone?' asked Catherine.

Danny nodded. 'I think Sergeant Rose was a close friend of Fletcher's. I'm not sure how much of Nigel's story the inspector believed but he seems hell bent on revenge.'

'A madman interrogating a madman,' observed Professor Taylor. He was standing by the kitchen door, staring out through into the fiery-coloured evening. 'I'm sure the inspector will find good company over at the cemetery,' he added half to himself.

Both Danny and Catherine looked at the professor without comment. The kitchen was bathed in a red half-light from outside but a shaft of candle light still splashed across the floor from the basement. Danny held up the Mini Disc player Mikey had given him and looked questioningly at Catherine.

'What is this supposed to be Catherine?' he whispered, not wanting Taylor to hear.

Catherine shrugged then turned as a shadow passed across the floor. With a candle in one hand and a full shopping basket in the other, Mikey stepped up into the kitchen. A lit cigarette protruded from one corner of his mouth; the rest of which was formed into a crooked grin.

'How's everyone doing?' he asked jovially.

'You are, of course, joking,' retorted the professor from the door.

Mikey dumped the basket onto the kitchen work top,

285

removed his cigarette and regarded the man with evident compassion. 'Sorry, prof',' Mikey replied. 'Probably not the best expression to use at a time like this.'

Catherine frowned and placed a hand on Mikey's arm. 'Are you okay?' she asked.

Mikey smiled back. 'Never better. I feel… Awake.'

Catherine returned the smile. The strangeness she had sensed in Mikey before was no longer there. She held up the Mini Disc player she had taken from him. 'Do you know what these do yet?' she asked.

Mikey looked at Catherine and then at Danny. Both were holding up the devices he had made and regarded them with complete bewilderment. Mikey chuckled.

'Sorry,' he said, hiding his smile behind his hand. He nodded and managed a straight face. 'Yes, I know what they do now.'

Mikey took the device from Catherine and slipped the headphones over her head so that they sat at the base of her neck. He held out the Mini Disc player to her. 'If you have a belt, clip this onto it but you must be able to get at the batteries easily.'

'Oookay,' replied Catherine. 'And if I don't have a belt?'

'We'll find something,' said Mikey.

Danny had followed Mikey's lead but did not possess a belt either. Mikey opened a kitchen cupboard in search of some string.

'You'll need to wear one of these as well, professor,' Mikey said as he rummaged by candle light in the cupboard.

'Oh, of course!' replied Taylor sarcastically.

Mikey removed a large roll of grey 'gaffer' tape and winked at Catherine. 'I can't say it's going to look fashionable but it'll do the job,' he said.

One by one, Mikey bound the Mini Disc players to Catherine and Danny's midriffs leaving the battery compartments exposed. He repeated the same procedure on himself then turned to the reluctant professor. 'Your turn, professor,' he said.

Professor Taylor held up a hand. 'No,' he replied with finality. 'I want nothing more to do with your mad behaviour.'

'Not even if your life depends on it?' asked Mikey.

The professor returned a humourless smile and pointed to a cupboard. 'I'm sure I'll find a tin of magic baked beans in there that will provide me with much the same level of protection,' he responded.

Mikey regarded the cupboard. 'I think I'm out of beans,' he replied.

Standing by the shopping basket, Danny had noticed a long handle sticking out from amongst the remaining Mini Disc players and headphones. He pulled it out to find a strange amalgam of objects connected to it. The handle was a camera flash grip attached to the base of a heavily modified CD Walkman and this in turn connected into the base of a camera. Danny turned the object over in his hands until the camera lens was pointing straight towards him.

'That's odd,' he said.

Mikey turned at the words and snatched the device from Danny hurriedly. 'Sorry,' he said. 'But this thing is dangerous.'

Danny nodded. 'That's okay,' he replied. 'I was just curious.' He pointed to the device now in Mikey's hand. 'From the front, that thing you've made looks just like an Ånkh.'

Professor Taylor let out a sigh. 'Please, Danny,' he protested. 'Don't encourage him. Things are bad enough as they are.'

Mikey regarded his own creation with curiosity. 'What's an Ånkh?'

Catherine too was looking closely as Mikey turned the object in his hands. 'It's an Egyptian talisman,' she said. 'A precursor to the Christian cross.'

'It's hardly that, dear lady!' exclaimed the professor, his professional pride overriding his outraged sensibilities. 'The Ånkh is the symbol of life – the rebirth of Osiris. It had nothing to do with the Christian cross.'

'But don't they both symbolise rebirth?' countered Danny.

'I am not in the mood to discuss semantics, Danny!' snapped the professor tersely. 'You are beginning to sound as mad as everyone else!'

Mikey had turned his attention to the professor but now his eyes narrowed on the half light outside.

'Get away from the door, professor,' he said slowly.

Professor Taylor stared back defiantly but Mikey grabbed his arm and pulled him away. Catherine and Danny had both been looking on with surprise. Now Catherine gasped.

'Oh, my god,' she said. 'It's Nigel!'

Beyond the door a misty shape had descended from the sky and formed itself into the figure of Nigel. It wavered for a moment as it coalesced, peering in through the window at the group. The large hole in the side of Nigel's temple was clearly visible as he stepped through the door into the kitchen.

'Told you I'd come back for you,' said the spirit with a sneer.

'Get in front of the professor!' shouted Mikey. He raised his camera.

Catherine instantly complied but neither Danny nor Professor Taylor could see or hear anything. Nigel's shape blurred rapidly across the kitchen towards the unsuspecting pair and Mikey fired the camera. He was too late, missing the ghost completely and the whole room was lit with a blinding flash. In the same instant, Danny gasped and flew through the air to hit the wall by the darkroom door.

The young Egyptologist slumped to the floor then climbed unsteadily to his feet as both Mikey and Catherine rushed to help him up.

'I… I saw him in the flash!' mouthed Danny in awe. 'He went straight into me!'

There was a moment of silence before their attention was drawn to the still sparking battery in Danny's Mini Disc player. Mikey reached out and removed the battery. He grinned.

'Is that…?' said Danny pointing to the battery. Mikey nodded.

'Meet Nigel,' he said then tossed the battery over his shoulder.

Catherine let out a nervous laugh. 'I think I know what these things do now,' she said.

Attempting to recover his wits, Danny was taking deep breaths. He looked down to see Professor Taylor curled up in the corner of the kitchen. The man's eyes were as wide as saucers.

'I've changed my mind,' said the professor weakly. He pointed to Danny's device. 'I want one of those things.'

Catherine helped the professor up. 'Did you see it?' she asked.

Professor Taylor shook his head. 'I'm not sure what I saw but…' He let out a deep sigh. 'I saw enough.'

Mikey fitted the professor with a device then offered Danny a fresh battery. Danny clicked it into place but seemed distracted. He stepped into the living room to look out through the broken windows.

'Can you hear that?' Danny asked as the others joined him.

Silently the others nodded as the noise of the engine grew louder until the shape of a grey van slowed to a stop before Mikey's house. Catherine instantly blew out the candle while Danny picked up his machine gun. Everyone held their breath and waited tensely in the darkness.

Chapter Fourteen

There was only one thing which Jane could do and that was to lay perfectly still. Any movement – even a deep breath – brought searing pain to her badly burnt body. Doggedly, she held the same, stiff position for what seemed like an eternity: slipping out of consciousness only to be awakened by another wave of pain as her body attempted to relax. She wanted to cry but knew that sobbing would jar her frail frame; so she gritted her teeth as best she could and hung on, hoping and praying that somehow, Mikey would find her.

During her bouts of consciousness she would hear vehicles and voices outside the chapel and, despite her painful state, Jane's inquiring mind would ponder the question of just what was going on outside. At one stage she was sure she could hear the hammering of stone, but Jane's condition was such that she was no longer sure if she was imagining it or not. After a long, countless time, a loud thump brought her out of her pain-wracked stupor and fearfully, Jane realised she was not alone.

'Oh, god,' whispered a voice. 'I'm so sorry.'

At the sound of the friendly voice Jane tried to open her eyes and, before the pain grew too great, briefly saw the slender figure of a red haired girl crouched before her. She felt the bonds which still held her being loosened. Jane tried to speak but agony overwhelmed the effort.

'Wait, don't move,' said the voice. 'I think I've got some Vaseline…'

Jane was not sure whether she nodded her head but the smile she attempted made her scream inside. She heard a brief rustling and then snowflakes seemed to be falling onto her face. She managed a sigh as the coldness spread through her lips and touched her eyelids.

'Careful,' warned the voice as Jane slowly opened her eyes.

'Thank…you…' Jane murmured weakly.

The girl nodded and settled down on her haunches before Jane. 'I'm Celia,' she said. 'And… Well, it's the least I could do.' She turned her head towards the closed chapel door. 'I'm not sure how much good it will do though…'

'…What's…?' managed Jane.

'Going on?' replied Celia, guessing the unfinished question. She sighed and her shoulders slumped. 'Well, I'm not sure how much you know, but Peter's master plan seems to be coming apart at the seams. He's acting stranger by the minute and a lot of us are beginning to question him. I was the first one to voice our doubts… That's why I've been put in here.'

'My…boy…friend… Get…my –' Jane winced and locked her limbs, stealing herself against the waves of agony which proceeded to wash over her.

'I'm really sorry,' replied Celia with feeling. 'I wish I could but I'm stuck in here with you until…' Jane saw the look of anguish which crossed Celia's face but the girl quickly managed to hide it behind a wan smile. 'If it's any consolation,' Celia continued. 'I don't think Garvin found your boyfriend – he got the book but, Mikey was it? Well, he wasn't there.' Celia gave a deeper sigh and crossed her legs. She picked up the little jar of Vaseline. 'Would you like me to put some on your hands?' she asked.

Jane managed an 'Mm' and Celia proceeded to dab the Vaseline onto Jane's cracked fingers.

'I can't believe Peter did this but, well… He's freaking us all out with that eye of his.' Celia shook her head. 'My father always said that students have three constants: education, enthusiasm and inexperience. He always said they were a lethal combination; I didn't take him seriously until today.'

Celia continued to gently apply the Vaseline for a few more minutes then sat back.

'Try that,' she said.

Jane carefully stretched her clenched fingers. 'Better,' she murmured.

Celia nodded. 'Like I said: it's the least I can do.' Her eyes wandered to the locked chapel door again.

'Phone?' asked Jane.

Celia shook her head and pointed up. 'The fire wall stops the signal. We're trapped until the temple powers down again – even Peter.' Celia gave a humourless laugh and tapped her wristwatch. 'Time's stopped too – apparently,' she said. 'Though it's still getting dark… Maybe because that's outside the barrier – I'm not really sure.'

A lot of what Celia was saying made no sense at all, but the conversation distracted Jane's attention from her pain. 'What…temple?' she asked.

Celia returned a pained smile. 'The Temple of the Hathnos,' she replied. 'It's right under our feet, along with the man who found it…'

Jane wanted to frown but fought the urge. 'Go… On,' she whispered.

Celia sighed and cupped her face in her hands. 'A long time ago, a man named Tenneshaw Wright came across an ancient, undiscovered site in Egypt. But when he uncovered it he found a lot more than he ever bargained for. There was this creature inside, named Åpep, who promised Wright eternal life – the keys to paradise if he would help the creature. Wright believed him and was rich enough to have the whole site shipped back to England and secretly buried on his estate. Under the cemetery – which wasn't there back then of course… So –' Celia frowned, collecting her thoughts. 'So, after all that effort Marcus was then informed by Åpep that he would still have to wait more than a hundred years for the gateway to paradise to open – some cosmic alignment of some sort, I think – but, though Åpep promised Marcus that he could survive all that time in the temple, Marcus wanted to make sure that neither he nor Åpep were going to be disturbed. Marcus's closest friend was a man named Charles Bradford who was given the task of watching out over the temple until the time was right. Marcus knew it would take several generations so, to keep the Bradford family's loyalty, he handed over his entire fortune to Charles in return for his continued vigilance. Peter says that, like his father and his grandfather before him, he was brought here to meet Marcus when he was a child –'

'– Photograph,' murmured Jane to herself.

'Yes!' exclaimed Celia. 'I saw it. Peter was trying to rally the troops with it a while ago… Anyway,' she continued on a more subdued note. 'We heard most of this story from Peter at college, but we didn't really believe him until we were introduced to Åpep…'

'In the… temple?'

Celia shook her head. 'That's the problem. It seems Åpep can get in and out of the temple at will but nobody else can. Peter has managed to make some sort of contact with Marcus again but neither one of them can open the door. The last I saw they had taken a sledge hammer to it.' Celia sighed. 'I suppose that's why Åpep is called the Gatekeeper. It seems we're all stuck outside until Åpep turns up or…'

Jane noticed the hesitation in Celia's voice and again she cast her gaze towards the chapel door.

'What?' Jane asked.

Celia dipped her head and shook it. 'It's nothing… Really,' she replied and returned the same weak smile. She frowned for a second, darted her eyes towards the thin chapel windows then returned her attention to Jane. 'Your boyfriend saw a ghost, didn't he?' she asked.

There was a clumsiness to the question which struck even

Jane's addled wits. '…Yes,' she replied.

Celia nodded. 'It wasn't Tenneshaw Wright though, was it?'

'No,' mouthed Jane.

'I think that's really upset Peter. He can't fathom out how another ghost could be connected to this thing… Do you know who this other ghost is?'

'No…' Jane replied. 'My – Mikey might know.'

Celia sighed. 'I wish I could find him for you but, like I say, he wasn't at his house and I'm stuck in here.' Celia frowned and chewed on her lip for a moment. She regarded the narrow, stained glass windows once again and a thin smile spread across her face. 'That window's broken!' she said, standing suddenly. 'I might be able to get out.' Celia regarded Jane with compassion. 'I've got an idea,' she said. 'If I can get out, I might be able to find your boyfriend – bring him back to help you… Do you have any idea where he might have gone?'

Jane had considered the question of Mikey's absence and her only conclusion was that he would have gone to her flat in Highgate. It was a slim chance that he was still there but it was the only hope she had. Slowly, Jane managed to tell Celia the address.

In response, Celia pulled a pen and paper from her bag and jotted the address down. 'How will I recognise him?' she asked.

'He's got red hair… needs cutting,' muttered Jane, 'and has worn the same smelly jump suit for years.' Jane wanted to smile: the thought of Celia finding Mikey made her spirits lift.

Celia nodded, made her final notes and returned the pad to her bag. 'Thanks,' she said brightly and slapped Jane soundly on the shoulder.

Jane's scream echoed around the chapel as Celia trotted quickly towards the door. She knocked twice and Garvin opened it.

'Any luck?' said Garvin.

Celia beamed. 'Got the silly cow's address,' she replied. 'She reckons that's where her boyfriend will be.'

Garvin smiled and looked over Celia's shoulder at the gasping figure of Jane. 'I hope this 'Mikey' character has some better answers than she did,' he said.

'Can Peter still not get inside?' Celia asked.

Garvin shook his head. 'Without Åpep here, it doesn't look like he will.'

Celia pulled her note pad out from her bag. 'Do you think finding this man will give us answers?'

Garvin shrugged. 'Mikey had the book. And if the boss thinks this bloke knows something about why we can't get into the temple, then it's worth finding him.' Garvin winked. 'And anyway,' he said, 'I don't like loose ends.'

Inspector Fletcher had left Mikey's house to search for fellow officers at the Hampstead Police Station; but the devastation and the dead bodies which he had found there diminished his grim resolve to confront Peter Bradford as soon as possible. The police station seemed now nothing more than a morgue and the silent ruin of the high street, dominated by the towering blaze of the fire wall, made the inspector reconsider his options. He was still determined to confront Bradford at Highgate Cemetery, but now – more than ever – Fletcher knew that he could not do it alone. He needed allies, and there was only one place he was going to find them.

On his way back towards Mikey's house, the inspector had reviewed Nigel's information on Bradford's activities: mulling over how best he could achieve his goal of bringing Bradford and his followers to justice. It seemed safe to assume that the murderous Garvin would be close at hand and also that Bradford's followers would be armed as Nigel had been. That meant that Fletcher would be asking a group of reluctant civilians to confront a group of well armed, well motivated criminals. That thought stopped the inspector in his tracks. He frowned up at the deepening sky, turned on his heals and headed back towards the station. As things stood the odds were against them yet Fletcher felt confident he would find something at the station to lower the risk. He would have to.

Stepping gingerly over the corpses which clogged the station entrance, Fletcher tried to keep his mind focused and not gaze at the rictus faces of former colleagues. Though the inspector did not know many of his fellow officers by name, he knew them by sight and now that sight was a harrowing one.

Fletcher inched further into the gloom, sliding one foot before the other to avoid tripping until his injured leg struck something which sounded like wood. The inspector's wound throbbed painfully at the impact and issuing a silent curse, he groped blindly until he felt the top of what he took to be the station's enquiry desk. Fletcher worked his way around until he was behind it then searched for the torch which he knew should be there. He ran his hands along the shelf beneath the desk – felt a truncheon, the alarm button and hand cuffs which he pocketed, until finally a solid, rubber gripped torch came within his grasp. Fletcher flicked it on and cast the beam to his left, past the dead officers and civilians slumped against the far wall and towards the security door which separated the front of the station from the rear. He was pleased to see that the door had been wedged open.

Less pleasing were the dozen or so bodies lining the corridor beyond and the sickly smell which made the inspector hold his breath. These victims were not contorted like the people littering the pavement and the entrance but the gruesome burns and bloody limbs which were now illuminated in the torchlight made them an equally upsetting sight.

The sound of a vehicle drawing up outside removed the dreadful scene from Fletcher's gaze. He flicked the torch off immediately and crouched down, moving to the side of the front desk until he could clearly see the grey van which was now parked in the road outside.

From the van, two young men climbed out to stand before the station entrance. They were dressed in the same yellow hazard suits which Nigel had worn but both had stripped them to their legs and tied the arms around their waists as makeshift belts. Both men shouldered sub-machine guns and while the driver waited for his passenger to walk around the van, Fletcher pulled his pistol from his pocket and took careful aim.

It was difficult for Fletcher to tell in the orange glow of the firewall but he thought the first figure's hair was probably blonde. Unlike his companion – whose hair had to be dark brown – the first man's head blazed like fire in the reflected glow of the sky. He was a good foot taller than his slighter companion and his build and heavy features made Fletcher instantly consider him as a budding rugby player. Both men, the inspector surmised, could not be more than twenty, but the blonde man's stature accentuated his companion's youth. The smaller man peered into the station entrance and looked nervously at his friend.

'There's no one there, Julian,' he said.

Julian sighed, shook his head and returned a condescending smile. 'All this death is making you timid, Timothy,' he replied. His smile broadened. 'Timid Timothy!' Julian guffawed. He reached out and ruffled his companion's hair. 'Aah! Is Timmy fwightened of da nasty police station?'

Timothy threw his head to one side to avoid further abuse and frowned. 'Bugger off, Jules!' he snapped. 'Just call for Nigel will you?'

With a smile still on his face, Julian cupped a hand to his

mouth. 'Ooh, Niigel!' he called merrily.

It was Timothy's turn to sigh. 'Nigel!' he called. 'If you're in there we've got to get back. The – er – radiation's getting worse.'

The pair waited in silence for a few seconds before Julian's jovial expression grew serious. 'I definitely saw somebody go in and I'm sure I saw a light.' Julian adjusted his grip on his machine gun and took a step towards the entrance. 'If there's anyone in there, you'd best come out. We're here to take you to safety.'

'Can you see anything?' asked Timothy. He too took a step closer to the doorway.

'Bodies,' replied Julian. 'It's too dark. Have we got a torch?' he asked, turning.

Timothy shook his head. 'Come on,' he said. 'Let's leave it. It could be anybody.'

'Unlucky for them if it is,' Julian answered, his tone firm. 'And if it's Nigel he might be injured.'

Timothy bit his lip and looked at the sky. 'Nigel could be anywhere and we've got to get back,' he urged. 'I don't have my talisman on.' He tapped at his throat. Julian smiled back and pulled at the piece of white cloth he had around his own neck.

'I do,' he replied with a wink. Julian ignored Timothy's frown and turned back to face the entrance. 'This won't take a minute,' he said and took one more step before the unseen inspector opened fire.

The flash and thunder of Fletcher's shot, coupled with his companion's sudden demise, froze Timothy for a vital second. Before his terrified senses could fully register the bloody mess of his friend's head striking the pavement, the inspector had taken aim and fired again; this time striking Timothy in the shoulder and dropping him to the floor.

As quickly as his injured leg would allow him, Fletcher ran from the station to disarm the writhing, screaming figure then handcuffed his good arm to the cast iron drainpipe which ran beside the door. While Timothy continued to wince and cry out, the inspector removed Julian's weapon and left both on the pavement out of his new captive's reach.

'You're mad!' gasped Timothy, staring wide-eyed for a second at the inspector. 'We're here to help!'

Fletcher returned an amused frown. 'Sure you are,' he replied as he checked Julian's pockets. 'Like you helped all the people lying around beside you.' The inspector jabbed a finger at the body strewn pavement.

'It was the radiation!' pleaded Timothy: panic and pain in his voice. 'You've got to listen to me!'

Fletcher nodded and pulled out a small plastic wallet from Julian's breast pocket. He flicked it open, smiled and turned it towards his captive. 'Hazard Bureau. That's you, is it?'

'Yes! Christ, let me go!'

Fletcher patted his own pockets and pulled out his ID card, holding it up beside Julian's. 'One of these is fake, and one of these is genuine,' the inspector said. 'And we both know which is which, don't we, Timmy?'

The realisation that he was dealing with a policeman seemed to quell Timothy's protestations. He gritted his teeth and shuffled into a sitting position against the wall, attempting vainly to bring his cuffed hand to his wound. He watched as the inspector opened the van door and pulled the keys from the ignition.

'You won't get very far!' said Timothy defiantly.

Fletcher pocketed the keys and moved to the kerb-side door of the van. 'Oh, I'm not planning on going far, Tim-Tim,' the inspector replied. He opened the side door, peered inside and smiled back at his captive. 'I thought I might take a trip up to

Highgate Cemetery. What do you think?'

Timothy's set jaw spoke volumes.

'That is where I'll find Mr Bradford at this time of night, isn't it?' Fletcher continued. 'Digging up temples with his friends…
'

Timothy lowered his gaze while Fletcher picked up the sub-machine guns and put them in the back of the van.

'Won't be long,' announced the inspector as he headed back towards the station. 'You stay here and guard the van.' With a wink, Fletcher disappeared inside.

It only took the inspector a few minutes to find what he was looking for but it took several trips to get all the equipment he wanted into the van. Satisfied that he had all he could possibly need, Fletcher slid the side door shut then regarded the surly figure of Timothy.

'Well, it's been fun,' said Fletcher, 'but now I've really got to be going.'

'You can't leave me here!' pleaded Timothy.

'Why not?' Fletcher replied, puzzled.

'I'm injured,' insisted Timothy, his eyes darting. 'You're a policeman, it's your duty to take me to a hospital.'

Fletcher crouched beside his captive and pointed down the hill. 'See that wall of flame which crosses the road down there?' he asked. 'Well, a few yards beyond that is a massive general hospital. But, because of you, Bradford and your dead friend here, nobody can get to it.' Fletcher smiled. 'I think that's what's called poetic justice.'

'You can't leave me here!' insisted Tim as Fletcher stood up. 'I'll die!'

Fletcher regarded the contorted bodies spread out on the pavement. 'I'd say you'd be in good company,' he said and moved towards the van.

'At least give me Julian's talisman!'

'Julian's what?' said Fletcher, turning.

'His talisman!' Timothy pointed furiously at his dead companion. 'It's the thing around his neck!'

The inspector walked to Julian and pulled the piece of cloth from his neck. It was almost identical to the one the professor had taken from Nigel. 'What's so special about this?' he asked.

'I... I just want it, that's all.'

'Not good enough,' replied Fletcher. He pocketed the talisman.

'Please!' Begged Timothy. 'I don't want to die!'

Fletcher regarded the pleading figure for a moment. 'Here's what I'll do,' he said, bringing the talisman back out of his pocket. 'You tell me why a crappy strip of cloth is so important and I'll let you have it.' Timothy went to speak but the inspector held up a hand. 'You've got one chance only,' he said, 'so don't fuck me around.'

Timothy bit his lip and studied the inspector's eyes for a moment. 'You wouldn't believe me,' he said.

'Maybe not,' replied Fletcher. 'But if it's the truth, I'll know it... And it can't be any stranger than anything else I've heard today.'

Again Timothy bit his lip. 'It's to protect me from the spirits,' he said slowly and looked pointedly into the sky.

'Up there?' asked Fletcher, pointing up. Timothy nodded gravely. Fletcher returned the nod – recalling Professor Taylor's jibe about Mikey seeing people in the sky. 'Now that is interesting,' he said to himself. He turned back to the van, tossed the talisman over his shoulder and climbed into the driver's seat.

Fletcher gunned the engine and set off on the short journey to Mikey's house, wondering just how he was going to convince civilians to take up arms against criminals. Outside the police station, Timothy struggled vainly to reach the piece of curb where the talisman had fallen.

Seated around the single candle which Catherine had placed on Mikey's coffee table, the group listened to Inspector Fletcher's proposal in silence. In the flickering light it was difficult for Fletcher to read their mainly down-cast expressions yet Professor Taylor's continually shaking head left the inspector in no doubt as to the archaeologist's thoughts on the matter.

'I know this is a difficult thing to ask of you,' concluded Fletcher, 'and under normal circumstances I'd obviously be doing this with fellow officers…' The inspector fingered the Mini Disc player which Mikey had strapped to his waist within seconds of him walking through the door. 'But I think we all know that we are not in a normal situation now and, well… I need your help.'

"Normal rules don't apply," sneered Professor Taylor. 'Wasn't that your expression, inspector? Just before you killed your suspect in cold blood.'

Fletcher frowned: dark lines creasing his face in the candle light. 'I know more than anybody, professor, what the result of my actions will be when sanity is returned to this place.' The inspector gestured around him. 'But if I have to take firm action to put an end to the slaughter of innocent civilians, then that's just what I'll do.'

'But now you're asking us to join you on your bloody crusade,' retorted Taylor. 'And you want to arm us so that we can help you gun down your suspects.'

Inspector Fletcher shook his head and reached for the packet of Gauloises which Mikey had left on the table. He lit one from the candle, grimaced at Mikey then returned his attention to the professor. 'In the back of that van outside,' he sighed, 'are full sets of riot gear – everything from bullet proof vests to CS gas launchers. I'm not asking you or anyone else here to 'gun down' anybody; I simply need your help in trying to subdue Bradford and his accomplices.'

'And what if you can't 'subdue' them, inspector?' asked Taylor. 'What then?'

'Then I will take whatever action necessary, professor,' replied Fletcher. 'However unpleasant that task may be.'

'Huh!' Professor Taylor gave a dismissive wave and turned away.

Catherine and Mikey had been seated on the sofa as the inspector had spoken but now, in unison, the pair inched forwards. Mikey raised his flash gun.

'Everybody be quiet – everybody freeze,' hissed Mikey.

Through the broken windows, the tall figure of a young man had floated into view and stood for a moment gazing intently at the group around the coffee table. Slowly, Mikey got to his feet.

'Don't move, inspector,' Mikey urged as Fletcher turned his head to see the empty space which had suddenly attracted Mikey's attention.

Fletcher frowned and turned completely to face the windows and with that Mikey saw the spirit suddenly smile and focus itself on the inspector. It stepped through the wall with a single stride and now Mikey could see that it seemed to be wearing a hazard suit similar to Nigel's yet tied off around its waist. Like the spirit of Nigel before, the apparition suddenly blurred as it sped towards the unseeing inspector but this time Mikey was ready.

'Christ, this better work,' he muttered and fired.

There was a blinding flash from the camera gun and a loud whine from the CD player connected to it. Inspector Fletcher, Danny and the professor all recoiled as the figure was suddenly exposed in the light: its body arcing towards the inspector's head.

'Jesus!' yelled Fletcher, recognising the distorted features of Julian as they suddenly appeared, mere inches before his face. He put his arms up to protect himself, felt no impact, then chanced a look to see the frozen image quickly fade to nothing.

'Well done, Mikey,' said Danny, his expression a mixture of admiration and relief.

Inspector Fletcher nodded rapid agreement and clutched at his galloping heart.

'I've got one condition before I agree to go with you, inspector,' Mikey said. 'And that is that I need to find my girlfriend first.'

Fletcher looked at the device which Mikey still held in his hand then up at the impassive features of the photographer. 'You've got it,' he said and took a huge gulp of air. The inspector hated to admit it, but he had never been so frightened in his life.

'Count me in,' said Catherine.

'And me,' said Danny as he stood up.

Mikey nodded and turned his attention to the professor. 'Professor Taylor, I know you don't want to get involved but it's probably safer if you stay with us. We've got a limited supply of batteries and there are hundreds more of those things up in the sky.'

'And you know more about the temple than any of us,' Danny added. 'Your help would be invaluable.'

Professor Taylor gave a deep sigh and stared at the carpet. 'This goes against my better judgment,' he said, 'but what choice do I have? Inspector, can you promise me that you will try to arrest Mr Bradford rather than simply gunning him down?'

Inspector Fletcher was now standing beside Mikey and he gazed down at the archeologist with evident sympathy. 'I wish

I could make such a promise professor. But if these 'White Knights' start shooting I may not have the luxury of choice. All I can promise is that I'll try my best to make them come quietly.'

Professor Taylor nodded, his face sad as he stood up. 'As long as it's understood that I will not take part in any violence, then I agree,' he said

Catherine put an arm around the professor's shoulder. 'Amen to that, professor,' she said softly.

Beside the van, Inspector Fletcher fitted each person with a bullet-proof jacket before re-strapping the Mini Disc players over the top. While this was going on, Mikey explained the workings of the second flash gun he had constructed to Catherine.

'Always keep the dial set to this symbol,' said Mikey, pointing to the selector on the top of the camera.

Catherine nodded and made a mental note of the little image of mountains. 'How do I aim?' she asked.

Mikey grinned and held the camera up to his eye, twisting the lens as he did so. 'Same as a normal camera,' he said. 'Whatever's in the centre will be hit.'

'Will it hurt us?' Catherine asked. She took the device from Mikey, pointed it at the sky and zoomed in on the wispy shape of a woman in stiff, formal dress, floating cloud-like far above.

Mikey too regarded the sky, checking to see that no more apparitions were heading their way. 'On that setting, no,' he said.

Catherine frowned and took the camera away from her eye. 'There are others?'

Mikey nodded and held up his own camera. 'See this lightning symbol? Well…' Mikey stepped away, turned the dial on his camera and pointed it towards a car parked across the street. 'Inspector?' he asked. 'Is it okay if I demonstrate?'

Fletcher had been adjusting the Velcro straps on Professor Taylor's bullet-proof jacket as well as instructing Danny in the operation of the CS gas launcher. He looked at Mikey, frowned at the camera and then regarded the car across the street. 'I wouldn't worry about setting off the alarm,' he said with a shrug.

Mikey nodded, took aim and a bright pulse of light flashed from the camera. There was a whoosh of sound as the beam struck the car and instantly the paint work was aflame.

'Bloody hell,' mouthed the inspector as first the windows and then the entire half of the car facing them melted.

'My god,' said Professor Taylor.

Mikey lowered the camera and turned back to Catherine who looked a little drawn.

'I'll make sure I don't have it on that setting,' she said.

Mikey nodded. 'Probably best not to,' he agreed.

With Fletcher driving and Mikey in the passenger seat, the others were consigned to the gloomy rear of the van. Seated on the bare metal floor they listened to the road rumble beneath them and tried to keep their minds from what awaited them at the cemetery.

'I hope you don't think that's some sort of new toy, young man,' said Professor Taylor. He nodded to the machine gun which Danny cradled in his lap.

'Do you know how to use it?' Catherine asked.

Danny nodded. 'The inspector showed me. It's quite simple.'

'It's also quite lethal,' the professor added. 'I trust it's for show only.'

Danny shrugged. 'I'm not going to fire the first shot, if that's what you mean,' he replied defensively. 'But I suppose I'll use it if I have no other choice.'

The professor sighed. 'How quickly we descend into the primeval abyss…'

'I'm not being primeval –' argued Danny, 'just protective. I don't want to get shot – and I don't want you to get shot either, professor.'

Professor Taylor's tone softened. 'Well, I suppose that is a noble sentiment,' he replied. 'Misguided, but noble.'

'Head's up back there!' called Mikey from the front of the van. 'Looks like we might have some company soon.'

Inspector Fletcher had driven through Hampstead until he reached the Spaniards Road. It was a short distance, but with abandoned cars littering the way, the journey had involved weaving continuously through gaps and driving on pavements. Now, with a straight stretch of road ahead and only a few cars to negotiate, Fletcher had speeded up – only to be slowed by Mikey's caution of what lay ahead. Frowning, the inspector scanned the bordering tree lines around Spaniards Road steeling himself for another unseen attack.

Mikey craned his neck to watch the sky, puzzled by the activity which was now taking place above them. Like flocking birds, the airborne spirits were beginning to descend en mass, flitting across the road at the tree line to disappear into the woods of Hampstead Heath.

'Go slowly,' advised Mikey. 'But keep going.'

'What's happening out there!' demanded the professor from the back of the van.

'I can't say I'm really sure, professor,' Mikey replied. 'The spirits appear to be swarming.'

'Perhaps they're looking for honey,' said Fletcher dryly, hiding his nervousness behind a thin smile. He too looked at the sky yet could see nothing but the same dull orange glow.

Catherine, Danny and the professor squeezed their heads

into the small open window in the back of the van which let them see into the cabin, and now Catherine urged Mikey to look down the road. Mikey did so and the pair fell silent.

'What?' asked Fletcher nervously. He cast a sideways glance at the photographer.

'Stop the van for a moment,' whispered Mikey.

Mikey felt a terrible sadness sweep over him as he watched the shambling, ghostly figure of Tom McDonald run down the road towards them. He had been too preoccupied with events in the sky to see Tom run the entire length of Spaniards Road but now, as he watched the ghost near the van he saw Tom turn his terrified gaze behind him, Mikey felt tears well up inside. He looked on as Tom turned back to face them with terror in his eyes before he stumbled to the right and disappeared into the southern tree line.

'It was Tom McDonald, inspector,' explained Catherine quietly. 'This must be the route he took that night.'

'Tragic business,' said Fletcher with a single nod. He tapped the steering wheel. 'Has he gone? Can I keep going?' he asked.

As Mikey nodded there was a thump in the back of the van and cries from Catherine and Danny were followed by a blinding flash. Both Fletcher and Mikey twisted in their seats to see through the small opening what was going on and the pair could just make out the forms of Catherine and Danny: hunched over the immobile shape of the professor. Mikey's gaze switched as the figure of a sallow-faced, bearded man swooped through the back doors into the rear of the van. He brought his flash gun to bear against the little window as quickly as he could and fired. His camera illuminated the rear compartment in an instant and the now frozen shape of the man evaporated inches from Catherine's head. Alarmed, Mikey turned and craned his neck out of the passenger window to view the sky and the space around the van. With concern he saw that at least a dozen more figures seemed to be bearing down from above the trees towards them.

'Hang on!' Mikey yelled. He pushed open his door, jumped out and ran round the front of the van. He threw open the side door to see three more spirits swoop into the van.

Inside, Danny had finally managed to replace the battery in the professor's pack but both he and the professor were hit again as the shapes of a small girl and an old man surged into them before Mikey could fire his flash gun. In the sudden blaze of light which stopped the third figure, Danny was thrown forwards onto the professor while, in the corner, Catherine seemed to have been similarly stricken. Mikey took a quick look at the sky: saw a continuing wave of bodies flying down towards them and slapped the side of the van.

'Drive! Drive on!' Mikey shouted. 'Get out of here!'

Instantly Fletcher had the van tyres spinning and the vehicle sped off down the road towards the Spaniards Inn leaving Mikey behind. For a moment, Mikey followed the receding vehicle, checking the sky to confirm his suspicion that there were no spirits further down the road then turned his attention to the rapidly descending forms above him. With a deft twist, Mikey adjusted his flash gun's focus, clicked the aperture as wide as it would go and swung the camera to his eye.

'Smile,' he muttered and filled the sky with light.

Fletcher kept his foot hard down until Mikey was all but lost in the fire tinted darkness. He called repeatedly to the others in the back of the van but got no response and, seeing the distant figure of Mikey suddenly illuminate the night behind him, the inspector hit the brakes and jumped out to see what had happened to his passengers.

Danny was getting unsteadily to his feet when Fletcher got to the side door and regarded the policeman blankly for a second before managing a pained smile. Professor Taylor gave groan and rolled over while Catherine held her hands to her temples and shook her head.

'That's the kind of psychic contact I can do without,' she muttered. She threw a sparking battery from her Mini Disc player, replaced it with a fresh one and turned her attention to the inspector. 'Where's Mikey?' she asked.

Fletcher glanced down the road and saw the flame-haired photographer running towards them.

'He's –' began the inspector.

Fletcher was turning to face Catherine when there was a deafening, metallic thud on the other side of the van and the vehicle span suddenly towards him. Unable to react in time, the van knocked the inspector from his feet. A terrifying roar joined Catherine's scream as Fletcher hit the ground.

Running as fast as he could, Mikey barely registered the grey shape before it had flashed from the cover of the trees and impacted with the van. He saw the vehicle wrenched sideways, the inspector thrown backwards and fired his flash gun as the towering figure sped around the rear of the vehicle.

Caught in the bright beam, the blood covered figure of Åpep stopped in its tracks behind the van and turned its hideous countenance in Mikey's direction. Shocked by the creature's ferocious appearance and its sudden attention, Mikey's pace slowed to a crawl. He fumbled nervously with the camera controls as the stationary beast continued to regard him intently with its single blazing eye.

Mikey risked a look down at the camera and satisfied himself that the dial was set to the lightning symbol. He raised the device to his eye, focused on the monster's gore spattered face but then paused as his finger applied pressure to the flash gun's trigger. In the view finder, Åpep was behaving curiously.

There was a deep, guttural growl from the creature and it raised a taloned hand before its face as if protecting itself. It

310

shook its head, its ember eye not wavering then slowly it settled into a crouch. With one hand still held up before its head, the other moved to place something on the ground. Now Åpep was nodding and rising, its frame still hunched and its attention still focused solely on Mikey who in turn could not shift his gaze from the monster. The single shot from Fletcher – mere feet from the creature – broke the spell.

The result was an explosion of movement from Åpep. In a single motion it lunged forwards, swiped the gun from Fletcher's hands then bounded off into the bushes at the top of Hampstead Heath as rapidly as it had appeared. For his troubles the inspector found himself sprawled on the road once again and, as he struggled to get up, Mikey came to his aid.

'What the fuck was that!?' yelled Fletcher as Mikey held out his hand.

Mikey shook his head and gazed into the dark tree line where the receding crash of ferns marked the monster's passage.

'I'm not sure,' he replied, 'but it looked... Frightened.'

The inspector's attention returned quickly to the others in the van while Mikey stared harder at the break in the undergrowth where the monster had entered the wood. He raised his flash gun and stepped closer as a familiar figure floated out from the darkness.

'It's time, Mikey,' said the preacher. 'The monster has kept its promise. Now it's up to you.'

'Wha – I don't understand,' Mikey replied with a frown.

'You have the key, now come to the temple – help Jane.'

'Jane!?' Mikey took a step closer, his empty hand balling to a fist.

'Now, Mikey,' said the preacher. The figure began to fade. 'Jane's in the chapel... Save her... Save us all...'

'You –' began Mikey but the preacher had disappeared.

311

'Mikey?'

The photographer turned to find Catherine standing behind him. The psychic looked drawn and leaned heavily on her stick while behind her the equally pale faces of the archaeologists stared out from the side of the van. Mikey hitched a thumb at the space where the preacher had been.

'Did you see?!' he asked.

Catherine nodded. 'Not very clearly. But I heard him.'

'He said Jane's in a chapel.'

Catherine nodded. 'There's a small chapel at the bottom of the cemetery: I suppose he means that. But what did he mean about you having a key?'

Mikey shook his head and pointed to where Åpep had crouched behind the van. 'I don't know,' he replied. 'He also said that thing had 'kept its promise'.' Mikey stared for a moment at the spot where the creature had been and took a few steps closer. In the dim evening light it was difficult to see but now, as Mikey crouched down, he saw a small golden object on the floor.

Catherine too had followed him and frowned as Mikey held up what looked like a large coin. It was roughly five millimetres thick, hexagonal in shape and as Mikey turned the object slowly between his fingers, she saw that a jewelled eye had been set into one of its sides. Fletcher, Danny and the professor now joined the pair and Catherine pointed to the coin.

'Is that the Eye of Horus, professor?' she asked.

Professor Taylor accepted the coin from Mikey and held it up while both he and Danny scrutinised it. 'No,' he said after a few seconds. 'It's exquisite, but it's not an Utchat. An Utchat always shows the left eye of Horus. For want of a better explanation, I would say that this appears to show a middle eye.'

'You didn't see the creature, did you?' said Fletcher.

Danny, Catherine and the professor shook their heads in unison.

'We saw the hole it made in the side of the van,' replied Danny.

'And the noise it made when it hit it,' added the professor. 'That was more than enough.'

Fletcher tapped his forehead. 'That thing had a single eye – right there,' he explained.

Taylor frowned at Mikey. 'Are you saying the beast dropped this thing when you fought it?'

Mikey returned a grim smile. 'We didn't fight it, professor,' he pointed to Fletcher. 'The inspector shot it, but that only seemed to annoy it.'

Fletcher nodded. 'I was lucky. I stood there for what seemed like an age while I plucked up the courage to shoot, but the thing seemed to be completely focused on Mikey.'

Mikey retrieved the coin from the professor. 'The creature didn't drop it, it put it on the floor.' Mikey shrugged. 'I can't explain it, but it seemed deliberate.'

'Do you think that's the key the preacher mentioned?' Asked Catherine.

Mikey stood up. 'I don't know, but for Jane's sake, I think it's time we found out.'

Chapter Fifteen

At the top of the hill which joined Swain's Lane with Highgate, Fletcher cut the lights and the engine and rolled the van slowly down the steep incline towards the cemetery. The inspector knew the layout of Highgate Cemetery well enough to know that their likely objective – the Egyptian Avenue – could be better reached from Highgate Village itself, but Mikey was adamant that they check out the chapel by the main entrance first. For Fletcher this seemed like a bad tactical move and he stole himself for the expected conflict ahead.

Beside him, Mikey craned his neck to gaze out of the open window and kept careful watch on the sky. Like ragged clouds caught in a high wind the spirits were now speeding over the trees which bordered Swain's Lane and disappearing beyond the high wall which marked the cemetery's boundary. Mikey cast his mind back to the photograph his father had taken – the terror it had engendered in his young mind about Highgate Cemetery. He felt no such terror about visiting the place now, but a nagging sense of foreboding continued to plague his thoughts. Whoever the preacher was, he had guided Mikey's actions from the very start and now, Mikey was sure, he was close to finding out why.

Still only half way down the hill the van slowed and Mikey ducked his head back into the van. 'Why're you stopping?' he asked.

Fletcher pulled on the hand brake and pointed down the hill. Framed by the bowing branches of the trees and the bordering wall, the road beneath the hill could just be seen. Mikey nodded as he looked down at the grey vans parked on the road then frowned as he spotted the car which was parked amongst them.

'That's Jane's car!' exclaimed Mikey. He grabbed at the door

314

handle but the inspector clamped a restraining hand on his shoulder.

'Easy, son,' said the inspector, his grip instantly loosening. 'You knew she'd be here, so don't go charging in.' Fletcher nodded towards the parked vans. 'We don't know how many are down there or what position your girlfriend is in, so let's take this slow and let's make it quiet. Surprise is probably the only advantage we've got.'

Mikey took a deep breath and calmed himself, nodding to the inspector's words. Gripping his flash gun in one hand he climbed out of the van and kept a vigil on the sky while Fletcher opened the side door.

'Last stop,' said the inspector with a half-smile as he helped Catherine out.

Like Mikey, the paranormal investigator regarded the sky then bit her bottom lip and moved to join Mikey in front of the van. She noted Fletcher explaining again the operation of the gas launchers to the archaeologists beside the van and spoke quietly so they would not hear.

'There are one hell of a lot of spirits going over that wall, Mikey,' she said before tapping her Mini Disc player. 'Do you think these things are up to the job?'

Mikey too had continued to study the rapid flight of bodies above their heads but now he smiled down at the psychic. 'I don't think they're too bothered with us anymore,' he replied 'But can you hear that tone?' Again Mikey cast his gaze to the sky and tilted his head to listen.

Catherine joined him and quickly became aware of the sound to which Mikey was referring. At first it seemed like a flat hum but, the more she concentrated, the more the noise resolved itself into a sigh.

'Are you two alright?' asked Danny as he and the others joined the pair before the van.

'Yes,' said Mikey. 'We were just listening…' He pointed up by way of explanation.

The others peered up doubtfully.

'The spirits appear to be singing,' explained Catherine.

'As long as they do it well away from me that's just fine,' replied the professor.

Mikey smiled. 'I don't think they'll give us much trouble now, professor,' he said. 'They seem occupied.'

Inspector Fletcher nodded, glanced down the hill then stood before the others. 'Okay. Now listen. This is how I want us to proceed,' he began.

The entrance to the cemetery appeared deserted but the inspector carefully weaved between the assembled vans: removing every set of ignition keys he could find. He scanned the dark windows above the cemetery gates then scrutinised the bushes beyond the entrance railings before waving the others on.

Now armed with a CS gas launcher, Professor Taylor scuttled his way towards the policeman. 'We are far too old to be playing at soldiers,' complained the archeologist as he settled down beside the policeman.

Fletcher grinned, watching as Danny, his face set firm – machine gun swaying – followed behind. 'Some of us are, some of us aren't,' he shrugged and returned his attention to the view through the railings.

Feeling more comfortable with his flash gun, Mikey had declined to carry either a CS launcher or the remaining machine gun. Both he and Catherine crept their way towards the others then stopped as they got their first clear view of the cemetery.

Beyond the railings and the boundary wall, the overgrown hill of Highgate Cemetery rose up before them. Lit by the orange glow of the sky, pale alabaster headstones, angels and crosses poked from the cloying ivy which strangled every surface. They dotted the view as the pair lifted their gaze towards the skyline. Above the cemetery, a vortex of souls swirled through the air, spinning rapidly to a central point which surged down below the topmost trees.

'That's…amazing,' muttered Catherine.

Mikey nodded silently, then patted her on the shoulder. 'Come on,' he said and moved off to join the others.

Keeping low, Inspector Fletcher had now moved through the open gate and cast a glance through the chapel doorway as he passed it. He stopped, gave a deep frown then regarded Mikey grimly as the photographer drew near.

'I…' he began but could not find the words.

Mikey was already mirroring the inspector's grim expression before he looked inside the chapel but now, with a pained yell he rushed to Jane's side.

'Don't touch her!' cautioned Fletcher. 'She's badly burned.'

'Jesus! Jesus!' shouted Mikey. He threw his flash camera onto the flagstones and bent over the pitiful shape of his girlfriend.

Hovering in the doorway, Fletcher turned to Danny and pointed to the dark border of the cemetery. 'Shoot anything that isn't already buried,' he said and went to join the photographer.

Mikey hung his head and wept, unable to comprehend how someone could inflict so much damage, so much suffering on another person. He felt the firm hand of the inspector on his shoulder as Fletcher knelt beside him then gasped as a voice he thought he would never hear again whispered his name.

'Mikey?…'

Elation and disbelief combined to choke Mikey for a second and he opened his tear streaming eyes to see Jane looking back at him.

'I'm here! I'm here!' he replied joyfully and tried with all his might not to clasp her by the hands.

'Knew… you'd… come…' muttered Jane, her red-rimmed eyes fluttering. 'Knew… it.'

A burst of machine gun fire sounded from outside and Fletcher instantly ran back to the door. He got there to find Danny, Catherine and the professor flat on the entrance floor as another rattle of bullets sounded in the distance.

'It wasn't at us, I think it's up there!' said Danny. He got back to his feet and pointed at the trees which obscured their view.

Fletcher, his machine gun at the ready, crouched in the doorway and listened. He thought he heard a cry carry through the air before prolonged bursts of gunfire from several different points flashed in the darkness.

'It must be coming from the Egyptian Avenue – don't you think?' said Catherine.

The psychic had moved close to the inspector and now she too assumed a crouch. She took a look into the chapel and found Mikey striding towards her purposefully. A deep frown set on his brow.

'Mikey?'

Without reply, Mikey brushed between Catherine and the inspector and strode quickly past Danny and the still prostrate professor. 'I'm going up there,' he said without turning.

'Wait!' yelled Fletcher. 'Mikey – there's a fucking gun-fight going on up there!'

'I want this over with right now,' replied Mikey without breaking stride. 'Jane will die if I don't stop this.'

Behind the chapel and the entrance was a small paved area which centred on a war memorial. Beyond that the rest of the cemetery was lost in waves of foliage but the remains of a shingle path still marked the route upwards through the graveyard. Mikey had almost reached the path.

'Fuck!' muttered Fletcher. He climbed to his feet. 'Come on, we'll have to help him,' he said and limped off in pursuit.

Danny frowned at the professor, shrugged and followed the inspector while Professor Taylor regarded Catherine with the same expression.

Catherine patted the professor on the shoulder. 'Look after Jane,' she said and hurried as best she could to catch up.

The pathway wound up through the plinths, tombs and angled gravestones of the wealthy but long-forgotten until it reached a junction where the path was barely discernible beneath the deep shade of the overhanging trees. Mikey stopped briefly, cocked his head to one side, then followed the sound of gunfire down the right hand path.

'For Christ's sake slow down!' hissed Fletcher from the darkness behind him but Mikey continued to increase his pace.

At the junction the inspector stopped to massage his bandaged leg, heard a scream echo somewhere through the night and waited impatiently for Danny and Catherine to catch him up. 'Come on!' he urged and hobbled after Mikey.

Mikey continued to march on, his mind set on one single task. He didn't need a doctor to realise Jane was close to death and that meant he had to get her to a hospital – quickly. To do that he would have to put an end to whatever it was this Bradford character was doing and he had to do it fast. He was not going to negotiate, he was not going to reason: he had stood by helplessly as Geoff had died – he was not going to do that with Jane.

A plastered wall suddenly broke through the flowing plant life to Mikey's left and following its pale line he spotted a dark arch framed by Egyptian columns. Though it seemed ancient, the red brickwork which showed beneath the occasional patch of cracked plaster belied its true, Victorian age and Mikey quickened his pace. He raised his flash gun as he saw two figures lying on the ground ahead.

Beneath the wide entrance to the Egyptian Avenue, the bloody corpses of a young man and woman lay broken on the shingle track. Bullet holes had arced shattered paths across the columns which framed the archway but the wounds which had stilled the figures at Mikey's feet had not been produced by any gun.

The man's head was separated from his body: his limbs splayed doll-like with his machine gun still clasped in one hand. Beside him the girl stared blindly at the night sky, her torso slashed and brutally punctured. Mikey had no doubt that Åpep was the cause of their deaths, but what puzzled him was why the vicious creature had seemed so cowed beside the van. Sporadic gunfire still echoed through the night air but Mikey's attention was suddenly drawn to the pulsing light which had begun to emanate from the far end of the Egyptian Avenue. The very fabric of the place seemed to be glowing.

Lined with the dark doors of family crypts, the avenue climbed gently until it reached the roundway – the sunken, circular centre piece of the cemetery. Though Mikey had never dared set foot in the place before, he recognised it instantly from the many photographs his father had taken of it. The single doorway which stood framed by the end of the avenue looked particularly familiar.

A figure ran past the doorway as Mikey advanced up the avenue, a scream on his lips and his machine gun flashing. Mikey raised his own weapon but the man disappeared – oblivious to Mikey's presence. The pulsing light from the stonework was growing stronger as the photographer drew closer to the roundway and now a second figure stepped into view. Seemingly in less of a hurry than the first man, he sauntered past the crypt door as Mikey looked on then paused in mid step. A thin smile spread across his face and slowly he turned to face Mikey.

Mikey recognised him instantly, but the crying boy he had seen in his father's photograph – in exactly the same spot – was now a man. Peter Bradford placed his hands on his hips and smiled more broadly.

'Come to take another photograph?' he asked.

Mikey frowned and raised the flash gun. 'Who the fuck are you?!' he snarled.

Bradford took a step closer and scratched the wound which sat upon his forehead. 'I might ask you the same question, Mr Dayville. By the way,' he added with a grin, 'how's your girlfriend?'

In a sudden rush of anger, Mikey raised his flash gun and pulled the trigger.

There was a whine from the device and a brief surge of light illuminated the avenue around Mikey. Dismayed, he grabbed at the dial to set it to flash but found that it already was. Mikey looked up at Bradford just in time to see that he appeared to have his own flash gun: set in the centre of his forehead.

A wall of intense heat knocked Mikey from his feet and tumbled him back down the avenue. For a moment it seemed that his entire body was aflame and Mikey gasped for breath before the searing pain suddenly disappeared. A volley of deafening shots sounded close to his ears, quickly followed by running feet. In the distance he heard someone shout: "It's open!" and an acrid smell of burning plastic reached his nostrils before unconsciousness overwhelmed him.

Pacing the flagstones beside the prostrate figure of Jane, Professor Taylor chewed on his lip and listened to the sporadic gunfire still sounding through the darkness. Keeping one

321

worried eye on Jane's shallow breathing, the professor strode to and from the chapel door: willing the others to return while his hands wrung the barrel of the CS gas launcher. He breathed a sigh of relief when at last he heard footsteps approaching but his joy was short-lived as Garvin stepped through the doorway.

In the time it took Professor Taylor to recognise the man he had seen leaving Mikey's house, Garvin had dropped the large canvas bag he was carrying, raised his .45 Colt and fired. A deafening explosion reverberated around the confines of the chapel while the professor hit the floor screaming: writhing in agony as he clutched his shattered shin.

Garvin frowned at the dark cemetery beyond, fished out his silencer from the bag at his feet and fitted it to his Colt. He tried to listen for any activity in the darkness but the professor's constant cries drowned out even the sound of his own sigh. Garvin knew waiting for Mikey to show up at Jane's had been a long shot, but he had not foreseen his target heading straight for the cemetery. It did not make tactical sense. Unless the screaming old man had nothing to do with Jane's boyfriend.

Garvin reloaded his gun, gave a final glance at the cemetery and strolled over to the now whimpering professor. He placed a foot on the man's chest, his gun against his temple and shouted over the cries.

'Stop screaming – start talking!'

There was still a terrible smell of burning plastic in Mikey's nostrils as he sat up but his attention was immediately grabbed by Inspector Fletcher's singed eyebrows.

'What happened to you?' Mikey asked with a frown.

'Same as you,' Fletcher replied. 'That bastard Bradford.'

The inspector tapped Mikey's chest and looking down, the photographer saw that the earphones he had placed around his neck were now nothing more than misshapen strands of plastic.

'Christ…' mouthed Mikey. He stood up, brushed himself down and smiled wearily at Catherine and Danny who had their weapons trained on the end of the avenue.

'Looks like you took the worst of it,' observed Danny. 'We just caught the tail end.' The archeologist patted his own, intact earphones.

Mikey nodded and retrieved his flash gun from the ground. 'I must have damaged this when I threw it on the floor of the chapel,' Mikey said as he looked the device over. There was a loose connection between the camera and the CD player which Mikey quickly rectified. He pointed the flash gun towards the bottom of the Egyptian Avenue and watched with satisfaction as a bush suddenly sprang into flame.

'Looks like Bradford has a similar weapon,' said Fletcher.

Mikey shook his head. 'That light came straight out of his forehead, inspector. Bradford was unarmed.'

'Like a third eye?' asked Catherine while Fletcher returned a deep frown.

Mikey shrugged. 'I don't know what you'd call it – it looked more like a miner's lamp from where I was standing: and felt like a blow torch.'

Inspector Fletcher fingered the singed hair of his eyebrows and sighed, eying the end of the avenue where the two corpses lay. 'Whatever that freak has done to himself, it looks like our monster friend is no longer on his side.'

Danny let out a hollow laugh. 'That makes me feel easier.'

Fletcher shrugged. 'Thank heaven for small mercies, son. Would you rather have fought him back at the van?'

'I don't want to have to fight him now: or ever,' Danny replied.

Mikey was watching the door which Bradford had stood in

front of, recalling the pulsing light which had glowed through the surrounding brickwork but had now stopped. He cast a glance at Catherine then peered up into the mesh of ivy which enclosed the Egyptian Avenue; attempting to view the sky.

'Can you hear the spirits anymore, Catherine?' he asked.

Catherine shook her head and stood up. 'No, it's gone quiet.'

'There's certainly no more gunfire,' added Danny.

Mikey walked to the roundway and checked each way before looking up. The sky was still the colour of fire but the spirits had disappeared. Mikey waved the others on. Cautiously, they gathered behind him and scanned the area.

The sunken circle which formed the roundway was, like the Egyptian Avenue before it, dotted with blank crypt doors and bricked up entrances. Moss and weeds sprouted from every crack in the plaster while the ever present ivy hung like curtains from the walls.

'There's another body,' whispered Fletcher. He pointed his machine gun at a grey shape lying half obscured by the right hand curve.

Straining their ears for the slightest sound the group moved forward cautiously until the corpse was at their feet. The inspector regarded the bloody torso and its raking wounds with a shake of his head.

'Nigel said that monster was difficult to control. Looks like he was right.'

'So do you think the shooting we heard was the White Knights trying to stop it?' asked Danny.

Fletcher shrugged. 'Probably. What worries me is that they're armed with the same weapons we have: and I haven't seen the monster's body lying anywhere.'

'Look at this,' said Mikey.

While Fletcher had been debating with Danny, Mikey had moved further around the curve until he had reached the rear

324

of the roundway. Here a crypt door had been wrenched from its hinges and the dark space beyond was littered with tools.

'Looks like our friends had difficulty getting in here,' observed Mikey as the others joined him.

Fletcher pulled a torch from his pocket and shone it into the darkness. There were pickaxes and sledgehammers lent against the walls and the battered stone floor indicated that their use had been both frantic and futile. In the centre of the floor however a large square hole showed where the White Knights had finally broken through. Fletcher moved to the hole and peered down, immediately flicking off his torch.

'There's light down there,' he said as the others gathered around the hole.

Danny gave a low whistle. 'That's some drop.' He crouched down and pointed to the cavernous space below. 'See the columns? Just like in Tenneshaw Wright's book.'

Catherine grimaced at the hole in the floor and hugged herself. 'It feels like Tenneshaw Wright's book,' she replied cryptically.

'What does that mean?' queried Danny.

'Catherine means it feels 'weird' – for want of a better word,' answered Mikey. 'I can feel it too… It's a kind of vibration.'

Danny nodded but seemed unfazed. 'So how do we get down?' he asked, looking briefly around the gloomy chamber. 'If Bradford's lot climbed down, where's their rope?'

'Good point,' Fletcher replied. He flicked his torch back on and scanned the crypt from floor to ceiling, stopping when a small depression sprang into stark relief on the wall behind the hole.

'Keyhole…' Mikey mused, remembering the words of the preacher. He stepped closer and studied the octagonal hole for a second before pulling the jewelled coin from his pocket. As the others looked on with curiosity, Mikey fitted the coin snugly into the shallow depression.

The jewel in the centre of the coin glowed brightly and Mikey stepped back. Without a sound, the hole at their feet was suddenly filled as a block of stone rushed up from the floor below. Fletcher shook his head in wonder.

'That's some lift,' he said. 'I had no idea the Victorians had them.'

'I'm not sure they did, inspector,' Danny replied. 'And the Egyptians certainly didn't.'

'Do you think it's safe?' Mused Catherine. The psychic seemed nervous.

Mikey shrugged and tapped the stone block with a foot. 'Only one way to find out, I suppose,' he said. He held his breath and stepped onto the slab.

Instantly the stone began to slowly descend. Throwing caution to the wind, both Fletcher and Danny leapt on while Catherine hung back.

'C'mon, Catherine!' Mikey urged as the floor of the crypt reached the level of his knees. He held out a hand and steadied the psychic as she jumped down to join them.

'Keep your eyes peeled and your weapons ready,' advised Fletcher as the crypt disappeared from view. 'We don't know how many of those White Knights are still around.'

In silence the four watched as a metre thick stone ceiling gave way to a large, columned chamber. Without any visible means of support, the square block descended into the well lit interior of the temple and the group scanned the distant, brightly painted walls for signs of movement.

'This is incredible!' sighed Danny. 'The professor is going to have a field day down here!'

'Very colourful,' nodded Fletcher. 'But there's still the small matter of catching Bradford first, Danny. So don't act like a tourist just yet.'

Danny nodded. 'If I remember the plan in Tenneshaw Wright's book, this is the first chamber of many.' He shook his head. 'I had no idea it was going to be so huge!'

Mikey cast his gaze around the gaudily painted columns supporting the chamber and directed Catherine's attention to a larger, central pillar. 'Is it my imagination,' he asked, 'or is that column pulsing?'

Catherine looked and nodded. 'Do you think that's where the spirits went?' she replied. Mikey shrugged and, as the pair looked on, the pulsing seemed to subside.

They were a metre from the floor when Fletcher spotted a shape suddenly dart past a column. 'Jump!' he shouted.

A burst of machine gun fire rattled through the chamber as the four leapt from the lift and Mikey grabbed out to steady Catherine as she hit the floor and stumbled.

'Christ!' she yelled as her bad leg buckled beneath her.

Mikey's arms were instantly around her waist and he threw them both behind the safety of a column as bullets sprayed across the stone floor behind them. Another burst of shots rattled close by and Mikey saw that both Fletcher and Danny had taken similar refuge behind pillars and were firing back. Mikey flinched as the pillar beside him exploded under the impact of another volley of bullets and he threw himself sideways and raised his flash gun.

Both Danny and the inspector were firing again and Mikey saw a figure duck down behind a far column as their bullets stuttered patterns in the ancient paint work.

'Gotcha!' said Mikey through clenched teeth and fired.

A blazing pulse of light surged from Mikey's flash gun and struck the bottom of the pillar which hid their adversary. In an instant the lower part of the column evaporated and Mikey's heart leapt into his mouth as the pillar and part of the roof

327

thundered down into the chamber.

'Fuck!' yelled Fletcher, running to throw himself down beside Catherine and Mikey. He was instantly followed by Danny and both men covered their heads with their arms as the temple shook ominously.

Frozen, Mikey looked on as massive chunks of stone rained in on the far end of the chamber before a billowing cloud of dust obscured his destructive feat. A nervous, wooden grin fixed itself on his face and he turned to find Catherine staring wide-eyed at him.

'Oops...' he muttered.

The temple continued to tremble around them but the grinding sounds of tumbling rock quickly subsided. The whole chamber was now fogged with dust and Fletcher coughed as he lifted his head. He regarded Mikey with a pained smile.

'Was that you?' he asked.

Mikey nodded mutely.

The inspector climbed to his feet, dusted himself down and squinted into the thinning cloud around them. 'Well...' he began. 'I think you got him.'

'Us too, almost,' added Danny. He shook his head at Mikey as he stood up but there was no animosity in his tone.

'Yeah, sorry about that,' said Mikey sheepishly.

Catherine tugged Mikey's sleeve and pointed to the centre of the chamber. 'Look,' she said.

The pulsing in the large, central column had begun again, but this time it was both faster and brighter.

'What the hell is that?' queried the inspector.

'I don't know,' replied Catherine. 'But I don't think it's good.'

'We've got to find Bradford,' said Mikey. He got to his feet and studied the walls for signs of a doorway. 'Danny, do you remember seeing a way down in Tenneshaw Wright's book?'

'Er... Yes,' the archeologist replied. He took a few steps to the right and pointed to a dark arch set in the eastern wall of the chamber. 'That way – I think,' Danny announced.

Mikey helped Catherine to her feet and took a final look behind them as they moved towards the arch. The north west corner of the chamber was now dirt covered rubble but the temple itself seemed to have resisted the worst of the cave in. Mikey hoped that he could finally find some answers in this strange place and tried not to think about the tortured images of Jane which kept forming in his mind. He would save her. And if it meant destroying the temple he would do just that. He turned and jogged after the others and did notice the stone elevator as it began to rise again.

Beyond the chamber, several wide ramps led down to another columned space and it was at the bottom of the final slope that the group found another body. Beside it were three leather bound books stuffed into a carrier bag.

'This one's different,' said Fletcher, crouching down beside the corpse.

The slender shape of the figure indicated it was female but the blackened clothes and roasted flesh made any further identification difficult.

'Looks like Bradford's turning on his own people,' observed Mikey.

Fletcher nodded and stood up. 'Between that madman and the monster, we might just win this thing.' The inspector frowned. 'I haven't seen the man who shot up my police station yet though, so –' Fletcher let the sentence tail away and turned to regard Danny.

The archeologist had recognised the leather books in the carrier bag as belonging to Tenneshaw Wright and had checked them to find that one of them was the one taken from Mikey's house.

'It's your book again, Mikey,' he announced, tapping the tome's cover.

'And the others?' Mikey asked.

Danny flicked a few pages of another volume, whistled and pointed to the centre of the chamber where another pulsing column stood. 'This one seems to be about that flashing pillar but I can barely make head nor tail of the annotations. It seems to be some strange form of Egyptian mathematics.'

'Just find a map of the place, Danny,' advised Fletcher. 'You can study later.'

Danny nodded and picked up Mikey's book. 'I'm not sure where you want to go, but down is that way.' He pointed to the far end of the chamber.

The group moved cautiously across the second chamber and passed close to the central column. Both Mikey and Catherine felt a vague disorientation as they approached the glowing pillar but the discomfort had passed by the time they reached the next set of ramps.

'It gets bigger as we go down,' said Danny with a smile.

'Just keep your eyes peeled,' said Fletcher. 'And if you know which way we should go, get rid of the book and keep your trigger finger free.'

Danny nodded, placed the book on the floor and adjusted his machine gun. 'This way,' he said and led them down the ramp.

The temple did indeed get bigger as they descended and the third chamber was cathedral-like in scale. An open ramp way zigzagged down the western side of the chamber and the floor of the vast space was dominated by a polished, copper-coloured dome. From the ceiling far above, the pulsing column descended into its top.

'How the hell did Tenneshaw Wright get this back here?' mused Fletcher as the group finally made it to the bottom.

'Think 'Bill Gates' type wealth, inspector,' Danny answered. 'The Victorians were not only rich, but immensely resourceful and Wright owned an entire merchant fleet.'

'Where there's a will, there's a way,' said Catherine as the group started across the floor.

Keeping a steady pace the group skirted the base of the towering copper dome and headed towards the eastern exit. The same feeling of disorientation gripped Mikey and Catherine as they moved near the gleaming centre piece of the chamber but now the others appeared to sense it too.

'What is that humming?' asked Fletcher with a frown. He grimaced at Mikey who pointed to the copper dome.

'It's that thing, inspector,' he replied. 'Catherine and I think it's where the spirits went.'

'Freaky,' replied Fletcher. He turned his attention to Danny who looked equally uncomfortable. 'Is there anything else like this in Egypt?' He asked.

Danny puffed out his cheeks, gave a sigh and shrugged. 'Frankly, inspector,' he said, 'I think this has about as much to do with Egyptology as Heathrow Airport has to do with Stonehenge.'

Fletcher snorted. 'Meaning what, exactly?'

'Meaning...' continued Danny with another shrug, 'that everything about this place is wrong. The architecture, the hieroglyphs, the scale. The Egyptians built many wonders, but they never constructed anything even remotely like this. If it wasn't for the fact that there's evidence to support its discovery in Egypt I – well, I wouldn't be able to tell you where it came from nor who built it.'

'Aliens,' said Mikey, almost to himself.

'Aliens!' echoed the inspector with surprise – his voice booming across the cavernous space. Fletcher grinned: 'Do you think we'll find E. T. in here somewhere?!'

331

'We've already met him, inspector,' Mikey replied casually. 'Or do you think Åpep escaped from a zoo?'

Fletcher's smile waned as he considered Mikey's words. He stared narrowly at the photographer for a second then shook his head. 'Let's get keep moving, shall we? We'll deal with the 'Close Encounter' scenario when the time comes.'

They picked up their pace and jogged towards the arch which was the only feature on the eastern wall. They were yards away from it when a loud slap sounded and Danny stumbled forwards.

'Fuck!' he yelped, sprawling onto the floor.

'Shit!' cried the inspector, instantly recognising the sound as a bullet striking the rear of Danny's Kevlar vest. 'Take cover!'

Catherine sprinted as best she could towards the arch as another bullet chipped the stone floor inches from the prostrate Danny's head. Both Mikey and Fletcher grabbed the stunned archeologist by the arms and dragged him to his feet as they darted for the rampway. A third bullet struck the wall beside them as they left the chamber and Mikey was suddenly chilled by a gruesome image of Catherine which flashed through his mind.

In a single frozen moment he saw the psychic – like Geoff before her – receive a fatal gunshot wound to the head and jerk backwards. Only Mikey was not currently looking at Catherine. He was staring at the floor.

Without thinking, Mikey let go of Danny's arm and had thrown himself across the corridor before he had even looked up. He struck Catherine in the midriff and knocked her to the ground. A few feet beyond the startled psychic, a bullet ricocheted off of the wall and whizzed away harmlessly.

'Keep running!' Mikey shouted.

He picked Catherine up and launched himself down the first

ramp, glancing quickly to his left to see both Danny and the inspector keeping pace. They hurtled down two more ramps before Catherine demanded to stop.

Both she and Fletcher massaged their legs while Mikey and Danny kept a wary watch on the rampway.

'What the hell was that?!' demanded Catherine, her exasperation plain.

'A fuckin' sniper rifle –' growled Fletcher. '– that's what that was. And a fucking silenced one as well.'

Danny tapped his chest. 'Thank God I was wearing this vest,' he said with relief. 'And thanks for dragging me out of there.'

Mikey nodded. 'Did anyone see where the shots came from?' he asked.

The inspector shook his head. 'No. I reckon the sniper was up on the other ramp: but what I want to know is how he got behind us. Is there another way up?'

Danny shook his head. 'I can't be one hundred percent, but I'm pretty certain this is the only way up or down.'

'So there must have been more of Bradford's people up top,' said Catherine. She stood up and stretched her leg.

The inspector nodded. 'I think it's the man I was expecting,' he replied. 'This 'Garvin' character.'

'So what do we do now?' asked Danny. 'Wait for him?'

'No,' answered Mikey bluntly. 'We keep moving.'

Fletcher held up a hand. 'Now, wait a minute, Mikey – Danny might have a good point.'

'I can't afford to wait, inspector,' urged Mikey. 'I have to stop whatever is going on here and get Jane to a hospital. How far is it to the bottom, Danny?'

'Um,' said Danny, pointing his machine gun down the rampway. 'The next chamber is as big as the last, then two levels of rooms, then the bottom – I think.'

'We can't possibly fight a sniper in a large chamber,' said Fletcher hitching a thumb over his shoulder. 'You saw it back there; he can pick us off from miles away. We're better off in a smaller space.'

'Then we get to these room levels Danny just mentioned: fight him there.'

'And what's to stop him picking us off while we're crossing the next chamber?' responded Fletcher with a shrug.

Mikey tapped the CS gas launcher slung around Danny's waist. 'We gas the stairway,' he replied, 'that'll slow him down.' Fletcher did not look convinced. 'I'm sorry, inspector, but I have to keep moving,' said Mikey earnestly. 'I have to find this 'preacher' – my girlfriend's life depends on it.'

Fletcher nodded silently for a moment. 'Alright,' he said, 'we keep on moving: but we'd better move bloody fast.' He pointed up the rampway. 'Danny, fire some gas up there now – I don't want that bastard creeping up on me until I'm ready for him.'

Danny nodded, dropped his machine gun on its shoulder strap then swung his launcher round. He pulled the trigger and fired up the ramp. With a pop the gas canister struck squarely against the wall and ricocheted back towards them.

'Fuckin' hell, Danny!' shouted the inspector as the returning canister began spewing a white plume of gas. Holding their breath, the group ran from the choking mist as fast as their legs would carry them.

It took several minutes before they reached the final ramp and, though they had expected to see another grand chamber, none of the group were prepared for the sight which greeted them. The next chamber was as vast as the last but here a colossal cylinder occupied the centre of the space from floor to ceiling. It was made from the same copper-like material of the dome in the previous chamber but this time the massive structure was pulsing frantically. A deafening, warbling roar accompanied the flashing light.

Grimacing at the noise, Fletcher patted Danny on the shoulder and pointed to the ramp they had just descended. 'No time to sight see!' he shouted. 'Fire another canister up there!'

Danny nodded, reloaded the launcher then took careful aim to deflect the projectile away. The canister bounced up onto the next flight of the ramp and this time did not return. Fletcher gave a happy thumbs up and with wary glances back, the four of them continued on towards the giant drum.

The noise from the structure beat relentlessly upon the group as they skirted its wide base but, despite its hostile blare, they still found themselves slowing to look at the angled slabs which surrounded the bottom of the drum. Made of stone, the tops of each slab were covered in coloured hieroglyphs: some of which were winking on and off in time to the pulse from the drum.

'That's incredible!' shouted Danny, veering off from the others to get a closer look.

He barely had a second's chance to study the strange array of flashing symbols before Fletcher's hand had gripped his collar and dragged him backwards.

'Do you want to get shot?!' yelled the inspector in Danny's ear as he pulled him away.

Reluctantly, Danny craned his neck to regard the towering drum a final time then turned and trotted off to join the others. Like the inspector, the archeologist had felt dismissive of Mikey's alien hypothesis, but now he considered it with a new-found respect. In the brief moment he had studied the top of the slab, he had seen that the hieroglyphs looked just like buttons – each shape outlined by a dark groove cut into the stone. He shook his head and smiled, scarcely noticing now the violent pounding from the drum. Just what would

Professor Taylor make of it all, he wondered.

The next set of ramps led quickly to a more enclosed level where the ceiling sat less than four metres above the group's heads and the noise from the last chamber was muffled by robust walls. A long, blank corridor of pale stone led off from the rampway and at its end a highly decorated arch surrounded the first door they had so far encountered in the temple. Realising their path was blocked, the group stopped a few metres away and saw that the dark material of the door was inlaid with rows of large hieroglyphs.

'Now what?' said Fletcher. The inspector turned and kept a close eye on the distant rampway while Danny stepped forwards to study the door.

'This is a tomb!' exclaimed Danny. He scanned the lines of glyphs on the door and read aloud: "Rest – something – traveller of the – something – sleep." The archeologist turned and grinned at the others. 'The syntax is odd, but the wording is very similar to hieroglyphs found in early dynastic tombs.'

'This must be where the preacher is.' said Catherine. She looked at Mikey, who frowned.

'Tenneshaw Wright will be here too,' he said.

'And Bradford,' added Fletcher. 'Does it say how we get in, Danny?' he asked.

Danny shrugged, moved closer to the door and placed a finger beneath one of the hieroglyphs. 'This –,' he began then stopped as the doorway paled: quickly disappearing to reveal the chamber beyond. 'Er?… Never mind,' said Danny with a nervous glance back at the others. Cautiously he led the group through the now open doorway.

Beyond the door was a long chamber lined on each side with upright, closed stone sarcophagi. The centre of the room was occupied by a row of the same stone slabs they had seen around the base of the pulsing drum.

'Stunning!' exclaimed Danny. He clapped his hands together and moved quickly to the first of the slabs, examining the glowing hieroglyphs with eager eyes.

'Is this were the preacher is, Mikey?' asked Catherine.

Mikey frowned, concentrating for a moment. 'I don't really know, but I don't think he's in this chamber.'

'How can you be sure?' asked Danny. He looked up from the panel and pointed to the stone sarcophagi. 'Maybe he's in one of these?'

Mikey shrugged and massaged his temple. 'Maybe – I don't know. But I'm getting the strangest feeling of déjà vu. Is there another chamber beyond this one?'

'Yes, and then another floor of chambers,' Danny replied.

Though the noise from the drum chamber had completely faded, the group now felt a tremor run through the floor.

'What the hell was that?' muttered Fletcher suspiciously. The inspector stepped away from the door where he had been watching the corridor and at once the doorway reappeared to block his view. The floor trembled again.

'Whatever it is, we should keep going,' insisted Mikey.

'It doesn't feel right,' said Catherine as a third tremor shook the chamber. 'Do you think it might be from that pillar you knocked down?'

Mikey shook his head. 'I don't know, but the sooner we find some answers, the sooner we can get out.'

'Agreed,' said Fletcher. He patted Danny who still leant over the panel of symbols. 'C'mon,' he urged and led them towards the end of the room.

A second doorway disappeared as soon as they touched it and led to a hexagonal chamber where a copper dome descended from the ceiling into a glowing pillar. Immense energy seemed to be thrusting down the column for the whole room shook relentlessly as the group ran for the next door.

337

Beyond was a another sarcophagi chamber identical to the first and as the doorway reappeared behind them, the group paused to let the ringing in their ears subside.

'It feels like the temple's going to take off,' observed Danny.

'Or shake itself to pieces trying,' added Fletcher.

There was a final, violent rumble through the stonework and the four staggered to the walls to steady themselves. A thin haze of dust fell from the ceiling and, as suddenly as they had started, the tremors stopped.

Catherine eyed the door they had just passed through and tilted her head to one side: listening. 'Can anybody else hear that?' she asked.

Fletcher and Danny followed her gaze. 'What?' they asked in unison.

Catherine shook her head. 'I'm sure I heard someone calling... Mikey, did you? –'

Catherine turned to see that Mikey was walking along the central, illuminated slabs which ran, once again through the middle of the latest sarcophagus chamber. There was a frown on his face as he studied the hieroglyphic panels and when he reached the third slab he punched down blindly onto the glyphs. The tremors began again.

'Mikey?!' cried Catherine.

Danny raced round to see which hieroglyph Mikey had struck while the photographer stared at his hand as if seeing it for the first time. He looked first to Danny then regarded Catherine with a puzzled expression.

'What happened?' Mikey asked.

'You'd better see this,' said Danny to the others. He pointed to the panel and both Catherine and Fletcher moved closer. In the centre of the bright hieroglyphs was a circle of polished stone upon which now flashed sets of rapidly changing symbols.

'What did I do?' asked Mikey. He took a step back from the panel then yelled as he felt a hand upon his shoulder. He span round to find himself face to face with the preacher.

'That really isn't necessary,' said the preacher as the rest turned and reflexively raised their weapons. He shook his head. 'I can assure you that I'm not a threat.'

'So just what the fuck are you then?' growled Fletcher, his weapon still pointed firmly at the clergyman's chest. 'And where the hell did you spring from?'

The questions elicited a pained expression from the preacher. 'That really is the most disagreeable phrase, inspector. Have good grace and manners completely disappeared?' He sighed. 'In answer to your first question: I am, or rather I once was, a minister of the church of St. Anne's in Lower Hampstead. As for springing from the fires of hell well, perhaps that is an apt description.' He pointed to the open sarcophagus behind him. 'I have spent a timeless spell inside this God-less place waiting for my time of redemption.' He smiled at Mikey and placed a gentle hand upon his shoulder. 'Thanks to you, my dear boy, that time is at hand.'

'I don't understand,' replied Mikey.

'I know,' responded the preacher in a soft tone, 'but all will soon become clear to you...' The preacher paused and glanced – almost furtively – towards the door the group had entered through.

'How long have you been in here?' asked Danny.

The preacher smiled, though it seemed edged with pain. 'A long time, Mr Trent.'

'How do you know our names?' asked Catherine.

This time the furtive glance was aimed at Mikey. 'My.. contact with Michael has – um,' began the preacher. He held out his hands. 'It really is rather difficult to explain, my dear.'

'The first one to move gets a bullet through the head,' said a calm voice from the doorway behind them. 'I want to see everybody's weapon on the floor and your hands up in the air –'

Fletcher, his machine gun still gripped firmly at his waist, span around to spray the doorway with bullets but the sight which greeted him stayed his hand for a crucial fraction of a second. In the doorway which led through to the hexagonal chamber, Garvin was crouched behind a wheelbarrow in which was splayed the unconscious figure of Jane. The inspector barely had time to register the fact before a savage blow to his chest threw him back against the wall.

Having felled one adversary, Garvin now found himself staring down the barrel of another machine gun and two camera lenses. Completely thrown by such a strange sight and seemingly outnumbered, Garvin quickly reconsidered his options and pressed the barrel of his pistol against Jane's head.

'She ain't dead yet, but you make one wrong move and she will be,' he said, his face a mask of hostile intent.

'Don't listen to him!' said Fletcher's pained voice from the floor. Clutching his chest the inspector slowly got back to his feet and re-aimed his machine gun at the doorway.

'The man's a killer, Mikey,' continued the inspector. 'Don't forget that. The first chance he gets he'll top the lot of us.'

'If I wanted you dead, you wouldn't be talkin' now,' countered Garvin. His eyes darted around the room, taking in the distance to the next door, calculating his next move. He licked his dry lips. 'I'm just tryin' to find a friend of mine, that's all. I don't want trouble.'

'You should've thought of that before you shot up my police station,' replied Fletcher icily.

'Where's Professor Taylor?' asked Danny, suddenly realising his colleague had been with Jane.

Garvin's eyes focused hard on Danny. 'He's alright,' he lied.

'Just unconscious.' His gaze shifted quickly to the inspector. 'You let me go an' nobody else gets hurt.'

'No fucking deal,' growled Fletcher. 'You drop the gun and I'll let you live.'

A thin smile split Garvin's sweaty countenance. 'I don't think so.'

The preacher moved a fraction closer to Mikey and whispered. 'I can save Jane if I put her in my chamber, Mikey. Take Garvin down to the bottom level – the answers you seek are down there.' Before Mikey could respond, the preacher was addressing Garvin. 'Mister Bradford is in the lower chamber, Mister Garvin, as well as Marcus Wright.'

Garvin fixed the preacher with a puzzled gaze while Mikey lowered his flash gun. 'Leave Jane here,' Mikey said. 'I'll take you to them.'

'Mikey?!' protested Catherine.

'What's the catch?' asked Garvin suspiciously.

'No catch,' Mikey replied. 'I just don't want my girlfriend to suffer any more.' Mikey placed his flash gun on the slab before him and raised his hands.

'You shouldn't do this, Mikey,' Fletcher warned as Mikey moved to stand in front of Garvin.

'Shut up!' snapped Garvin. He kept the gun pointed at Jane for a second longer then, in a flash he was behind Mikey with the .45 Colt jammed against the side of his head. 'Right, nice and easy… Nice and easy,' said Garvin to the others as he walked Mikey backwards towards the distant doorway.

'Do as he says,' said Mikey, nodding to the worried faces. Only the preacher seemed to show no concern. 'I'll be fine.'

Garvin chuckled. 'Yeah,' he whispered as they backed away. 'You keep thinkin' that, Mikey.'

Fletcher and the others looked on until the pair had finally disappeared behind the next doorway. 'That was a stupid thing to do,' the inspector said, lowering his machine gun. 'We should go after them.'

'You'll do no such thing,' said the preacher firmly. 'Now help me with Jane.'

The preacher moved quickly to the wheelbarrow and gripped Jane under her arms. Danny put down his machine gun and grabbed her legs.

'What are you planning to do?' asked Catherine.

'Put her in my chamber,' replied the preacher. 'I can't explain how this place works but it does have some marvellous effects on the body – miraculous one might almost say.'

Together they placed Jane's limp body into the chamber before the preacher turned to inspect the hieroglyphic panel. His finger hovered for a few moments above the symbols. 'This one, I think,' he said and pressed one of the glyphs.

The front of Jane's sarcophagus reappeared as solid stone and another tremor shook the room. The preacher nodded with satisfaction then moved to the next panel and pressed another symbol. A stream of glyphs flashed brightly across the centre circle and the sarcophagus beside Jane's opened.

'That's not possible,' said Catherine, wide-eyed at the sight of the figure who was now revealed.

'But…?' was all the inspector could manage. Confused, he pointed to the doorway which Mikey and Garvin had passed through.

The preacher smiled and picked up the flash gun which Mikey had discarded. 'He will explain,' he said as the figure stepped out and grinned broadly at the awe struck group. 'And now I must go and meet an old friend.' The preacher paused and smiled at the newcomer. 'Thank you, my dear boy,' he said then rushed off into the depths of the temple.

With Garvin pacing a few yards behind, Mikey led the way through the next level of the temple: an identical version of the level above. As the minutes passed and their distance from the others increased, Garvin seemed to relax and become conversational.

'You know, it's funny,' he said as they entered the first chamber of the second sarcophagus level. 'I spent about an hour waiting at your girlfriend's flat for the opportunity to get my hands on you, and you went and handed yourself over.' Garvin grinned. 'Despite the combat clothing and the bullet-proof vest, you obviously haven't got a clue about tactics.'

Mikey continued in silence for a few paces. 'I'm no expert,' he said at length, 'but I'm pretty sure there's only one way in and one way out of this place.' He glanced over his shoulder. 'That means that if I don't walk back out to meet my friends, Inspector Fletcher will take great satisfaction in blowing you to pieces.'

'Brave words,' replied Garvin. 'I think Mr Bradford will have some fun with you.'

Mikey remembered the burnt corpse they had found at the foot of the first rampway and its implication that Bradford was killing his own followers. 'How much do you trust your glorious leader?' he asked.

The question seemed to catch Garvin off-guard. 'What the fuck do you mean by that?!' he snapped.

'I mean how much do you really know about what's going on?' replied Mikey with a shrug.

'A lot more than you, Dayville,' said Garvin defensively. 'Now shut up and keep moving.

'Certainly,' responded Mikey. 'But one final thing. If I were you, I wouldn't keep that gun trained on me – I'm the last of your worries.'

'And I'm the first of yours – so shut up!'

They passed through the central hexagonal chamber and into the second sarcophagus area. Far down on the right side of the long room a single sarcophagus had been opened. Mikey noted it but did not communicate the fact that it was probably where Tenneshaw Wright had been. Instead he asked:

'What are you getting out of this, Garvin?'

Garvin chuckled. 'Wealth, immortality; the usual stuff.'

'Immortality?' queried Mikey. He glanced over his shoulder to find his captor grinning back at him.

'That's right,' he said and waved an arm. 'This temple has the power to make dreams come true, Mike. Once Åpep has revived Tenneshaw Wright, we can start reaping the rewards of this place.'

Mikey stopped and turned to face Garvin. 'You did see the bodies outside, didn't you? Your White Knight friends were hacked to death by Åpep.'

A frown creased Garvin's face. With frightening speed he moved towards Mikey and clubbed him to the floor with the butt of his gun. 'You're out of your depth an' out of yer league!' he snarled, pointing down at the prostrate photographer. 'If you wanna live a little longer you'll do as I say an' shut the fuck up!'

Mikey, his head ringing from the blow, rubbed the back of his head and climbed warily to his feet. Perhaps it was the promise that Jane would be okay, or the fact that answers lay at the base of the temple which had made him feel so unconcerned, but now common sense suggested he do as his captor ordered and stay quiet. His last question had clearly unsettled Garvin and, though he had no idea what lay ahead, he was determined to live long enough to see it.

With a shove from the now hostile Garvin, Mikey continued leading the way. Beyond the final sarcophagus chamber the vibrations and noise returned and, as they zigzagged down the next set of rampways, a pale blue light from the chamber below began to spill onto the walls around them.

Half way down the ramps, the pair found the source of the light. A large open archway on their right revealed what Mikey could only assume was some form of control room. There were a dozen hieroglyphic slabs arranged around the wide room but, by comparison with the ones above, these were monumental in scale. At the end of the room a large window seemed to be the source of the blue light and a dig in the back from the equally curious Garvin prompted Mikey to investigate. The tremors and the noise were more oppressive here but both men found their attention taken by the sight which was revealed as they got closer to the window.

Far below, another giant chamber of stone stretched out before them and in its centre a circular podium seemed to contain a waterfall of blue light. Mikey marvelled at the pale cascades of colour and while he was noting how its speed and strength shifted with every tremor he spotted a figure close to the podium.

'Tenneshaw Wright,' said Mikey with a slow shake of his head. He recognised the man instantly from the photograph his father had taken but could scarcely believe the man was really alive. He watched as Wright approached the falling light then saw his figure fade as he passed inside.

'C'mon,' said Garvin with a frown. He waggled his gun towards the archway and, with a shrug, Mikey led the way back onto the ramps.

A final, long ramp descended directly into the cascade chamber and as they reached floor level the pair got their first clear view of the central podium. Viewed from above the falling light had seemed bright and solid but now it was possible to see not just inside but completely through. The podium was empty.

'Put your hands on your head,' Garvin ordered as they moved closer.

Mikey glanced back as he complied then began to veer to the left as he crossed the floor. Apart from the disappearance of Tenneshaw Wright he had the nagging suspicion that there was something not quite right with the interior of the podium.

Focused on the cascade and puzzled by the disappearance of Wright, Garvin did not notice Mikey moving further to the left. But when the photographer stopped, moved right, then back again to the left, Garvin raised his gun and advanced towards him.

'What the fuck do you think you're doin'?' he snapped.

'Now you see them,' said Mikey with a smile. He moved a few paces closer to Garvin. 'Now you don't.' Mikey nodded towards the cascade.

With a furrowed brow, Garvin looked into the falling light and took a few more paces to his left. Suddenly both Peter Bradford and Tenneshaw Wright could be seen but both men seemed to be beyond the confines of the podium.

'What the fuck?' muttered Garvin.

'Interesting, isn't it?' replied Mikey.

Garvin levelled his gun at Mikey's head. 'Move,' he ordered and pointed towards the cascade.

Mikey regarded the structure for a second, sighed and walked until he was right beside it. He turned to find himself staring down the barrel of Garvin's Colt.

'Go on,' urged Garvin, 'see how 'interesting' it is.'

Standing so close to the cascade, Mikey could feel the energy surging through the falling light; powered, he supposed, by the enormous structures on the levels above. He closed his eyes, held his breath and stepped forward.

Mikey felt his stomach flutter, his equilibrium spin as if, in that single stride, he had fallen down a mine shaft. Unnerved and dizzy, he opened his eyes to find that his feet were planted firmly on the ground beyond the cascade. He turned to see that Garvin was still behind the barrier of light but for some reason he had moved about two metres to Mikey's left – his gun was no longer trained on Mikey. Then Garvin stepped forward and seemed to jump the gap, appearing right beside Mikey with his Colt once again inches from his captive's head.

It was plain to Mikey that Garvin too had suffered a similar disorientation in that single step, but the man's gun arm barely wavered. Garvin narrowed his gaze. 'Get moving!' he barked.

Whatever the cascade was, concluded Mikey as he took in his surroundings, it was more than just a pretty light show. Though the podium was still behind them, the room they were now in was not the grand space they had entered. This chamber was smaller, brighter and – though Mikey could not quite put his finger on it – more unsettling than the rest of the temple. There were the now familiar hieroglyphic slabs arranged down the left hand wall of the room while on the right were large, translucent panels through which sunlight seemed to be streaming. Has the barrier gone down? Mikey mused, then turned his attention, like Garvin, to the activity at the far end of the chamber.

Dressed in stiff, cream linen, Marcus Tenneshaw Wright was frantically pounding the hieroglyphic slab beside a large, arched door while Peter Bradford stood directly before it – his hands placed upon his temples. Wisps of smoke were curling from the dark surface of the door and, though Bradford had his back to Mikey, the photographer guessed that he was using his strange third eye to try and burn through the barrier.

'Peter!' Garvin shouted, pushing Mikey forwards. 'What's going on?!'

Both Wright and Bradford turned and regarded the newcomers with shocked expressions. Despite his stiff,

347

Victorian attire, Tenneshaw Wright looked younger than Mikey had expected while Bradford, his face sweat stained and the wound on his forehead a livid red, seemed old and haggard by comparison.

'Where the hell have you been, Garvin!?' snapped Bradford, his anger plain.

'I got delayed,' Garvin replied. He waved his pistol at Mikey. 'I brought you a present.'

Bradford sneered. 'How – fucking – thoughtful.'

'I thought you wanted to speak to him?' replied Garvin defensively.

'Yeah! Two fucking hours ago!' Peter stabbed an arm towards the floor. 'I needed you here!'

'Steady, my boy,' cautioned Wright.

'STOP TELLING ME WHAT TO DO!' screamed Bradford. His face flushed crimson and the eye in his forehead fluttered. 'All my bloody life you've been telling me what to do and now you can't even open a fucking door!'

There was fear in the Victorian's eyes and he edged away along the slab. Garvin stepped forwards and attempted to placate his employer.

'What's the problem, Peter?' he asked. 'Where's Åpep?'

'He doesn't fucking know!' barked Bradford, waving an arm at Wright. 'All we know is that he must have gone through here!' Peter seemed on the point of hysteria and slammed his fist against the door in fury.

'He can't have gone far, Peter,' said Wright soothingly. 'We will find him – I promise you.'

'Like you promised me eternal life?!' spat Bradford, his face contorted. 'The keys to paradise?! You don't even know where the fuck we are!'

Wright held his hands before him defensively. 'I'm positive that this is the gateway to paradise, Peter,' he said. 'You must trust me…'

Unnoticed, Mikey inched himself further away during Bradford's tirades in the vain hope that he could make it all the way back to the cascade without being spotted. And, having seen the scorched body on the second level of the temple as well as Jane's injuries, Mikey had a sneaking suspicion of just how Bradford's anger tended to resolve itself. The photographer had felt Bradford's fury once and lived to tell the tale but the fused earphones around his neck meant he would not be so lucky a second time.

As Bradford's rage continued unabated, Mikey continued to inch back and puzzled over the words of the preacher. He had said that the answers Mikey sought would be found here, yet the photographer could see nothing enlightening within this new chamber, just more mysteries: like why he still felt light-headed. With the cascade still some twenty metres distant, Mikey was half-tempted to make a dash for it; but Garvin's prowess with a rifle made him discount the idea. Mikey did not want to find out the hard way how good a shot Garvin was with a pistol.

He kept his eyes glued on the feuding trio by the door who did not once glance back at him. Perhaps, Mikey thought, the distraction Bradford's temper was causing might be enough for him to simply slip away. As if to confirm this, a crimson-faced Bradford suddenly grabbed Wright by the lapels.

As Garvin acted as referee and prized the two men apart, Mikey reversed faster until his heel struck a narrow hieroglyphic slab set beneath one of the large translucent panels. Glancing round, Mikey saw that there was a single flashing glyph in the centre of the slab and, without thinking, Mikey touched it.

The top of the slab disappeared to reveal a row of identical objects made of crystal which instantly reminded Mikey of the flash gun devices the preacher had instructed him to make. A short handle of dark blue crystal merged into a clear, angular middle above which sat a circle of white crystal inset with a beautifully crafted ruby. They looked, Mikey thought, like the Egyptian Ånkh Danny had mentioned.

Distracted by their continuing argument, Mikey looked back to find that Garvin had taken sides against his employer and a now silent, scowling Bradford had a .45 Colt aimed at his head. Buoyed by Garvin's sudden change of loyalty, Tenneshaw Wright was taking the opportunity to berate his prodigy.

'You're a disgrace to your family!' Marcus was barking. 'Unfit to hold the trust I placed in you!' There was something else about being a 'monster' but a sudden breeze on Mikey's cheek caused him to glance towards the large translucent panel on the wall. It was no longer there. Neither, it seemed, was Highgate.

The sky beyond the window was a bright mauve and a small red sun blazed high above a bank of pink-tinged cloud. There were rust red mountains on a misty horizon while steaming marshlands flecked with yellow plant life occupied the middle distance for a far as Mikey could see. Immediately below the window stretched a city of pristine white stone which buzzed with life and, looking down, Mikey saw that they were at least fifteen stories above the ground. Mikey focused on a wide plaza which sat at the base of the building and saw that a large group of people were moving closer at some speed. It was difficult to tell from such a height, but there was something disconcerting about their shapes and disjointed in their movements.

'Aliens…' mouthed Mikey.

A single, sharp klaxon call sounded from the direction of the door and Garvin, suddenly realising Mikey had moved, instantly fired a warning shot. It missed his head by inches and ricocheted off of the wall behind him. Mikey ducked reflexively and put his hands up.

'What the fuck did you touch?!' shouted Garvin, his other arm pointing to the now open door behind them.

Mikey shrugged. 'Nothing,' he lied. He nodded to the mauve sky. 'This window opened on its own.'

Marcus took a few steps towards the window, gazing out onto the alien day with a look of wonder. 'Paradise…' he sighed, then turned on Bradford. 'Did I not tell you so!?'

Peter scowled in response and struck the distracted Garvin on the back of his head as hard as he could. Garvin stumbled, dropped his gun and before he could get to his feet, Bradford made a vain dash for freedom down the long corridor beyond the open door. He did not get far. Running back towards the chamber was the blood stained figure of Åpep, pursued by several of the creatures Mikey had seen in the plaza moments before.

Peter stopped at the sight of Åpep's rapid advance and looked back to find Garvin taking aim at him. In desperation Bradford turned again and, attempting to force a passage, unleashed his fury upon the onrushing aliens. A heat haze swept down the confines of the corridor, erupting into flame as it struck first Åpep then his pursuers. His body smoking, Åpep roared out in pain, staggered into the wall then slowly moved forwards as Bradford continued to pour heat upon heat. Behind him the aliens were now nothing more than thrashing torches.

Unsure which was the more dangerous and fascinated by the contest, Garvin held his fire to watch the duel between Bradford and Åpep reach a conclusion. He would most likely shoot Bradford in the back of his head the second Åpep went down but, for the moment at least, he was satisfied to see if the burning monster could stagger close enough to use its lethal talons. Peter was screaming with the exertion his fire wave demanded but still Åpep, its skin a mass of steaming blisters pushed forwards. It got to within ten feet before it began to waver then braced itself against the wall and pointed an arm at Peter. Clutched within its talons was a jewelled Ånkh which only Mikey recognised from the cabinet he had opened and, as the central ruby flashed into life, Mikey realised that it did not just look like the flash gun he had made, it acted like it too.

Bradford's scream rose suddenly in pitch as his clothes ignited and streamers of flame danced behind him as the blow torch effect of Åpep's weapon engulfed his body. His hair burned brightly for a second, his flesh scorched black and he tumbled forwards before Garvin ended the fight. Aiming carefully at Åpep's single eye, he slammed four rounds into Åpep's head and watched with satisfaction as the once imposing creature slipped down the wall.

'He who lives by the sword...' said Tenneshaw Wright. He shook his head at the burnt corpses in the corridor then shrugged at Garvin.

'Will die by the sword, Marcus!' shouted a voice from the other end of the chamber.

Advancing from the cascade with Mikey's flash gun raised, talisman-like before him, came the preacher.

'Dunne?!' exclaimed Wright, dumbfounded. 'What the devil –?!'

'The devil takes many forms, Marcus,' replied the preacher, still advancing. 'And I have come to shine God's holy light upon you.'

'Do you know this nut?' asked Garvin as the preacher continued to stride forwards.

Marcus gave a half nod and frowned. 'Well, yes, but –'

352

Garvin nodded in response, aimed casually and shot the preacher in the stomach.

Still by the window, Mikey screamed as Father Dunne collapsed and grabbed one of the crystal Ånkh's from the cabinet. He could instantly feel power surging up his arm as he gripped the device but when he pointed the weapon towards Garvin he realised too late that he had no idea of how to work it. The ruby glowed momentarily but quickly faded and Mikey felt a chill run down his spine as Garvin levelled his pistol and fired.

Mikey heard a hollow click, followed by another as Garvin rapidly fired his now empty automatic. He raced towards Father Dunne as Garvin hastily searched his pockets to reload. The preacher, his teeth gritted, was singing as he tried to rise.

'Who so beset him round,' he muttered, climbing onto one knee, 'with dismal stories…' He raised the flash gun and fired blindly towards Tenneshaw Wright, blasting a hole into the hieroglyphic slab by the door and blowing both Wright and Garvin from their feet. Garvin's ammunition spilled from his hand as he rolled for safety and a shudder ran through the room accompanied by a loud bang from the direction of the cascade. Mikey glanced back to see the light stream was now sparking and flashing wildly.

'Do but themselves confound,' continued Dunne, getting painfully back to his feet, 'his strength the more is. No foe shall stay his might, though he with monsters fight…'

Garvin was scrabbling to reach his ammunition while Marcus had disappeared behind what remained of the control slab. Father Dunne, one bloody hand clutched at his midriff, stepped forwards and fired again.

'He will make good his right,' he sang at the top of his voice, 'to be a pilgrim!'

The floor beside Garvin dissolved in a blaze of light, forcing him away from his bullets. He rolled into a crouch, snapped the ammunition clip into the base of the Colt and hit the preacher in the shoulder with the single round he had managed to retrieve.

Father Dunne fell heavily to his knees while Garvin again scrambled for the remaining ammunition. Mikey took the flash gun from the preacher's slack grasp and in a single motion brought the device to his eye: zooming into perfect focus on Garvin's face.

'This one's for my album!' shouted Mikey and pulled the trigger.

Garvin's head disappeared in a lethal flash to leave a smoking semi-circle between his shoulders. One hand was still moving a bullet towards his pistol but it wavered in mid-motion. The cartridge dropped from his fingers and Garvin's headless corpse fell backwards.

Mikey discarded the flash gun and knelt behind the preacher, cradling his head as the injured cleric managed a pained smile.

'You must go back, Mikey,' said Father Dunne. He coughed and blood spilled from his lips.

'We'll both go back,' insisted Mikey as the preacher clutched his hand tightly.

Father Dunne shook his head. 'No, no,' he whispered. 'My repentance is done, my –' another wracking cough shook his body but he smiled through the pain. 'My glory is finally at hand.' He nodded and fixed Mikey with an intense stare. 'You must go back, Michael –'

A shot ricocheted from the stone floor inches to Mikey's right and he looked up to see Tenneshaw Wright gripping Garvin's discarded pistol.

'I will not be denied paradise!' bellowed Marcus. With some difficulty, he cocked the unfamiliar weapon and levelled it at Mikey as he backed away towards the archway. Behind

Wright, three more aliens appeared at the far end of the corridor and sped towards the chamber.

There was a grin of triumph on Tenneshaw Wright's face but, when it was mirrored by Mikey, he heard too late the sound of running feet behind him.

Marcus turned and fired at point blank range at the leading alien, striking him square in the chest and knocking him from his feet. The other two came on regardless and placed their hands around the gun before Wright could fire again.

Both creatures vaguely resembled Åpep in shape but not in size or stature. They were both slender, with dog-like heads and though they did not appear to possess mouths, Mikey was suddenly aware of a flood of information from them.

They were the Hathnos – who were Marcus and his companions? What were they doing in the museum? Where had the criminal Åpep been for the last five thousand years? Did they not know of the suffering Åpep's experiments had caused? Why were they killing each other?

Mikey felt the stream of questions slow as the aliens seemed to tune themselves into Mikey's sub-conscious then the torrent of information began again…

…He could see Åpep creating a gateway and a temple on this planet – using the murdered spirits of his fellow creatures to give it power, distorting space and time in the process so that he and his followers could escape to worlds uncharted by the Hathnos. They had disappeared through the cascade but all except Åpep had returned one hundred years later, just before the alignment with their home planet had been lost. Åpep's followers returned to face their punishment with tales of a desert world populated by barbarian aliens. Here Åpep had been hailed as a god but, disconcerted by the primitive nature of these 'Egyptians' Åpep and his followers had decided to move on. They had used Åpep's 'god' status to construct a second temple and a second gateway on earth and convinced the ruling elite of Egypt that eternal life awaited them after death. They needed the deaths to power the temple and, to begin with, so many Egyptian dignitaries were happily buried around the building. But for the cascade to work so that Åpep and his followers could escape, thousands had to be slain within the boundary of the fire wall. Unfortunately, such was the status of Åpep in the eyes of these Egyptians, that only a chosen few were allowed anywhere near the isolated temple and they jealously guarded its secrets from the masses. Without the complicity of the Egyptian elite to bring a massive number of people within the boundary of the fire wall, the Hathnos were completely trapped. But the Egyptian elite were adamant – even to Åpep himself – that they did not want their prize gods disturbed. As almost a century passed however, successive generations of Egyptians began to slowly tease out the secrets of the temple until some amongst the elite came to the conclusion that the Hathnos were not gods. Whether it was out of the anger caused by this realisation, or just greed to wrest the secrets of the temple from the Hathnos, Åpep and his followers never knew. All they were aware of was that some of the Egyptian elite rebelled and suddenly the humans were at war with one another with the temple as the prize.

Conversely, the seeds of their destruction reaped salvation for Åpep's followers. As the war raged, Åpep convinced the humans still loyal that a massive army was needed to protect the temple. In return this army would be given a pill which would make each man invincible. The loyal priests, not wanting to loose their gods, complied and an army of men was brought within the boundary markers of the temple. They were instructed to take their tablets at the same moment and died to a man in neat ranks. In the bedlam which followed their merciless act of mass murder, all but Åpep escaped via the cascade back to their home planet.

Mikey was still staring at the silent aliens in the corridor but images and information continued to flood into his mind. He could see the workings of the temple and its devices – ancient museum pieces to these aliens – and understood, though how he did not fully comprehend, exactly how it all worked. Everything, the cascade, the fire weapons. The temple was nothing more than a transport link, the sarcophagi regeneration-stasis chambers. It was how Åpep had survived so long, how Tenneshaw Wright and the preacher had stayed alive. Åpep had promised Marcus paradise, but it had been a lie. All Åpep wanted to do was to get home but, so far was his journey, it had been five thousand years before the correct celestial alignment could be reached again. And, as before, Åpep had needed a mass death to power the temple. And gullible followers to do his bidding.

Mikey's thoughts were interrupted by questions from the aliens and it seemed that, as well as transmitting information, they were also receiving from all three humans. Were they the barbarians – the Egyptians the Hathnos had heard of? No... Not Egyptian, but still more intelligent and devious than Åpep had realised (this sentiment seemed tinged with wonder). No such thing as paradise. Who is God? Do not return through the gateway, the time stream is corrupt. Humans. Prize exhibits – add to museum. No, do not return through the cascade –

Mikey felt the preacher's firm grip on his hand. 'Run, Mikey!' he gasped.

Mikey shook his head, attempting to clear his thoughts of the mass of jumbled information pouring into his mind. He looked up from Father Dunne to see that more aliens were running down the corridor while the two with Tenneshaw

Wright suddenly broke away to begin advancing on him.

Stay. Do not use the gateway. The time stream is corrupted. Stay. Do not use the gateway...

'Go!' croaked the preacher as the aliens moved towards him.

'I can't,' replied Mikey. He glanced at the cascade. The flashing and fluctuating lights had become more pronounced and, with the information Mikey had received, he now knew what the aliens meant. The time stream was broken. He could still pass through it back to earth but when he would arrive was no longer predictable. It could be at any moment since its construction five thousand years ago.

'Yes! Mikey!' pleaded the preacher. 'You've done it before. My dear boy, you – ' Father Dunne gasped for breath. 'You return and save me! You save Jane. This...This has always been all about you...'

Father Dunne went limp, his eyes staring vacantly up at the photographer. There was the vaguest impression of a smile on the preacher's lips before his face slackened. Mikey grabbed the flash gun and levelled it as the aliens bore down upon him.

'Get back!' shouted Mikey. He turned and ran as fast as he could towards the sparking cascade.

Epilogue: Hampstead Heath 1847

Father Dunne had sinned. He had stepped away from the righteous path and allowed the savage, carnal lusts of man to lead him into an unholy wilderness. From his rural parish of Lower Hampstead, through the putrid gin palaces and whore-strewn back streets of London, Dunne had pursued his rutting urges once too often and now he had paid the price. Forced by his own, base weakness to take part in hell's own scheme.

How Marcus Tenneshaw Wright had found out about his secret crimes of the flesh, Father Dunne did not know, but he was driven by his own shame to do Wright's bidding or else suffer the ignominious consequences. And, with the devil's own tongue, Marcus had made his proposal seem so simple.

Father Dunne was to consecrate the new cemetery Marcus was building beneath Highgate Village and preside over Marcus's own funeral. Suicide was, of course, a crime against God, Marcus had freely admitted, but then so was whoring through the East End of London. Who was Dunne to judge a man's destiny? In return for Father Dunne's co-operation, his vile sins of the flesh would remain a secret.

And so Dunne had carried out the unholy ceremony in the promise that his own crimes would be saved for God's judgment alone and had watched as Tenneshaw Wright – still very much alive – had waved his farewells and entered his secret, underground monument. And, when Father Dunne had glimpsed the demon which lived inside the tomb, he realised he had been tricked into aiding Lucifer himself.

Charles Bradford, Tenneshaw Wright's beneficiary in their perverse scheme had laughed out loud at Dunne's horror. He had slapped the cleric on the back and said:

'Go and hide in your church, Father, and pray the devil does not come looking for you. For if you breath a word of this to anyone I can assure you that he will come for you.'

After two weeks, Father Dunne's conscience had finally overcome his fear. But, before he could tell the world of the evil which lurked beneath the cemetery, he found that once again the devil had tricked him. A parade of women, none of whom he had ever had the misfortune to know in any sense of the word, came forward to detail his crimes of lust and, in an instant, the Father had found himself defrocked and all but destitute.

With the meagre money his family's estate yielded he had bought himself a small cottage in Lower Hampstead and promised God that he would dedicate himself to one single task. He would inform the public of the evil which sat in their midst – festering beneath the soil of Highgate. He was not believed of course, by the polite society which promenaded itself every Sunday through the trim gardens of the cemetery, but still Father Dunne persevered. Every day of every year, without fail, he left his house in Lower Hampstead and, with Holy Bible raised before him, would march across the Hampstead heath land until he reached the gates of Highgate Cemetery – telling the world of the devil which was waiting to rise from its tomb. And then, one day, something miraculous happened.

Father Dunne was crossing the grassland below Parliament Hill on his daily march to the cemetery when he spotted a strange figure sitting beneath the oak saplings which had recently been planted on the lower slope of the hill.

'Beware the devil, young man!' Dunne had cried as he marched towards the green clad figure. 'For he sleeps beneath your very feet!'

'I know, Father Dunne,' replied the red-haired man. 'I've just come from the temple and now that I've seen you I finally understand.' The red-haired man stood up and smiled. 'My name is Mikey Dayville, Father, and I have a very strange tale of redemption to tell you...'

You may also like...

Book One of the REILAN Trilogy

The King
of Nothing

Gordon Ian Barrick

Available now in paperback and for Kindle.

www.ingramcontent.com/pod-product-compliance
Lightning Source LLC
Chambersburg PA
CBHW070801180626
46818CB00001B/44